ALICIA DURST

Psychosomatic Slaughter

OSMOND
press

First published by Osmond Press 2025

First edition

ISBN (paperback): 979-8-218-60186-7
ISBN (hardcover): 979-8-9988442-1-8

Cover art by Sarah Derr

This book was professionally typeset on Reedsy.
Find out more at reedsy.com

For Michael and for my Mom
Thank you for believing in me

And for the lovers of rock and roll, enjoy this sincere homage to the 1980s.

Contents

Playlist

- "In the Beginning/Shout at the Devil" by Mötley Crüe
- "Into the Void" by Black Sabbath
- "Sympathy for the Devil" by The Rolling Stones
- "Rats in the Cellar" by Aerosmith
- "Twist of Cain" by Danzig
- "Number of the Beast" by Iron Maiden
- "Cross Road Blues" by Robert Johnson
- "The Conjuring" by Megadeath
- "Rats" by Ghost
- "Sad But True" by Metallica
- "It's So Easy" by Guns N' Roses
- "Year Zero" by Ghost
- "Master of Puppets" by Metallica
- "Sabbath Bloody Sabbath" by Black Sabbath
- "Love You To Death" by Type O Negative
- "Live Wire" by Mötley Crüe
- "Slipping Through My Fingers" by ABBA
- "Sweating Bullets" by Megadeath
- "Black Sabbath" by Black Sabbath
- "Holy Holy Holy" by The Newton Brothers

Content Warnings

This book contains sensitive topics, including but not limited to:

- Child abuse & neglect
- Alcoholism
- Self-harm
- Depictions of blood, death & gore
- Acts of violence
- Drug use
- Explicit language
- Animal cruelty
- Body horror & dismemberment
- Possession
- Murder
- Sexual situations
- Struggles with sexuality & sexual orientation
- Torture
- The Occult
- Knife Violence
- The Devil, Satan, Satanic Rituals & Sacrifices

This book is intended for a mature readership. Please read at your own risk and be aware of potential triggers.

The Many Faces to Evil

There are many faces to evil. True evil is disguised; it can wear the mask of a friend, a parent, a politician, or a clown who will twist balloons at your child's birthday party. The Devil himself has taken on many forms throughout history. If you were to gaze upon the Devil, what would you see? Would you see a beautiful fallen angel with an affinity for stringed instruments or a red man with hooves and blackened eyes in a pit of fire? When Leon Holman stood face-to-face with him in 1983, he possessed the face of a man and introduced himself as Lucius Wolfe.

Since 1976, when he fell in love with rock and roll and, ultimately, the occult, this meeting between Leon and Lucius had been predestined to occur.

I

Part One: Coming to the Crossroads

1976

1

Blood Brothers

"If you play "Stairway to Heaven" backward, you can hear a message to the Devil," Leon Holman said as he slipped the vinyl out of its sleeve and placed it carefully on the turntable. It looked shiny and beautiful, the diamond in his parents' double-wide, wood-paneled rough. He peered over at Jimmy sitting beside him on the floor. Mrs. Ballard dropped off her son earlier that day, not trusting him to balance the turntable he got for his 11th birthday on his bike. Despite her polite but persistent protests, he insisted on bringing it over to show Leon. As she drove, she warned her son to be careful with the fresh new present he held tenderly in his lap in the passenger seat.

"Wanna hear it?" The corners of Leon's mouth turned up in a conspiratory grin.

"You're so full of shit." Jimmy got up and went to his friend's unmade bed, flopping down. Leon walked on his knees over to the turntable.

"No, I'm not! My dad told me. He showed me, even."

Jimmy sighed and nervously wiped his sweaty palms on his shorts. He'd always heard the rumors about the song but didn't care to find out if there was any truth to them. Leon had been his closest friend since first grade. Jimmy had a tough time back in those days—some older boys had thrown him into a garbage can for being a 'mama's boy.' To make things worse, he was adopted and often teased for that, too. When he finally managed to get himself out of the trash can, the kids egged on a chant—"Junkyard

Jimmy"—and taunted him for smelling like sour milk and leftover mystery meat.

Leon was the only one who didn't join in on the name-calling. He cringed hearing Jimmy get made fun of, considering those same kids called him "ginger-vitis" every day. Leon, a scrawny and lanky redhead that stuck out like a sore thumb, never fit in with anyone. And because of his family's lack of funds, he had been in Jimmy's shoes more days than not. He had to wear the same outfit to school every day, and by Friday, he reeked of mildew and Mr. Holman's cigarettes. Not to mention that his mom forgot to register him for kindergarten on time, making him one of the oldest kids in the class. He never quite fit in and didn't care to, but having a friend would have been nice.

He'd never spoken to Jimmy before that day—he thought that Jimmy was too richy-rich to be friends with him. But he knew how badly that taunting hurt and wished someone was there for him. Leon got up and went to have lunch with Jimmy, who sat defeated at a table littered with discarded wrappers and spilled juice. Leon gave Jimmy the bigger half of his peanut butter and banana sandwich, which was unusual since he rarely had lunch, let alone food to share. The grumbling of an empty stomach was all too familiar to him, and he didn't want that for his new friend.

They'd been inseparable ever since. Even though Jimmy had always trusted Leon and they had been through a lot together, he didn't want to hear a message to the Devil. He wanted to go over there, grab his turntable, and go home. But it was best not to poke the bear when Leon was in these moods. Sighing heavily through his nose, he dug his short nails into his palms.

"Fine, just play it," Jimmy relented as Leon's eyes sparked.

"Okay, ready?" Appeased, Leon dropped the needle onto the record. "We've gotta listen to the whole thing normal first to build up to it."

Finger-picked acoustic guitars and medieval-inspired flutes filled Leon's small room and transported him into another world where people didn't pick on him for being trailer trash. In this world, he performed for hoards of screaming fans, girls who wanted him, and guys who wanted to be him.

4

He looked over his shoulder at Jimmy. "Just wait. You need to experience the whole song."

"I've heard the song before. It's like ten years old. I love this song. I don't want you to ruin it." Jimmy got up and grabbed his records off of the foot of the bed.

"It's not ten years old, doofus. The song came out in 1971. It's only five years old. And you've never heard it like this, so stop being such a pussy and listen."

Jimmy locked his knees and clenched his fists. Heat surged through his body, causing his face to redden. He hoped Leon was too captivated by the music to notice. He threw the records back onto the bed and slumped down beside Leon. "I'm not a pussy. Just play it."

Leon rolled his eyes, swallowing a grumble at the ruined moment. He re-positioned the needle, placed his middle finger gently on the label, and spun the record in the opposite direction. It began slow and distorted, with John Bonham's introduction hammering in reverse. Leon tapped into the rhythm and timed the record spin precisely, falling to the groove of the song. Jimmy's muscles tensed, and a chill raced down his back as he made out the jumbled words. He could have sworn that Robert Plant's warped voice sang about 666, referring to the Devil affectionately. *Sweet Satan?* Jimmy was unsure if he was hearing the messages or if it was Leon's power of suggestion by invoking the myth. Either way, Leon sat in astonishment, gazing down at the album with a wonderstruck grin spreading across his face. Jimmy wasn't sure which frightened him more: Leon's face or the alleged backmasking. He slapped Leon's hand away from the turntable.

"Stop!" Jimmy whined, making Leon giggle.

"Stooooop," Leon taunted in falsetto.

"I'm serious, Leon. I want to go home." Jimmy's eyes flicked downward, embarrassed that he had gotten scared. He began winding the wires to his birthday present, gathering his things to leave. Leon watched as the beautiful gift threatened to leave, forcing him to listen to his hand-me-down, scratched records on his dad's turntable, which was worse for wear.

"Oh, come on, man. I'm sorry, I just wanted to show you."

Jimmy reached down, took the vinyl off the turntable, and slipped it back into the record cover for Led Zeppelin's *Untitled*. Jimmy looked at the album cover, soaking in the image of an older man with a bundle of sticks on his back before looking up at Leon. Leon's lips pouted out, making him look even younger than 12. A wave of compassion washed over Jimmy when he noticed how innocent Leon looked with his red hair and fair skin.

"I mean, it's okay. It was pretty cool, even if it's a stupid rumor." Jimmy shrugged, cocking his head to one side. He smirked as he looked up, feeling silly now. "I always got confused when he started singing about a May Queen. It makes sense now that it could maybe be secret code."

"If it is, Jimmy Page is a fucking genius." Jimmy laughed, hearing how unnatural *"fucking"* sounded coming out of Leon's mouth. It sounded clumsy over his tongue.

"You're fucking right," Jimmy added, trying out the swear for himself. Leon busted out laughing.

"It's cool if you think about it," Jimmy said as he sat next to Leon, fidgeting with the album sleeve. "If you listen to it normally, it *is* Heaven's entrance. You're climbing up the stairs to the pearly gates. But, if you listen to it backward, you go down to Hell. Instead of finding God at the end of the song, you find Satan." Jimmy shuddered as he said the name *Satan*. Leon's head snapped up.

"Whoa," he whispered as his eyes widened. "That's awesome. And he says that you still can change your choice." Leon sucked in his cheek, considering. "Where would you want to end up?"

Jimmy furrowed his brow. "Isn't it obvious?"

Leon shrugged. "If rock and roll is the Devil's music, wouldn't Hell be more fun?"

Jimmy's eyes narrowed as he tried to decipher whether Leon was joking. Leon always said odd things, but he didn't always mean them. Jimmy studied Leon's face: he laughed, but not with his eyes. His eyes looked almost *empty*. Jimmy had never seen that expression before on anybody. Despite Leon's unblinking eyes, he hesitantly chuckled.

"Jimmy, I'm joking. Get your panties out of your ass."

They spent the rest of the night listening to Led Zeppelin, Black Sabbath, and The Rolling Stones, pouring over the liner notes and dissecting each lyric. The music drowned out Leon's sister's constant knocking on the door. They listened to *Night at the Opera* as Leon's mother shouted at his father for being a useless alcoholic who treats her like shit. Jimmy and Leon sang along to "The Twilight Zone," impersonating Getty Lee in their pubescent voices. At the same time, Leon's father reminded his mother that she deserved to be treated like shit since she had turned into a lazy, disgusting sow since they got married.

Mr. Holman had gone to the bar by nine o'clock, his sister had exhausted herself, and Mrs. Holman was smoking her final pack of the day in front of the television. Jimmy had never experienced peace at the Holman house before, and he couldn't understand how Leon survived there. Jimmy's parents lavished him with affection; he never went hungry, and they never argued in front of him. It made Jimmy sorry for Leon, but he was glad Leon could find comfort in music.

The boys absorbed the enchantment of *Dark Side of the Moon,* unwinding as the nighttime hours turned to morning.

"Jimmy?" Leon glanced at his friend lying on the bed with his head hanging off the side, eyes closed, immersed in the music.

"What?"

"I want to play guitar, like Tony Iommi and Jimmy Page."

"So learn," Jimmy said without opening his eyes.

"How? I don't have a guitar."

Jimmy rolled onto his stomach and propped himself up with his elbows to see Leon staring at the demonic entanglement on the *Sabbath Bloody Sabbath* album cover.

"Do you get an allowance?"

Leon's jaw clenched, and his neck stiffened. "No. I saved up $3.00, but that won't get me a guitar."

Jimmy sucked in his cheeks and puckered his lips in thought. "Maybe I could help."

Leon put *Sabbath Bloody Sabbath* back on the floor in front of him. "No,

Jimmy, it's okay. I shouldn't have said nothin'."

Jimmy's face lit up. "No, I want to. No, Leon, listen!" Jimmy sat down next to his friend and picked up *Led Zeppelin II*.

"This could be us." He pointed to Robert Plant and Jimmy Page sitting together in a World War I recreation photo. "I can help you get a guitar! I have some birthday money from my grandma, and I can give you some of my allowances every week, and then you put in your $3.00. It won't be a Gibson, but you can learn!"

Leon's eyes got wide, and a smile grew across Jimmy's face.

"I could mow some lawns for money too! Old Mrs. Fincher always tips well. We'll have enough in no time!" Leon paused, gasping in an excited breath. "And you can be the singer. I've heard you sing along to these records all day. You're really good."

Jimmy blushed a little and ran his finger over the corners of the record in his hands. "Thanks. I wasn't even trying. I bet if I tried to sound good, I could do much better."

"If we are going to start a band, we have to learn how to look cool." Leon pressed his lips together, attempting to conceal his smile that threatened to reveal his secret. He rose slowly, walked to his bed, and lifted the stained mattress. He took out a cigarette box and opened it, revealing one single cigarette that he had stolen from his mother. He gave it to Jimmy, who reveled at it, having never held one before. Leon was always too nervous to smoke it because he was afraid of getting caught and getting a beating for stealing. But if this wasn't the perfect time, he didn't know when else he would have such a perfect opportunity.

Jimmy's eyes widened as he knelt next to the redhead. Leon lit the cigarette and held the lighter before his face, concentrating hard to get the perfect light. The smell of tobacco overpowered the mildew smell of the trailer's old carpet. He slid the cigarette back between his index and middle fingers, his unpracticed hands shaking slightly.

"This is how my old man smokes it," he explained, holding the cigarette to his lips. He took a little inhale and let out a tiny puff of smoke. Jimmy's mouth gaped open, impressed by how cool Leon looked. Leon smirked, overconfident, as he inhaled deeply and took a long pull.

This drag did not go as planned. He coughed so hard he wanted to gag as he sputtered the smoke out. "Your turn," he said, gasping for breath as he pushed the cigarette into his friend's face.

"All right," Jimmy said in a barely audible voice. He reached for the cigarette, his fingers grappling with it in a clumsy attempt to mirror the way Leon held it. The cigarette was cautiously handled as if it were a bomb ready to detonate with the slightest mishandling. He took a careful puff, ensuring not to inhale too much, and exhaled as little smoke as he possibly could.

"You didn't even blow any smoke out!" Leon swung his arm toward Jimmy, pointing with his open palm at the cigarette that was hoarding ashes at the tip.

"Yes, I did! You were coughing too hard to see me."

"The only smoke you're blowing is out of your ass." Leon took the cigarette back and dangled it leisurely between his lips. He leaned back against the wood paneling, resting his arms on his knees and cocking his head. "Do I look cool, though?"

"The coolest," Jimmy said as he put on a new record, placing the needle precisely on the third track on the B side. The main riff of Aerosmith's "Round and Round," drenched in distortion, flooded the room. Leon leaned forward toward Jimmy, cigarette ashes flying.

"Are you serious about this?" The cigarette bobbed on his lips with each word. Leon let a smile creep across his face as he looked up at his friend through pale lashes. Jimmy nodded, his nods fast and his eyes bright.

"Let's make a pact."

"A pact for what?" Jimmy whispered. Leon ran over to the window and opened it, tapping the cigarette's tip on the side of the trailer and dropping it. He shut the window, picked up his pocket knife, and sliced a small cut in the middle of his palm as he sat down. Unflinching, he looked up at Jimmy. "That we won't let this dream die. That we will always stick together, no matter what."

Jimmy's heart rate quickened as he gazed in shock at the blood oozing from Leon's wounded palm. Though unease grew under the weight of Leon's intense, penetrating stare, he could not look away. The dark pools of Leon's dilated pupils swallowed everything in their path, leaving Jimmy staring into an endless void.

He wordlessly extended his palm, allowing Leon to make an identical cut on his hand. Jimmy flinched, hissing an inhale through his clenched teeth. He watched the blood flow from his hand even though it made him queasy. The cut penetrated the lifeline, severing it a quarter of the way through.

At that moment, a sense of unity and acceptance overwhelmed Jimmy, overpowering his unease. This act—this ritual—struck him as significant. Almost *sacred*. It was as if he had finally found his place in the world.

"Brothers?" Leon reached his hand out, the blood trickling down his wrist.

"Brothers." Jimmy took Leon's hand, mixing their gore. Their blood squelched between their palms as they shook.

With their hands held together, they united their wounds and pledged to become one of the most famous rock duos in music history, superseding the Toxic Twins, Lennon and McCartney, or Jagger and Richards. Jimmy would take on the lead vocals, while Leon would aspire to become a legendary guitarist like Hendrix.

More importantly, they became blood brothers late that June night in 1976, irrevocably intertwining their life forces.

It was a bond they would take to the grave—an unbreakable, dedicated, and doomed connection.

This was Leon Holman's first deal that was bound in blood, and it certainly wasn't the last.

2

Music In His Blood

Early the following day, around eight, Janice Ballard arrived to pick up her son. She honked twice to let Jimmy know it was time to leave, clucking her tongue in distaste as she glanced around. She dreaded it whenever Jimmy visited Leon's house, especially if he spent the night. Each time, he came back starving. The floors at the Holman's were so dirty that it left a coating of filth on the bottom of Jimmy's socks, which made them stick to the linoleum floors in the kitchen.

Despite her dislike of the trailer park, she had a soft spot for Leon. She always ensured he left her home well-fed and with a clean shirt. When the week was through, she even offered to wash his gym clothes for him. God forbid his mother would do such a thing. After a few weeks of doing this, Janice noticed Leon would slip a spare shirt or pair of pants inside his gym bag. She never said anything about it; instead, she merely smiled and folded them carefully before putting them back in his bag, fresh and clean. If only she could have been fortunate enough to be Leon's mother—he would have been adored.

She accidentally made eye contact with two men sitting in lawn chairs on a makeshift porch on the opposite side of the street. They leered at her, raising their morning beers in appreciation. She averted her gaze back to the Holman's door, honking the horn again. Mrs. Holman swatted at the curtains to investigate the commotion while sporting a curler in her bangs.

She held a cup of coffee in one hand and a cigarette in the other as she pulled the curtain open. Janice leaned over the passenger seat to roll down the window.

"Morning, Lorraine! Is Jimmy about ready?"

Mrs. Holman sneered and waved dismissively as she dropped the curtain. Janice sighed, forcibly turning the downturned corners of her mouth into a bright smile as her son appeared in the doorway, awkwardly waving the hand that supported the bottom of the turntable.

Jimmy raced out, his turntable delicately poised in his arms. With a broad grin, Leon stood in the entryway, holding the door open.

"Hi, Mrs. Ballard! Thanks for letting Jimmy stay over!"

Janice gave him a warm smile and a wave. "Good morning, Leon! I hope you boys had a nice time!"

Behind Leon, Mrs. Holman peered out the door at the Ballards' station wagon. She creased her brow and shoved Leon's shoulder.

"What are you doing?" She glared down at her son as she leaned against the doorway, jutting a hip out to block Leon's path back into the house.

Leon turned away from his mother and toward Jimmy, who had stopped halfway between the Holman's trailer and his mother's car. "I'm saying bye to Jimmy…" He made an uncertain pointing motion toward his friend.

"Why aren't you goin'? Your little friend spent the night in *my* house, so now I'm stuck with you all goddamned day?" She yanked the cigarette out of her pursed lips and waved it around, sending ashes flying all over her son. "I don't want to look at your face today. Go get in that car." She brought the cigarette back to her lips as she pushed Leon out of the way and closed the door, waving to Mrs. Ballard. "Bye, Janet."

Leon said under his breath, "It's Janice." He turned toward the car with his head down, making Janice's heart ache.

"Come on in, Leon. When we get back home, I'll make a big breakfast."

Leon looked in the open passenger side window as Jimmy hopped into the backseat.

"I'll just walk around town 'til it gets dark, Mrs. Ballard. That's all right. I don't want to be a bother." Leon kicked up some dirt as he looked down at his worn sneakers.

"I insist," she said as she jutted her thumb over her shoulder. "I don't have all day, so hurry up. Get in!"

Jimmy pushed open the door and scooted over to let his friend in. Leon gave Mrs. Ballard a wan smile and climbed inside.

"Thank you, Mrs. Ballard," he said quietly.

"Alright," she said as she put the car in drive. "What are you boys thinking: eggs and bacon or pancakes?"

"Eggs and bacon!" Jimmy piped up.

Leon's stomach grumbled. Both options sounded delicious. He was glad his mother forced him out because now, he would enjoy a hot breakfast while she chowed down on cold noodles and tuna. He stifled a smirk and stared down at his thumbs.

Jimmy nudged him. "Does that sound good?"

Leon glanced from his friend to the front seat. Mrs. Ballard winked at him in the rear-view mirror, and he grinned back at her. "Yup, sounds good to me."

Jimmy's house was in a beautiful neighborhood, where wives put flowerbeds in their windowsills and husbands meticulously manicured the lawn against the driveway. Leon loved going to Jimmy's. No matter what the scent was—whether it was Spic and Span, fabric softener, or freshly brewed coffee—it always smelled good. Family portraits covered the walls, their adoring smiles frozen over time. Jimmy stood out in the pictures because of how his tawny skin and black hair contrasted with his mother's blonde hair and hazel eyes. Leon thought about that a lot—how a Portuguese teen had given birth to Jimmy and how he had been adopted as a newborn. Although the young mother who gave birth to him didn't want him, the Ballards sure did. They took Jimmy in by choice and loved him unconditionally, something Leon couldn't fathom. He imagined what it would be like to experience that kind of love and belonging. Even though the Ballards enveloped him with an abundance of love and affection every time he visited, he couldn't help the resentment that squeezed his heart. That resentment grew like a void in the pit of his stomach. The longing.

Why wasn't he able to have that?

Why couldn't I be loved like that?

Leon and Jimmy hurried to Jimmy's room as Mrs. Ballard prepared breakfast. Jimmy placed his turntable in the designated music corner. Leon jumped onto the perfectly made bed, glancing around at the posters hanging from the walls while Ted Nugent and the members of KISS stared back at him. Leon wished that his room could look like this. Everything had a place. All of Jimmy's clothes smelled like fresh fabric conditioner, and each shirt and pair of socks was folded and organized. The carpet wasn't crusty from built-up spills. The sheets smelled like warm summer air, like fabric softener marinating in the sun on the clothesline. Jimmy had a brand-new turntable, all the music he wanted to listen to, plus a desk to work at. If Leon had homework, he had to do it in the kitchen or balance a book on his lap so his pencil wouldn't poke holes in the paper. He usually opted for the latter since being in the kitchen usually landed him in the crossfire of his parents' aggression.

Jimmy turned on *Physical Graffiti* after he had set up the turntable. What better music could set the mood than Led Zeppelin, who gave birth to their dream? He shuffled over to the desk in the corner, picked up a birthday card, and slid two bills out of it.

"I got this from my grandmother for my birthday." Jimmy offered Leon the two bills—a total of $30. Jimmy raised his eyebrows in encouragement.

Looking down and away from his friend's big brown eyes, Leon accepted the cash. He folded it in his hands, wringing them slowly. His family forgot his last birthday.

Jimmy picked up his piggy bank and gave it a shake. Coins bounced around from inside the delicate pig, clanging loudly against the sides. "This ought to make a nice dent in your guitar fund, too!"

Leon glared at the pig, dumb and pink. "How do you get the money out?"

"You've got to smash it." Jimmy shrugged and draped a t-shirt around the bank. "Here goes nothing," he said, banging the bundle into the desk corner. It shattered, loudly smacking against the wood.

"What was that?" Mrs. Ballard called from the bottom of the stairs.

"Nothing!" Jimmy yelled back, kneeling down to unwrap the shirt from around the damage. Leon climbed off the bed and sat beside Jimmy, who was slumped over the mess. They separated the broken piggy bank parts from the cash, slapping chalky bisque off of their hands. They divided the money into heaps and ended up with one five, eleven ones, two quarters, five dimes, and 22 nickels.

"Holy shit!" Leon yelled, but when he remembered Mrs. Ballard was downstairs, he quickly ducked his head and covered his mouth with his hands. Jimmy laughed gleefully, tapping his finger over his mouth to keep Leon quiet.

"That's more than I thought I had!" Jimmy gathered all the money into one pile as Leon leered at the cash. That was more than he was expecting, too. Way more.

"Okay, so $18.10 plus the $30 from my grandma is…" Jimmy paused as his eyeballs darted back and forth, mirroring his mental math. "$48.10! You said you had $3, right?"

Leon sucked in a breath. "Well, I thought I did, but I forgot I bought a bottle of Coke the other day. I only have $2.75." He lowered his gaze so he wouldn't have to look Jimmy in the eyes. Jimmy was all but buying a guitar for him. He had no idea Jimmy had saved so much money. He fidgeted with his hands as he stared down at them, caressing the smooth tops of his short, bitten nails.

Jimmy pushed the pile of money in front of Leon. "Well, now you have $50.85."

Leon raised his head, stunned. He shook it slowly, back and forth.

"No way, Jimmy, I can't do it." Leon shoved the pile aside and stood up, turning toward the bed, hoping Jimmy didn't notice his eyes welling up with tears. Jimmy prodded Leon to turn around by placing his hand on his shoulder.

"No, it's all right. You should have it, please." Jimmy thought back to that peanut butter and banana sandwich from first grade when Leon had nothing to share, but he did anyway. "You're my brother, remember?"

Leon stroked the scab that began forming on his palm's wound. He wiped his eyes with the back of his arm and ran his hands through his frizzy ginger hair as he turned to face his friend. Jimmy gave him a hopeful smile. Leon nodded, pulling Jimmy in for a hug.

It felt foreign to him. Leon had never been touchy-feely and couldn't remember the last time he received a hug from anyone, let alone gave one, so he wasn't sure what made him pull Jimmy in. Nevertheless, at that time, it seemed fitting. Jimmy returned the embrace. "We're going to rock."

Leon squeezed him firmly before pushing him away. "Yeah, alright. Nothing fruity like that again. Rock stars are tough."

* * *

"Boys, dinner!" Mrs. Ballard called later that night. Jimmy and Leon thundered down the carpeted stairs, exhilarated by their day of planning. They would collect cans and mow lawns to save money, and Jimmy volunteered to do extra chores. Leon would begin learning to read music so that when he got his guitar, he could go right into playing.

"Hey, you boys look excited," Roland Ballard said as he smiled over his newspapers from the head of the table. "What did you get into today?"

"We listened to records," Jimmy said.

"I trust you weren't listening to any of that Devil's music, right boys?" Leon's heart skipped a beat before realizing Mr. Ballard was laughing. Jimmy was, too, until he saw the look on Leon's face.

"He's kidding, Leon," Jimmy reassured him.

"That's what my parents always said to me when I was young," he said, gesturing in Mrs. Ballard's direction with the base of his wine glass as he raised it to his lips for a sip. "They were mortified that I met your mother at an Elvis concert."

Does he even appreciate them? Leon thought, glancing at Jimmy's smiling face.

"Now, what are you telling them about the olden days?" Mrs. Ballard came into the dining room carrying a casserole dish. The smell of melted cheese and seasoned beef made Leon's mouth water. He couldn't remember the last time his mom made a meal, let alone a hot one. It was usually every man for themselves in the Holman household, with cold cereal or a can of beans being the best-case scenario. Leon greedily eyed the heaping scoop that Mrs. Ballard put onto his plate while her husband rambled on about how they first met, what it was like to see Elvis perform live, and the way that people lost their minds in the crowd when The King moved his hips.

"Leon and I are going to start a band," Jimmy said proudly. Leon folded his lips in, the corners of his mouth turning up.

"Oh yeah?" Mr. Ballard chuckled.

"Yeah! We were listening to music last night, and we decided that we wanted to start a band. We pooled our money so Leon could get a guitar to learn to play. We're going to work together to save enough money to buy one."

Mrs. Ballard's eyes softened as she took in the innocent joy on her son's face. "That is very nice of you, Jimmy. But…" Jimmy looked at her with a spark in his eyes while Leon looked down at his plate, pushing around the crispy top of the casserole.

"Whose idea was this?" She asked gently, pausing as she looked between the two boys. "To buy a guitar?"

"Mine," Jimmy said. "Leon almost didn't take the money, but I made him take it." Leon's cheeks began to color, making her throat tighten with guilt. She glanced up at her husband, and he gave her a slight nod.

"I'm sure you will play beautifully, Leon," she reassured him as she reached over and squeezed his arm. He gave her a small smile, keeping his eyes on his fork.

"And, Jim, what would you do in this band?" Mr. Ballard smirked into his wine glass, garnering him a piercing glare from his wife.

"I'm going to be the singer." Jimmy looked down, his face flushing with red blotches. "Leon said I'm really good," he said, quickly turning to Leon to back him up, who nodded fervently in agreement. Janice used her hand to prop up her chin, attempting to hide the smile spreading across her face with her palm. "But I wasn't even trying to sound good. I'm sure I could be even better if I tried."

"Well, when you make it big, remember your dear old dad, okay?" Jimmy smiled as his dad winked at him.

After supper, Leon argued that he could easily walk home, but Mrs. Ballard insisted on driving him. He pretended to reach for the doorknob as he waved goodbye, waiting until she was out of sight to scurry around the side of the trailer to climb through his bedroom window. The sun was still up, and if his mother saw him enter the house before it was dark, he would be in serious trouble. He would never be in the house if it were up to her. At 10 o'clock, when the PSA came on the television asking parents if they knew where their children were, her answer would always be, "Don't know, don't care." In any case, he wanted to get a head start on getting to sleep so he could wake up early and visit the record shop as soon as it opened.

* * *

The dull sound of the neighbor's push mower droned in through the window, bringing with it the earthy, clean smell of freshly cut grass. On any normal day, Leon would be annoyed to be woken up so early on a summer day, but he had already been up for hours. He wanted to be ready when he had enough money, so he began drafting his lesson plan. The boys agreed that Jimmy should keep the cash at his place. If Leon's parents had come into his room and discovered that he had money, it would have been long gone by the time he realized it was missing.

Until they saved enough, he planned to write out all of his guitar goals and make a checklist of everything he wanted to learn from his idols. Leon slipped out of his room to get a pen and paper, hopping over the garbage, laundry piles, and dolls his sister had left in the hall. As soon as he entered the kitchen, he pried open the junk drawer. Layers upon layers of paint coated the cabinets, and the summer heat made the caked-on varnish sticky. He pulled on the handle, causing it to finally crack open, but not before peeling the paint off the top of the drawer.

Leon's mother shrieked at him from the couch, "Leon, what the fuck are you doing?"

"All I need is a pen and paper. Have we got any?"

"Shut up, you little shit." She waved her hand in his general direction, scattering ashes on the ground and thickening the layer of filth. "I can't hear my show."

"I got it. Sorry, Mom." An empty beer bottle whizzed past his face and crashed into the kitchen cabinet. Leon stood there, stunned, as the shattered glass swirled around him.

"Get out of the kitchen and leave me alone," she hissed, sighing in exasperation at what he had just made her do.

Leon's lip trembled, and he wasn't sure if it was from rage or tears. He marched into his room and slammed the door shut with all the strength his body could muster. To drown out his mother and the max-volume television, he put on some music and began preparing a list of all the songs we wanted to learn:

"Stairway to Heaven" - Led Zeppelin

"Sweet Leaf" - Black Sabbath

"Temple of the King" - Rainbow

"Seasons of Wither" - Aerosmith

"Sabbath Bloody Sabbath" - Black Sabbath

"Voodoo Chile" - Jimi Hendrix

Leon climbed out of his bedroom window and headed down to *For the Record*, a grungy record and music store he enjoyed visiting, armed with his list of songs. Posters of Janis Joplin, Nazareth, and Deep Purple members covered the walls and watched you as you browsed. The smell was always a little musty, but he welcomed the scent. It smelled like home, the good kind of home: soft, safe, and familiar. He was secure, surrounded by his favorite things while he was there. Walls filled with cassettes and record bins sitting around the store organized by genre stood by, ready to be sifted through by punks, rockers, and new wavers. Shelves stocked with music waited to be explored, and racks boasting guitars, basses, and the occasional banjo hung in anticipation of being played. He loved running his fingers over the guitar bodies. One of those guitars would be his golden ticket. Even though he had no idea what the sheet music meant, he liked browsing through it, looking at all of the notes and the ornate swirls that decorated the lines. Little did he know that music wasn't for guitar; it was for piano.

As Leon came in, Rufus restrung a Gibson Les Paul behind the counter. Rufus put his life savings into opening *For The Record*, working hard to ensure every customer left with something they would love. One of his most-loved aspects about music as a veteran rock and roll enthusiast was how the soul could flow through a guitarist's fingers as they played. His favorite was blues music; the blues led him to pick up a guitar for the first time. The steady progression from blues to rock, the British Invasion, and the rise of heavy metal kept his passion for music alive.

With his waist-length graying beard and low braid, Rufus had a hard look to him. Yet nothing made him happier than seeing young people like Leon come in and show an interest in music. This redheaded hellion reminded him of some kids he met at Woodstock in 1969. He traveled alone and was glad to meet a group of young hippies. They looked to be in their 20s but were more than willing to include this middle-aged man in their group, sharing their drugs, van, and experience with him. He was grateful to those kids for proving to him that nothing else has the power to unite people and transcend time and age the way music does.

Woodstock was unlike anything he had ever known. He'd gone to concerts before; the enthusiasm is always contagious. But the energy at Woodstock was *infectious*. Years later, the memory of that excitement still made him euphoric, as if the vibrations from the stage still fueled his soul.

Rufus watched Leon float around through the shelves of sheet music. Leon's tongue stuck out in concentration as he tried deciphering the notes on the pages.

"What can I help you with, kiddo?" Rufus put the guitar on a display stand and walked over to Leon. The kid sucked in his lips and raised his eyebrows.

"Oh! Um—" he put down the sheet music and looked at the toes of his sneakers. Once upon a time, the scuffed brown toecaps were white. Threads hung from the fabric of his shoes, and his toes peeked out from a hole in the mudguard on his left foot.

Great. Something else to embarrass me.

Rufus looked at the top of Leon's ginger head, a sympathetic smile turning down the corners of his mouth. "What do you play? Do you play piano?"

"No, I don't play anything yet. I want to learn how to play guitar."

"Well then!" Rufus grinned. "I play guitar, too. Maybe I can help you."

Leon's head snapped up, his eyes bright with admiration. "You do?"

Rufus chuckled. "Since I was smaller than you. I reckon I'll be more helpful than that old sheet of piano music."

Leon set down the music and looked at Rufus like God himself. "Can you play "Stairway to Heaven"? That one is my favorite."

"I sure can. Would you like to learn?"

"Yes!" Leon bounced on the balls of his feet. He reached out and ran a dirt-encrusted finger over an Ibanez hollow body. "I'm saving up for a guitar. My best friend and I are going to start a band. I have $50.85 saved up right now, so hopefully, by the end of the summer, I can come in here and choose one." Leon looked around at all of the guitars lining the walls. "Maybe once I have the guitar and save up some more money, I can come to learn. Would that be okay? How much would a lesson be?"

Rufus couldn't hold back his laughter. This scrawny little thing gave the impression of having a strong sense of entrepreneurship. "What's your name, kid?"

"Leon."

"I'll tell you what, Leon. Once you get your guitar, I'll give you lessons for three bucks a pop. Until then, I'll teach you the basics on me."

"Oh, Mister, I couldn't—"

"Call me Rufus. And yes, you could. Once you get the basics down, it's all in the ears from there. What kind of guitar are you looking to get?"

Leon looked down at his shoes, trying to hide the smile on his face. "Thank you, sir. And I'm not sure. I want an acoustic to start because I can't afford an amp and cables and all that. I just need a guitar to get me started."

Rufus turned and walked up to the hanging rack of guitars and pulled a parlor guitar down.

"See, regardless of the type of music you like or want to play, an acoustic guitar is a good first guitar," he said as he sat down and placed the guitar on his lap. He fingerpicked some open chords, filling the store with a sweet and gentle sound. "Because these strings are thicker than electric guitar strings, so your fingers will be stronger. Acoustics will help you create calluses. You'll need tough fingers to play like Hendrix and Richards."

"Really?"

"Really! My uncle taught me how to play when I was a kid, and I learned on an acoustic, too. He hooked me on Robert Johnson; I fell in love with the acoustic guitar when I heard him play."

"Who is Robert Johnson?" Leon leaned in, close enough to see his reflection in the guitar's shiny varnish.

Rufus smiled and began plucking a bluesy riff. "Robert Johnson is the father of blues music. He was a real man, just like you and me, but he is also a legend." Rufus stopped playing and lowered his voice, leaning over his guitar. "Some people believe that supernatural forces were at work in giving him his talent."

Leon gasped a sharp inhale. "Like magic?"

Rufus nodded. "Like magic. According to folklore, he went to the crossroads and met the Devil. He is said to have made a deal with the Devil, trading his soul to be a master on the guitar."

Reeling from what he learned, Leon sat beside Rufus on a practice stool. "He sold his soul to play guitar? What happened to him?"

Rufus ran his tongue along the backs of his teeth, stalling an answer. He realized talking to this kid about the Devil might not have been a good idea. He stopped strumming and lifted the guitar off of his lap.

"I think that is enough darkness for today, Leon."

"No!" Leon squeaked. "I can take it. I'm 12 years old, not a baby. I've seen *The Exorcist*. I can handle scary things."

"Well, in that case," Rufus let out a good-natured laugh. Putting his hands on his knees, he leaned in to see the boy eye to eye. "He was poisoned."

"What!"

"Yep, poisoned. Some people believe that he fulfilled his end of the bargain with the Devil, so the contract was up."

Leon considered this, taking out his song list from his pocket and studying it.

"Do you have a pen? I want to add him to my list of songs I want to learn to play."

"I certainly do," Rufus replied, handing him a pen from the cash register. Leon paused as the pen's tip made contact with the paper, realizing he didn't know any of his songs.

"Can you tell me your favorite Robert Johnson song?"

"His most well-known song is "Crossroad Blues," which tells the story of making the deal at the crossroads."

Leon grinned. He wrote down the tune and returned the pen, exclaiming, "So he DID do it!"

Leon and Rufus planned to have an hour-long lesson the following week, and Rufus sent Leon home with a copy of Robert Johnson's *King of the Delta Blues Singers* to listen to, free of charge. Six times that night, he listened to the album from beginning to end, savoring the words, the chord progressions, and the soul that went into each note. Tinny vocals and eerie acoustic melodies filled his room. Leon listened to the lyrics to "Me and the Devil Blues," in which Robert Johnson sings about strolling alongside Satan after he arrived at his door one morning. Leon couldn't help but feel that, if there was any truth to the legend, the deal was well worth it despite having a hellhound on his trail.

* * *

Leon arrived at *For The Record* at exactly 4:00 for his first guitar lesson on Tuesday. He rushed to the door, relieved that no one was inside. There usually wasn't, but there couldn't be any interruptions. He wanted to learn everything he could about the guitar in that hour.

Rufus greeted him, mentally checking off his good deed for the day, excited to help Leon learn how to play. He let Leon borrow a Fender dreadnought for the hour and brought his Gibson Hummingbird, his most valued possession, in for himself.

Once they were settled, they commenced the lesson. Leon learned the open string notes, practiced his finger dexterity, and mastered the minor pentatonic scale in the first 30 minutes. Rufus had written down every detail for Leon to take home and practice with once he had his guitar, but he thought Leon would be fine without it. The dexterity and ease with which Leon handled the instrument amazed him. Rufus anticipated they would get to the pentatonic scale at the tail end of the hour, so he stopped writing the lesson notes there. There was no way that he thought Leon would have the innate skill and stamina to blow through the lesson plan so quickly. It usually took students months to develop that level of coordination. *A gift from God, it must be.* He realized he would have to improvise the remaining lesson material, so he introduced the sliding scale utilizing E-type and A-type scales.

"You know what you just learned?" Rufus asked as he re-tuned his guitar.

Leon gave Rufus a puzzled glance. "The sliding scale? I think that's what you called it."

Rufus smiled as we twisted the tuning peg. "Well, yeah. But you just learned all the tools you need to solo. Soloing and improving is a snap after you're comfortable moving up and down the neck and know where all of your root notes are."

Since the shop was slow after the lesson time was up, they worked on power chords. Leon's hunger for knowledge hadn't been satiated, and no customers roamed the store. Rufus taught him the chord forms for major and minor power chords and dominant 7th and 9th chords. By the end of the lesson, he was strumming the chords and performing nearly seamless chord changes while Rufus outlined the rest of the lesson on scrap paper, using a music stand as a makeshift table.

"I've gotta say, kiddo. You blew me away today." Rufus placed his pen on the ledge of the music stand and smacked his palms against his knees. "I'll be damned if you can't play Led Zeppelin solos by the time you go back to school."

Leon's face brightened. "Do you honestly believe I'm that good?"

Rufus slapped his palm on Leon's shoulder as he stood up. "You're a quick learner; what you learned today would take other people months. Now, I want you to go home and practice the finger dexterity up to the fifth fret and back down. Then, I want you to practice the pentatonic scale up 12 positions and back down the neck. Try the sliding scale if your fingers feel up for it. But pace yourself—your fingers will be hurting as you build up calluses."

Before Leon could say, *'But I don't have a guitar to practice on,'* Rufus entered the back room and emerged with a guitar. It had seen better days—a nasty crack extended from the sound hole up the body, and there were no D or B strings. Almost all of the varnish had been chipped away in some places, and the body bore many pick marks and deep scratches.

"Someone left this behind a long time ago. I can't sell it like this. I almost threw it away but couldn't bring myself to do it. It'll do you fine until you save up enough to come in here and have your pick."

Leon opened his mouth to object, but Rufus raised a meaty palm before he could finish. He looked sternly at Leon, his eyes crinkling with kindness at the corners."Ah-ach. If you don't take it, I'm taking it to the dumpster."

Leon nodded as he took the neck of the old guitar, running his eyes up and down the instrument.

"Thank you. Not just for the guitar but also for the lesson and for saying I was good."

"I don't think you're good. I think you have the potential to be one of the greats." Rufus looked at him with gentle eyes, his smile lines running deep along the corners. He clapped Leon on the back and thought, *he has music in his blood.*

3

Running For the Hills

Leon cradled his new guitar with tender care on the walk home. His head told him that he didn't have to be careful, it's not like he could have done any more damage to it. But his heart put the instrument on a pedestal, despite the damage. It belonged to him, and that was what mattered. It was his first guitar, and it was perfect.

He returned to the trailer park, hiding behind his neighbor's linens on the clothesline like a Halloween slasher and creeping through Mrs. Coltson's neglected garden. No one could see him with this guitar, so he had to be stealthy. If his dad caught him with that guitar, hell, if Mr. Holman knew that he took a free lesson with Rufus, he would get an ass-whooping. He would get an ass-whooping if his mom learned he was given a guitar, even though it was falling apart and cost zero dollars. And if either of them discovered that Jimmy offered him money? They would open a fresh can of whoop ass for him.

Leon loved his dad, as complicated as that feeling was. His dad was the one that introduced him to rock and roll. They used to sit on the floor together, playing old records. Some of Leon's happiest childhood memories were playing air guitar to their favorite solos, with his dad always allowing him to play the lead while he happily strummed along to the rhythm guitar. Leon shredded the air, using the sunbeam shining through the window as a spotlight while dust floated around him like a personal fog machine.

They would laugh and sing along for hours. At one point in time, their relationship ran much deeper than father and son. The love between them used to be so strong, but Mr. Holman's love for the bottle was ultimately stronger than his love for his son.

The more he drank, the further he slipped away. His soft, air-guitar hands became hardened from the iron fist he squeezed his family with, keeping everyone but himself in line. Kind eyes were replaced with sallow bags, dragging his face down. Alcohol transformed the Holman household into a desolate, lonely dictatorship. The further the facade of the family fell, the more distant his mother became, distraught at what had become of her family. Sadness turned to anger, and anger turned to rage before ultimately fizzling out into numbness. That was the worst—the disconnection. Leon craved the family he once had. He was so small when he had it that he wondered if it was even real. It could have been a dream; it felt that far away.

His dad still liked to sing, but only to himself. Only when he was so drunk did all of the words blend together in an incomprehensible tune, rambling on until he passed out. Leon could hear his dad's slurred voice reverberating in his head.

You take nothin' from nobody. You wanna be in no one's debt.

Leon heard that phrase from his dad more and more as he got older, and now, he was in Rufus's debt. He approached the trailer and gently leaned the guitar against the tin wall below his bedroom window. As he ran around the side, his heart pounded when he saw his dad's beat-up Ford in front of the house. He pushed the front door open, sliding his sweaty palms over his pale, freckled arms.

"Jesus Christ, Leon, don't slam the goddamn door."

"Sorry, Dad." Leon rushed past the living room, trying to get to his room before anyone could see the guitar outside. Before he could open the door, he was pulled backward and put into a headlock. Knuckles dragged across the crown of his head, matting his already unkempt hair.

"Where have you been today, dude?"

Leon wriggled out of his dad's grip. They used to horse around, but now that move passed for a power play instead of an innocent joke.

"I went over to Jimmy's. We went over to *For The Record* and looked around." Leon combed his hair with his fingers. He was trying to grow it out, thinking he'd look like Joe Perry with long, shaggy hair, but it was in an awkward phase that was constantly in his face.

Mr. Holman looked at his son, squinting his eyes as he sized him up. Leon twitched, shifting his weight and bouncing on the balls of his feet. His eyes darted from his dad to the crack in the wall behind him, and when he realized his eyes probably looked shifty, he looked down at his feet.

"You didn't steal anything, did you?"

Leon swallowed hard, remembering the copy of "Disraeli Gears" that he stole from that store and snuck into the house. He used the same window method but slipped the record through, waiting to hear the soft thunk against the frayed edge of the carpet. Mr. Holman heard the muffled music late that night and had beat Leon so hard with his belt that he couldn't sit comfortably for the three days. He never forced him to return the record or apologize to Rufus. Leon was taught two lessons that day: one was that stealing was wrong. The other was that if you do something wrong, it's okay, as long as you get away with it. After beating his son raw, Mr. Holman laughed and congratulated him for having the good sense of not getting caught.

"I'm getting a paper route. T-to make some money," Leon blurted and immediately wished he didn't. He briefly considered getting a paper route, but that was where the idea died. Forcing himself to maintain eye contact, Leon curled his toes in his battered sneakers. He couldn't look away, he couldn't move—that would show weakness. So he scratched the sole of his sneaker with his toenail through his sock, fighting with himself not to back down.

"A paper route? Mm-hmm." A nasty sneer spread across his thin lips as he narrowed his eyes even more. "You better not act out, kid, or play any games. If I find out any funny business is going on with you, you're on your own. My dad kicked me out when I was 13. I turned out just fine. If anything, it built character, stopped me from being such a fucking pansy ass, and turned me into a man." Mr. Holman grabbed his son by the shoulder and pulled him in. "Being a klepto is one thing. Being a liar is another. You best not be lying to me."

Leon locked his eyes on his dad's. Sometimes, he wished they would just kick him out. Anywhere would be better than there. He could go stay with Jimmy and be loved. Mrs. Ballard would probably get him lessons and put candles on a cake for his birthday. Maybe she would sing with him, and he and Jimmy would be brothers. *Real* brothers, in every sense of the word. He shook his head 'no' and flinched back as Mr. Holman tightened his grip on his shoulder.

"Use your words, Leon," he hissed.

"I—I'm not-t lying." He could've died for stuttering in his dad's face. His face flushed as his hands balled into fits at his side. The taste of pennies filled Leon's mouth. Mr. Holman let go, pushing him into the bedroom door.

"I ought to throw you out just for that. Look at how red your face is." Blowing a laugh out of his nose, he flicked Leon hard between the eyebrows before returning to the couch. "Toughen up." He threw the words over his shoulder as he slumped back into his seat, cracking open the tab of another beer.

Leon pushed open the door and slid into his room as fast as he could, his face burning with years of internalized rage. He padded over to his window and quietly opened it, careful not to make any noise. Leaning out the window, he grabbed the stock of the guitar and lifted the instrument into his room with as much care as he could muster.

Once he safely brought it inside, he ran his finger over the fretboard. He traced the spots where oily fingers had rubbed away the finish after years of use. Scanning his room, he realized that there was no good hiding spot for something this big. He concealed the guitar as best he could in the back of his closet until he could safely pull it out to practice.

* * *

Leon practiced his guitar whenever he had the chance throughout the following few days. He took it out and began to play as quietly as he could, barely touching a single string as he raced through the exercises and scales, moving his fingers from fret to fret, even on the phantom strings. He looked forward to his father's nightly trips to the bar. After a while, he would hope that he would discover his mother passed out from one too many beers while his father was out. She had taken up his habit somewhere along the line, and for the first time in his life, he was grateful for that. He was improving; his chord changes were fluid, and his fingers moved easily up and down the neck.

Each day, he could feel the calluses getting stronger and the ease of the movements flowing through his hands. He didn't have to think about what to do anymore. His brain didn't have to consciously connect to his fingers to direct them where to go. They just *knew*. They could dance along the fretboard, making music with the rhythmic tapping of his fingertips against the fretboard in lieu of strings.

To give his fingers a break, Leon would ride bikes with Jimmy. They would practice tricks as they raced through the streets, getting honked at by impatient, jaded adults. Leon's favorite thing to do when he wasn't practicing was to go down in the woods and skip rocks on the creek. It was quiet, and it smelled earthy and wet. Jimmy would pack them sandwiches that they would eat with dirty hands before going to hunt for frogs. Leon loved finding frogs. He loved the way their slimy bodies felt in his hands. Sometimes, when Jimmy wasn't looking, he would pull on their legs to watch their skin stretch to the point of tearing. Most of the time, he would get the skin to that point and let them go, watching as they hopped away a little off-kilter. The more unlucky frogs got their limbs torn off as Leon pulled on their femurs, dislocating their legs from the rest of their bodies with little *cracks*. He would place the body down to free up his hand to run his finger up the little bone, separating the muscles from it. Leon stroked the little bones, rubbing the bodily fluid between his fingers. He would wash the gore off of his hands in the creek, raking his fingers through the pebbles to get them extra clean before rejoining Jimmy, who was none the wiser to what had just happened. It made him feel powerful, being able to pluck up another living being and alter them to his liking. He may have grown to hate his dad, but he did understand him. Getting to inflict pain on others made his own a little more bearable because now he wasn't the mouse. He was the cat.

It was a normal, sunny Thursday when Leon got a strange feeling in his gut as he pushed his bike up the dirt street to his house. Otherwise, it had been the perfect summer day. But he could hear his mother shouting and banging as he drew nearer. Leon considered turning around and running back into the woods with the frogs. Against his better judgment, he silently opened the front door and crept inside, brushing his sweaty hair off his red face. His stomach lurched when he realized that his bedroom was the source of the ranting. His heart was racing as he made a few steps toward his bedroom. He came to a stop when he noticed his mother around the corner.

She turned to look at him, her eyes rimmed by black smudged circles. Chunks of frizzy russet hair stuck to the sides of her cheeks. She had a wild look in her eye that made him want to heave. The vein in her neck pulsed from the tension in her body—it was hunched over like a werewolf in the moonlight resisting the change.

"I thought I heard you come in," she sneered at him, a cigarette bobbing loosely from her lips. "I need you to explain something to me." In false delight, she made a grand motion toward his room. Leon cautiously entered and saw that it had been destroyed. His records lay scattered in pieces across the floor and his few pieces of clothing lay shredded and scattered around the room. Ashes littered the pile of debris as she stooped to pick up one of the few surviving records. Hurling her weight into the motion, she slammed *Welcome to My Nightmare* against the wall, screaming as it broke in half.

"You want to explain to me where you've been getting all these records?" She threw her still-lit cigarette onto the floor. The end singed the liner notes of Janis Joplin's *Pearl*, erasing the lyrics as it burned. He watched as the paper burned away in rings, dissolving the words to "Cry Baby" as panic ripped through his little body. It was mocking. Intentional. The light hairs on his freckled arms stood on end as he found his voice.

"I—they're not mine! Stop, Mom!" She tore through his collection, throwing, trampling, and smashing them with her hands while Leon watched in horror.

"Don't lie to me, you little shit!"

"I'm not! I swear, Mama."

"You're just like your father. Thinking you can pull a fast one on me."

"I'm not Ma—"

She snarled, "Then how did you buy these? With what money?"

"Mama, those are Jimmy's old records. Please stop." In the heat of the moment, his voice broke, his legs locked, and his muscles tensed.

"What, are you accepting charity from your little fucking friend? I'm so sorry that you weren't born into that family." Her voice dripped with sarcasm as her face contorted into an exaggerated expression of mock sympathy. "I'm soooo sorry your parents aren't rich enough to give you every fucking thing you've ever wanted. You must be so neglected. I'm just the worst mother ever, huh?"

She slammed another record into the wall and turned wild-eyed at her son.

"No, Mama, please. He just wanted to share them with me!"

"Mmm, right. How the fuck do you explain that?" She spun around and hurled a record into the closet at the broken-down guitar. Leon cried; his stomach grumbled, and he began to sweat. A few fragments of the record fell into the sound hole as it broke against the back of the closet and scraped the guitar's body.

Leon cried out in desperation, "The trash! It was about to be thrown away, so I took it."

Mrs. Holman smirked menacingly, and Leon received his mother's undivided attention for the first time in two years.

"Oh, trust me, Leon. It will be thrown away."

Leon's hands secreted sweat as he reached out toward his mother. He extended his arm to keep her from reaching for the guitar, throwing himself into her path. But it was too late.

"No! Stop—"

Before he could finish speaking, his guitar crashed into the dresser. The giant crack by the sound hole severed the entire front of the instrument. As the guitar split, the strings dangled hopelessly between the fractured sections. When the guitar's neck severed from the body, Leon's lungs also took the impact out of pure shock. He gasped to catch his breath as if the wind had been knocked out of him like when he was five years old and had fallen flat on his back after dropping out of the tree he'd been climbing. Only watching the splintered pieces of wood litter the ground was more painful. He stood there frozen as if his feet had become rooted to the ground, forcing him to watch the events unfold through a distorted lens as tears filled his eyes. She appeared to move in slow motion—this moment in time suspended in the cosmos with every hit and every bash slowed down so that Leon could absorb each blow to its full effect. The only item of value he had ever owned lay in pieces on the floor, destroyed by his own mother, who was meant to love him the most in the world. His mother betrayed him, letting him fully comprehend the depth of the wound that the violation could create.

"What in the fuck is going on in here?" Leon tensed up as the tears that had brimmed began silently streaming down his face.

Dad was home.

Mrs. Holman gave her son a condescending sneer that screamed *you're going to get it now*. She threw the guitar's neck atop the rest of the shattered fragments. "Come look at everything your son stole," she called to her husband, spatting the words out.

Prickly heat spread over Leon's entire body. He glared at his mother with a look of betrayal, helplessness, and utter wrath beneath the surface. In that instant, he became alienated from himself by his unadulterated hatred for her. She repulsed him. He was ashamed of her and his attachment to her. He imagined himself hitting her in the face with the severed guitar neck that lay limply on the floor, bludgeoning her face until it was incapable of ever again giving him a condescending smile. Mr. Holman interrupted his fantasy by seizing him by the neck and pushing him against the wall. Rage filled Leon's entire body as he gasped for air.

"Let go of me," he said as evenly as he could, his voice rasping from the pressure on his throat. Mr. Holman laughed, his breath smelling like whiskey, plaque, and stale cigarettes. He put more pressure on his son's neck.

"Or what?" Mr. Holman leered, his voice low. "I'm going to put the fear of God into you, boy."

Leon's eyes flicked to the cross necklace gleaming in the fluorescent light. This was his father's favorite line. He was always threatening to fill him with the fear of God. *Fear of God.* Jimmy went to church with his family, and he never talked about fearing God. He spoke about a loving God. A forgiving one. A God that gave his son as a sacrifice for humankind. That didn't sound like a God to be feared.

Why should I have to live in fear?

Leon, caught in a cycle of fear and moral turmoil, always had someone to fear, whether it was his father or God. His father. A man who wore a cross, yet was a sinner in every sense. A prideful man. His pride and gluttony, manifested in his excessive drinking and subsequent wrath, were painful reminders of the hypocrisy that governed their lives.

I'm done being afraid.

Years of rage boiled to the surface. With as much strength as he had in his underdeveloped body, Leon kicked between his father's legs. With a stomach-lurching groan, Mr. Holman dropped, letting go of Leon's throat. Leon crossed the room and wrapped the bit of the guitar that still had the string attached to it around his neck. He dragged the string deep into his throat with all the vigor he could conjure, creating a bloody path.

His mother, who had begun to lunge for him, came to a stop. She screamed as she froze, reaching for her son to unwrap the guitar string.

Leon threw himself into the dresser violently and split his forehead open. He experienced no pain as a thin trail of blood dripped down his eyebrow, little droplets of blood pooling on his light eyelashes. The rage pent up in his little body released itself with the blood. He felt nothing but loathing.

He basked in his power as he watched his mother weep for him, imploring

34

him to stop and attempting to wrap her arms around him. Leon's father, who had hardly gathered himself up off the floor, stared at him in utter horror.

He wanted to ruin them.

Leon reveled in their sympathy, worry, and terror. He had them eating out of the palm of his hand, too afraid of his next move to look away. It was a sensation he never wanted to lose. He wished to drive them—his mother—even closer to the breaking point. He leaned down cautiously and picked up a fragment of a broken record. It looked sharp—the closest thing he could get to a weapon in that moment. He grinned as he gripped the piece to the blue vein that stood out so prominently in his pale forearm.

"I swear to God I'll do it," Leon growled. "I'll do it, and I'll call the police. You will go to jail." He spoke carefully and clearly with that final statement, enunciating each word. *Don't go too deep,* he told himself, *just deep enough that they let you go. And if they don't? Drive it deeper and end it.*

"Leon," Mrs. Holman cried, crouching over her husband writhing on the floor. "Leon, please, you can't treat me like this. Baby, Mommy loves you."

Leon snorted. "Yeah, right. You're a liar and a bitch."

Mrs. Holman let out a primal cry. "They'll take you away from me," she whined.

"Yeah, and Emmy too. And we'd both be better for it. I'd love for someone to come here and take me away." Leon's hand shook as he pushed the shard into his skin, causing a small bead of blood to form at the point. "No one needs to know about this. Don't put your hands on me, don't talk to me, don't talk to anyone *about* me. You no longer have a son, okay? If you agree, I'll put this shard down and be on my way. You and your piece of shit abusive husband can live unhappily ever after together. Deal?"

They locked their gazes on each other. Her spirit pleaded with his as they bore into one another's souls. The freckles sprinkled across his mother's nose made her look girlish, almost pretty. Just like that, he almost felt sorry for her as he looked into her wide eyes. She crumbled when she saw he wasn't going to break. Raking her hands through her hair, she pulled the muscles in her face taut, erasing all the sorrow and the worry from her eyes and mouth.

"You promise you won't call?"

Leon inhaled a sharp breath that hurt worse than the gash in his forehead or his bleeding neck. This pain was in his heart. Of course, her self-preservation kicked in instead of her motherly instinct.

"Promise," he spat, hissing out the last syllable.

"Alright," she said, indifferent. The only sign of emotion she displayed was a single tear that fell from her eye. Her tone turned hard, albeit hoarse, as she huffed at him. "I never wanted you anyway."

A bitter laugh came from Leon's chest as he glared at her. He nodded and tossed the fragment into the heap of his ruined possessions. "Fine," he said with an edge in his voice.

Leon looked into his mother's eyes—his eyes, green with yellow and brown flecks—and said the last words he'd ever speak to her: "You are a worthless whore. Fuck you."

He kept his gaze fixed on her to see her response. He watched the blatant anguish spread across her entire face, the corners of her mouth pulling downward, giving her a grotesque frown.

His father's angry face, already crimson from drinking, became much redder as Leon gazed down at him. He shakily stood up, ripping off his belt while maintaining constant eye contact with his son. He wavered as he rose, his movements clumsy and fumbling.

Leon straightened his shoulders and stood tall to confront his father, who wobbled slightly from the pain. Leon's eyes blazed, even though the corners of his lips twitched downward, threatening to reveal his fear of his father. He refused to let him enjoy his fear. Leon angled his chin downward, staring toward his old man through his eyebrows—a challenge—as his father looped the belt over his hand.

"Todd—" Leon heard his mother speak softly for the first time. "Don't. Just…just let him go." Her voice broke, and defeat overtook her as she slid down the side of the dresser onto the floor.

Mr. Holman's mouth curled in disgust as he watched a spark ignite in Leon's eyes. Leon realized he had the upper hand. He grinned, but not before imitating his father's expression.

Leon escaped from the trailer. His parents' neglect and cruelty had never made him feel more liberated; they had taken the burden off his shoulders. He ran for the hills, breathing in the evening breeze and gazing at the stars.

* * *

He hadn't seen his parents since that night in 1976. They could have tracked him down; he didn't travel far. Mrs. Ballard took him in when he showed up at her doorstep that night, dried blood running down his throat from the guitar string amidst the nasty bruise where his dad had pinned him up against the wall. Blood from the wound on his forehead spilled down his face, leaving red-tinted stains as he wiped it away. Tears trickled down in streams, washing away some of the mess.

Without asking any questions, she took him in, fixed him up, and gave him a place to call home. Finally, he had enough food to eat and clean clothes to wear. He was accepted into their family, and for the first time in his life, he was given the most essential thing in the world: love. Instead of only being blood brothers through the pact, he and Jimmy became a real family. Despite the Ballards' affection and acceptance, Leon couldn't help but resent their attention because he suspected they didn't truly love him—they merely pitied him.

Leon didn't have a guitar after the ordeal with his mother. The coloring of the bruises deepened to a greenish-yellow by Tuesday when he showed up empty-handed for his weekly lesson. Rufus made a deal with him: he could keep the money he had saved and work shifts at the store. Leon's earnings from those hours would go toward the purchase of whatever instrument and equipment he wanted. They would carry on with their lessons in the meantime. Leon, deeply touched by Rufus's generosity, decided on the cheapest amp in the store and a tobacco burst Les Paul replica.

He excelled in his lessons with Rufus. Every day, he would go home and show Jimmy everything he had learned. Jimmy's parents bought him an acoustic dreadnought guitar from the Sears catalog so that he and

Leon could practice playing together and come up with their own chord progressions. Jimmy began penning lyrics about the girls in his class and the abuses of power he observed from the teachers. Leon, consumed by his passion, skipped classes and eventually stopped attending altogether when he was fifteen. Occasionally, he wondered whether the truancy officers had ever hauled in his parents.

Before his shifts at *For The Record*, he had begun to sell drugs at the loading dock behind the strip mall. He began coming home less often, either from putting in longer hours at the record shop or dropping LSD alone in a graveyard to write better songs. It became a ritual for him, as he thought that the spirits of the deceased used his body as a vessel to write poetic lyrics. He always returned sooner or later because Jimmy kept his beloved instrument safe and sound.

* * *

In an era when rock and roll took over the famous Sunset Strip, Leon and Jimmy grew into men. They fell into the trap of fate as destined bonds and deals were forged, leading us to our story of the ill-fated band called Psychosomatic Slaughter.

II

PART TWO: A Deal With The Devil

1983

4

Strike Up The Band

When the razor's blades slid over Leon's jaw and down his neck, he cocked his chin toward the mirror. He examined his face after wiping off the shaving cream with a damp towel. It wasn't the face of a scrawny 12-year-old boy anymore. He had a sinister allure to him thanks to an expressive face that was sharp and defined due to his broad jawline and straight, well-defined nose. Auburn brows accented his green eyes, making them look piercing and fierce. He hated his eyes—they belonged to his mother.

He looked at the crumbling tile wall and the dark, moldy grout that lined his bathroom. At some point, the grout was probably white, tarnished by the neglect of tenant after tenant. He despised his face. As he grew older, he could see his mother's hair falling over his shoulders and his father's square chin emerging. He would rather stare at that filth on the wall and the rotting grout than at himself. Flipping the mirrored door of his medicine cabinet open, he stashed the razor inside.

Leon dabbed on some aftershave; the musky leather scent was overpowered by the alcohol, which burned his pale skin before he closed the mirror cabinet. Taking one final look in the mirror, he ran his fingers over his long hair that had been cut into a shag, framing his face. He grabbed a comb and brushed it through his overgrown bangs, but it made them frizzy. Yanking the comb through the rest of his hair in frustration, a small clump of coppery strands was torn out, creating a tangled knot around the teeth of the comb. Shaking his head, he gave up on his appearance for the day and put the comb behind the faucet on the sink.

Leon stepped out of the bathroom and into his small apartment's main living space. The living room, kitchen, and bedroom were all situated in the same area. The scent of mildew and incense made the air thick. He leaned against the chipped laminate countertop, pulling the edge and releasing it to hear it clap back into place.

Steam rose off of a bowl of hot water on the countertop. He reached out, pulling on the corner of the plastic baggie steeping in it. The bag bobbed as the weight of the rat inside settled back into the water. He ran his fingers over the nicked rim of the bowl, scraping the moisture into the raw bisque where the glaze had cracked away. It had been about 40 minutes, the perfect amount of time.

"Breakfast is served, buddy!" Leon crooned as he reached into the bag, pulling out the stiff body with feeding tongs. He slid open the glass aquarium that sat beside the unmade bed. Calling it a bed was an overstatement; the threadbare mattress sat directly on the floor. Leon didn't own a single set of sheets, so a pile of blankets concealed layers of mystery stains.

The bedding in the aquarium crunched as a ball python slithered out from beneath a log hideout. Its head twisted about like a wave, extending to accept the sacrifice. Its tongue slithered as its head leaned back before striking, yanking the rodent from the tongs. Leon chuckled with pride as the python devoured its meal, swallowing the rodent bit by bit.

"Good boy," he praised the serpent, securing the enclosure. He checked it twice before heading to his afternoon shift at *For The Record*. The stairs leading down from his apartment creaked loudly with each of his heavy-footed steps, shaking under his weight.

Please be dead.

Leon hoped for a slow day so that he could pick out an instrument from the ones for sale on the wall and practice. He and Jimmy had been looking for the right people to jam with and take their music to the next level, but they had yet to find the perfect fit.

Puffing on a cigarette, he walked along the busy street to *For The Record* as cars whizzed by him, cruising up the Sunset Strip. Blaring music filled the air, and the voices of Michael Jackson, Madonna, and The Police wafted by Leon.

He walked past the large storefront windows showcasing the newest records, shiniest instruments, and most popular merchandise. Since he was a kid, the store had come a long way, largely thanks to his ideas. Rufus had taken Leon's suggestions and set them into action throughout the years, transforming the store from a run-down, hole-in-the-wall record store into a gathering spot for music lovers and musicians alike.

Leon pulled on the door and was greeted with the familiar scent of vinyl records and the aged wood of used guitars, their fingerboards bearing the marks of countless melodies. He helped Rufus replace the bins of albums and tapes with aisles of record and cassette racks, each meticulously organized by genre and artist. Guitars and basses still hung on the walls, and Rufus cleared out a space in the back of the store for keyboards and drum equipment. The instruments glittered under the soft glow of the overhead lights, luring musicians of all skill levels to pick them up and give them a play.

Despite all the changes, Leon still experienced a wave of overwhelming nostalgia when he walked in every day. He gave a slight nod and wave to the couple sifting through music as he made his way to Rufus, who was sitting on one of the chairs in front of the listening booths where people could sample new albums. He looked the same as when Leon first met him, except for the extra plumpness around his waist and the fact that the gray in his hair and beard had turned white.

"Hey, Rufus." Leon slipped behind the cash register and leaned on the glass case displaying guitar strings, fingerboard oil, pedals, and anything else you could need or want for your instrument. "Sweet guitar."

Rufus grinned as he tuned a cherry hollow body guitar with a black pickguard. "Sure is, kiddo." He stood up, carried the guitar to the wall, and rehung it. "Sadie called out. She is studying for her 'final final,' as she calls it." Rufus held out his hand and circled it around, trying to conjure some sense out of the air. He let out a gruff sigh. "I'm not sure why she cares so much now. One passing grade won't make up for the rest of the year."

Leon snorted, giving his boss a downturned smile. "Aren't you glad you have a strapping young employee who doesn't have to worry about graduation?"

Leaning against the edge of the display case, Rufus spread his palms out in front of him as he faced Leon squarely. "It's not like I didn't try and talk you out of it," he said and head cocked to the side, "but you try and talk a wise-ass little brat out of what they think is good for him."

Leon locked his gaze on Rufus's kind eyes, and his lips twisted to stifle a laugh. He couldn't hide it anymore—his shoulders began to shake with laughter.

"Listen," Leon protested, pushing off the display case and leaning back in a cocky stretch. "When you have so much talent in such a rugged, hard body, what good is school?" Leon sucked on his teeth and swung his hands out, giving Rufus a dramatic shrug before slapping them back down on the counter. Rufus let out a sigh that hitched into a laugh.

"Cocky son of a bitch." He pushed his palm into the side of Leon's head, giving him a good-natured shove.

"Are you gonna be sticking around tonight?" Leon hoped for a yes. He loved closing with Rufus. As the night wound down, they would sit and have a jam session, taking turns improvising solos. They would sit there riffing together, sometimes until midnight. Those were the best nights.

"Yeah, I'll be around," Rufus drummed on the glass case. "But I'm not doing shit. You're doing all the work."

"Just call me Cinder-fuckin'-rella," Leon called after Rufus, who waved at him as he strode into the back office.

The front bell chimed as it opened, and a woman's high-pitched laughter poured in. Leon's lips curled into a grin, knowing exactly whose arm she was dangling off of.

Dallas Jacobson.

Dallas came in every day with a different girl, each hotter than the last, despite his gaudy sense of style. His typical look included tight shirts, bandanas, scarves, and leather or spandex pants. This time, he wore regular jeans, a Harley Davidson t-shirt, and a spiked leather jacket. The heels of snakeskin boots clopped dully on the floor as he strutted in. Bracelets snaked up his wrist, a cross necklace hung around his neck, and a cigarette dangled behind his ear. His hairstyle was almost identical to that of the girl he was with today—jet-black, long, and tousled with bangs that fell into his eyes. A black leather fedora rested atop his teased hair, tilted just so on his head.

Leon couldn't help but admire Dallas's theatrics, and his eyes involuntarily gave the day's girl an appreciative up-and-down. Dallas, always quick to notice, puckered his lips into a smug smile. His large mouth and naturally upturned lip corners gave his face a sly, mischievous expression as if he were perpetually smirking, which, to his credit, he usually was. Dallas put his hand on the girl's ass, forming an "O" with his thumb and pointer finger before giving it a squeeze. He winked at Leon, his eyes smudged with black eyeliner that made them look sleepy and seductive.

Leon found this man *fascinating*. Despite the makeup and overt flamboyance, he oozed sensuality. Dallas harnessed that, exuding an unabashed sexual magnetism wherever he went. He might not be conventionally attractive, with a large hooked nose contrasting his pronouncedly high cheekbones, but it *worked* for him. Leon watched him come in day after day, strutting around with a chick on his arm and an intoxicating arrogance. His confidence was contagious from across the store.

When a girl approached the counter to buy a Bonnie Tyler album and a Rick Springfield poster, Leon's attention was diverted from the colorful couple. He rang her up and turned back to find the girl of the day standing alone, studying the album cover of a newly released pop album. Leon's eyes darted around the store to find Dallas standing in front of the bass guitars.

He had never seen Dallas stray off by himself. He was usually too busy groping, kissing, or petting the girl he brought in. Dallas was a creature of routine; he had a shtick that he stuck to. First, he would bring the girl with him around the store, and together, they would sit in the lounge area, where he would choose a bass from the wall and give her a little performance. He never used a bass pick, bragging about how well he knew how to use his two fingers. The set list was always the same: "Under Pressure" by David Bowie and Queen opened the performance, followed by Iggy Pop's "The Passenger," which led into the grand finale of Pink Floyd's "Money." Leon noticed how Dallas would finesse the tunes and add his own flair, adding fills between riffs and improvising the bridge. There was undoubtedly technical skill there. That much was clear, but his groove overshadowed it.

That groove. One cannot learn to have groove like that through imitation or by practicing with books of sheet music. It's a natural rhythm, as fluid as breathing, that Dallas effortlessly brought to life.

As luck would have it, it was not a typical day. Leon slipped out from behind the register to approach the bassist. Dallas welcomed him with an over-the-shoulder smile.

"She's a beauty," he said in a deep, raspy voice. "When did you get her in?"

"We must've just got it last night. This is the first I've seen it here," Leon said as he inspected the beauty in question: a used white Gibson Firebird III. The instrument had been well-loved, with some scuffs and missing finish, but there was no denying that it was still stunning.

"She must have quite the story." Dallas delicately rubbed a black scratch with the tips of his ring-adorned fingers.

"How long have you been playing?"

"Since I was a kid," he said, his wide mouth stretching into a smile. "My brother was quite the prodigy and taught me." His smile faded as his lips pursed into a slight considering pout. He looked the instrument up and down before flicking his eyes to the floor.

"Does he still play?" If this guy taught Dallas, he must be a God.

"He—uh, he died of a drug overdose a couple of years ago. Heroin." Dallas gnashed his teeth together, shifting his weight. "I feel close to him when I play." He shrugged, rolling off the sentiment as he looked back at the bass. He busied his hands by running his thumb along the E string.

Leon puckered his lips, not knowing where exactly he should look. "I'm sorry, man."

Dallas's eyes darted from Leon to the floor as he fidgeted, twisting his toe on the old carpet. With a jolt, he smirked and laughed out of his nose, clearing his throat as he pulled his spine up straight.

"Yeah, that's the story I tell chicks. It makes them feel sad and makes me look vulnerable. They eat that shit up," he laughed, elbowing Leon in the arm. His gaze lingered on Leon's face, gauging the redhead's expression as his own faltered with each passing millisecond. When Leon didn't look impressed, he quickly added, "I play with a band a couple of nights a week. Nothing serious, but it sure brings in a lot of opportunities."

Dallas ran his tongue over his bottom teeth and raised his eyebrows toward the girl he came in with. "Today's opportunity is Diana."

Leon bit back a smile and nodded. He leaned back as Dallas encroached on his personal space, taking the acknowledgment of the joke as a positive sign. Leon could smell Diana's cherry chapstick on Dallas's neck, mixing with his overwhelmingly strong cologne.

"Would you be interested in getting serious with a band, or are you just in it for chicks?" Leon asked.

Dallas cocked his head to the side, bridging the space Leon put between them only a moment before. "I don't do it just for chicks, dude," Dallas balked. "There's drugs, too."

The expression on Leon's face hardened, his eyes bugging slightly as he squinted at Dallas, trying to figure out if he was joking again. He wanted nothing to get in between him and his music, especially smack. Heroin was the cruel mistress of rock and roll, leading many of the greats astray. He refused to let drugs be the Yoko of his band. Dallas scoffed.

"I'm not into the hard stuff, dude. Just grass," he rolled his eyes up to the side and pricked his head up. "I dropped acid once and bugged out. I do coke, but...who doesn't do snow?" Dallas swayed his head from side to side, puckering his lips so intensely that they almost touched the tip of his beaked nose. "All jokes aside, I think I would. You know, get serious. I just need to find the right guys to go there with."

Bingo.

"I'll tell you what," Leon said, stretching back and peering over his shoulder toward Rufus in the back office. He made a show of leaning covertly toward Dallas, who turned to look at the Firebird while cocking an ear toward

Leon, playing into the ruse.

"I've heard you play," Leon muttered out of the corner of his mouth. "I'll take 50 bucks off the bass if you come to meet me and my friend for a jam session. See if we're the right guys."

Dallas's eyes sparkled with intensity at the offer. Leon wondered if Dallas might also be a gambler, given how his eyes shone at the proposition. He held out his hand.

"Do we have a deal?"

Dallas pursed his lips with a sly, upturned smile. He tilted his chin up, gazing down at Leon through thick, black lashes.

"We sure do."

* * *

Jimmy closed his locker for the last time after taking his final high school exam in music theory. He had to compose and notate a melody in a specific key with a range of intervals and cadences. The test was easy for him; being a guitarist gave him an advantage. Leon taught Jimmy to play rhythm guitar while he played lead.

As he strolled down the hallway, a group of girls intercepted him and wished him a flirty farewell for the summer.

"I know you're graduating, but you better come back and visit us," they giggled.

Gone were the days of ridicule that he had once endured from his peers, especially from the girls. While he wasn't the most popular guy around, his charismatic personality could easily win anyone over. His rock star style, with band tees, tight Levi's, and an oversized belt buckle, was irresistible to rebellious teenage girls. Every girl in his class fantasized about removing that belt buckle with their teeth.

He ditched the feathered shags and mullets his buddies wore and embraced his straight black locks, which he grew out long enough to graze the end of his rib cage. Jimmy had a striking blend of delicate beauty and masculine appeal, giving him a perfectly harmonious face with a strong nose, full lips, and deep brown eyes. Those dark eyes and his charming smile made women of all ages swoon. As he made his way out to the parking lot, he flashed that irresistible smile at Sissy Anderson.

The June afternoon smelled like nostalgia and freedom. He breathed in the fresh breeze coming from the newly mowed football field. The breeze mingled with smoke from students loitering in the parking lot. Some younger kids were getting hazed by the outgoing seniors, others were making plans to meet up and drive around that night, some were getting high, and some were hustling to their cars to get out of that hellhole and never look back. Jimmy, on the other hand, planned on going to Leon's apartment and hanging out there by himself until Leon got off work.

As he strolled towards the parking lot, Jimmy's thoughts were interrupted by a sudden collision. He stumbled back, the keys to his black 1980 Camaro clattering to the ground. A black canvas rucksack fell from the person he had collided with, scattering its contents.

"Ow, fuck!" It was a wonder that Jimmy wasn't on the pavement, too. A brick shit house had nothing on this guy.

"Shit, dude, I'm sorry," Jimmy said and stooped down to help collect the items on the ground. He scooped up a few dropped objects, including a battered paperback edition of *The Return of the King* by J.R.R. Tolkien, a hardcover copy of *Dungeon Master's Guide for Advanced DND*, and an unopened package of slinky electric guitar strings.

"Hey, that's okay," the hulking figure said, shifting his weight awkwardly before squatting down next to Jimmy, opening his bag so that he could slide the items back in. "Thanks, man."

"No problem." Jimmy stood up. "What's your name again?"

After he asked the question, Jimmy remembered his name. He had crashed into Cameron Tulley, better known around school as Cam, the class clown and the Dungeon Master for the Dungeons and Dragons club. People would go out of their way to stop by the black box in the art wing on Tuesdays to see what he was cooking up, regardless of whether they understood the game because of how seriously he took campaigns. Despite being the resident outcast, he could surely draw the interest of the masses. No one would ever admit it, but he made the game look cool.

"You can just call me Cam," he laughed awkwardly. Cam's arched, extremely expressive eyebrows gave his otherwise innocent face a hint of menace. His nose was slightly curved and had a strong bridge that gave his face a masculine look, otherwise offset by his prominent cupid's bow.

"You're Jimmy, right? I see you down at *For the Record* all the time."

"Really?" Jimmy always hung out there, lazing by the register with Leon, discussing music theory with Rufus, or hauling up in a listening booth for hours, but he'd never noticed Cam there. "What kind of stuff are you into?"

"Zeppelin, Rush, Genesis," Cam tilted his head as his eyes darted around, trying to visualize his music collection in the sky. He began naming artists on his fingertips like a toddler learning how to count to ten: "Ozzy, Deep Purple, Jethro Tull."

"What do you play?" Jimmy asked, his curiosity piqued.

"An Ibanez hollow body." Cam noticed the corners of Jimmy's mouth turn down in consideration—he obviously wasn't expecting that answer. The guitarist rubbed the nape of his neck, bouncing on the balls of his feet. "With the right pedals, I can get any sound I want."

"Oh yeah?"

"Yeah, man!" Cam laughed, his words drawn out in an authentically Californian rhythm. Cam would have appeared relatively feminine if his frame hadn't been so large, with his high brow, oval face, and overall soft features. He stood out next to the rest of the D&D clan. Cam embodied California health with his tanned skin and toned physique, which he developed by designing his own obstacle courses. His friends made fun of him for what he dubbed his "warrior training." He laughed along with them, teasing that he would actually be able to pull Arwen, flexing his arms as the joke's punchline.

"Would you maybe want to come play with me and my friend? You've probably seen him, too. He's the redhead that works at the music shop."

Cam used his hand to comb the long, golden-brown waves out of his face. The bright sun shone straight into his eyes, causing him to squint as he looked at Jimmy. He broke into a broad smile, revealing straight teeth.

"Hell yeah, brother!" His lips curled in an animated grin. His bobbing head abruptly stopped as his expression turned serious. "I can go get my guitar right now."

To stop himself from smiling, Jimmy bit his lower lip. This guy was unusual and lived up to his reputation, but Jimmy didn't mind. It felt good to see Cam confident and comfortable with himself, not worried about others' opinions. He came across as a calm, carefree, and genuinely nice guy. Plus, he may be able to balance out Leon's volatile personality.

"Hop in." Jimmy gestured to the car's passenger side. Cam gave a tiny skip in place before bouncing into long strides to the car's passenger door. Jimmy chuckled under his breath as he settled in behind the wheel, adjusting the rear-view mirror. Cam threw himself into the car and slapped his hands on his knees.

"So, are you in a band?"

"We're trying to put something together," Jimmy said as he backed out of his spot, carefully avoiding the student bodies lingering in the middle of the parking lot. "The redhead, his name is Leon. We've had this idea of being in a band together for…shit…it must be five or six years now. He plays guitar. He's a good lead man, and I've been playing rhythm just until we can find someone better than me and who can mesh with Leon."

"And that's where I come in," Cam said confidently, jutting himself in the chest with his thumb. He mimed a guitar resting in his lap, giving it a hard strum and a headbang. "Is Leon tough to mesh with or something?" Cam flipped his head back, blowing his hair out of his face.

Jimmy chewed his lower lip and tugged on his earlobe, keeping his eyes fixed on the road.

"He's—he's got a big personality," he admitted. "He has a flare for the dramatics and is extremely…passionate." Jimmy nodded, satisfied with how well that characterized Leon without being truthful enough to scare Cam away.

"Like me," Cam said excitedly.

"Eh—sort of," Jimmy grimaced.

Cam chewed this over, stroking an imaginary beard on his clean-shaven face. "He's got a temper, doesn't he?"

Jimmy burst out laughing. "Yeah. Yeah, he does."

"Noted," Cam said. "I think we'll get along just fine. I get along with pretty much everyone."

Jimmy pulled up in front of Cam's house, a small single-family home painted bright yellow. Multi-color stained glass diamonds decorated the windows facing the street. The outside of the home garnered as much personality as the inside. Cam walked Jimmy through colorfully painted rooms with bright carpets. Toys littered the floor, and almost every inch of the walls gave glimpses into the family that lived there. Memories, children's art, and school photos hung on an endless collage throughout the living room and up the stairs into the hallway.

"Let's make this fast before my mom gets home," Cam said as he pushed open a light green door.

"What, she won't let you go out?" Jimmy took one last look at the art on the wall and followed Cam into the room, wishing they didn't have to make it fast. He let his eyes drift around Cam's bedroom, taking in Cam's broad collection of movie memorabilia. A replica of the Millennium Falcon spaceship decorated his dresser, with tiny stormtroopers positioned around it. Michael Myers stood 9 inches tall on the bedside table, a little knife held mid-stab, next to an E.T. lamp with a glowing red heart. Band and movie posters adorned the walls, while fantasy maps hung above the desk, surrounded by notes and hand-drawn pictures.

"Something like that," Cam coiled an amp cord lying on the floor and secured it under his armpit. "Those are from old campaigns," he huffed a little laugh to himself. "I think they're cool."

"They are." Jimmy inspected the drawings further. "Did you draw these?"

"Yup." Cam reached under his dresser and pulled out a tiny pedal board with a delay pedal, a distortion pedal, and a wah pedal. "I like to draw when I listen to music."

Cam reached under his bed and slid out a hardback case. He gave his new friend a knowing glance as he clicked the buckles open. Gauging Jimmy's interest, he paused like a magician about to pull a rabbit out of his hat. Cam popped the lid of the case open, revealing a shiny hollowbody guitar with a worn black pickguard. The scratches on the instrument documented years of passionate playing, etching his performances into the surface of the instrument.

Before Jimmy could express his admiration, Cam dropped the lid and latched the case like a gangster on a heist. He stood and shoved his amp into Jimmy's arms, stacking the peddle board on top.

"Let's go," Cam bopped past him, guitar case in hand.

Cam treated his guitar the way most people would care for a human child. He carefully opened the car door, slowly swinging it open to keep from knocking the case. Cam gently strapped it in the rear seat with the seat belt, tugging on the strap lightly to tighten it.

"She's not going anywhere," Cam announced, hurling himself into the passenger seat.

"Alright," Jimmy laughed as he fired up the engine and shifted the car into gear. "Let's rock and roll."

"Hell yeah!" Cam cheered, rooting through Jimmy's tape collection in the center console. Jimmy understood why teachers always put Cam in the back of the classroom; the dude could not sit still.

"Good tunes, man." Cam nodded in approval as he sorted through Aerosmith, Led Zeppelin, and The Who.

Cam selected a tape and stuck it in the cassette deck. Geezer Butler's pulsating bass line and Tony Iommi's slow, powerful guitar riff filled the car. The thundering pulse of the drums heightened the song's ominous tone. Cam bobbed his head with each hit of the hi-hat.

"Duh-nuh!" Cam sang the guitar hit as Ozzy's voice rang out. Jimmy joined Ozzy Osbourne in singing while Cam air-guitared beside him and sang along to the guitar riffs under his breath.

When Jimmy looked in his passenger side mirror to pull onto the street where Leon's apartment was, he saw Cam headbanging in the seat next to him, a mass of flying hair. He put the gearshift into park and switched off the ignition as Cam raised his head and shook his hair out of his face.

"You never told me, but I'm guessing you're the singer in this band."

"Yeah, I am," Jimmy laughed, racking his hand through his mussed-up hair.

Cam grinned approvingly and tapped his palms on his thighs. "Shit, dude, this is going to be good. I can feel it."

As they unpacked the guitar and equipment from Jimmy's Camaro, Cam stepped back and shielded his eyes from the light.

"You know, if we start playing gigs, having this as our home base would make for easy transport." The Sunset Strip, just a stone's throw away, was home to a vibrant nightlife culture with clubs that were home base for the L.A. rock scene.

"Yeah." Jimmy slammed the car door shut. He grabbed the guitar case with one hand and rested his free arm against the car. "Most nights, Leon and I'll walk down there and see whatever bands are playing."

"You live here too?" Cam picked up the rest of his equipment and followed Jimmy up the wobbly stairs to Leon's apartment. Jimmy balanced the guitar case gingerly on his thigh so it wouldn't hit the railing. Cam followed behind, thundering extra hard to make the stairs sway.

"Nah, I might as well, though," Jimmy said as he fumbled with his keys. "I live with my parents, but I spend most of my time here when I'm not in school. They don't seem to mind. They never question where I'm at. They'd rather us play here than in the house, I guess. My parents don't care about the noise, but the neighbors do."

Jimmy slid the key into the keyhole and pushed the door open. Cam stepped in, coughing a bit as he inhaled the pungent aroma of stale incense.

Leon tried his hardest to make the apartment his own. He attempted to cover the peeling wallpaper by hanging rock posters, layering them to create his own heavy-metal worshiping wallpaper. Scratched records were nailed to the wall, breaking up the array of posters. A large tapestry depicting Baphomet, the humanoid beast with a goat's head, served as the main focal point of this homemade wallpaper. A pentagram was inscribed on the goat's forehead, with a torch illuminating the way to enlightenment perched between its two enormous horns.

Cam skimmed over the spines of the music books, ranging from rock and blues guitar to the occasional sheet music compilation. Leon's collection of books dedicated to the occult filled the other half of the bookshelf. His books about possession, the Devil, seances, witchcraft, pagan rites, and the paranormal lined the shelves. Cam ran a finger along the worn spine of a paperback copy of *Michelle Remembers*. He pulled it out, running a hand over the deep creases in the cover from being accidentally folded.

Multiple copies of both books that Anton Szandor LaVey wrote adorned the shelves, their pages tattered and worn from repeated reading. One book had its cover facing outwards, showcasing the Sigil of Baphomet.

The Satanic Bible.

Strange discoveries kept in jars sat between the stacks and rows of books. One was full of cockroach carcasses floating in liquid. One had desiccated bird bones. Leon kept one jar full of shedded snake skin and another brimming with what looked to be mouse tails.

"I take it this is where the skin came from," Cam said as he squatted in front of the tank containing the ball python. The serpent lay lazily along the front of the enclosure, satiated from the morning feeding.

"Ah, yeah," Jimmy flopped down on the couch he had helped Leon bring in from the curb down the block. "What can I say? He's got interesting taste."

"Yeah, he sure does," Cam said, not taking his eyes off the snake.

"That's Stevie."

"As in Nicks?"

"No, as in Ray Vaughn," Jimmy replied.

"Is your friend, like, a Satanist or something?" He stopped to scan Leon's tape collection. His eyes glazed over, not reading a single one. His attention shifted back to the jars on the bookshelf. Cam slid his hands into his pockets and walked around the rest of the apartment.

"I don't think so," Jimmy said, pivoting to face Cam and resting his head against the back of the couch.

"You don't know?" Cam plopped down next to Jimmy, deflating the couch. He sunk into it uncomfortably.

"He's always been a little...," Jimmy pushed out his lips and swayed his head back and forth, searching for the right word, "off-kilter. He's always been a little strange, interested in darkness, the macabre. But I don't think he's ever crossed that line, though. At least, I hope not."

Cam nodded and rubbed his palms against the worn leather, feeling its scratchiness on his skin. "Do you think he'd tell you?"

"I think so." Jimmy paused as he considered this. "I mean, I hope he would. When we were kids, he was obsessed with Jimmy Page. He's probably just trying to emulate him with this occult stuff, to share an interest with an idol." His words hung in the air for a moment. The silence made him question if he was telling Cam the truth or trying to convince himself that Leon wasn't wandering down a dark path.

"That makes sense, I guess." Cam's voice broke the quiet as he picked at a worn spot on the couch's arm and twirled loose threads between his fingertips. Jimmy watched the blood bloat Cam's fingertip as he tightened one of the threads.

"I do get worried sometimes," Jimmy admitted. "He's a good guy, though. He's a good dude. I think you'll like him."

* * *

"Alright, Rufus," Leon yelled as he closed the register. "Money's counted, doors are locked, and I'm out."

Rufus emerged from the office and leaned against the door frame.

"Unless you wanna jam for a bit," Leon added, hoping he'd say yes.

Rufus sighed and shut the door to the listening booth. "I wish I could, buddy, but who would've thought owning a business meant I'd have to do business."

Leon sighed, dissatisfied. "Alright, old man, have fun with that."

"I will, you little shit," Rufus grunted a laugh.

Leon grinned and waved two fingers over his shoulder while he walked out the door, Rufus locking it behind him. He looked back at the old man, who was flipping him off through the glass before waving goodbye. Leon chuckled and returned the gesture as he embarked on his walk home.

The Sunset Strip hummed with music and pulsing with activity. Teenagers cruised up and down Sunset Boulevard, smoking and drinking as they searched for the clubs with the coolest bands. Music boomed out of cars. Girls screeched as guys sped after them down the boulevard. Men and women alike painted their faces with too much makeup. Leon passed drag queens with high eyebrows and contoured cheeks. He bumped into a man with blue hair dressed in a leather trench coat. People lined the walls outside of clubs, loitering on the sidewalk, waiting to get in to see a band. Seedy characters sealed deals in alleyways, and drunks vomited on the curb.

Despite their differences, everyone on that Strip loved the euphoria that came with the high, the sound of music, and the constant party.

It was chaos. It was dirty. It was depraved.

It was *invigorating*.

Leon quickly made his way up his home street and headed for his apartment. As he approached, he saw that the lights were on, meaning Jimmy was already there. *Perfect.* He had to tell him about Dallas. Their band was coming together. He grabbed onto the steel railing with chipped white paint and hurled himself up the stairs.

About halfway up, he stopped. Straining to hear, he slowly climbed the rest of the stairs. Leon could recognize Jimmy's voice, but he was singing an unfamiliar song accompanied by a smooth electric guitar.

What the fuck?

He swung open the door to find Jimmy singing with a long-haired stranger. A notebook rested on Jimmy's lap, and he was tapping it in time with a pen. The stranger strummed rhythm guitar, his head bowed to the side, objectively listening to what he was playing. Neither of them heard Leon come in, so he slammed the door behind him without turning away from the two. The guitarist abruptly stopped playing as the door closed and stood up. He looked like he'd just been caught with his pants down. He shifted, clutching the neck of the guitar at his side.

Jimmy whipped around. "Leon!"

"Jimmy," Leon muttered nervously, a sly smile creeping across his face. He pointed toward Cam. "Who are you?" The smile blossomed into a grin

57

before he could finish his question. It was all coming together.

"I'm Cam." The hulking stranger waved a hand stiffly in front of him.

"You guys sounded good," Leon said, not bothering to introduce himself as he crossed the room and pulled a chair away from his small kitchen table. He set it down in front of the couch, straddling it and resting his arms on the back support. "What were you playing?"

Jimmy handed the notebook to Leon. "We were just fucking around with some lyrics." He tapped the pen in the middle of the page. Cam slumped back onto his seat on the couch and ran his fingers along the smooth edge of his guitar pick as he watched Leon read.

Returning from the hero's journey
To the homeland of the heart
Finding that time has had no mercy
And one last villain to outsmart

"It's just for fun," Cam added a caveat as Leon read.

"Is this about the Scouring of the Shire?" Leon asked, noticeably surprised. Cam's face lit up.

"Yeah! It was a poem I wrote between finals. I've been re-reading the book and was feeling inspired. Jimmy was helping me put a melody to it."

Leon gave Cam an upside-down smile and lifted the notebook. "It's not bad," he said, gesturing to Jimmy for the pen. He tipped the chair forward to reach it. The chair creaked in protest. "Very Zeppelin-esque. What if we added our own destruction in here?"

Leon wrote beneath Cam's poem:

Swallowed in a pit of fire
Fear unrolls like pollution
To the ones still in the Shire
Longing to see the Spring sun
Through the flames of his hellfire

"That's wicked," Cam said, taking the notebook back and tapping his finger on the new lyrics. "Hey, Jimmy, do you think this will work with the melody?"

The singer looked over Cam's shoulder at the changes.

"Yeah, it should," Jimmy said, taking the notebook. He hummed along to the melody as he read the new words. "I like it."

"Hang on, let me get my shit." Leon jumped up and headed toward the single closet in the apartment. He moved aside the minimal clothing hanging in there and brought out his Les Paul copy and amp. The guitar rested comfortably across his body, humming to life as he plugged it in.

"Ah, dude, that's a beautiful guitar," Cam remarked, slack-jawed.

"She's the best girl in my life," Leon said, tuning up the strings. "She is beautiful, doesn't nag me, and screams when I ask her to." He ran through a few test chords. "Can you run through what you were playing before?"

Cam took his guitar and perched himself on the couch's arm, playing the progression Leon heard when he walked in. Jimmy began singing the melody. Leon improvised the second time after figuring out the key and gaining a sense of the progression. They wrote a chorus and a second verse during their breaks from playing. By the time they reached the bridge, Leon had improvised a raw and passionate blues-based solo, the bends wailing out in sympathy with the Hobbits. They had written a song, practiced it, and developed their playing chemistry over the course of the night.

"When you invited me over, I didn't think we'd write something this cool," Cam said as he picked up his notebook and examined their evening's effort. Their handwriting combined to cross out the initial poem, circle parts, reposition them, and scatter new lyrics across the remaining space on the page with chord progressions above them.

"What should we call it?"

" 'Shire on Fire,' " Jimmy suggested. "It's short, sweet, and rhymes."

" 'Shire on Fire,' " Cam scribbled the title across the top of the page while speaking each word slowly. "I like it."

Cam got up and grabbed his bag from beside his amplifier. He flopped back onto the couch, digging through the bag between his feet. He pulled out his copy of *Return of the King* and began penning the lyrics on a blank page in the back of the book. While he was still writing, Leon strolled over to the mildewed refrigerator and pulled three beers out, allowing the cool air to dry the sweat that prickled up on his face from the exhilaration of playing. He used his teeth to open one of the beers, spitting the cap onto the beige-gray countertop before taking a long swig. He held the remaining two beers in his other hand, gave Jimmy one, and placed one in front of Cam's bag.

He plopped down next to Cam's feet, leaning against the couch and flinging his stringy red hair onto the seat. Leon closed his eyes as he thought about Cam's poem. Cam was easy to work with; they all collaborated well together. The ideas flowed, and trying new things and experimenting with lyrics and riffs felt natural. Cam came off odd, but hell, Leon was strange himself.

"So," Cam said without looking up. "What's the story with the jars?"

"The jars?" Leon looked up, rolled his head onto his shoulder, and peered over Cam's knee at the lyrics he was writing. Cam pointed to the bookcase with his pencil.

"Oh, the jars." Smirking, Leon hoisted himself to his feet and walked over to the shelves. He picked up the jar of cockroach carcasses. They floated as he shook the jar like a macabre snow globe. "A lot of these I found in the apartment. I used to have a pretty bad roach problem." The carcasses floated back to the bottom of the jar. He studied them before putting them back on the shelf.

"What are they floating in?"

"Alcohol," Leon answered, straightening the jar. "Science was my favorite subject in school before I dropped out."

"Did you have Mr. Furguson?" Cam spread his knees a little wider, resting his elbows on them.

"Yeah," Leon sat back down at Cam's feet, resting his head on the couch. "He was a badass."

"I figured," Cam nodded, wagging the pencil toward the redhead in a knowing gesture. "He had all kinds of stuff like that in his classroom."

"He taught me everything I know," Leon chuckled. Mr. Furguson was an interesting character: an unsuspecting man with thick bifocals and a hunchback with a collection of jarred specimens. He taught biology and was known for bringing in roadkill found on his commute to school to use in his lessons. Leon took a special interest in these lessons, particularly how these lessons became specimens. He would stay after school and help the teacher preserve and jar the animals.

"Did you have a favorite jar?" Cam asked, tapping the pencil against the pages in his lap. "I liked the fawn the best. I named it Walter."

"No," Leon laughed, swallowing it when he caught a glimpse of Jimmy's bewildered face. "I liked them all. I always thought they were so cool. Death is beautiful, and preserving it into something that can be enjoyed was always something I liked about him. He inspired my humble little collection."

"That's wicked, dude," Cam shook his light-brown hair off his shoulders as he leaned down to put his book and pencil away. "I dig it."

Cam's hands drew Leon's eyes to a book sticking out of the bag. He reached over Cam's foot and pulled the book out—*Advanced D&D Dungeon Master's Guide*. Leon mused at the cover.

A horned beast with a crimson body towered over warriors wielding swords and shields on the book's cover. This beast held a woman in one hand and a sword in the other. Flames enveloped his muscular frame. He possessed keen, sharp teeth and black, flame-reflecting eyes like a demon in hell.

"What is this thing?" Leon tipped the book toward Cam. Cam tilted his head, thrilled that someone was asking him about D&D without poking fun.

"It's an Efreeti," Cam said, thoroughly entertaining Leon's curiosity. "They are super powerful."

"Is he some sort of demon or something?"

"No, they get mistaken for devils, though," Cam explained. "It's because their bodies are covered in burning skin. They live in the Elemental Plane of Fire."

"Sounds pretty demonic to me, even down to the pit of fire."

"*Plane* of fire," Cam reiterated, enunciating the first word. "*Plane.*"

"Right," Leon snorted, bouncing the book in his hand. "Pretty blasphemous stuff here."

"Nah," Cam shook his head, scooping the book out of Leon's fingertips.

"It's just fantasy."

"That's not what the news says," Leon instigated, lowering his voice mockingly and sitting up perfectly straight. "The game is a vessel for Satan, and drives clean-nosed kids to devil-worship and opens up demonic portals." He punctuated the imitation with a grunt.

"It's not like that," Cam said, tapping his fingers on the hardcover. "That's just an excuse parents make when their kid goes apeshit one day, and they need to blame something other than themselves for their bad seed."

"How do you play?" Jimmy asked.

"How much time do you have?" Cam chuckled, picking up his beer and taking a greedy sip. "It feels like a lot of information when you get started, but you just need a little creativity to get into it."

"Fuck that, man." Leon grabbed the book off of Cam's lap and stuffed it back into the rucksack before tossing the bag out of reach. "If I'm putting creativity into anything, it will be music."

"Half of Led Zeppelin's catalog is about Lord of the Rings," Cam reminded him. He raised his eyebrows and cocked his head. "I think Jimmy Page and Robert Plant would have a blast with this."

"Get the fuck out of here with that shit," Leon chuckled, flicking a guitar pick at the Dungeon Master's face. Cam looked up at Jimmy, expecting him to defend his claim, but was met with the singer smirking into his beer bottle, taking a sip to remain neutral.

"Dude," Cam let out a disappointed sigh. "They totally would. Maybe not Robert Plant, but Jimmy Page would *for sure*."

Jimmy and Leon locked eyes, telepathically discussing what they should do about Cam. Leon raised his eyebrows, turned down the corners of his mouth, and cocked his head slightly in Cam's direction. Jimmy lifted his chin in agreement before tilting his head back to pour beer into his mouth.

"So, what do you think?" Leon asked.

"About what?" Cam asked while flicking his finger over the end of the guitar pick that had just hit him in the nose.

"About playing with us," Jimmy said. "About being the first official member of our band."

Cam turned his head from Jimmy to Leon, who held his beer bottle up to him, waiting for a tap of approval.

"Hell yeah," Cam clinked his beer bottle against Leon's.

"I'll drink to that." Jimmy held out his bottle to them before taking a long swig.

* * *

Leon breathed in the warm summer air wafting through his open windows. He didn't open them often because the layers of chipped paint would rain down thick white flakes at the slightest disturbance. This Sunday morning was an exception, though—the sky looked bluer, and the air smelled fresher. The breeze blew through the musty old apartment, starkly contrasting the stagnant air it whisked away.

It would have been a perfect morning if he could rehearse with Jimmy— they had unfinished lyrics to hammer out. Cam had fit into their duo well, bringing a new energy they desperately needed. He chomped at the bit to spend every waking second with them, writing, playing, and developing their chemistry as musicians. His passion for music, for their dream, burned bright, ready to steal his every waking moment.

But *no*.

God stole Jimmy's Sunday mornings.

Leon couldn't imagine wasting his day away in a wooden pew, shaking hands with people, wishing them peace when those same holier-than-thou strangers looked down upon him. The hypocrisy of those people: indulging in their own illicit affairs, embezzlement schemes, or pornography addictions.

He couldn't fathom giving money to the Church in the offering basket only to have the same Church line their pockets and use that money to buy a bigger steeple than the Church down the street rather than paying it forward to the homeless. It was a bitter pill to swallow. Leon believed that if Jesus were real, he would be so disappointed in what God's followers have become.

Leon seethed. Church became a sham through the centuries, leading a flock of stupid sheep with blind faith. The idea that an all-seeing God, who supposedly had a hand in everything that ever happened to everyone, could let so many awful things happen to good people infuriated him.

The Church's manipulation of the concept of God into something idealistic, accompanied by a strict set of rules to follow, raised his blood pressure. Gullibility triumphed over these people; they believed every word out of the preacher's mouth without question as if that preacher didn't have his own agenda.

The Bible interwove itself into a social construct to keep people in line—a rule book to keep a well-oiled machine running with each cog performing its assigned purpose.

Leon refused to be a cog.

5

A Message From a Spirit

Leon promised Jimmy he would attend his graduation. Now, the night before the ceremony, he regretted making that promise.

Leon would be standing next to Jimmy in a parallel universe or a different timeline, wearing his own idiotic cap and gown. In that universe, Leon would also receive his diploma and have a tassel falling in his face as he walked across the stage. But he would arrive as a guest in this universe, ready to applaud.

He licked the edge of the paper before running his finger up the seam of his joint. Leon held it between his teeth as he lit a match, hearing the paper sizzle in the flame. He inhaled the smoke as he shook out the match, admiring his music collection.

The collection evolved from vinyl records to cassette tapes, but he preferred a select few in record form for nostalgia's sake. He splurged on a rack system turntable with a dual tape deck, a luxury well worth the money. One of the first records he bought for his collection was a copy of Robert Johnson's *King of the Delta Blues Singers*. It was the first of many albums Rufus introduced him to and was his primary influence in incorporating blues techniques into his playing. In his loneliness, he decided to spend time with his best friend: the blues.

Slipping the record out of the sleeve, he positioned it gingerly on the turntable. He dropped the needle, and gritty scratches filled the room as the needle fell into the grooves. Robert Johnson's haunting guitar riffs rang out, and the metallic-sounding strings echoed, revealing the age of the recordings. Johnson's long-dead vocals singing about the crossroads brought back memories of bloody fingers not yet callused from months upon months of running scales. It brought back memories of sitting in Jimmy's bedroom with Mrs. Ballard's freshly squeezed lemonade quenching the thirst brought on by hours of rehearsing acoustic covers. Playing the electric guitar was easy compared to the thick acoustic strings; Rufus was right about that.

He puffed away at his joint, reminiscing over choosing his first and only electric guitar: the tobacco burst Les Paul copy. Feeling guilty about stashing it in his closet, it now rested next to his stereo on the floor, much adored but lacking a stand to display his prized possession. He'd always meant to buy a stand for it, but he figured it didn't matter, considering it spent more time in his hands than sitting idle looking pretty.

By the time Johnson began singing about hellhounds hunting him down, the effects of the drugs set in. *Hellhounds.* He put out his joint, tapping it against his tongue to save the rest for later. His opinion never changed over the years: if he stood in Robert Johnson's shoes, he would have sold his soul, too. Whether the Devil slipped him a poisoned whiskey bottle or if there indeed was a hellhound on his trail, it was well worth it, despite being young.

A deal is a deal.

Leon peeled himself off of his couch to sift through his other records laced with sentimentality and stopped at *Led Zeppelin IV.* He took in the image of the hermit on the cover, reminiscent of a tarot card—the Ten of Wands. The hermit, hunched over under the weight of a pile of sticks, reminded him of the card, representing burden. When pulled upright, the card symbolized weight, obligation, and responsibility. A state of overwhelm and overwork. Leon's mind worked fast, spinning a story in which this became symbolic. *What if Jimmy Page sold his soul? Could he be the one carrying the burden of success?*

Leon's eyes widened as he took in the album artwork, blown away by the fictitious epiphany the drugs help him to illuminate. *Why did I never realize this before?* He flipped open the cover, slipped out the inner sleeve, and studied the sigils above the track listing. This was the album where the band members' symbols first appeared, which gained notoriety for the band. Leon was always most intrigued by Page's symbol, ZOSO. In his THC-induced haze, he connected it to Zozo, a demon known to communicate through the Ouija board.

He slipped the record out, replacing Robert Johnson on the turntable. "Black Dog" blared, filling the apartment with Robert Plant's howling vocals. He picked up the needle and dropped it on the indented groove that indicated the beginning of "Stairway to Heaven."

The sound of flutes and guitar brought him back to the night when he and Jimmy became blood brothers. He would sell his soul for this kind of success, if not for himself, for Jimmy. They deserved it.

ZOSO ran through his mind. *What a genius.*

ZOSO. ZOSO. ZOSO.ZOSO.ZOSO.ZOSO.

ZOZO.

A small occult shop that Leon liked to explore called the outskirts of the city home. It sat tucked away, nestled in a seedy strip mall. He would run his fingers over the small cast iron ritual cauldrons that could be used for one-off spells. The taxidermy fascinated him most, especially the baby ducklings dressed up in Victorian garb—those were his favorite. He always wanted a home filled with the strange and unusual and promised himself that one day, he would have ducks of his own. His mind kept a running list of everything he wanted from that shop, but he only allowed himself to purchase an old Ouija board. It looked to be from the 1930s, and he couldn't leave without it—he brought it home after falling in love with it upon first sight.

Leon closed his eyes and let his head fall back as he unboxed the spirit board. He placed the board before himself and lightly touched the planchette, ready to communicate with lost souls. He rolled his shoulders back, feeling self-assured about initiating communication.

"Are there any spirits present tonight?" His voice sounded like it belonged to someone else. It sounded out of place emanating from his body, alone in the night. He swallowed hard as the planchette moved smoothly across the board.

"YES."

A tingle of adrenaline spread to Leon's fingertips, causing them to tremble lightly. *Holy shit.* The wooden chair groaned in protest beneath him as he shifted his weight. The record produced raw white noise as the needle scraped the vinyl, denoting the end of side A.

"Thank you. Do you want to talk to me?"

The board creaked as the planchette moved slowly across it, grinding a groove into the musty wood with its weight as it pivoted to reset.

"YES."

Leon's curiosity piqued. He leaned in closer to the board, eager to communicate with anyone. *Anything.*

"Are you trapped in my apartment?"

The planchette traveled slightly nearer to the middle of the board before sliding over to "NO."

His brows furrowed as the planchette stopped rolling, and his fingers twitched as they settled onto the unmoving piece.

"Then why are you here?"

"Y—"

Leon's teeth gnashed together as he tightened his jaw, grinding them in impatience. The sound of his molars rubbing together reverberated in his eardrums, the soundtrack to the mounting tension as the planchette moved to the—

"O—"

His muscles contracted, causing tension in his spinal column. A chill ran down his neck and spread through his limbs, through the fingertips gliding across the board to "U."

He gasped, holding in the air for a few moments too long. A shuddering breath escaped his lips, permeating the silence.

"You're here for me?"

The planchette swiftly crossed to "YES," making the wheels squeal. It paused for a beat before moving to the "W." Leon's eyes darted across the board, trying to figure out the next letter.

"A—"

He could no longer feel the seat beneath him. He had no peripheral vision as he focused on the board before him. Leon's stomach flipped like he was being suspended in the air. It was as if he were a part of the intro for The Twilight Zone—floating in a black abyss where only he, the spirit, and the board existed. The planchette stopped at the letter 'N,' its pointed top curved to the right, causing Leon's hands to contort toward the letters.

WANT.

"Only if I want?"

The planchette pulsated under his fingertips, carefully extending itself.

"YES."

Leon's eyes rolled back into his head, his eyelids fluttering shut. A smile broke across his face. He possessed power. *Good.*

He tilted his head downward and stretched his neck. This thing was here for him. He opened his eyes and gazed at his fingertips, his short nails clawing at the planchette impatiently.

"Who are you?"

"F—"

"A—"

"N."

Leon furrowed his brow, lurching his body closer to the spirit board. Ginger hair grazed the vintage wood. He sat there, hunched over it, like Smeagol. His precious fan. He had a *fan.*

"What is your given name?"

"W—"

As Leon stared at the Ouija board, the letters forming the word in his brain, he became acutely aware of the subtle sounds around him. He could hear the gentle flow of air as it entered and exited his nostrils, and he took note of the worn scratches on the board's surface that had accumulated over time. The black paint on the letters had faded, aging the board. His pet snake flicked its tongue, creating a soft clicking sound in the background.

It sounded like a ribbon flowing in the breeze, flapping and folding around the fluid air. He watched his hands be guided around the board, carefully keeping score of the letters in his head.

WOLFE.

The scent of the wood used to construct the board wafted up to his nostrils, filling the air with its earthy aroma. He took deep breaths, feeling his lungs expand and deflate with each lungful, becoming fully immersed in the present moment.

"Thank you," he sighed. "Why are you here, Wolfe?"

The planchette stayed put on the "E." Leon stared at it, willing it to move with his mind.

It didn't move.

Instead, the needle on the record scratched behind him. Angling his head, he listened to the needle drop where John Bonham entered "Stairway to Heaven." The vinyl began to spin counterclockwise. Goose flesh spread like dandelion seeds blowing in the wind. It was turning too slowly; Robert Plant's distorted voice sounded like it was trudging through hot tar. The verse played out until Leon thought he could make out the Devil's namesake, to which it abruptly scratched off, creating a loop of white noise once again.

The planchette moved before Leon could ask anything else, gradually gaining speed beneath his fingertips. It was now heavily weighted, creating deep scratches on the wood. The board screamed at Leon as the planchette slid frantically from letter to letter, dragging tiny paint chips with it.

Leon's gut lurched. He wanted to cover his ears; the shrieking wheels grated his nerves, but he couldn't break contact with the board.

It was a rule.

He cringed, pushing his shoulder into his ear. It was trying to spell something out, but he lost track of all the letters in the frantic motions until the speed abruptly depleted.

The planchette moved slowly toward the board's edge before turning and returning to the middle. As soon as it reached the opposite side of the board, it looped back, moving in frenzied figure-eight patterns. Velocity built. Without warning, the planchette soared off of the board.

The sudden blaring sound of the stereo across the room startled Leon as the planchette hit the wall. Bruce Dickinson's banshee scream pierced through the silence, leading into the second verse of "Number of the Beast."

Leon's heart raced as the vibrations gurgled his organs. Every fiber of his being was on high alert as he became too aware of himself. His bones became too heavy in his body, the blood cells flowing too quickly, causing him to detest how wet his bones were trapped beneath his skin. He could sense the oxygen drifting through his bloodstream, and his senses acutely tuned to every sound and movement in the room.

He jumped out of his seat, fumbling with every button on the tape deck. He ejected the tape, feeling his nerves still tingling with adrenaline as they reacclimated to the silence. The noise from the record player's needle was too loud, so he turned off his stereo completely.

Leon turned slowly, taking a deep breath to steady his nerves as he returned to the table. The music didn't cause the vibration throughout his body—it was the pure adrenaline pumping through his veins like heroin. He picked the planchette off the floor with a shaky hand and placed it back on the board.

He laughed, watching awestruck in deafening silence as the planchette glided calmly across the board with no fingers to weigh it down. The little wheels whimpered as one of the back ones rotated freely, curving the path of the little wooded piece before straightening back out. It rolled to a stop.

"GOODBYE."

6

Black Sheep

Leon fiddled with his tie before yanking it out from beneath his collar in frustration. His body twisted awkwardly as he threw the tie on the mattress behind him.

Creeping into the bathroom, he gave himself a thorough once-over. Dark circles shadowed his eyes. The blue button-down swallowed his thin frame, and the plain black slacks hung off of his hips. Though he managed to steal the clothes without getting caught, he figured he should have looked at the size tag beforehand. Stealing was never a habit he got into, his father made sure of that, but he didn't own any dress clothes. Never in his life did he have a reason to look nice.

Leon dampened his comb and pulled it through his hair in an attempt to tame his unruly mane, combing it back into a low ponytail. His side-parted bangs refused to be tamed and kept getting frizzier with every pass. He turned the faucet on with too much force, causing water to spit out in all directions. Leaning down into the sink, he soaked his bangs, combing the flyaways back into place.

Fuck it, he thought. *Good enough. No one will be looking at me anyway.*

He put his sole belt—a concho belt—through the fabric loops before he left, not bothering to see how it looked before slamming the door behind him. For the time being, it would have to do.

Leon spent a mere couple of months at Trinity High School, having dropped out his freshman year. Although years had passed, the campus made him feel the same way it did back then. Small. Stupid. Insignificant. He would have been predestined to barely graduate and follow in his father's footsteps, who would pass his seat at the bar on to his son to repeat the vicious cycle of being miserable. Being out of the classroom, he could put his destiny in his own hands. He didn't have to waste his youth in a building at a desk. He could make his own way, but the path proved to be lonely.

Parents, siblings, family members, and friends crowded the parking lot outside of the football field. Leon stayed back, watching people mill about as they talked, laughed, and celebrated. He listened as fathers reminisced about their golden days. Mothers dabbed tears as they discussed this milestone in their children's lives, puffing on cigarettes held in sparkling red fingertips, their pink lipstick leaving chunky streaks on the filters. He wondered if his parents would be there to celebrate with him if he graduated in that parallel universe. Almost certainly not. He wondered if they were even still alive.

He heard his name called, and it pulled him back to reality. A pair of recognizable faces emerged from his sweep of the crowd. The woman smiled warmly and extended her arms to him.

"Mrs. Ballard," Leon said as he embraced her. The years weaved white strands into her blonde hair, creating a light glow around her face. She drew her surrogate son in and hugged him even tighter before letting go. She sighed with a smile as she stared at him, holding his shoulders.

"Look at you," she said fondly. "You boys are all grown up." She pulled back her hands and gave him a teasing shove. "And how dare you make yourself a stranger at our house. You haven't been by for dinner in ages."

"I promise I will come by for dinner," Leon assured her.

"Good," she nodded. "You better."

"I will," he promised. "Where's Jimmy?"

"Oh—" she waved her hands absentmindedly toward the school. "All the graduates had to meet in the gym. They're going to put them all alphabetically to give the right kid the right diploma."

Mr. Ballard clapped him on the shoulder. "Which means you're stuck with us old folks. What do you say we go find a seat?"

They found rows of folding chairs before a makeshift stage as they walked onto the football field, claiming an almost empty row. As the ceremony began, the graduating students walked down the aisle between two groups of applauding family members before settling into their seats in the front few rows. With a proud smile, Jimmy waved to them as he passed their row. His mother enthusiastically applauded him, nudging Leon with pride as he waved.

Leon gently clapped, keeping his hands low on his lap and his eyes down as the graduates filed in. He remembered nearly every one of these people. They used to be his peers, his classmates. But never his friends. Leon remembered Scotty McDowl snatching his clothes while showering in the locker room after gym class. He recalled Claire Peterson asking him out as a prank and how he eagerly accepted, hoping to get some attention from a pretty girl. Later, he realized she only asked him out to make fun of him with her friends.

Leon was relieved he wasn't seated among them as their peer—their equal. He despised them—loathed every one of them. He hated their stupid grins, so proud of themselves for making it to graduation. Prideful. Smiles laced with condescension and the superior sense of a job well done spread across their faces as if any of them knew what hard work felt like.

Stupid, pompous assholes.

Leon raised his head in response to the muffled fumbling reverberating through the microphone as Principle Atwood adjusted it to the perfect height before delivering the formal opening address. Leon searched the rows of graduates as the speeches dragged on and found Cam moving around in his seat and bobbing his head in search of his family. His face contorted the longer he searched, the corners of his mouth pulling downward when he realized they weren't there. He whipped his head repeatedly as the tassel flicked him in the nose. Cam spotted Leon in the crowd. Recognition and excitement spread across his face as he raised his arm and waved frantically. It drew attention away from the ceremony, eliciting laughter from the audience. Leon chuckled and held up his hand in a small wave.

Principal Atwood began reading off the graduates' names, each one eagerly awaiting their chance to shake his hand and receive their passport to adulthood.

"James Christopher Ballard," he announced. Jimmy walked confidently across the improvised stage to accept his diploma. He shook the principal's hand and gazed out into the crowd. Leon and the Ballards cheered as loudly as they could, and Leon noticed that Cam and a number of the girls in the audience gave him extra whoops as well. Holding his diploma triumphantly in both hands above his head, Jimmy finished his walk across the stage.

The graduates each basked in their seminal moment. They strutted across the stage, reveling in the applause and admiration of the crowd, with a self-absorbed simper on their face. Others walked meekly to Principle Atwood, their necks shrinking into their shoulders, trying to block the attention that was inevitably on them for that brief moment. Cam danced across the stage, pumping his diploma in the air.

"To the class of 1983, I want to give you one final task before you move on. I want you to move your tassels to signify the end of your academic journey and the start of your next adventure."

The air was filled with the sound of the graduates grabbing their tassels in unison. They peeled their caps off of their sweaty heads to toss them in the air, the last moment of carefree whimsy before real life stepped in to steal their youth.

Leon waited for Jimmy after the ceremony—his eyes fixed on the bustling crowd. As he waited, his gaze wandered to Cam, who was at the helm of a group of outcasts. They engrossed themselves in a playful game of make-believe. Leon watched as they pretended that their tassels held magical powers. Although undeniably weird, he still yearned for their strong bond. He had Jimmy, but he wanted a tribe—a *band*.

His arms were crossed tightly across his chest as he watched the group through narrowed eyes. He sucked in his cheeks, realizing how shallow and fleeting his relationships were. Aside from Rufus, Jimmy was the only true friend that he had. The others who came and went through his life were merely transient acquaintances who were only interested in chasing their next high. The closest Leon ever got to experiencing a love connection was the sex that he had with junkies in exchange for the coveted baggie. It was a form of payment that he happily accepted; however, the whole thing seemed sad in the harsh daylight surrounded by joy.

His reverie broke when Mrs. Ballard squealed with delight as Jimmy walked up, holding his diploma and cap. He removed the gown as soon as the ceremony concluded, draping it neatly over his arm. She embraced her son and expressed how proud she was of him, while his dad responded with a proud wink and nod from over her shoulder.

"Oh, you boys, get together." She held up her camera, poised to take a picture. The camera pressed against her glasses as she squeezed her one eye shut, waving them together with her free hand.

"Ma—" Jimmy rolled his head to the side. "Come on. You've got enough."

"Not of the two of you, I don't." She lowered the camera to glare at her son. "Put your cap back on and get together."

"One picture, no cap," Jimmy bargained.

"Deal, now scoot." She waved in Jimmy's direction, instructing him to get close to his lifelong friend.

Leon stood with his arm around Jimmy, smiling at the camera. Mrs. Ballard took one photo, then another as soon as the camera spit the first out in a mechanical whir. She handed the second photo to Leon, who could barely look at the picture before a weight on his back shoved him forward.

"The band's all here!" Cam exclaimed, draping an arm around each of his friends.

"Oh, how cute," Mrs. Ballard squealed. "Smile!"

A final photo emerged from the camera. As it developed, blackness gave way to Jimmy and Cam's carefree grins, illuminated by the dancing rays of the sun.

Meanwhile, gloominess filled Leon's face. Even as the photo developed, Leon still looked to be surrounded by darkness as resentment crept into his eyes, unable to muster a smile for the candid photo.

7

Jam Session

Dallas meticulously checked his appearance in the sun visor's mirror, ensuring his smudged black eyeliner was perfectly diffused. He flipped up the sun visor, rubbing his pointer finger and thumb together to flick off the eyeliner dust. Puckering his lips and swiveling his jaw from side to side, he tousled his hair, running his fingers through the roots to re-fluff the tease. Dilated eyes scrutinized his reflection in the rear-view mirror. Looking up at Leon's apartment, he could see the shadows of his potential new bandmates through the window. Every so often, he caught the sound of one of them noodling around with an electric guitar, and it was more than merely a sound; it was a captivating melody that filled the air.

Dallas stared intently at his reflection as he waited. His eyes fixated on his mouth as he ran his fingers over his top teeth, feeling the smooth surface of the enamel. Nervousness settled in the pit of his stomach. He thought it would subside the longer he sat in the car, but that apprehension persisted. Cycling through all of the usual suspects, he couldn't quite pinpoint the source of his anxiety, but, at this point, he knew that stalling wouldn't help him figure it out.

Dallas had a history with this jittery foreboding. He auditioned for bands in the past and played with quite a few of them. This audition gave him the undeniable feeling of being different. The usual emotions all bubbled on the surface: the excitement, the anxiety, the nervous energy. However, beneath it all was an almost tangible sense of dread.

Inner turmoil be damned. Dallas was hell-bent on giving the audition of a lifetime.

He unscrewed the silver-encased top of his antique gemstone necklace, revealing a tiny spoon, onto which we prepared a bump of cocaine. Powder poured out as he tilted the gemstone to one side. He held it to his nose and sniffed, returning his attention to the window while massaging the base of his nostril. The sting of the drugs through his sinuses barely fazed him anymore. The only sign he was flying high was the blown-out pupils staring back at him as he reassessed his reflection. Reaching under his passenger seat, he pulled out a flask. He took a swig of vodka, reveling in the burn as it dispersed throughout his insides. Life was all about balance: one upper, one downer.

As he stepped out of his gleaming red 1970 Chevelle with black racing strips, he couldn't resist running his fingers over the car with a sense of pride. The golden hour illuminated the shiny paint. The sun accentuated every curve and line as Dallas made his way around the car to the trunk. He unlocked the trunk with a satisfying click and took out his hardshell protective case.

Inside the case was his pre-owned, yet new to him, Gibson Firebird III bass guitar. He took it out gently, admiring the sleek design and superior craftsmanship. The sight of the bass gave him the boost his spirits needed. He situated the instrument back into the case and secured it by flipping the buckles to lock it.

Placing the case gingerly against the bumper, he began unloading the rest of his equipment, careful to not scratch the paint or dent the metal. After gathering all of his belongings off the curb, he took a deep breath, letting it cleanse away the remaining fear.

Dallas crossed the street, walking with his usual swagger in a faux show of confidence. His heart beat faster in anticipation with every step he climbed up to the front door. He knocked firmly, struggling to keep his hands from shaking, and eagerly waited for Leon to answer.

The door flung open, and Dallas was greeted with a familiar face surrounded by a halo of red hair reflecting the dull glow of the apartment's fluorescent lights. Without hesitation, he reached out for Dallas's amp to start the session.

"Hey, man," Leon said as he stepped aside, letting Dallas in. He set the amp down next to the door, enthusiastically rubbing his hands together as he stood back up. "Glad you could make it."

"Glad to be here," Dallas rasped as he entered the apartment and placed the bass case against the window frame beside the door. He muttered a hello to Jimmy and Cam, who sat on the couch working out some lyrics. Cam casually laid his strumming hand over the guitar's body as he took in the flamboyant stranger.

The stench of too much Brut cologne emanating from Dallas overwhelmed their senses. Cam waved, discreetly using the same hand to shield his nose from the overpowering scent. Jimmy smiled and stood up to cover for Cam's indiscretion.

"Hey, I'm Jimmy," he said as he reached for Dallas's hand, shaking it firmly before gesturing over his shoulder. "That's Cam. He's our rhythm guitarist." As their handshake broke, Jimmy noticed that Dallas's hands were sweaty.

"What's up, my dude?" Cam gave an upward nod of acknowledgment, getting used to the reek of Dallas. He picked up his guitar and plucked each string, tuning them again so he wouldn't have to shake his hand.

"So you're a bassist?" Jimmy returned to his seat, discreetly wiping Dallas's sweat off his palms on his pants.

"Sure am." Dallas leaned down and unbuckled his case, keenly aware of everyone's eyes on him as he ran his thumb over the instrument's fretboard. "Thanks again for helping me score this beauty," Dallas said, pointing toward Leon. He winked as if they shared an inside joke.

"No problem," Leon said. He handed Dallas a beer and sat on a kitchen chair, straddling it backward. Resting his arms on the back of the chair, he leaned forward as he sipped from his bottle. Leon studied Dallas, noticing that he appeared more jittery than he had in the store. He was calm, relaxed, and smooth with the ladies—completely in control. But at that moment, he didn't convey that same impression.

Dallas set the beer on the windowsill and took the bass out of the case. He scanned the room, looking for a place to sit that wouldn't require too much movement to get to, already feeling self-conscious. Fidgeting with his rings, he twisted the oversized cross on his middle finger.

"You look familiar," Jimmy said as he squinted. "Did you go to Trinity High?"

"No," Dallas snorted as he rested the bass against the window and picked up his beer. An awkward pause hung in the air as they waited for him to elaborate or divulge more details about himself. "Well, I guess I did. I was supposed to…" He rubbed his thumb against the tip of his nose before abruptly throwing his hand out to the side. "I got suspended when I was a sophomore."

Dallas tittered, taking a sip of his beer. *Fuck*, Dallas thought. *Too much, too fast.*

"What did you do?" Cam leaned forward, looking across Jimmy. Dallas rubbed his eyes with one hand and crossed the other arm over his body. He huffed a laugh despite himself—he was making quite the first impression. A mischievous smile spread across his wide mouth as he sighed in a deep inhale.

"I lit the gas in the science room and flicked my lighter. It set the cat I was supposed to dissect on fire. Dude, when I tell you that thing went up like a Roman candle." He bulged out his eyes and sucked his cheeks in. "I was not expecting it."

"Formaldehyde, my dude," Cam shook his head. "Flammable as fuck. That thing didn't stand a chance."

As Cam said the word, memories flushed back to Leon. Scent is a fascinating sense—it possesses the ability to trigger a memory better than sight, touch or sound. The recollection of the smell transported him back to his short high school career, sitting in Mr. Furguson's classroom with the burn of formaldehyde stinging his sinuses. The corpse of a cat laid stomach-up on his dissection tray, its fur clumpy from the preservation fluid. He followed along step-by-step with his classmates as they created an incision along the belly. Pinned the skin of the chest open. Handled the stomach, studied the heart, extracted arteries, and prodded at muscle. He treasured every second of it, feeling the slimy cold remains through his gloved hands, wishing to slip off the gloves to caress the preserved skin against his own.

"Whatever, it was already dead." Dallas took a sip of beer, shrugging off the memory and breaking Leon out of his. The bassist held out an open palm, realizing how his words sounded. "I didn't mean to do it. I hope Whiskers is resting in peace."

"I remember hearing about that. You were a grade above us," Jimmy said as Leon imagined what that burning cat must have smelled like. The phantom aroma tickled his nostrils.

"So that's it? You just never went back?" Leon flicked a guitar pick between his fingers.

"No, I would've been expelled, but I played dumb like I didn't know what would happen." He swallowed a burp, the yeast rising in his throat. Dallas opened his arms, swinging his beer to the side as he pointed at the group. "To be fair, I didn't have to play hard. I didn't know it would be that bad. That part was true. I went back when I felt like it to scope out the crop in the parking lot."

"Didn't your parents get in trouble?"

"For what?" Dallas squawked.

"Truancy." Leon raised an eyebrow, tucking his chin down. Dallas bounced his snakeskin boot's heel off the couch, jutting his bottom lip out. "Shit, man, after my brother died, I got a free pass. They just thought I was, how did they put it?" He brought their words to life by leaning on the arm of the couch, gesturing with his hands, and adding air quotes to emphasize each one. With a playful tone, he recited them in a silly voice. "Processing my emotions by acting out."

"I'm sorry, man," Jimmy offered. Cam grabbed the neck of his guitar and set it down on the floor in front of him. He put his pick between his teeth and got up to get a beer. When he returned, he sat on the floor next to Leon, putting some distance between himself and Dallas, whom he realized was a close talker.

"It's alright," Dallas waved off the condolences. "Heroin's a bitch."

Cam lowered his gaze and nodded in agreement as he reached for his guitar. He rested his back against Leon's chair, cradled the instrument in his lap, and began quietly fingerpicking a melody. Irked by Dallas's comment about getting into trouble, Jimmy asked for more details to satisfy his curiosity.

"Shit, dude," Dallas drawled, making bouncy, childlike motions, unable to sit still for a minute. The corners of his wide mouth turned up, and Dallas threw his head back, his black hair swaying with the sudden motion. He flailed his arms outwards instinctively to maintain balance while perched on the edge of the couch arm. His stack of bracelets jingled on his wrist at the sudden movement.

"The police department has a file on me as big as my dick," he bragged, grabbing at his crotch for emphasis. *Shut the fuck up, Dallas*, he reprimanded himself. But once the words began flowing—

"I got hauled in for petty theft for stealing a bottle of booze and a pack of smokes from the corner store. They were going to let me go, but I got *belligerent*." He rolled his eyes in exasperation, saying 'belligerent' in the same voice wives use to make fun of their husbands, dropping his voice to sound dopey and froggy. Cam stopped playing, his hands frozen in place as he listened.

"Then I got busted outside a Rolling Stones show for possession." He glanced up and to the side, picturing his rap sheet on the ceiling and counting his infractions on his fingers. "Public fornication, disturbing the peace for streaking, possession again, and public intoxication." He nodded in satisfaction. "Those are the main ones."

Dallas hoped that giving away all of the dirty details would at least earn him some street credit with these guys after seeing Cam's exaggerated frown, clearly displaying his amazement at Dallas's arrest record. Jimmy's expression, with his downturned mouth and raised eyebrows, gave him less confidence in that hope. Leon roared in a fit of laughter, catching Jimmy off guard.

"Oh, come on." Dallas became abruptly serious. His spine straightened as he shoved his hands into the pockets of his velvet blazer. "You better not tell me that having a record is a deal breaker. I thought this was a rock band. Sex, drugs, and rock and roll?"

"We are." Leon reconsidered his words. "Well, we want to be," he amended with a shrug. "It's not a deal breaker. You're just an idiot for getting caught that many times."

"Yeah, I guess I deserve that." Dallas twisted his body, sliding off the arm and sinking into what was Cam's seat. He situated himself, leaning in toward Jimmy. "What's the vibe you're going for? Who are your influences?"

"Jesus, it's all over the place," Leon admitted. "I learned guitar on the Delta Blues, guys like Robert Johnson and Big Joe Williams. Ozzy is a God. But my favorite record when I was a kid was *Led Zeppelin IV*. Jimmy and I listened to it all the when we were kids."

"Sweet," Dallas put his elbows on his knees and twisted his rings. "So you've all been friends for a while now, huh?"

"Just me and Jimmy. He's like my brother." Leon made a grabbing motion with his hand and placed it on Cam's head, gently shoving forward in a playful gesture. "Cam just joined the ranks last week."

Dallas hummed his understanding, glad he wasn't the odd man out. He pursed his lips, the corners turning up as he turned his attention to Jimmy. "What about you?"

"I grew up on Elvis and The Doors. My parents were big fans," Jimmy cracked his knuckles absentmindedly. "I started listening to Elton John as I got older, The Stones, Sabbath, Zeppelin. Leon and I used to listen to all those together when we were kids. We ate that shit up." Jimmy's face lit up with nostalgia. "I also like singer-songwriter-type stuff."

"Singer-songwriter?" Dallas scoffed.

"Yeah." As Jimmy began, he was interrupted by groans from Leon and Dallas. He leaned back against the couch and opened his chest, projecting as much confidence as he could as he prepared to defend himself. "Listen, Jim Croce is the shit. *Time In A Bottle* is a masterpiece."

"Fucking depressing is what it is," Leon said into his beer bottle.

"You're just too shallow to listen to the lyrics."

Leon swallowed his beer, letting out a belch. "Or," he pointed toward Jimmy with his bottle. "It just sucks."

Jimmy clucked his tongue. "You never grasped the moral of the story, Leon. That album teaches you a valuable lesson."

"What lesson is that, that it's a snooze-fest?"

"Nope, that you don't want to mess around with Jim." Cam snickered. Jimmy smiled slyly as he raised his palms in victory.

"You're such a fucking nerd, Jimmy," Leon chuckled, tossing his empty bottle to the corner of the room before cracking open a new one. "It hurts my soul what a fucking nerd you are."

"At least you have your looks," Dallas pursed his lips, nodding. "As long as you're good-looking, chicks will come." He winked at Jimmy with a downward nod. "Am I right, Jimmy?"

"I don't know," Jimmy waved him off dismissively. "I've always put music first. I've gone out with a bunch of girls, but nothing serious."

Leon snorted. "Yeah, right." Half the songs in that notebook are about Mandy."

"Mandy, huh?" Dallas perked up. "I knew a Mandy once. She was a minx." He ran his tongue over his teeth in a suggestive expression.

"Yeah, well, that's over." Jimmy threw a pencil at Leon.

"Yeah, well, depending on how this audition goes tonight, let's just call it what it is: it's an audition," Dallas rolled his head toward Leon, who smirked in confirmation. "I'm taking you guys out, and you're gonna drown in pus—"

"Okay," Jimmy laughed, cutting him off. He placed a cigarette between his lips and searched his lap. Leon flicked a lighter to get his attention before throwing it into Jimmy's open palms.

"What?" Dallas said in a breathy, naive voice as Jimmy lit his cigarette and tossed the lighter back to the guitarist. "I'm just saying that we're gonna go out, and we are gonna get fucked up and get fucked. That's all." He held his hands up in surrender, jutting his head forward to punctuate his point.

"You're on." Leon shoved the lighter back into his pocket as he pointed at the bassist with the top of his bottle. He downed the rest of his beer and picked up his guitar, strumming a few quiet chords before hooking it up to the amp.

"What about you, geek?" Dallas tilted his chin toward Cam.

"What do you mean, 'geek'?" Cam questioned in defense.

"I can smell it from across the room. You probably like Rush."

"I *do* like Rush," Cam said with wide eyes, eliciting a disappointed sigh from Dallas.

"What else you got?" Dallas asked.

"Zeppelin, Aerosmith," Cam paused, putting his guitar pick between his teeth and shrugging off his denim jacket. He grabbed the guitar pick from his mouth with his thumb and middle fingers and pointed at Dallas. "Genesis."

"Alright, you got me with Genesis," Dallas gave him a wry smile. "I can get on board with all of you guys; I'm into the Sabbath and the Stones. The Runaways are the shit, those chicks can rock."

"Agreed," Cam said.

"I'm also into Billy Squier, Nazareth, Queen," Dallas said.

"Yeah, we can tell," Leon snorted as he flicked on the amp with his toe, strumming a chord before Dallas could retort. Dallas shot up from the couch to grab his instrument, averting his eyes from Leon. He threw his body down, shifting his weight to settle the instrument on his lap. Rolling his shoulders back, he plucked the bass strings to ensure they were all in tune. They were; he made sure of it three times before putting the bass in his car.

"I learned guitar playing the blues," Leon gave his guitar a couple of test strums. "What do you say we try a minor I-IV-V progression in E? See if we can keep up with each other."

Jimmy tapped his foot to keep time in lieu of a drummer. On the fourth count, Cam and Leon introduced a slow melody. Dallas listened, taking in their rhythm and tapping his own foot in time. After the first run-through of the progression, they repeated it, but this time, Dallas let his natural groove shine through. He embellished the rhythm, playing off of Leon's improvisation. Leon raised a brow at him, matching his energy. As they fell into the groove of the progression, their instruments came alive with soulful energy.

"What do you say we try something out here," Leon played a lick, incorporating emotional bends into the mix. Dallas waited a few measures before coming in with the bassline, with Cam coming in with the rhythm. They played a rag-tag rendition of a blues-rock classic. The familiar chords of Jimi Hendrix's "Red House" filled the room, and the band settled into a natural and effortless rhythm. Leon skillfully enhanced the melody with a captivating solo, perfectly complementing Cam's provocative rhythm guitar. Throughout it all, Dallas provided the steady and unwavering rhythm that held the whole song together.

They paused before Jimmy could come in with the vocals and took it from the beginning to tighten things up. They played through the song again, and it was entirely as raw as the first time but perfect in a technical sense. Cam and Dallas communicated easily through eye cues, creating a fluid, strong rhythm section. The bassist seamlessly fit into their group. For each one of those musicians, it was an unspoken understanding that Dallas had indeed made himself a part of the band.

"I guess all we need is a drummer, huh?" Dallas said, causing them all to snicker at his boldness. Leon appreciated the balls it took to be that self-assured. Without uttering a single word, the members of the group came to a unanimous decision, basking in the strong sense of camaraderie among them. The Devil himself could not have created such perfect chemistry.

8

Paint the Town Red

"For The Record, what can I do ya for?" Leon answered the phone in a bored voice, disassociating while staring at the instrument wall. Aside from Jimmy, the aisles of records remained untouched. Guitars hung unplayed on the wall, and no one snorted a line in the sticker-covered bathroom. The cords in the listening rooms remained neatly coiled. The only sound filling the store besides the faint overhead music pumping through the speakers was the swishing of plastic sleeves as Jimmy thumbed through the archives of the same tired albums, looking for something new. Leon drummed his fingers on the glass countertop as he waited for the voice on the other end to answer, annoyed with the crackling on the other end of the receiver.

"Are you with Jimmy?" The familiar voice sounded far away amidst the city's hustle and bustle.

"Dallas?" Leon perked up, squinting at Jimmy, who stopped sifting through the discount bin and looked up, tilting his head to one side and furrowing his brow. Leon nodded, his eyes falling to look into the display case below the glass.

"No, it's Bert," Dallas said sarcastically. "Listen, man, I'm not made of quarters here. Are you with Jimmy?"

"Yeah, he's right here, Jesus Christ." Leon stooped to straighten a rogue distortion pedal in the case. "Why?"

"Today's his birthday," Dallas said in a derisive tone.

"No kidding," Leon feigned astonishment. "I would've had no idea. Thank you, Dallas, for filling me in."

The floor squeaked as Jimmy wandered over to the used instruments. A warm hum mused from an old acoustic Fender as he ran his fingers across the strings.

"Smart-ass," Dallas grumbled, almost being drowned out by a honking horn. "Is he doing anything tonight?"

Leon mumbled, "Hold on," as he dropped the phone into his other hand, which was resting on the counter. "Are you doing anything for your birthday tonight?"

Jimmy took the Fender off the stand and sat down with it, fingering a soft melody. He leaned back, getting comfortable with the instrument as he played. Peering up at the ceiling, he said, "I think my parents—"

"No," Leon returned the phone to his ear, interrupting Jimmy, who stopped playing. He shook his head and curled his lip, glaring at Jimmy through an exasperated squint. *Dweeb.* "No, he's not doing anything."

Jimmy sneered back at him, wrapping his fretting hand around the neck of the guitar.

"Beautiful," Dallas singsonged. "Keep him there. We're going out."

"Copy that," Leon said as he hung up the phone. It dropped back on the receiver with a *ting*.

"What was that all about?" Jimmy asked, getting up to put the Fender back on its display.

"Dallas is on his way here," Leon said, crossing his arms over his chest and resting his elbows on the edge of the counter. "He said we're going out tonight for your birthday."

"Really?" Even though he didn't smile, Leon noticed a glimmer of happiness on his face.

"Hey, Rufus," Leon called out. "You there, old man?"

"Yeah, keep your pants on," Rufus huffed, leaning out from the back room. "Hey, if you've got time to lean, you've got time to clean."

Leon pressed his thumb against the glass, smirking, creating an oily fingerprint. He wiped it away with the hem of his shirt before proudly splaying his hands out.

"Done," Leon quipped as he leaned back down. Rufus snorted an exasperated chuckle.

"What do you want, kid?" Rufus took a peek into the listening rooms, making sure that everything was in order.

"It's dead. Do you mind if I head out early? It's this guy's birthday." Leon walked around the case and clapped Jimmy on the shoulder.

"Oh yeah?" Rufus smiled as he looked around the empty store, taking in the woody scent of guitars and the chemical smell of records. The instruments were dusted, gleaming in the light, and there wasn't a single stray tape in the aisles. "Sure thing. Happy Birthday, Jimmy."

"Thank you," Jimmy nodded and turned his gaze downward to hide a smile. Rufus sized up the two boys, now men that had grown up right before his eyes. He'd heard them talking from the office about forming a band for years, and now, they had recruited two new members. The old man's heart warmed, looking at them, itching to get out of the store and be set loose on the Strip.

"Oh! You know what?" Rufus wagged a finger at them. "You have to do something for me if you're gonna head out early. Both of you."

"Sure thing," Leon leaned against the front of the counter. "What's the damage?"

"I know that soon, I'll be stocking your record on my shelves. You boys better come back here to my little ole' shop when you make it big and sign some records and posters. I think you owe me that much, considering I taught you everything you know," he said, waggling a finger at Leon.

"Shit, Rufus," Leon clapped Rufus on the back. "That's a done deal."

"Alright," Rufus's eyes twinkled. "You gonna stay out of trouble?"

"It's Dallas," Leon said in a sarcastic tone as if this statement was self-explanatory.

"Call me if you need me to bail you out of jail, Jimmy." Rufus turned back into his office, chuckled, and waved over his shoulder.

"What about me?" Leon bound over to the listening rooms, leaning against one of the separating walls to peer into the back office.

"Come on, Leon," Rufus spun around in his chair, his beer gut resting on his lap as he hoisted his feet onto his desk. "The guy has a squeaky clean reputation. I'm not letting his parents deal with that. You'd feel right at home spending a night with a couple of degenerates, anyways."

The corners of his mouth perked up as he flipped off the old man and received the gesture in return.

Dallas burst into the door approximately twenty minutes later, causing the bells to clang against it so hard that they swung and hit the wall.

"You're legal!" He announced to Jimmy from across the store, raising his arms in a triumphant 'V' shape. Bracelets jingled down both arms as he walked over to Jimmy and slung his arm over his shoulder. "I remember 18 like it was yesterday."

"Wasn't it last year?" The guitarist shook his red hair out from the low ponytail it was in, running his fingers along his scalp.

"Watch it," Dallas warned with a light and playful voice despite his flaring nostrils. Turning back to Jimmy, he tightened his arm around his neck.

"Let's get you laid," he chanted through gritted teeth in Jimmy's ear, who squirmed out of Dallas's grip.

"Let's do it," Jimmy tapped Dallas on the chest and walked toward the door, away from the cloud of Brut cologne that perpetually hung around the bassist.

"You dog, you," Leon said sarcastically through a snicker as they walked out the door. The door's bells clanged as it shut behind them, bouncing off the glass covered in band flyers and peeled stickers. Air polluted with car exhaust, cigarette smoke, and hairspray filled their lungs as they made their way to Dallas' car, glittering like a candy apple in the last slivers of sunlight.

"Should we invite Cam?" Jimmy asked as he propped open the passenger side door, careful not to handle it too roughly.

"Already called him," Dallas said out of the side of his mouth as he lit a cigarette, resting one elbow on the roof of the car and the other on the open car door as he huddled his hands around the lighter. He swung the cigarette over the car door, tapping off ashes into the street. "He's doing a campaign tonight, whatever the fuck that is."

"It's a D&D thing," Jimmy explained. "Apparently, this is a big night for him."

"Shit, dude," Dallas scoffed, blowing out a puff of smoke."He's lucky he's talented. Get in the back, Howdy Doody, the Birthday Boy gets shotgun."

"You son of a bitch," Leon chuckled, climbing in the backseat. "You ever call me Howdy Doody again? I'll knock your fucking teeth out."

"Ooo, I'm shaking," Dallas mocked through his teeth, holding the cigarette firmly in his mouth as he swung himself into the car. He took a final drag and tossed the butt out the door before closing it. Unscrewing the top of his necklace, Dallas scooped out some powder and snorted it. He scooped out a little more and turned to Jimmy. Dallas wedged his tongue in his cheek, nodding his chin down toward his hands. Jimmy gazed at Dallas, then at the tiny spoon. The bassist raised his eyebrows, gesturing to the spoon with his eyes.

"C'mon," Dallas encouraged. "Up your nose with it."

Jimmy looked back at Leon before leaning over and cleaning the spoon with a quick sniff. He rubbed the base of his nose, grunting at the sensation. Shaking his head, he ran his fingers through his black hair. He looked at Dallas with glazed, watery eyes.

"Jesus Christ," Dallas said, screwing the top back on his necklace. "Was this your first time doing blow?"

"No," Jimmy said, wiping at his septum. "I just don't like to make a habit of it."

He began laughing, which made Dallas laugh, which made Jimmy laugh even harder. Maybe Dallas was a good influence for Jimmy to not be such a pussy. With a gaping mouth, Leon raised his eyebrows and waved into the front seat.

"Hello," Leon drawled. "I'm still here. I'm not going to be the only sober one. Hook me up."

"Sorry, dude." Dallas scooped out a bump and offered it over his shoulder. "Bon appetite."

The powder stung Leon's sinuses as he sniffed it. A cold head rush incited instantly, invigorating all of his senses. He pinched his nose before allowing himself a deep breath in, letting fresh air dance through his head. It trickled through his sinuses in a cool tingle, reawakening his mind and body.

Dallas pulled a baggie from his pocket, bit a small hole in the corner, and replenished the necklace before screwing it back up.

"Alright," Dallas shot Jimmy a crooked smile. "Now, if you're feeling drunk, take a bump, got it? We don't need you blacking out. You've got fake IDs, right?"

"Have you met me?" Leon asked in mock-offense. "I've had that base covered for years."

"Beautiful," Dallas singsonged. Jimmy's face twisted, and he shot Dallas with a sharp look. Dallas chuckled.

"Coke drip, you're fine. Don't be a wuss," Dallas waved him off, slipping a flask out of his jacket pocket. "Drink."

"God damn," Jimmy took a swig and let out a relaxed breath. "Where are we going?"

"I—" Dallas crooned as he pulled into traffic, jerking everyone around with his choppy merge. A yellow Datsun laid on their horn and yelled profanities out their window. "Fuck," he grimaced. "Don't know yet. We're just going to drive around until inspiration strikes. In the meantime," he pushed the flask back up to Jimmy's lips with a menacing grin. "Drink up."

They cruised up and down the Sunset Strip, hanging out of the car's windows and catcalling the girls walking to the clubs. Cigarettes hung from their fingers out the open windows, ashes flying behind the car like a trail of breadcrumbs. They passed around a brown paper bag of Night Train wine, which, thanks to its high alcohol content, gave them a sufficient buzz. Dallas took a red light as an opportunity to take a bump to bring him back down to normal.

Dallas slowed down the car upon seeing a vertical sign with a vintage carnival-inspired font surrounded by an ornate border: "Tattoos," the sign said. His mouth turned up, spreading into that shit-eating grin that was nearly ever-present on his face.

"This will be a good time," Dallas said as he opened his door and bounded to the curb. Jimmy stayed in the car, his hand poised on the door handle.

"Is this really a good idea?" Jimmy mumbled out of the corner of his mouth, twisting to look back at Leon. Shrugging, Leon nudged him to open the door.

"Fuck it," he slurred. "Live a little, Jimmy."

With a deep sigh, Jimmy drank the last of the wine and shoved the bottle under the seat. The motley crew ventured inside and were greeted by a man with long blue hair wearing a leather trench coat. Blue Hair stroked the death's head moth ink that wrapped around his neck as he looked up at the rag-tag bunch of rockers that stumbled into his tattoo parlor. Running his tongue across the snakebite piercings in his lip, he considered these guys to be an easy sell.

"What can I do for you, gentleman?" He rolled his tongue piercing in between his teeth as Dallas considered the flash art on the wall.

"You can make us look badass," Dallas demanded, jokingly pinching the breasts of a flash tattoo of a pin-up girl.

Leon and Jimmy spent most of their time at the parlor talking Dallas out of getting a Prince Albert piercing. The bassist was insistent but conceded when Leon said that infection could cause him to lose all feeling down there, which would simply not do. Instead, he got a tattoo just below his belly button that said, "Eat Me."

While Dallas was getting inked, Jimmy got his nostril pierced, barely flinching as the needle was pushed through the cartilage of his nose. His eyes watered as the piercer threaded the simple gold hoop through the end of the needle and pulled it back through the new hole in his face. She adjusted it, looping it in place. Jimmy crinkled his nose, getting used to the new piece of jewelry.

"That's hot." The piercer winked at Jimmy, sucking in her cheeks in mock concentration as her hand lingered under his chin under the guise of steadying his face. Jimmy kept his eyes fixed on her as she adjusted the hoop longer than she needed to. He gave her a close-mouthed smile that showed off the dimples on his cheek.

"Thank you, darling," he crooned in a low voice. "You were so gentle, I barely felt a thing."

Leon cleared his throat, ready to get Jimmy out of the chair. The piercer didn't even acknowledge him. She leaned in toward Jimmy and cleaned around the piercing with a cotton swab. Leon pressed his lips together, tapping the heel of his boot against the metal leg of the chair.

"Alright, sugar, you're all done." She finally turned her attention toward Leon, snapping off her gloves and running her fingers through her bleached blonde hair. "What can I do you for?"

Leon rose and took his shirt off, flexing his chest as he told her to pierce his nipple. She smirked, licking her lips as she replaced her piercing tray and chose a stainless-steel hoop for him.

"Christ, are you sure?" Jimmy put a hand over his own peck.

"It'll look bitchin.' I can take a little pain." Leon flicked his eyes over to the piercer. "I might even like it."

"Yeah, okay," she said dryly as she snapped a fresh pair of gloves on and pinched his nipple between the piercing clamps. "Take a deep breath in."

He inhaled the sterile smell of antiseptic, the buzzing of the tattoo gun drowning out the punk music playing through the stereo.

"And breathe out," she said as she exhaled with him, shoving the needle through. Leon gnashed his teeth together, running his tongue over the gritty backsides of his bottom teeth as Jimmy winced in sympathy. He opened his eyes, and sure enough, the needle was barred straight through his nipple.

"You did good," the piercer raised her brows. "You're a tough guy, aren't you."

"I'd like to think so," Leon met her eyes as she screwed the ball on the hoop to secure the jewelry in place. She smiled politely without meeting his eyes, her fingers not lingering on him like they lingered on Jimmy. Squaring his jaw, he got up and tugged his shirt back on, careful not to pull it over the fresh jewelry.

Dallas fed his bandmates some more powder when they got back into the car. After making sure their pupils were good and blown out, he leaned forward in his seat, tugging his shirt off clumsily over the steering wheel. Taking a switchblade out of his boot, he cut the hem off of his Cathouse tee shirt.

"This will show off the goods," he ran his tongue over his teeth as he pulled the shirt back on. The bottom of the shirt rolled up just enough to be able to read his new tattoo. Dallas rolled his head to Jimmy, waggling his eyebrows. "Eh?"

"Looks good," Jimmy's voice cracked as he held back a laugh, twisting the hoop in his nose so his hand would cover his smile. The sun had set entirely as dusk set in, and the lights of the city guided them on their way. Inspiration struck again on Clark Street when Dallas swung into the alley behind the Whiskey A Go-Go.

"I've got some friends playing here tonight," Dallas said as he pulled in behind a black Trans Am. A guy with more makeup on than Dallas got out of the front seat.

"Jamie!" Dallas called out of the window, waving wildly. The guy looked up, straightening his white leather vest over his bare chest. Dallas rolled the window up and got out of the car, forgetting entirely about Jimmy and Leon. They followed him out, resting their thumbs in their belt loops a safe distance behind their bassist.

"What the hell are you doing here?" Jamie jested. "Did you get sick of slumming it with The Dog House?"

"The Dog House?" Leon shifted his weight, adopting a mock-confrontational stance.

"My old band," Dallas explained, running his fingers along the waistband of his leather pants, feeling the fresh tattoo with his thumb.

"What a shitty name for a band," Jimmy taunted.

"Fuckin' A right it is," Jamie agreed, not bothering to introduce himself and not caring to be introduced. "Are you still playing with them?"

"No." Dallas rolled his eyes to the side and held up his hands in a *don't shoot* gesture. "They were a mess. I'm with these guys now. We're prowling for a drummer, but tonight, we're celebrating this guy's birthday."

Dallas elbowed Jimmy in the ribs playfully.

"Ah, okay, okay," Jamie tittered, puckering his over-lined lips. His hair was bleached so blonde that it lay in white tufts around his face, making his makeup stand out that much more. "Come on in. Just bring in the rest of this equipment so you look useful, and you don't have to pay."

Jamie thrust an amp into Leon's arms and brought them in through the back door.

They hung out with the band, a little too glam for Leon and Jimmy's tastes, but they were nice enough guys who put on one hell of a show. Their name wasn't memorable enough for Leon to take note of; he was barely even listening as they talked about music, drugs, and women. As far as he was concerned, these guys were his competition. *If only we could find a drummer,* Leon thought, *we would be so much better than them.*

After the show, the band was greeted by a hoard of girls in the alley behind The Whiskey. Jamie's lip liner was smeared all over a tall brunette's face. Leon and Jimmy stuck together, searching over bobbing heads for their bassist as they made their way back to his car. Dallas could be anywhere in the crowd: all of them were wearing heeled snakeskin boots, tight leather, and teased hair. He fit right in with this group.

"Do you see him?" Leon surveyed the masses, skimming the midriff of everyone looking for the suggestive new tattoo.

"No." Jimmy looked, too, propping his elbow on the hood of Dallas's car. He finally spotted Dallas, making an exchange with Jamie.

"There he is." Jimmy pointed and whistled to get his attention. Dallas's head snapped up. Guilt filled his eyes for a split second before a smile spread across his face. He said goodbye to Jamie, tapping him twice on the cheek, and made his way to the car.

"See anything you like, Jimmy Boy?"

"Nah," Jimmy shrugged, his face flushing as he looked around at the flocks of women making advances toward the band.

"Too easy?" Dallas asked, nodding his understanding. He squinted. "You like a chase?"

"I guess so," Jimmy cocked his head to the side, swinging himself into the car.

"No," Leon scoffed, snorting at his friend. "He has to wine and dine her and learn her innermost thoughts and feelings before he makes a move."

"This was a great birthday," Jimmy said, ignoring Leon, who rolled his eyes and looked out the window. "Thanks for taking us out, Dallas."

"Shit, the night is still young," Dallas hollered, putting the car in gear and whipping the car around the crowd, honking as he drove by them. He put a cigarette between his lips and jutted his chin up at Jimmy in a wordless command.

"Where are we going?" Jimmy asked, flicking the lighter and holding the flame up to Dallas's cigarette.

"I don't know yet." Dallas took a puff and released a plume of smoke over the dash. He stuck his head out the window so he could see the road as it dispersed. "I think we'll stop by the Guardian Warehouse."

"The storage unit?"

"Yeah. My old band used to rehearse down here, and they would throw some wicked parties." Dallas smiled fondly as he remembered the delinquency and wildness of those parties, resting his arm out the window. "More often than not, the cops would be called to break things up. But until that happens, it is a lawless fun land."

As they turned the corner, they could already see floods of people milling around. Music blasted, and people stumbled about, too drunk to know who was unzipping their pants.

"Just as I suspected." Dallas spun the wheel to back into a parking spot between two other cars. He swung in, kissing the bumper of the car behind him. They bounced off the bumper, and Dallas quickly straightened out the car. "Nothing to see here," he drawled as he checked his side mirrors. "As I was saying, they've always got something going. It doesn't matter if it's a Tuesday or a Saturday."

He put the car in park and opened the glove box. It was empty, besides a few condoms and two baggies: one filled with white powder and the other filled with a clumpy green mass. Dallas took out one of the condoms and tossed it in Jimmy's lap.

"Use this," he said, his face completely serious. "Me and every single guy in that band picked something up at one point or another at these parties."

"Ew, Dallas," Jimmy rolled his head toward the car door as he pocketed the rubber.

"What? It's no big deal," Dallas knitted his brow. "Nothing some fish antibiotics can't fix."

"You're so full of shit," Jimmy chuckled as he got out of the car.

"I'm serious." Dallas got out of the car and looked at Jimmy over the roof. "I saved so much money not going to the doctor and stopping by the pet shop."

"I will use it," Jimmy said, shooting Dallas a look to shut him up as he slammed the door.

"Attaboy," Dallas swiveled around the front of the car and locked Jimmy's head under his arm, his wide mouth spreading into a smile. "Shall we?"

Leon got out, looking around at the crowd. He watched Dallas introduce Jimmy to his friends, the guys in his old band. *What a stupid way to spend your time,* Leon thought. *They're taking their eye off the prize.* What good is partying when you have nothing to celebrate yet? As far as he was concerned, these guys were as good as the washed-up has-beens strolling the Strip. *They will still be partying and trying to make it in the same clothes thirty years from now, but it will be less cool then.*

Girls flocked to Jimmy, quickly making him the center of attention. Dallas left him alone after picking up the first girl he saw, pulling her onto the ratty couch that someone had dragged in from an abandoned unit. A woman approached Jimmy and wrapped her arms around his neck, falling into him. Her lipstick was smeared, and her bra strap had fallen down her arm.

"You're exotic," she babbled as she ran her lips over Jimmy's neck. Her breath smelled like cigarettes and vomit. "Where are you from?"

"I'm from here," Jimmy gave a half-suppressed laugh as he leaned away from her.

"But what *are* you?"

"I'm Portuguese," he answered as he tried to stand her up straight.

"You're beautiful," she crooned as she fell right back into him, too drunk or doped up to hold herself upright. She wrapped her fingers in his long black hair.

"Thank you," Jimmy said, keeping his body tense. He untangled her fingers from his hair and held her hand steady. "What's your name?"

"Cindy," she mumbled, her name coming out like 'sin-nee.' She ran her hands down his body and clumsily stuck her hand down his jeans.

"Sweetheart, you are completely intoxicated." Jimmy pulled her hand out of his pants, holding her firmly by the shoulders as he stepped away from her. He patted her shoulders gently, trying to keep her upright.

"That just makes it more fun, Jim," Dallas quipped.

"Pig," the girl on Dallas's lap teased as she knelt on the floor, unzipping his fly. Dallas gestured to her now-bobbing head, pursing his lips in an 'I told you so' expression.

"See!" Dallas took a sip of his beer and laid his head on the back of the couch. Cindy leaned into Jimmy again.

"Darlin', I won't take advantage of you," Jimmy said, holding Cindy's hand as he gently pushed her away. "I'm sorry."

"Whatever—" she slurred, clumsily straightening herself up. "You look like a lousy lay anyway."

Dallas burst out laughing, running his fingers through his girl's hair as Cindy made a wobbly exit. Jimmy wiped his palms on his jeans before walking outside. He found Leon leaning against the car, lighting up a joint.

"Hey," Leon's eyes lit up when he saw Jimmy and held the joint out to him.

"Nah, thanks."

"You okay?"

"Yeah," Jimmy sighed. "This just doesn't do it for me. This isn't my scene. I just want to make music."

Leon nodded in agreement. He would rather spend his nights strumming the strings of his beloved guitar, losing himself in his songs and letting his troubles fade away. In the melodies he played, he found an escape from the chaos of life. He knew they would outgrow the life eventually. They would age out of the women and wear out the drugs, but they would be forever young in their music.

"What do you say we leave Dallas here and go make our own fun?"

Jimmy gave Leon a wan smile. "Tempting, but we can't just leave him here."

"Yes, we can." Leon snuffed the joint out on his tongue and reached into his pocket, pulling out a set of keys with a rabbit's foot dangling off the keychain. "The dumbass left his keys in the ignition. He's in no state to drive anyway."

Pursing his lips, Jimmy looked from the keys back over his shoulder at the party.

"He probably won't even notice we're gone," Jimmy reasoned, jumping in the passenger's side. Leon twirled the keys around his finger, rounding the car to the swing in behind the wheel.

They stopped at a liquor store first, the clerk barely looking at them long enough to care that they were obviously underage. They took their Jack Daniels and case of beer on their merry way. Before heading out to one of their favorite places, they picked up some flashlights and a radio from Leon's apartment.

Dante's View in Griffith Park, a serene spot that overlooked the cityscape of Los Angeles, provided a tranquil escape from the hustle and bustle of the city. Jimmy and Leon sat on the wooden guard rails, passing their bottle of whiskey back and forth as they looked at the blur of the lights from their place within the trees. The city noise was drowned out by the soft breeze in the trees and the cicadas singing their summer song. Lynyrd Skynyrd played on their radio, the volume turned down low enough to hear the sounds of nature. Nighttime had cooled the June air, chilling the breeze in a way that made them feel more alive to breathe it in.

This was one of their favorite places to go, a spot they had been visiting since they were kids on bikes. Their friendship was unique. They never felt the need to fill the silence with meaningless small talk and overflowing words. Out here, they could simply *be*.

"Happy Birthday, Jimmy." Leon handed the bottle to Jimmy, breaking the silence. Jimmy took it with an affirming nod, and they settled back into peace and quiet.

9

Come Together

Lonnie Herring lit a cigarette and leaned back as he perused the newest edition of *The Recycler*. He had been playing drums in a punk band, but the constant turnover of musicians wore him down. He despised the revolving door and, with it, the entire band.

Lonnie's search for a new band had become a constant routine. Every week, he would meticulously scan the classifieds in the latest *Recycler*, reading ads from musicians seeking new talent to jam with or bands that needed that final missing piece. With each new edition, he clung to the hope of stumbling upon an ad seeking a drummer like him to fill their musical void.

Lonnie let out a deep sigh, a cloud of smoke escaping his lips. He scanned the ads that searched for singers, guitarists, and songwriters to collaborate with. He couldn't help the disillusionment that crept up his gut as he read the naïvety between each ad's lines.

Once upon a time, he had been full of hope—a young, starry-eyed teenager eager to make it big with his first band. But the revolving door had begun: egos, drugs, girlfriends, creative differences—they all got in the way. At only 22 years old, Lonnie had lost the stars in his eyes. Who were these people who believed that all they needed was one more member to become rich and famous? Who were they to think *they* had what it took over anyone else? They dared to believe themselves to be so talented. The audacity. *How embarrassing*, he thought, sipping coffee in between drags. Then again, who was he to judge when he had once believed the same thing himself? Hell, he was still believing it. *I'm no better than they are.*

Week after week, he searched for a band that needed a drummer, but bands interested in him were always either too soft or too glam. He was never the right fit. The perfect fit. This week, however, one ad in particular caught his eye:

```
In search of a cool, crude dude who likes banging drums as much
as he likes banging chicks. Influenced by Sabbath, Aerosmith,
Zeppelin, SRV, Iggy Pop. Call Leon: 310-555-6663.
```

The wittiness of the ad made him chuckle. He immediately liked the first impression he got of these guys. Their music taste was diverse, including blues, hard rock, and punk, which promised a blended sound. *That* was the kind of sound that Lonnie wanted to be a part of. This group came off as being the brash, confident, and unapologetic band that Lonnie sought to join.

He straightened the paper; the ad not only caught his attention but also piqued his curiosity enough to make a move. He got up from the dinette table and dialed Leon's number. Walking back over to the small table, he stretched the spiral cord across the wall as he sat back down. Lonnie cocked his head in impatience as he drummed his fingers on the tabletop. The phone rang and rang. Lonnie slapped his restless fingers over the newspaper, ready to hang up when Leon answered.

"Is this Leon?" Lonnie ran his tongue over his bottom lip, his irritability getting the best of him.

"Who's asking?" The voice at the other end of the phone was deep and gravelly.

"Lonnie Herring. You're lucky you didn't put Lynyrd Skynyrd on this ad. You would've been shit out of luck."

Leon chuckled. "I take it you're a drummer, huh?"

"Nothing gets by you," Lonnie huffed a laugh, pressing the phone against his ear with his shoulder as he poured himself another cup of coffee. He was at the end of the pot, and clumps of coffee grounds floated to the top of his mug. Frowning, he poured it down the drain.

"I actually started out on guitar before starting on drums. I played bass for a while there, too, before figuring out drums were my calling."

"So you're a one-man rhythm section. Impressive."

"I'm all you'd need."

"Why did you settle on drumming?"

Lonnie considered this. "They scratch the creative itch while giving me an outlet for my aggression."

Leon laughed and said something indistinct to someone in the background. "Well, you've got the crude part of the ad down. Let's see if you've got the talent. Thursday, say 4?"

"I'll have my secretary mark you down." He stretched back to hide the excitement that was bubbling up under the surface. Lonnie didn't let himself get excited, not anymore. He'd been burned too many times by hacks and has-beens looking for their 15 minutes. He needed more than 15 minutes—he wanted a legacy.

Lonnie jotted down the address, hung up the phone, and reread the ad. There was something different about these guys, but he couldn't discern if it was a good or bad feeling. The acidity from his coffee burned his throat, mixing with bile from his stomach. He explained the nerves away, attributing them to the impending audition. A voice in his head told him to go—that he had to go. He had no other choice.

* * *

The guys evaluated their prospective drummer: he had a strong jawline and a somewhat rounded, angular-shaped face. One of Lonnie's most distinguishing traits was the color of his eyes, which stood out against his fair skin. His small but expressive eyes were a striking blue. His intense and confident stare instinctively made them feel a little inferior. He had a messy mane of thick, wavy brown hair with a mullet that was tucked behind his ears. Simply by virtue of his appearance, he belonged in their band.

It took a couple of trips to haul all of Lonnie's equipment into the apartment. The snare drum almost fell victim to the wobbly stairs, being extremely close to meeting a violent end on the concrete below. As Lonnie set up his drum kit, Leon realized it would be a tight fit to give them enough room to jam and rehearse comfortably all together. With Cam and Jimmy's help, he moved the couch back and the table off to the side while Dallas tapped out a cigarette in the kitchen sink. Jimmy stacked the collection of amps in the corner of the kitchen, resting the instruments on the wall by Stevie's enclosure.

"You guys must suck if the drummer is the last member you recruit for your band. How the hell do you keep any time?" Lonnie finished setting up his drum kit as the rest of the band looked around at one another, brows raised. Dallas waved his hand in a dismissive gesture.

"Our songs are tight. We don't need to rely on you or any other drummer."

Lonnie looked up; his face looked perpetually pinched. "Is that so?" He picked up a drumstick, twirling it between his fingers as he walked up to Dallas. Lonnie looked him up and down, smirking at Dallas's white leather pants. He tugged on the belt loops of his jeans and leaned, stretching his back. "Let me guess. Bassist."

Dallas wrinkled his brow, leaning against the arm of the couch. "Yeah. How'd you guess?"

Lonnie walked back over to his drum kit, pointing with his stick. "Because only bassists can have that kind of superior attitude dressed like that." He clucked his tongue, looking over Dallas's scarves again, and laughed.

Leon scoffed and clapped Lonnie on the back. "Don't bother setting up the rest of your kit. You're in."

Jimmy smirked as he looked over at Dallas, who had a flushed face and curled lips.

"Whatever," Dallas spat, pulling up on his belt loops. "Nice denim on denim."

"I think your scarves are cool." Cam flashed Dallas a downturned smile. He looked bug-eyed at Jimmy and shrugged his shoulders.

"Whenever you're ready, drummer." Jimmy crossed his arms and leaned back on the table.

Lonnie sat at his drum kit, twirling a drumstick in his right hand. He silenced the room by tapping the kick drum pedal twice with his foot. Giving the hi-hat four quick taps, he established a rhythm by adding a double bass pattern. He launched into a storm of rapid fills, smoothly switching between diverse drumming techniques. Each hit of his drumstick looked perfectly calculated, his movements flowing naturally as he showed off his skills, utilizing every component of the drum kit.

As the solo neared its conclusion, Lonnie unleashed a barrage of lightning-fast drum rolls, concluding with a thunderous smash.

The band erupted in cheers and whistles. Despite his ego taking a hit, Dallas joined in on the applause as Lonnie rose to take a bow.

Lonnie stood up, soaking it in. "Anything to say, bassist?"

Dallas jutted his lips out, shaking his head. A hint of a smile appeared on Lonnie's face, causing an identical expression to form on Dallas's.

"No," Dallas shrugged. "I think we could work well together."

Lonnie had the urge to widen his smile and maybe even laugh, but he would rather stick his drumstick up his nose and swirl his brains around than show these guys any more joy. He carefully observed each of them: the glam rocker, the blues guy, the soul, the whimsy, and he brought the punk attitude that every band needs to succeed. Lonnie knew that to make it on the Strip and beyond the Strip, you couldn't conform to fit into a box. These guys, though, were diverse enough to break the mold and leave their mark.

"What do you say we test it out?" Lonnie sat at the kit, bouncing on the stool a bit. He tapped the kick drum twice and did a drum roll on the snare.

The musicians all strapped on their instruments, plugged in their amps, and tiptoed dangerously close to setting Leon's apartment on fire with the amount of equipment they had plugged in. After tuning their instruments, they decided to play a cover of Nazareth's "Changin' Times" to give their chemistry an audition. Lonnie counted them in, and they kicked off strong, playing the bluesy opening riff. The drummer was impressed by how well they played together and how much grit these guys had. He had underestimated Dallas, writing him off too quickly. The bassist had a natural knack for going beyond the fundamental job of a bassist and adding groovy sustenance to the music. When Jimmy began singing with his smoky, raspy voice, Lonnie couldn't help but break into an extremely rare smile. It felt appropriate: these guys were rare.

The band continued jamming, trying different covers, and improvising over simple 12-bar blues progressions. Everyone brought Lonnie up to speed on their musical influences, and he added his own to the list: The Sex Pistols, the Misfits, and Judas Priest.

They took a smoke break, giving their fingers and ears a few minutes to recuperate before abusing them for another couple of hours. The band was deep in a discussion about its direction, and everyone except Dallas nixed the idea of going glam. Instead, they wanted to focus on creating a pure rock sound that incorporated elements of metal, punk, and blues. They all agreed that to achieve the sound they wanted, they would collaborate on the lyrics, and no one would be the designated lyricist. The music should be a product of all of their voices and a blend of their individual styles.

"I've been tossing around an idea for a while," Lonnie took a drag of his cigarette. "It's a song about Charles Manson and the Manson Murders. I've been calling it "Teen Killer," but it's just a clusterfuck right now."

" 'Teen Killer?' " Leon asked. "They didn't kill any teenagers. They killed that actress, right?"

"You're missing the point, man." Lonnie shook his head and took a long drag. "It's not about the physical murder. It's about how this hippie fuck brainwashed hitchhiking teenagers and lonely fucking kids into killing innocent people in the most brutal way they could imagine. He killed their *souls*. It's about the evil in the world."

"Damn, dude," Cam said, wide-eyed. "That's deep shit."

"Yeah, it is," Jimmy agreed. "I like it. What do you have?"

Lonnie took a final puff from his cigarette before pulling a crumpled paper from his back pocket. He unfolded it and smoothed it out, revealing a bunch of hastily scribbled notes:

Yes, Charlie. Please, Charlie.
Goodbye, little piggies
Come, little piggies, say goodbye to Mom and Dad
Tell them you've made yourself a new family.
I'll huff little piggies, and I'll puff little piggies,
And I'll blow your humanity in
Heads full of dope and dreams.
Free love and living in sin
Waiting to wage the war - it's about to begin
Won't you tell me, Charlie?
Will you lead me, Charlie?
Lead the little piggies to slaughter
Butcher the piggies, do it for them, make it grisly for them
He's a prophet of God. He's speaking the truth.
Leading little piggies to sacrifice their youth
Their heads full of dope and dreams

"Free love and free hate," Cam said, taking a sip from his drink and passing the paper to Leon, who was immediately intrigued by the dark and twisted nature of the lyrics. While all band members had a penchant for the macabre, it was clear that Lonnie's ideas were particularly unsettling and disturbing. Leon loved it.

"I think we have the start of a new song on our hands," Leon said as he passed the paper to Jimmy.

"I think so, too," Jimmy agreed. Lonnie smirked, proud to have made his first contribution to the band.

"What if we do a real rocked-out rhythm that is inspired by the 60s?" Dallas considered the lyrics. I could do a tuned-down, "Day Tripper" inspired bassline, and we could layer the vocals. Be reminiscent of the Beach Boys, the Mamas and the Papas." Dallas extended the lyric sheet back to Lonnie, who was squinting at him through dark lashes.

"What?" Dallas asked, shrinking into himself. "Isn't that the kind of music Charlie liked?"

107

"I underestimated you, bassist," Lonnie admitted, snatching the lyrics back and shoving them in his back pocket. "Let's make it happen."

They hammered out the opening riff and chorus for the song before losing steam, needing to refuel their bodies with food, alcohol, and drugs.

The five of them celebrated at The Rainbow Bar & Grill. Growing up, Jimmy and Leon sneaked in with fake I.D.s that Leon made. They loved seeing all the musicians who used the place as a hangout. A place where they could be themselves and let loose. They always said that they would go there when they had a band. They couldn't wait to grow up.

They slid in at a booth illuminated by multicolored Christmas lights left up year-round. Ambient lighting created a warm glow against the red booths that still smelled like leather, no matter how many fluids (bodily or otherwise) were spilled on them. Lonnie ordered a round of shots, taking in the moment.

"To the first of many times coming here as a band," Jimmy toasted.

"And to all of the success that lies before us," Leon added.

"And to sex, drugs, and rock n roll!" Dallas announced, tapping the glass on the table and taking his shot. The rest of the band followed suit.

The energy throughout the night was electric. Their noses burned with the sting of powder. Rounds upon rounds of drinks were consumed as they jotted down lyric ideas on flimsy bar napkins. They brainstormed show ideas, coming up with wild antics to pull on stage for shock value. A band's success heavily relies on chemistry, and it was evident that they had found the perfect formula. Each one of those men stumbled home that night, buzzed and buzzing with promise.

10

A Sacrificial Offering

Booze stung Leon's throat, threatening to make a reappearance as he made his way up the stairs to his apartment. The stairs swayed, doubling in front of his eyes. He clumsily made his way up to the door, leaning all his weight on the guardrail. It creaked, but he was too preoccupied with the night, the band. It was late enough to be considered morning but too early for the sun to be up. Leon should have been blacked out, but thanks to the amount of cocaine in his system, he was coherent enough for his thoughts to race. It was a recipe that was damning for creatives, sentencing him to be tortured by his own ideas, never ceasing until he made a move to silence the voices.

The key dangled around the keyhole, tauntingly circling around, keeping Leon from the idea that had been torturing him since the first shot at The Rainbow. This was it, the culmination of daydreams and nightmares. Leon had found his tribe, the four other guys who could sink their teeth into the Sunset Strip, chew it up, and spit out success.

He was on a high, not from the drugs but from the dream: it was falling into place. But they would need connections, and he knew that. They needed help to get there. Leon knew that fate was on his side. It had to be. He had a fan beyond the veil, and he wanted to call in a favor—perhaps even call in a favor to the Chief of Demons himself.

The key finally slid into the keyhole. Leon jammed it in, twisting it to the side, and shoved the door open. He swung himself inside, slamming the door shut behind him in case any of the guys followed him back. The faint click as he twisted the deadbolt completely sobered him. The lock was useless, having been pried open too many times actually to protect him from danger. He never cared about the lock before, but now he had something to protect.

Scanning the dark room, he took in the mess of cords that littered the floor and the instruments that leaned against the walls, no doubt creating scuffs on the chipped paint. He hoped there were scuffs, something to ingrain their history into the fabric of this room—the room where his band was formed.

A low hum came from an amp that someone had forgotten to turn off before heading out on the town. Leon took a step into his apartment, searching for something to put in front of the door as an extra layer of security. He slammed his toe into the foot of the couch.

FUCK!

He had forgotten that they had moved the furniture—hell, he'd forgotten he'd owned furniture. He rounded the couch and pushed it up against the door. His bandmates would have to pick up their equipment later. *His bandmates.*

He straightened, satisfied with his new arrangement. The only light in the apartment radiated from Stevie's enclosure, who had slithered out to peek at all the commotion. Its tongue flicked in excitement, feeding off of the energy that Leon was emanating.

Leon kept the lights off—he didn't want anyone to know he was home, especially Jimmy. Clearing his table of clutter, he swept cigarette ashes, beer bottles, trash, and broken guitar strings onto the floor. He arranged three black candles along the back of the table and ceremoniously flicked a match to light them. The wicks sparked as they let themselves be enveloped by the flame, the twisted threads unraveling at the heat.

Sliding his Ouija board from beneath his couch, he placed it on the back of the table, balancing it carefully against the wall. The last time he used it, he discovered his only fan. A good luck charm—bridging the gap between him and whoever or whatever was on the other side.

He looked around for something to write with that could be easily wiped away, something that could be erased so that no one else would know about this little covenant. The answer lay within his hands. He held his athame—a ritual knife with a black handle and two sharp edges—tenderly in his hands, running his fingers along the smooth face of the blade. Ultimately deciding that he couldn't cut his fretting hand—those calluses were precious and needed to remain intact—he pressed the tip of the athame into his right hand's pointer finger, making a small slice.

Blood dribbled down his hand, streaming down his wrist and dripping off of his elbow. It was running fast, faster than he anticipated. He pulled his shirt over his head, wrapping the fabric around his wrist.

Placing the bloody finger on the table, he drew an inverted pentagram, carefully plotting his motions to emulate his ultimate goal: to invoke.

He hurried to his bookcase and snatched a couple of specimen jars, his eyes sweeping over his collection of books. All the books had different rules for spells and rituals, depending on who penned them and what practice the author believed in. The Wiccan ones preached the Rule of Three. Those were Leon's least favorite books; he hated the idea of karma.

He found that a common denominator among all the various practices was respect for the earth and its elements. He put down the jars so that the snakeskin rested on the leftmost point, the cockroach carcasses and tiny animal bones were at the bottom, and the mouse tails lay to the right. A bird skull sat upon the top point in front of the candles: the element of fire. The remaining elements—salt for the earth, water, and a feather for the air—were placed in three shot glasses. He picked up the shot glasses and arranged them alongside the candles.

He set his athame on one side of the pentagram and presented an offering of red wine in a gold chalice he had stolen from a swap meet. He lit an incense cone, tilting it into the flame of one of the candles. It charred, the tip of the cone blackening. It let out a whispering whir as it seared. Leon set the cone down, inhaling a deep, spicy breath.

As he pulled his hand away, a slight breeze caused the top of the feather to float. He straightened the feather, feeling the silky-smooth texture on his fingertip. The finger was still oozing blood, staining the purity of the white feather red.

The source of the feather cooed in a box beside Leon. While buying food for Stevie earlier that day, he purchased the white dove at the pet store. Anticipation got the best of him, and he bought the dove on a whim. He figured if the audition went well, it was a sign that this dove was meant to be a part of their journey. He stashed the box in his bathroom, hoping that no one needed to use it. To his luck, they didn't.

He opened the box and wrapped his fingers around its plump body, feeling the vibration of its heartbeat. The dove crooned in his hands as he carefully took it out of the box. With pure, foolish innocence, the bird's beady eyes bore into his own. Leon held the bird firmly in his palms and stroked its wings.

Leon pulled his right hand away, slowly reaching for his knife to avoid setting off the bird. He tightened his grip on the dove to compensate for having only one hand on it. As he enclosed his fingers around the knife, the bird settled into his hand, wrapping its feet around his finger. He brought the bird to his chest, securing it to him. The bird tried to flap its wings as sounds of terror replaced the cooing.

Blood poured from the bird's breast from the fatal wound inflicted by the athame. He held the dove out, letting the blood pour into the center of the altar. He placed the body down, letting it lay in a pool of its own blood. The feathers soaked some up, creating sticky clumps.

Leon took in a slow breath, letting the air fully fill his lungs. He held his breath until it burned, rolling his eyes into the back of his head, basking in the energy he had created on the table. It radiated, calling to him. He let his breath out, ready to call upon the entity that had helped so many people succeed before him. Leon picked up a piece of parchment paper that he had meticulously cut and began chanting these words as he penned them:

I conjure the serpent
I summon the keeper of souls
I give you all that I am
For your power, your glory, and keeping

The air around him changed. It grew heavy. Humid.

There was a disruption in the static energy; the quiet in his apartment now hummed with the power of something else. Some*one* else. Someone was looming over his shoulder, watching him delicately tuck the carefully folded paper underneath the bleeding dove's limp body. Watching his eyes roll back into his skull. Listening to his chant, answering the call to his words.

Leon sensed the presence behind him, a breath hitching in his chest as he continued to chant.

How long do I need to chant? How will I know it worked?

The temperature in the apartment plummeted unexpectedly. The hair on his arms and neck stood up, the root of the hairs prickling into goosebumps that spread over his entire body. It sent a ripple through him as if he had been permeated by a cloud filled with cool mist. Despite the sudden cold, the humidity hung over him, the hum turning into a ringing in his ear that got louder and louder, and the pressure bore on his shoulders.

He sat motionless, observing as the candle flames frantically flickered and swayed. A sharp gust of air extinguished the candles, blowing his hair into his face. The melted black wax dripped onto the tables, forming large puddles, while he watched the wispy smoke dance off of the wicks.

Leon felt as if someone strung up his limbs, pulling him out of the chair by a string in his head. He rose from the altar, his head heavy with disorientation. Something was plucking skillfully at the set of strings to pick up his feet, putting one in front of the other.

A marionette, obediently following the directions of his Master.

Of course, there were no strings. Leon lifted his hand as he walked with heavy footsteps, checking to see if he still had autonomy over his body. He did.

Didn't he?

Seeking comfort, he fell onto his mattress. He blinked, his eyelids beginning to sag. The distinct noise of sharp scratching emanated from the altar as if something was being dragged across the tabletop's surface. It was a heavy sound, like whatever was being dragged had been slowed down by passing through the congealed blood of the dove. Inching closer to the edge, the athame slid off the tabletop. The blade perfectly pierced the floor as it fell, leaving the dagger standing completely upright.

He jumped, his eyelids flying open to see what made the noise, but he found it too difficult to keep them open. The invisible strings pulled Leon's head back down onto the bed. He fought the exhaustion that washed over him, prying his eyelids open with his last bit of energy. A shadowy figure loomed near the table where he had completed his ritual. The darkness swallowed the light from Stevie's enclosure.

It was too heavy, he couldn't fight it anymore. Submitting, he let his eyelids flutter down, erasing the image of the figure standing before him. His big toe got pinched as he began to unwind, but he couldn't open his eyes to see what had done it. He fell asleep as the blanket covering him began to be peeled off, exposing him to the room's cold yet suffocating air.

Dense energy coursed through the apartment. Leon's snake slithered quickly, thrilled by the intensity. It flicked its tongue at the being whose energy was audibly vibrating low beyond the glass as it slithered around its enclosure.

Leon opened his eyes and was greeted by the familiar smell of the stage. Booze, smoky cigarettes, hairspray, and musky colognes intermingled into a familiar cloud. The room was dark, the flashing stage lights illuminating it in a dim, colorful glow.

No longer in his apartment, he recognized the light-up sign in the middle of the stage's backdrop.

The Troubadour.

With a sweeping glance, Leon surveyed the room. He should have been jostled around for taking up too much space. People should have been elbowing and shouldering him out of the way with how packed it was, but they weren't. Most wore casual denim and leather clothes, but a select few stood out in their long vinyl trench coats, colored hair, and spikes, standing on the sidelines. Everyone in the throng talked and laughed with their friends, excited to see the band whose instruments sat propped up on stage, primed and ready to be played.

Nobody noticed Leon as he made his way through the crowd. *I'm dreaming*, he concluded. It was the strangest sensation: he knew he was dreaming, but all the information he needed to understand his experience poured into his head within an instant. He knew that he was at the Troubadour and had to grab a seat at the bar immediately or risk missing the meeting.

What meeting? That was the only seed of knowledge he was missing.

It was all so real. He sensed the pulsating energy around him, feeling it in his chest. The hairs on his arms stuck to the bar as he leaned on it, scanning the crowd. He could feel the cold surface of the bar beneath his forearms and the reverberating buzz beneath his feet.

Leon spun around on his bar stool, not knowing who he was looking for until he found him.

The presence of an incredibly imposing man leaning his muscular frame casually against one of the support beams below the showroom balcony took Leon aback as he wondered how he could have missed him. Two women were clinging to his arms, one of whom was a brunette running her fingers through his long black locks, while the other was a blonde admiring his chiseled chest. A third woman approached him, vying for his attention. But the man's deep-set green eyes focused on Leon, and a seductive gaze filled with recognition and intensity pierced him. The man tilted his squared chin up and kept his unwavering watch fixed on Leon.

The three women withdrew their hands off the brooding man's body and disappeared into the crowd as if on cue, wordlessly peeling themselves off of him in unison. Leon didn't see the man take one step as he approached the bar. There was no bounce, stride, or dull thud from his leather boots on the floor. Instead, the man appeared to glide across the floor. His ferocity made Leon's heart rise into his throat and the blood thump in his ears, drowning out the crowd's chatter.

The stranger stopped next to Leon and lowered himself onto the bar stool. His elbow rested on the bar, and his legs parted casually. With a wave of two fingers, the bartender immediately set down a whiskey on the rocks before disappearing. Never taking his eyes off of Leon, he picked up the liquor and took a sip.

The meeting was in session.

The man grinned like a Cheshire cat, his teeth shockingly white, even against his porcelain skin. The canines tapered into vampiric points.

"Do you understand what you're conjuring up?" He taunted in a low, raspy voice that vibrated in Leon's chest.

"I'm dreaming," Leon said, as much to himself as to the stranger before him. The stranger laughed and shook his head. Up close, he appeared even more bone-chillingly exquisite. His skin looked to be chiseled from stone because of its milkiness. Sideburns that tapered into the contours of his face accentuated his high cheekbones. His black hair was parted down the middle and spilled over his broad shoulders, making him seem all the more pale. His lips were a deep pink as if someone had bitten them, and blood had rushed to the surface. This man would look almost like a beautiful corpse risen from the dead if it weren't for his bright green eyes.

"I have access to you any time I feel like. I can enter your mind. I can enter your dreams. I can possess your body. I have zero limitations."

"What's your name?" Leon's cheeks burned.

The man chuckled as he swirled the whiskey in his glass, the ice clinking the edges. "It depends on who you ask," he paused, considering. "You can call me Lucius. Lucius Wolfe."

"Leon." Leon reached out his hand and examined Lucius's, adorned with a wolf ring denoting his surname. Recognition lit up Leon's face as Lucius's laughter rumbled like a growl.

"Don't shake unless you know what you're doing. I know who you are. That's why I came to you. And you know who I am. That's why you called to me."

Leon observed Lucius, clad in leather chaps, acid-washed Levi jeans, and a denim battle vest over a leather jacket. As Leon's fingertips tingled, a new wave of information washed over him as he scanned over the patches on the vest. Each patch was a visual representation of a soul that Lucius possessed. Each person had made the ultimate sacrifice for their art, wealth, and fame. Leon's eyes raked over the patches, recognizing his idols among them. A surge of excitement filled his chest as he noticed the empty spot on the vest, a place reserved for him. His band. This meeting, he realized, was about claiming that spot. It was his if he so desired.

"I do," Leon said with a heartfelt nod. He was ready for anything that came his way. If this were the Devil, he would give his soul to rock and roll.

Lucius took a swig of his drink. "I can give you success, I can make you a legend, but I am going to need pieces of you. Pieces of human morality. The slaughter of all of the societal conditioning, the religious conditioning, the moral conditioning."

"I don't have religious conditioning," Leon said. "I don't believe in God."

Lucius's eyes burned with a glorious rage as his mouth twisted into a smile. He glared at Leon, his eyebrows straight.

"Why, of course, there is a God. Without God, there is no Heaven. Without God, there is no Hell." Lucius's eyes darkened, narrowing as he tipped his glass to his lips and tilted his chin in a downward nod. "And there is a Hell, Leon." He stared into Leon's soul, burning with a passion that held Leon's eyes and created tightness in his chest. "God has many, many angels," Lucius said, almost in a whisper. "He used to have a favorite, the angel of music."

Lucius's gaze grasped him tighter, like a snake about to strike his prey. "He was cast out," Lucius spat. "Cast away," he said, smiling, "for being proud."

He ran his finger along the empty spot on his battle jacket. "I can help you to become immortal in your music. Your physical body will die, eventually, and your soul will be cast away from Earth. But you, your music, will live on. Forever." Lucius tossed the rest of his drink back, his lips curling away from his teeth as he swallowed the liquor. His Adam's apple bobbed in his thick neck. "In return, you'll serve me." Lucius leaned toward Leon, nodding.

Leon felt his own head bob up and down slowly in imitation.

"You will be loyal to me until *I* feel you've held up your end of the bargain. When I say you're done, *you're done*. Do we have a deal?"

Lucius stopped nodding, and Leon's head slowly came to a stop. The word was on the tip of his tongue. *Yes.* But something stopped him.

Jimmy. What about Jimmy?

Lucius clicked his tongue in displeasure, shaking his head slowly from side to side.

"Hesitation." He twisted his lips and looked at Leon through thick black lashes. "What a pity."

Lucius stood up and threw a 100-dollar bill onto the counter. Leon only then realized that there was no longer a bartender behind the bar. They had been sitting there alone with no one else in sight. The girls surrounding Lucius had vanished; the entire crowd had vanished. No band played. The venue was silent, albeit from the sound of their two voices. Leon's brain shocked his body back into reality. He shook his head, attempting to form words, the letters battling for dominance on his tongue.

No, please. I'm ready now.

"Conjure me up when you're ready. When you're ready, your patch will go..." the corners of his mouth turned up as he traced the empty spot on his vest, "...right here. Cross your heart and hope to die."

A grin spread across Leon's face involuntarily. It quickly faded as a low, ominous laugh emanated from Lucius, whose pupils contracted into thin slits as he let out a sharp hiss.

"Crossssss your heart."

Leon's heart skipped a beat as he struggled to catch his breath. Writhing snakes coiled tightly around his ankles, wrists, and neck, their scales shining in the dim light. The serpents' split tongues reverberated in his ears, creating a deafening roar that made his entire body vibrate.

Leon struggled, gasping for little breaths as the snakes tightened around his veins and airway.

"Lucius," Leon tried to speak but only got out a barely audible first syllable. The more Leon fought, the harder Lucius cackled, never moving his gaze away from Leon. The bar light illuminated a set of pointed teeth. Lucius extended his hand, the wolf's head now watching the struggle. Leon stumbled backward as Lucius jabbed his finger into his forehead, sinking mindlessly into total darkness. Nothingness.

The sun's morning rays jolted him awake, burning his eyes as he lay in bed in his shitty apartment. A chuckle escaped him as he looked around the apartment, at the sticky black blood on his table and the knife sticking out of his floor. As terrifying as Lucius was, Leon was determined to meet him again—to gratify him, to be owned by him.

11

Grimoire

Leon's head throbbed. Was it because the snakes coiled themselves around his throat so tightly that it cut off oxygen flow to his brain? Maybe, but it was more likely that it was throbbing from the partying he'd done the night before with his band.

His band.

Leon's hunger to create intensified after meeting Lucius. A dormant fire had been ignited deep in his gut. A newfound confidence, like a potent drug, coursed through his veins. It was a sign, a confirmation that fate guided him on the right path.

He wanted to remember every detail about Lucius, from the spirit board session that introduced them to the ritual he performed to meet him face-to-face. The memories deserved to be preserved and logged into a history book, his personal history. His legacy. Leon never wanted to lose that fire, crackling with every beat of his heart. He never wanted to let it burn out.

Leon ventured into the occult shop and purchased a book. But it was not just any book. It was a genuine black leather-bound journal with ornate metal brass corners. An antique clasp secured the handmade cotton paper inside. Leon ran his finger over the deckled edges, feeling the weight of his decision to spill his knowledge and experiences into this sacred book.

Every letter and phrase in this book would hold power. He planned to write his songs on these pages, letting the lyrics soak in the magic of the words around them and charging each word with the energy of his craft.

This book satisfied his yearning for a place where he could worship his own God—Hell's God. It allowed him to express his spirituality in a way that resonated with him, free from the constraints of organized religion.

It was at this moment that Leon recognized the difference between his sacred books and the Bible, between his God and Jimmy's: in response to his call for guidance, Lucius didn't leave him suffering in turmoil. No—he materialized in Leon's subconscious mind and extended a helping hand, providing him with solutions to all his woes. Feeling a wave of relief, he was grateful for Lucius and his perfectly-timed intervention.

Leon, in a moment of profound realization and acceptance, uttered his own hallelujah for the first time in his life: *Hail Satan.*

Hail, Satan, indeed.

12

Pulling the Strings

Leon's apartment had become the unspoken rehearsal space. He kept a stash of weed, cocaine, and beer to take the edge off living the starving artist's life. The posters on the walls fueled their passion to play until their fingers bled and to write until there were no more words to be written, their dedication to their craft unwavering under the eyes of their idols.

Lonnie had an apartment across town, but Leon's place was their hub, their heavy metal bubble. Jimmy was usually there anyway—he crashed at Leon's place most nights and had become his surrogate roommate. They would go out on the Strip, bring back girls, and write songs together until sunrise. Dallas would show up on nights when he wasn't staying with Lonnie or his on-again-off-again girlfriend. Although Dallas never admitted it, he sometimes stayed at Leon's because he wanted to, not because he had to.

Their band was like an infant, a living and breathing being that needed nurturing and feeding. Every free moment was spent together, running riffs and smoothing out hooks. The Rainbow or The Whiskey nurtured their bonds through nights of partying. A watchful eye was kept on other bands performing on the Strip, assessing the presence, the music, and the look, all while honing their own image, mapping out the impression they wanted to brand on the public with a hot iron.

With every rehearsal, they blossomed into a creative powerhouse. They became a group that could put everything on the table and make magic out of thin air. Their jam sessions became sacred times. Baphomet kept a close eye on them—watching from the confines of the tapestry's fabric on Leon's wall as they put together songs for their catalog, fanning at the creative spark to keep it alive as they polished new riffs and wrote new verses.

The band finished a long stint of rehearsing on an exceptionally crisp night in early September, rewarding themselves with cheap wine, beer, and Chinese takeout. Leon had braved the wrath of the chipped paint that rained down off of the window sill to let some of that early fall air in. The breeze lightened the weight of the air that had become bogged down with the sweat of five men performing in Leon's apartment, the furniture all pushed to the side once again to open up the floor as a makeshift stage.

They realized they had yet to name their band as they ate through boxes of Kung Pao chicken and wonton soup. Floating that decision for as long as possible had become an unspoken rule. What a significant responsibility it was, to name something so much bigger than the five of them. Leon racked his brain for names that could be chanted by fans begging for an encore.

"Crimson Death." Cam made brackets with his hands, emphasizing each word before holding up his hands in a triumphant gesture.

"Starting out strong," Jimmy considered it with a nod.

"It could work," Lonnie added. "How did you think of that?"

Cam leaned forward, resting his elbows on his knees.

"Okay, so…"

"Is this a fucking D&D thing?" Lonnie squinted at Cam, tilting his head to the side.

"Well," Cam wiggled into an awkward shrug. "Yeah, but—"

"Forget it," Lonnie snapped, cutting him off again. "Veto." He forcefully wiped his lips, threw the napkin on the table, and pointed at Cam. "Is there some timer in your head that makes you say nerdy shit every three and a half minutes? Turn it off, dude."

"Lonnie—" Jimmy groaned.

"Jesus Christ," Lonnie mumbled, rolling his eyes. "Sorry."

"We need something…sexy," Dallas interjected, taking a swig of his beer. "The Slippery Pussies."

Jimmy erupted into laughter, contrasting Leon's irritated eye roll and Lonnie's theatrical head-hanging expression of hopelessness.

"Absolutely not," Jimmy declared, biting on a dumpling to keep himself from laughing.

"What about Damned Passion," Lonnie suggested.

"I like that better than The Slippery Pussies," Jimmy chuckled as he turned to face Dallas. "The fuck is wrong with you?"

"I've got about four more in the chamber," Dallas retorted. "The Rocking Dolls."

"Fuck no," Lonnie waved him off.

"Isn't that already a band?" Jimmy asked. Dallas shrugged and took a sip of wine.

"Bloodthirsty."

"No."

"Essence of Sin."

"Now we're getting somewhere."

"Do you guys ever think about how easy it was to form this band?" Cam shoveled lo mien into his mouth, not bothering to finish chewing before continuing. "Think about it. Jimmy and Leon have known each other their entire lives. They auditioned one guitarist," his eyes bulged out as he pointed a finger at his chest. "They met one bass player," he pointed at Dallas. "And Lonnie! Lonnie was the first guy to answer our ad."

"Yeah, we shoulda kept shopping around." Dallas rolled his eyes and looked at Lonnie, who gave him a mocking snarl.

"Ha-ha, bassist," Lonnie pointed his chopsticks at Dallas. "They only kept me around because I'm the only one to call you on your weird shit."

"No, seriously," Cam nodded earnestly while they all laughed. "It's true. It's like fate." His eyes lit up, and he threw his box of lo mien on the table. "Shit, that's it. The Fates. We could be The Fates!"

"The…*Fates?*" Leon mocked in disapproval. "I'm not playing in a band called The Fates. It sounds like chick rock. I'm not doing that."

"No, it could be bitchin'," Cam said, extending a hand in front of Leon to prevent him from further criticizing the idea. "The Fates are goddesses in Greek mythology. There are three of them, and they weave the fate of mortals through threads. And when you die, your thread gets cut. But they determine your destiny. The five of us were destined to meet and form this band."

"Oh, good. Not only do you suggest a puss name for us, but now you're getting mushy, too?" Leon groaned.

"You're done, Cam," Lonnie threw a dumpling at him. It bounced off his forehead onto the floor. Cam picked the dumpling off the floor and popped it in his mouth despite the piece of lint now stuck to it.

"But—" he protested through a dumpling-stuffed mouth.

Lonnie jabbed his chopstick in Cam's direction. "I swear to God, if you suggest The Fates or repeat the word destiny, I will cut your thread myself."

Sighing indignantly, Cam snatched his carton of food off the table, stuffing noodles into his pouting mouth. "You didn't have to make fun of it like that."

"Cam's right, though," Jimmy cocked his chin toward the guitarist. "It's like there was an invisible force bringing us together. It was way too easy to form this band."

As Leon mulled this over, it all became so clear. They were right—the stars had aligned somewhere in the universe to bring them together. A higher power had chosen them, each hand-picked to be destined for greatness. Something took their fates into its hands and stitched them together with a red thread. *A blood tie.* Leon took a long look at Jimmy, stroking the scar on his palm. Blood—blood ties you together.

A picture of Lucius appeared in his head, a tiny needle in his massive hands, sewing his life to Jimmy's, then to Cam's, then to Dallas and Lonnie's. Lucius and his patchwork of souls standing by on watch, ready to accept him. Leon could smell the leather and tobacco essence of him and could feel the darkness that surrounded him. That sucked him in.

The dream was extraordinarily vivid, like a movie fueled by psychedelics. Lucius's words bounced off the walls of his skull, his low voice repeated over and over: *I can make you a legend, but I am going to need pieces of you. Pieces of human morality. The slaughter of all of the societal conditioning, the religious conditioning, the moral conditioning.*

Leon's pulse quickened as he sucked in a fast gulp of air. Before he could give Lucius those pieces, he would have to kill those parts of himself. A moral suicide. A psychosomatic solution.

His tongue ran across his bottom teeth. "What about Psychosomatic Slaughter?" Leon dared not make eye contact with any of his bandmates as they debated his idea. He fixed his gaze on the table at the splatter of soy sauce and stray grains of rice. Dallas was the one who broke the silence.

"What the hell does that mean?"

"The link between body and mind. How the mind can affect your whole being."

"The ultimate suicide," Cam added. Lonnie winced at the word *suicide*. He drew back, assessing the words.

"That could work," Lonnie mused, drumming on his knees with a pair of chopsticks. "Going mental for metal."

"Psychosomatic Slaughter," Leon said, slower this time.

"Psychosomatic Slaughter." Murmurings bubbled on everyone's tongues as they tried the words out on their own lips.

"That...that is fucking *metal*," Dallas laughed menacingly, thrusting out his tongue and shaking it. An impressed downward smile crept across Lonnie's lips as he nodded in agreement. Cam chuckled, enthusiastically nodding as his body moved back and forth with each excited nod.

"That's wicked," Jimmy nodded, reaching out to give Leon a proud clap on the back.

"Alright, alright," Leon threw up his hands, relinquishing his place in the spotlight. He picked up his beer bottle from the table and held it up.

"To Psychosomatic Slaughter and making music to melt their fucking faces off." A shout erupted from the newly-named band as five beer bottles clattered together in celebration.

Leon pressed his smile into his beer bottle, watching the lineup of his band eating up the breadcrumbs he was throwing down, leading them to Lucius. The stars that aligned to bring them all together shined in their eyes.

Dallas slipped a baggie out of his pocket and dipped a stray guitar pick in, scooping out a bump to keep his adrenaline high. Jimmy raised his bottle in a silent toast to Leon, a wordless acknowledgment of their pact as he took another sip.

The name "Psychosomatic Slaughter" would look great on a patch sewn over Lucius's heart, if he had one. It would be a tribute to Lucius contaminated with hidden symbolism, a secret code, a tip-off. A sign that he was ready.

13

Strike a Chord

With their name established, Psychosomatic Slaughter embarked on creating their setlist. Having assembled all its members, the band was able to refine and polish "Shire on Fire" into a Led Zeppelin-inspired anthem of destruction. Leon set the tone with a foreboding opening riff infused with a sense of whimsy and impending doom.

"Teen Killer" had evolved significantly since the band's initial session. Lonnie embraced Dallas's concept, and the bassist crafted a song with a 1960s-inspired bass line that carried the entire piece. Harmonized vocals were layered over the chorus, the rest of the band acting as background vocalists while performing their parts as Jimmy taunted the little piggies. The track was designed to incite a cult-like frenzy in the crowd with an interactive chorus that could be chanted back to them during their performances. They would be Charlie, reveling in the love and devotion of their fans as they sweated under the stage lights.

Dallas never claimed to be a lyricist. He never fancied himself a writer, but he had an idea for a song that nagged in the back of his head, begging to be written down. The idea was sparked after a night of rehearsing. The lineup had gone home, leaving him and Lonnie alone in the bachelor pad. Instead of caressing a woman, he caressed his bass, fingering a rhythm that was tight and steady. Repeating it over and over, he allowed his mind to wander, thinking about his brother. Bruce would kill to have the bass he was playing on right now. He remembered hearing the groove of the instrument through their paper-thin walls at night. Everything transferred—he heard everything, including his mom's screaming when she found him with white foam pouring out of his mouth with a needle in his arm. That gnawing idea broke out, inspiring Dallas to give himself the grace to put pen to paper and let the words pour out. He brought lyrics for "White Horse" to Jimmy, who helped him write the chorus and incorporate drug-related metaphors:

White horse, valiant steed

Charging in to do dirty deeds

Psychosomatic Slaughter embodied sex and drugs into their music with gritty guitars and heavy vocals, but at the root of it all, the blues were the glue that held the composition of their songs together. Digging beneath the parties and the women, they found rage, trauma, and anguish. They harnessed the ugly parts of life into their music to create something beautiful out of something painful. Leon let the pain bleed into the guitar for "White Horse," the instrument crying out during the solo.

Cam transposed the keys section of Stevie Ray Vaughn's "Crossfire" into a soulful rhythm guitar part. Of all the songs they covered, this was the one that allowed them all to shine.

They began booking gigs, performing as Psychosomatic Slaughter, and playing shows at house parties for friends. None of these shows ended well. If they were promised cash, they seldom got paid. The cops raided a couple of parties, forcing the band to sprint down the street with as much equipment as they could carry. During one show, Dallas mixed the wrong pill with vodka and ended up vomiting behind their makeshift stage throughout their entire performance. Lonnie ended up taking him home that night to dry out.

Once they had completed their time on the party circuit, they advanced to Chinese Restaurants and small hole-in-the-wall venues. Lonnie was elated to play at Madame Wong's—he deeply loved and respected the Godmother of Punk.

The first flyer posted on a Sunset Strip telephone pole marked a momentous occasion. Posting a flyer on the Strip symbolized a rite of passage for aspiring musicians. Getting those flyers took a lot of work from Dallas, who seduced a photographer named Connie. Dallas met her through a mutual friend named Natasha, an adult film actress who would let Dallas crash at her place every now and then, keeping him in line.

Connie's services were, for all intents and purposes, free. Dallas's body was the only form of payment that she would accept, and he never complained about that one bit.

Their first photo shoot featured a mix of styles, each member of the lineup letting their personal style shine through. Dallas made love to the camera, his already-high cheekbones accentuated with blush. His smudged black eyeliner contributed to his sex appeal with a slept-in look. Dressed in only leather pants and a leather vest, his patchwork tattoos were fully displayed, the "EAT ME" on his lower abdomen taking center stage.

Lonnie wore denim on denim, his signature look. He begrudgingly took his headshots, only mildly entertaining the idea of being in the group shot for publicity's sake. Jimmy went for a more daring look, wearing only tight leather pants and a bullet belt, showing off his lean and muscular body. His long black hair grazed his rib cage, shining blue in the sun. Leon chose leather chaps over jeans and a tight black shirt, adorning his wrists with leather cuffs. Cam embraced the whimsical style, wearing a loose button-down shirt tucked into jeans and pairing it with an embroidered velvet waistcoat, ala Jimmy Page.

Connie's live photos of the band's set at Gazzarri's encapsulated the band's energy, showcasing them in full action. The images froze moments in time, like Dallas glamming it up on his knees, rocking out on the bass while a girl's hand reached up to touch his. They captured Cam, completely backlit; his hair splayed out around him as he headbanged. Lonnie's direct gaze bore into the camera as he twirled a drumstick. One photo caught Jimmy leaning on Leon, feeling the music resonate through his body as Leon played his soulful solo, tilting his head back to savor every lingering note. These photos immortalized a motley crew of metalheads, each with a unique style, coming together to conjure pure magic on stage.

They pooled their money to print hundreds of flyers for distribution and stapled their band's flyers up and down the Sunset Strip. Dallas used his sex appeal to his advantage, dressing up in his stage clothes to drive to local high schools around Los Angeles. He would tease up his black hair, letting it cascade around a scarf tied around his forehead. Eyeliner smoked out around his hazel eyes, making them look dreamy, especially to teenage girls. His light wash jeans were laced up the sides with black leather cord, showing peeks of the tattoos snaking up his legs. The tattoos always reeled them in—hook, line, and sinker. Timing his arrival to line up with the last bell of the day, he would sit on the hood of his car and pass out flyers to the senior girls, who would eat it up every time. They felt a part of something special and gave the band free marketing, taking piles of flyers to spread around. On show night, they would pile into their cars to pick up their friends and watch the band with the hot bassist, feeling like they were part of the band's journey.

Lonnie's apartment was the epitome of a bachelor pad, with little effort made to personalize the space aside from the oversized drum kit muffled with towels. The walls sported a yellowed, dingy white hue from years of cigarette smoke, and makeshift curtains made of old bed sheets and towels adorned the windows. Lonnie showed no interest in decorating, with his only furniture being a dinette table pushed against the wall near the small kitchen and a couch on the opposite wall, strategically positioned to allow ample space for the band's practice sessions. The couch pulled out into a mattress for Dallas when he chose to crash there.

The band had gathered bright and early to work on some fresh material when their session was abruptly interrupted by Lonnie's ringing phone. As he strode into the kitchen with drumsticks in hand to answer the call, the rest of the band took a breather, setting down their instruments and reaching for a swig of whiskey to mix in with their morning coffee.

"Hello?" Lonnie grumbled, furrowing his brow. He despised interruptions during rehearsals, but his expression brightened upon hearing the voice on the other end of the phone. "Dee," he cooed, his jaw unclenching. "How are you?"

Dallas's head snapped towards Jimmy, his eyes widening with intense curiosity. The corners of his mouth twitched in surprise, a suppressed chuckle escaping as he noticed a similar expression on Jimmy's face. Cam's eyes bulged, a mix of confusion and amusement dancing on his face. He mouthed, *"Dee?"* to Leon, who shook his head and raised his hand to signal for silence as he focused on listening.

"Yeah, we've been getting some good traction. We're playing the Whiskey on Saturday."

Dallas leaned in, straining to catch Dee's words on the other end of the receiver.

"I'm sorry," Lonnie groaned, rolling his neck. He propped himself up on the countertop with his elbows, running his fingers over the chipped laminate. "I didn't want to jump the gun before we were ready—okay," he squeezed his eyes shut and nodded, scratching a chip in the countertop. "Understood. I have a ticket for you, and we'll see you Saturday." There was another long pause as the drummer picked up his sticks, twirling them between his fingers. "Yes, ma'am."

Overwhelmed by a sudden burst of laughter, Dallas buried his face in his hands and crouched down, snorting to stifle it. The band sat there, shocked by the uncharacteristic soft tone from their drummer. Lonnie shot daggers in Dallas's direction, a silent warning to not let another snort escape. The bassist pushed the heel of his hand to his lips to stifle the laughter.

"Alright, I'll see you then," Lonnie said goodbye and hung up, giving the band an exasperated expression.

"What the *fuck* was that?" Dallas chided as Lonnie walked back to his drum kit. "No, more importantly, *who* the fuck was that?"

"Do you have a girlfriend, Lonnie?" Jimmy asked with genuine interest. Lonnie gave Jimmy a stern look, turning to Leon for support. Leon shrugged at him, giving him the floor to answer while Cam and Dallas tittered like children. Lonnie clenched his jaw, hitting the kick drum hard.

"No, Jimmy," Lonnie snapped. "I don't have a girlfriend, smart-ass. That was a woman named Deanna Slater. She's a manager that I met a couple of years ago."

"You knew a manager, and you've been holding out on us?" Leon's lips pulled back in a grimace. Lonnie shrugged.

"I know, I just thought get some more shows under our belt—"

"No, man," Leon cut him off. "This is when we need some guidance. Someone to help us as we get started."

"You bastard," Dallas uttered as he shook his head slowly, his tone teetering between sarcasm and seriousness.

"She worked with one of my other bands, and it didn't work out because the singer got too big of a head for us. We broke up, but she told me to call her if I ever started up something serious. I've meant to, but I didn't want it to be like last time."

"Okay," Jimmy nodded slowly, sipping his Irish coffee. "But she's coming to the Whiskey on Saturday?"

"She'll be there." Lonnie gave a single nod to confirm.

"Alright," Leon strapped on his guitar, running through a few chords. "Then we need to be tight."

On Saturday night, Psychosomatic Slaughter delivered an electrifying performance, and it was all thanks to the rowdy crowd. The audience, a pulsating, wild entity, came together as one, spilling drinks and sending hair flying. Their contagious energy fed the band, which in turn fed it back, creating a syncopated energy that culminated in an explosion of applause at the end of their finale.

As they stepped off the stage, Psychosomatic Slaughter was physically exhausted, running off the fumes of their performance's thrill. Their ears were ringing, their hearing partially gone. Drenched in sweat from the stage lights and the adrenaline coursing through their bodies, they felt the sting of their fingers, tingling from overuse after an epic show at the Whiskey A Go-Go. Running backstage, Lonnie ran his drumsticks along the wall, coming off of the best high there was.

Leon whipped around, taken aback by a woman's raspy voice that boomed down the hallway. It was clear that her voice had been warped by years of heavy smoking, not from screaming in the crowd during their show. A woman with a big figure and bigger hair filled the hallway. Her hair was bleached blonde with teased black roots. If her roots didn't out her dirty little secret of being a bottle-blonde, her thick eyebrows did. Her clothes were loud, and her voice was even more deafening. She leaned on the wall, a big smile spreading across her face when she saw him. Lonnie's face lit up as he got up to greet her."Dee!" he crooned affectionately, pulling her into a hug.

"Damn," Dallas said, giving her a once over. "I'd like a slice of that pie."

"Dallas, fuck off," Lonnie scowled. "Guys, this is Deanna Slater. She's a manager I know from way back."

"Pie's not on the menu, little boy. You get peanuts," Deanna quipped, shaking his hand.

"I'll take whatever you give me," he smirked. "I'm Dallas."

"I know. I was warned about you," Deanna flicked her eyes over to the rest of the band as she shook each of their hands. "It's nice meeting you boys. You put on a killer set, and I think we would work well together."

"That would be amazing," Jimmy sighed with relief.

"I want you to meet me at Zucco's Deli tomorrow at one o'clock sharp. Don't be late." She poked a finger at Dallas. "I mean it, I want a do-over from you tomorrow. I'll give you a pass tonight because of the post-show high, but that's it."

"Yes, ma'am," Dallas said, color flushing his cheeks. He looked at Jimmy and impressedly smiled, turning down the corners of his mouth. He looked back as Lonnie walked Deanna out of the wings."I think I need a cigarette after that, goddamn."

14

One Hell of a Woman

The band sat around a circular booth at Zucco's Deli with one empty chair reserved for Deanna. It was quarter to one; they took no chances to get on her bad side. Lonnie warned Dallas not to say anything funny to her—they needed her.

At 12:59, the welcome bell chimed, and Deanna strode in wearing cheetah-print boots. They all sat up straighter as she approached the table, her heels clicking against the scuffed floor. Lonnie stood up and pulled the chair out for her.

"Thanks, sweetheart." She pinched Lonnie's cheek and sat down. He frowned, eliciting a sneer from Dallas. Lonnie shot him a glare to stay in line, wiping the snicker off his face.

"Hey, doll," she called up to the teenage girl at the bar counter. "Can I get some coffee over here?" The girl brought over a mug and saucer and set it down in front of Deanna. "You guys want anything?" She asked as she poured the coffee. They all said no, too put off by the woman to have any appetite. They waited for her to get situated, letting her take a sip of coffee. Her red lipstick left a chunky stain on the rim of the white porcelain mug.

"Thank you for meeting us," Jimmy said, the only one brave enough to end the silence. "We really need a manager."

"The band really is missing a woman's touch," Dallas said smoothly. "When you said you could help us, I thought—"

"I'm going to cut you off right there." Deanna placed her coffee cup on her saucer and sliced the air with her hand. The saucer rattled with the force of her movements. "We are going to get one thing straight. Right off the bat. Don't fuck with me just because I'm a woman. I'm smarter than you." She gave them each a stern look as she surveyed their faces. "I'm stronger than you, and I won't hesitate to level your asses out if you cross a line with me, capisce?"

The band nodded in unison, speechless. She confirmed their understanding with a slight nod. She cocked her head toward Dallas.

"I mean it, Twinkle Toes." The rest of the band held back their laughter as she pointed at him. "You try to make a grab at me, and I'll cut off your God damned hand. Try playing bass with one hand."

"Twinkle—?" Dallas whispered under his breath, too hung up on his new nickname to hear the threat.

"Your hands," she held hers up and swiveled her wrists around, "are at risk. Understood?"

"Yeah, understood, God damn." Dallas held his hands up in surrender before tucking them firmly in his lap. "Jesus, Lonnie, was she a prison guard before hitting the music circuit?"

"Alright," she said as she nodded in Dallas's direction, cutting off any reply from Lonnie, and turned her attention to the rest of the band. "Now that we've got some housekeeping out of the way let's get down to business."

"Yes," Lonnie clapped his hands together. "Let's do it."

"Listen, guys. The only way you get anywhere in this industry is to have good people on your side. It's all about creating a network, okay? It's true what they say; it's all about who you know." She straightened her shoulders before folding her hands and leaning on the table, all business. "You've gotta play the game and play it well. Do you have a photographer?"

Jimmy pulled out a stack of printed photos: some headshots Connie took of each of them showcasing their personalities and posing with their instruments. He slid those over to Deanna, along with a few samples of the flyers they had made up for the last month's worth of shows. They sat in silence as they studied her face, watching her as she looked at each photo.

"Alright," she said, her voice trailing up at the end. "Yeah, these are good. They will do it until you can afford something better, but honestly, you could get away with slapping these photos on the inside sleeve of your album. Great—check. How are you marketing your shows?"

Dallas leaned back in the booth, a smile curling up at the ends of his mouth.

"I've got that covered. I've got a bunch of chicks at the high school, real sweethearts." He winked, and Deanna rolled her hand at him to finish talking. His confidence shaken, he cleared his throat before continuing. "They're really into the rock scene. I give them a bunch of flyers, and they do the work for me. Uh—us, I mean."

"We also each take a stack and put them along the Strip. In shop windows that will let us, on bulletin boards, telephone poles, that kind of thing," Cam added.

"Okay, not bad. Free promotion, that's good. Bringing in the girls is smart. They bring in their friends. If the girls are there, the men will follow like dogs—all good. I'll talk to some friends who're promoters to beef up your buzz."

"Thank you so much, Dee," Lonnie said. "That would be great."

"If you're all in here, so am I," Deanna stated, sipping her coffee. "I think you've got something that the Strip has never seen before."

"You're saying all the right things," Leon said, leaning forward and mirroring her stance. "But what's your story? We laid everything out on the table for you. What's your experience? How do we know we can trust you?"

"Leon," Lonnie hissed through gritted teeth. Deanna smirked.

"You're a straight shooter; I like that." She nodded in acknowledgment. "I assume Lonnie told you how we knew each other."

"He did," Leon confirmed, picking up a sugar packet and flicking it like a drug baggie.

"Okay. Then you'll know I am an entrepreneur that's passionate about music and the artists that create music. My girlfriend, Lisa, and I started Sonic Horse Entertainment to build legitimacy after we helped out some friends who had great success. We've built a network of connections that helped us get to where we are. Have you heard of Lord Reapers?"

"I have," Leon said, making sure not to let his admiration show on his face.

"They're good friends of mine. I helped them launch their career, and they were Sonic Horse Entertainment's first client."

Leon pursed his lips, ready to, as she said, *play the game and play it well.* He let her stew in silence for a moment.

"Listen. Lonnie's an old friend." Her voice softened as she patted the drummer on the arm. "I'd never screw you over. And no hard feelings if it comes down to it and we aren't the right fit. But I feel it in my bones. You guys are special. The Whiskey's a small venue, but you performed that show like you were playing Madison Square Garden. I want to be a part of this."

"You've got yourself a deal," Leon reached out his hand to seal the deal.

* * *

Deanna's sprightly business partner, Lisa, took all her fashion choices from Pat Benatar. She had short, cropped hair and wore clothes that made her features look especially angular. She loved fashion and helped the band elevate their signature looks. Lisa gifted Cam whimsical blazers and waistcoats that she would embroider and bead herself by hand. Lonnie initially hesitated to deviate from his usual Levis and Wrangler collection. Still, Lisa convinced him to try a statement belt buckle she found at a pawn shop, and he ended up making it one of his signature pieces.

By September 1983, Deanna's guidance had propelled Psychosomatic Slaughter to become one of the stand-out bands on the Sunset Strip. She refined their set list, adding transitional segues between songs to help the set flow more like a concert. She also assisted Jimmy in writing fun introductions, which he used when introducing the band to the audience toward the end of their set. As a result of her management, the demand for Psychosomatic Slaughter skyrocketed, leading to more show bookings and gigs almost every night. They even achieved the impressive feat of selling out the Whiskey A Go-Go two nights in a row.

After their second sold-out show, the band, now a hot topic on the Strip, made plans to go out and celebrate. Their growing fan base was a force to be reckoned with, and they were ready to show the world what they were made of. In the alley behind the Whiskey, Jimmy paused to catch his breath while the other guys loaded the last of their equipment into their cars. He lit a cigarette, taking a moment to soak it all in, and inhaled a deep drag.

"Can I bum a smoke?" A soft, sleepy voice asked, breaking him out of his musing.

The most stunning face Jimmy had ever seen met him as he gazed up to locate the source of the angelic voice. Her skin was like porcelain, her eyes a deep, captivating blue. She gave him a wide smile that reached her eyes, and her thick auburn hair reached the top of her high-waisted jeans, making her blue eyes pop.

"Absolutely," Jimmy smirked, making the cigarette in his mouth bob. He took a Marlboro pack from his pocket, opened it, and offered it to her. She accepted one, casting her eyes down as Jimmy lit it up for her. Leaning forward, she held the cigarette delicately between her fingers as she took her first puff. Her lips looked so smooth; he watched them as she took a pull, wondering what they would feel like against his.

"Thank you." She blew out a plume of smoke and gave him a closed-mouth smile that showed off her dimples. Looking down at her black leather boots, she shifted her weight nervously.

"Anytime, darlin'," He smirked at her profile, admiring her soft features. She looked out of place in this dimly lit alley, too soft and too elegant, like a beautiful flower blooming from a crack in the concrete.

"That was a really great show," she said, flicking her eyes to meet his, but only for an instant.

"Thank you."

"My friends and I have been to a few of your shows," she added before he could say any more. "I think you guys are really, really special."

"Oh yeah? I appreciate that, thank you." Jimmy chuckled as he tossed his cigarette onto the ground and twisted the toe of his boot on the butt, grinding it to ashes.

"Yeah," she giggled and ran her fingers through her hair. "I'm sorry, I'm talking really fast. I'm just a little nervous."

"Of what?" Jimmy teased.

"I usually don't do this," she murmured. Embarrassed, she smiled, but Jimmy thought her smile looked like pure sunshine.

"What? You mean you don't meet strange men in alleyways for a smoke?" Jimmy tried to banter, but his smile betrayed him.

"Oh my God," she threw her head back and squeezed her eyes closed. "That sounds awful."

She laughed and snuffed the butt of her cigarette on the wall behind her. Jimmy joined in, savoring their shared moment.

"What's your name?"

"Heather," she said, extending her hand. Her already-rosy complexion flushed even more.

"Jimmy." He took her hand, feeling how soft it was, like her voice, like velvet, and he didn't want to let it go. Her touch was bewitching; he wanted to forget about his band for the night.

"Jimmy, are you coming?" Leon called, leaning out of the passenger-side window of Lonnie's car. Jimmy glanced at Leon and quickly shifted his gaze back to Heather. The alley was filled with people wanting to party with them, but she was the only person that he wanted to spend the night with.

"Listen, Heather," Jimmy said, ignoring Leon. "I'm going to ditch the guys and go get some breakfast."

"Breakfast?" she giggled. The sound was music.

"Yeah," Jimmy chuckled, a little self-consciously. "They're gonna go out and get drunk. I, on the other hand, am going to get pancakes. Do you want to come with me?"

Heather paused and narrowed her blue eyes while pursing her smiling lips.

"Pancakes," she confirmed, her voice weary at the innocence of the word.

"Pancakes."

"I would love to."

"Go on without me," Jimmy yelled over his shoulder, not taking his eyes off of the woman in front of him. A whisper of a satisfied smile danced on his lips. "I'll see you guys tomorrow."

Leon and Dallas taunted him, with Dallas yelling vulgarities and Leon's loud moaning echoing off of the building's walls. Lonnie honked his horn in encouragement while Cam laughed in the backseat, giving Jimmy two thumbs up. Heather covered up her forehead with her hand, laughing.

"Ignore them," Jimmy waved them off. "They're just jealous I get to go out with a beautiful lady tonight."

The mom-and-pop diner that Jimmy took her to was always his favorite place to go, a spot where his parents always took him as a kid. He used to look forward to sliding into the shiny red vinyl booths and loved the vintage vibe of the place, with its black and white tiled floor, a tall, lit-up jukebox playing rockabilly music, and neon signs lighting up the walls.

The strong scent of brewing coffee filled the air as the night crowd stumbled in, looking for a cup of Joe to sober them up. Darlene, the waitress who had been old since Jimmy was ten, brought over their order, placing a short stack of pancakes in front of him and a burger, fries, and a strawberry milkshake in front of Heather. Darlene gave Jimmy a wink; she had always had a soft spot for the boy, and he had always had a soft spot for strawberry pancakes.

As they eased into a conversation beyond the music, he learned she worked at a video store and liked writing in her free time. She used to intern for a local paper, but she hated writing about the news. She would take those news stories home and put a creative spin on them, and in doing that, she realized she loved writing historical fiction.

"History was always my favorite subject in school. It's so fascinating and so petty." She sipped her milkshake, twirling the cherry in the whipped cream on top. "It's like being filled in on over a hundred years' worth of gossip. It's fun."

She propped her head up with her hand, feeling self-conscious. With his deep brown eyes fixed on her, Jimmy unconsciously mimicked her gesture.

"So, you like writing about history?"

141

"Yeah," she smiled, her eyes lighting up with a fire of passion. Her light ignited a spark in Jimmy's heart. "I'm working on a novel about the lost Roanoke colony. I've always had a weird fascination with that story. It always bugged me that no one knows what really happened. So, I made it up myself."

"That's so cool," Jimmy said, his eyes studying every inch of her face, his admiration shining through his expression. She laughed, plucking the cherry off of the stem with her teeth.

"Thank you, I think so too," she chirped, beaming with newfound confidence. "It's skewing a little toward horror. There's little supernatural element."

"You don't look like someone that likes horror."

"And you don't look like someone that ditches a party to bring a girl to a diner." She retorted playfully by tossing a french fry at him. Jimmy smirked at her and picked up her weaponized fry, taking a bite.

"Well, I'm full of surprises," he said with a grin. "In your book, what happens to the colony?" Heather looked thrilled that he'd asked, her eyes sparkling at the question. Her excitement grew as she began to speak.

Heather told the story of the Roanoke settlers building their colony on sacred land. Her take on the lost colony theory didn't blame Native Americans but instead brought forth angry elemental beings.

She spoke passionately about her interests; Jimmy watched in awe. He soaked in her creativity and beauty as he listened, not wanting to interrupt her. He could listen to her talk for hours and never feel the need to say a word. Eventually, she fell silent, her face dropping at the end of her tale.

"Is that stupid?" she asked in a small voice, her body shrinking into the booth.

"No—" Jimmy shook his head quickly. "No, I think it sounds interesting. I'd love to read it."

"Really?"

"Really," Jimmy assured her. "I'm sorry, I just liked listening to you talk. I've never heard of a story like that. I liked it."

She smiled and finished her milkshake. They sat together in a comfortable silence for a few moments.

"Jimmy, you're not how I imagined," she tilted her head and stared dreamily at him.

"Ouch," Jimmy said in mock offense, holding his hand to his chest. "I'm so sorry to disappoint."

"No, I mean that in a good way," she said. "You're sweet."

"So…" Jimmy puckered his lips and toyed with a sugar packet. "Does that mean you want to do this again?"

"Yeah," she smiled softly. "Yeah, I'd like that."

"Good," Jimmy said. "You'll need to come to my shows, though; I need to show you off."

"You've got a deal," she giggled. "I'll go to every show you have."

"We're pretty booked. That's a lot of time we'll be spending together."

"That's okay," Heather said. "I think I can handle it."

* * *

The innocence of young love, with its yearning, adoration, and giddiness, is sweet. Everyone was thrilled for Jimmy, finding someone who mirrored him so well. But in the midst of this sweet innocence, a shadow of jealousy was cast, souring the taste.

Leon loathed Heather and her constant presence. Distracting Jimmy. She was always there, in the wings, her eyes filled with a love that Leon saw as a threat. Jimmy's time was precious; they couldn't afford to have their singer's attention anywhere but with the band. What others saw as a devoted bond, he saw as a competition—a loss in his book.

For Leon, everyone had become a competitor, not just Heather. Other bands were a threat, a danger to Psychosomatic Slaughter's star. He kept a vigilant eye on them, especially those who dared to shine even a little brighter.

15

Master of Poppets

Hatred is a palpable emotion. Leon laid out his collection of Damien Moxie's DNA. Saliva stained the butt of the cigarette, the mustard yellow tipping paper crinkling where his lips touched. A strand of gummy, bleached-blond hair lay beside it. Leon ran a thumb over the crude doll cut from the cloth of one of Damien's t-shirts. He had taken it off mid-set, tossing it in the wings, only for it to end up in Leon's guitar case.

What a fucking douche.

The mix of cheap musk cologne and the sweat from the performance clung to the fabric. He placed the strand of hair and the cigarette remains into the belly of the poppet, handling each specimen with care in a gloved hand. Leon shed his glove, threaded a needle with red thread—the lifeline—and tenderly sewed up the body of the doll.

Channeling his hatred into his fingertips, he held the doll, transferring all of his disgust, all of his loathing into the limp fabric body.

Damien Moxie was a fraud. A poser. A stain on the name of rock and roll. Leon couldn't understand how Möxxy had cultivated such a following on the Sunset Strip. The entire band was based on unoriginality—a bunch of pretenders. Damien named the band after himself, ripping off the idea of adding the umlauts from another, more successful band. He cheapened himself to become a knock-off of that band, going so far as to bleach his hair to look like the lead singer. When he did it, disdain roiled in Leon's gut.

He saw right through Damian's shameful charade.

Other people couldn't. And that sent Leon down a spiral.

He began following Möxxy closely, attending all their shows and studying Damien's every move on stage. Leon dissected his stage presence, taking into account every cue, every embellishment, every time the microphone touched his lips as he sang and watched how the crowd reacted.

He befriended their drummer—a dumb brick of a man named Perry. Leon donned masks to integrate himself into their inner circle: the wide-eyed fan, the friendly face, the curious fellow musician. When the time was right, he introduced his band into the fold, sitting back to watch—the puppet master—orchestrating the formation of bonds between bands.

The closer they got, the easier it was to immerse himself and his band into their world. To gain exposure to Möxxy's fans by capitalizing on the popularity of posers. Psychosomatic Slaughter began playing as the opening act for Möxxy regularly at the big-name clubs on the Sunset Strip, and Leon's soul withered with each song he performed in preparation for them to take the stage. Each note he played was a nail in the coffin of his soul.

But it was time. Psychosomatic Slaughter was no longer an opening act.

Leon stabbed his needle into the poppet's face, the leftover red thread hanging off the eye of the needle like a trail of spurting blood. A light sense of joy filled his heart as he placed the doll in his sink and dowsed it with black candle wax. The candle wick stooped to make contact with the doll, spreading its flame up the seam that Leon had stitched. The fire spread, eating away at the fibers of the doll's skin and incinerating the strand of hair. The cigarette butt sizzled as it became ash. Leon pulled the pin on his fire extinguisher and suffocated the poppet in white foam, satisfied that the doll had suffered enough. He slung his guitar case over his shoulder and gave the mess one final look before heading out the door for soundcheck.

Soundcheck commenced as expected, kicking off with the headlining band's rhythm section. Once the guitarists ran through their clean, distortion, and overdrive tones, Damien strode up to test the center microphone.

The room filled with a symphony of faint humming, making Leon's heart vibrate in his chest. The electrical current droned through the wires and cables, coming to a head as Damien wrapped his hand around the microphone, bringing it to his lips. A charged zap reverberated through the singer's body. For a fraction of a moment, his white-blond hair glowed around a grotesque expression of surprise. The pungent stink of burnt hair wafted off the stage. As his lips touched the spit guard, ready to breathe life into the microphone, Damien's body convulsed on impact. The moment lasted far too long as a hiss whirred in the air.

Leon looked up in time to see the singer collapse onto the stage with a solid thud, punctuating the end of the droning current. His fingers fell away from the tuning knobs of his guitar as he took in the spectacle in front of him.

A miracle. Hail Satan.

Jimmy sprang to his feet as Möxxy crowded around their fallen member. Adrenaline coursed through their veins as they shook him, the chemical reaction in their bodies causing them to apply excessive force. Damien's head ebbed and bobbed from side to side. His body's tension relaxed, and his bladder released onto the stage. A dark patch spread over his light-wash jeans as he lost control of his body.

Jimmy bound to the stage, pushing his way through the crowd of musicians to kneel beside Damien, whose skin developed a pallid grey discoloration. He lowered his ear to the singer's chest, holding up his palm in a plea for silence. A hush fell over both bands as Jimmy listened, his face paling with each passing second. Jimmy moved Damien's dry and brittle hair to the side, the strands almost breaking off as he did so.

Two fingers to the neck confirmed that Möxxy's namesake had died.

Jimmy pulled his fingers off the corpse, letting them fall into his lap as he slumped down to sit on the stage. His eyes drank in the sight of the limp body strewn in front of him. He looked up to the rafters and the stage lights mounted there, wondering if the light Damien walked into moments ago was as bright as those.

Leon watched the scene like a movie. He sat back, never taking his guitar off his lap.

Hail! Hail Satan!

A deflated Jimmy looked to his band from the stage only to notice a flicker of sinister joy flash across Leon's green eyes. Jimmy squinted in an attempt to discern what he'd seen through the chaos, hoping it was merely a morbid trick of the mind.

Officially, Damien Moxie's cause of death was electrocution. An improperly grounded microphone.

Unofficially, Jimmy was certain that there was more to that story. He knew about Leon's deep-seated resentment towards the singer, a feeling that even Jimmy shared. Logically, there was no way that Leon could have killed him; they all witnessed Damien's electrocution. Yet, there was that flicker in Leon's eye that convinced Jimmy he was aware of the impending tragedy, and perhaps even welcomed it.

16

The Séance is About to Begin

Autumn had turned the leaves yellow, scattering them along the sidewalks of California suburbs. Fall wind carried them past Jack-O-Lanterns, who stood on watch on doorsteps.

After a weekend of performances, the band assembled their set list for the upcoming Friday and Saturday shows. Leon, in particular, brimmed with excitement. His favorite time of year was upon them, the weekend before Halloween—the perfect time for some new theatrics on stage. He was eager to see how far the band would let him push the envelope, perhaps even a touch of Ozzy-inspired gore.

Deanna and Heather sat on Leon's couch, captivated as the band rehearsed their latest set list, which featured a brand-new song. They all looked forward to the debut of Jimmy's heartfelt ballad, "Sweet Nothings," written especially for Heather.

As the last notes of their set faded, the band members relaxed. They slung off their instruments and settled around the apartment as Heather and Deanna whooped and applauded. Lonnie remained seated at his drum kit, leaning back against the wall. Cam sprawled out next to his amp on the floor, and Dallas perched himself on the couch arm, playfully tousling Deanna's hair. Jimmy planted a gentle kiss on Heather's forehead before settling down beside her. Leon grimaced at the tender moment between lovers.

"So, what did you think?" Cam asked the ladies, spinning his guitar pick between his thumb and middle finger.

"You guys were amazing as always," Heather grinned at Jimmy.

"You were good—" Deanna hesitated. "But I don't think you're ready."

"Excuse me?" Leon retorted, his brow knitting together. He set his beer on the table and stepped out of the kitchen to confront the manager. His face was almost the same shade of red as his hair as he planted his feet in front of her.

"I don't think you're ready," she repeated, meeting his eye. Deanna stood firm, remaining cool and calm under a look that could kill.

"What in the fuck does that mean?" He demanded, grabbing the kitchen chair. Leon swirled it in front of him, straddling the chair and resting his arms on the back of it. Leaning forward, he invaded Deanna's personal bubble. "We've been playing these songs for weeks. We've been selling out clubs. Psychosomatic Slaughter is hot. What do you mean you don't think we're ready." He mocked her as he quoted her words, pitching up his voice in an ugly falsetto.

"Yes, you are great," Deanna agreed, not shrinking away from Leon as he encroached on her. "But there are a lot of A&R reps sniffing around. You're gaining a lot of interest, but I don't think that you're ready for that next step. You are missing that one song—the song that will separate you from every other band playing the same kind of music that you're playing. You need your rhapsody."

"Rhapsody," Leon repeated, considering the concept as he tasted the word on his tongue. It tasted bitter.

"Your songs are impressive, don't get me wrong, but you need to write *the* song. The one that becomes synonymous with your name. Think about Queen with "Bohemian Rhapsody" or "Dream On" by Aerosmith. *That's* the kind of song you need."

Dallas took a bump. "Fuck," he exclaimed in a whispered snap, rubbing his nose. "You're right."

Leon clenched his jaw. *No!* His gums ached as he gnashed his teeth together. The grinding of his molars filled his ears with a vibration that made his eyes water. This was unacceptable. He dedicated his life to this dream, casting away all other human pleasures to put this band at the forefront of his life. At night, he would play until he spread blood over the strings of his guitar, smearing it around the fretboard. He would watch his blood soak into the wood, for he would rather keep playing and have the instrument weather the stains than to not play at all. Music was the air that filled his lungs, the motivation to get up in the morning and make something of himself. Without music, he was nothing. Tears would fall onto the paper as he would pen lyrics, the droplets spreading out the letters on the page into inky puddles. Those pages would always be rewritten after the ink dried because nobody could know that he cried, pouring his heart and soul into these songs.

His soul—there was the answer. A beacon of hope. Lucius was his Gatsby, flashing the green light across the bay to lead him home.

Lonnie packed up his drums, and Cam helped him bring his equipment to his car. The instruments were tucked away into their protective shells, put to sleep while the band wallowed in their inadequacy. They filed out slowly, parting ways to go home and torture their brains to squeeze out any ounce of greatness that might be lurking in the shadows.

Deanna was the last to leave, hanging back after the door had closed behind Heather and Jimmy. Her lips tightened into a flat line, watching Leon clean up the beer bottles.

"You're really close." He stopped to glare at her soft words. "There's just one more song you need to write, okay?"

Leon grunted, picking up the end of the couch and moving it back to its place on the floor. "Whatever, Dee. What's one more, right?" Scowling at her, he snatched up his guitar. He rested it on his lap, wrapping his arm around the neck to place his fingers on the fretboard. It was so intimate, the way he clung to that instrument. Deanna shifted her weight to remind him that she was still there.

"Close the door behind you," Leon said without looking over his shoulder, strumming a minor melody. The door latched softly behind him, and he let his strumming hand fall into his lap. Resting the guitar on the couch next to him, he leaned back, needing a moment of solitude to mull everything over.

Leon's mind raced as he pondered the dire need for their rhapsody. As much as he hated to admit it, Deanna was right—they were so close.

So close.

He could feel the tingle of success within his grasp as if he could reach out and touch it with his callused fingertips. The fingertips that bore the marks of his love for his guitar. That tingle electrocuted him with the frustrating feeling of reaching toward something barely out of reach. *So close.* The path to success was not always smooth sailing. Leon knew that. He needed guidance, a lighthouse in the storm, to show him the way, to help him navigate the treacherous waters of stardom.

Leon could not fathom any scenario, any path, that didn't have Lucius by his side, sharing in the thrill of his success. He was willing to do whatever it took to ensure Lucius was part of his journey. But there was a price to pay.

Energy surged through his body, seeking out the soul within. Where could he find his soul? Was it in his heart, beating life throughout his veins? Was it surrounded by memories, thoughts, and his innermost feelings in his head? Wherever it was, Leon was ready to surrender himself—to embrace the price. Even if he had to claw away at the essence of himself, raking through his depths to unearth his soul, he would find it. He would gently scoop it up, wrap his hands around it, and hold it in open palms for Lucius to devour.

I'm ready. I'm ready. Lucius, I'm ready.

The words repeated in his head on a loop, over and over and over. A maddening cycle that abruptly stopped.

The pit of Leon's stomach dropped, a void opening within himself. Standing alone, the silence was deafening.

I blew it.

FUCK.

I blew it.

Raking his fingers through his hair, he scored his scalp with his nails. The tracks burned, pulling with it clumps of hair that wafted to the floor as he flailed his arms. He had the opportunity to make this deal that night at the

Troubadour. Lucius was there specially for him, and he let him go. That was it—it was done.

Leon desperately yearned for Lucius, pining for that undivided attention once more to atone for what he'd done. He would plead for forgiveness. On his knees, he would hold his fragile soul in his palms over his head. It was a small sacrifice to make.

Why should he give me a second chance? He gave me a chance already, and I blew it. Because of Jimmy. Fucking Jimmy.

Thoughts created a whirlwind in his mind, wrapping him in a dizzying, maddening blur. He should have followed his gut, the fluttering butterflies in the pit of his body. Intuition guided him to Lucius, but he chose to ignore it. Jimmy was to blame. Jimmy, with his fucking moral compass. Morals had no business in rock and roll.

Regret over ignoring his intuition consumed Leon, roiling throughout every fiber of his being. A guttural scream ripped through his vocal cords, sending rabid lines of spit flying as he lost control over his rational mind. He paced his apartment, carving a worn trail with his dragging feet as his vision turned red. Shuddering breaths heaved his chest, each one a struggle as he gagged on the hyperventilation. He tore chunks of his hair out, ripping the root clean out of his scalp. His fists balled around the hair, clutching at them like a lifeline.

"Lucius," Leon pleaded, letting the torn-out strands of hair float to the floor. "Please... I'm ready. I'm—"

Fuck. I blew it.

Watching it like a movie, Leon replayed the conversation in his head. Be kind, rewind—it played again and again until Lucius's face became a distorted, faceless blob as his memory twisted the image. The faceless figure spoke to him in a warped voice, like he was low on batteries. He found the key in dissecting every word that left Lucius's lips:

Hesitation, what a pity. Conjure me up when you're ready. When you're ready, your patch will go right here. Cross your heart and hope to die.

Salvation!

Of course—the spot was already reserved for him. For his band, his coven.

What a cruel trick of fate, trying to convince him otherwise.

Weak from hyperventilating, Leon took a deep breath to calm his shaking hands. His scalp burned from the abuse, and his throat was raw from straining his vocal cords, each breath a painful reminder of his ordeal.

Leon walked to the bathroom in a zombie-like trance, thanks to the tension headache that was thumping in his skull. Turning on the faucet, he filled his cupped hands with cold water. He leaned down and splashed the water onto his face, rubbing off the worry and washing away the voices in his head, the ones that seemed to echo from the walls of his own mind. The water invigorated him, washing away the dried spit clinging to the corners of his mouth. Squeezing his eyes shut, he filled his hands again to give his face another splash. He ran his hands down his forehead and over his eyes before flicking the water off his jaw.

Opening his eyes, Leon looked into the mirror through his eyebrows, gripping the bowl of the sink with tense fingers. A presence darkened the mirror. Leon tilted his chin up in surprise, finding two reflections staring back at him: a distorted version of himself and a figure lurking in the shadows.

Lucius! Hail Satan!

The Devil's broad body barely fit in the bathroom, the crown of his head brushing against the ceiling. His large arms crossed over his chest, and a condescending smirk twisted his lips. Lucius's bright green eyes stared into the mirror, directly into Leon's reflection.

"You're not ready yet," Lucius mocked. Though the gravel remained in his voice, it wasn't the deep booming sound that Leon had replayed time and time again. This voice was higher. Familiar. Leon's reflection contorted, gaping at the presence. The muscle under his eye spasmed as Deanna's voice continued through Lucius's lips. "But you're close. You need to write your rhapsody."

"How do I do it?" Leon pleaded into the reflection. The splashes of water that landed on the mirror distorted his face. "I need your help."

A vicious smile crept across Lucius's lips. He uncrossed his arms and hooked his fingers around his belt loops. Sucking in his cheeks, he looked away coyly, jutting his jaw out in a condescending expression.

"Lucius!" Leon screamed, whipping around to face him. Little droplets of water flew off of his nose, and chunks of hair stuck to his wet cheek. Lucius pursed his lips, the corners pulling up into a cheeky grin as he let out a deep, booming laugh. The sound rattled the mirror on the wall.

"I already told you that you were ready," Lucius taunted, tilting his head to the side. "And you *hesitated* in taking my help. I offered you the key to success. It was yours, and you hesitated. Now, some *woman* tells you you're not ready, and the first thought you have is to call on me for help. Tsk, tsk." He clicked his tongue, casting his eyes down in a mockery of sympathy.

"I'm sorry." Leon squeezed his eyes shut, his voice catching in his throat.

" 'Sorry' doesn't buy you success. 'Sorry' gives you nothing. Never, ever be sorry for anything."

Lucius lifted himself off the wall and walked out of the bathroom, stooping so as not to hit his head on the low door frame. He crossed Leon's apartment in only three gliding strides, sending a breeze behind his hulking body. The air that trailed him smelled like warm leather, vanilla tobacco, and amber spirits. It wafted through the apartment, replacing the stink of disappointment from that afternoon's rehearsal.

Stevie slithered up to the glass, flicking its tongue at Lucius, who slid the enclosure open and offered Stevie his hand. The snake caressed Lucius's hand with its cheek, its tongue flicking slowly. Lucius stroked Stevie under the chin, and the serpent accepted the affection. It wound itself up Lucius's arm as if summoned from Eden to be joined by an old friend. They seemed to share a unique bond, an intimate one. The snake tightened its body around Lucius's forearm, perching itself around his bicep to bore eyes into its pleading owner.

"Lucius!" Leon pleaded, his voice barely escaping his constricted throat. A wave of vulnerability washed over him. It reminded him of his childhood when his mother would give him the silent treatment for making small, childish mistakes. He used to wish she would yell at him and get it over with rather than endure the prolonged agony of her silence.

"I see you, Leon," Lucius assured, his eyes never leaving the snake. His voice was a masterful display of control, dripping with a patronizing evenness that sent shivers down Leon's spine. "I see you even when you think you're alone. I'm like Santa Claus that way." A wink. "I heard you calling to me. I heard you loud and clear. But calling is different than conjuring."

The menacing serpent coiled tighter around Lucius, attempting to cling to the Devil as he unwrapped the serpent from his arm. Despite Stevie's protest, he placed the snake back into its enclosure, gingerly sliding the glass closed. Turning toward the guitarist, Lucius floated to him in a split second, rushing at him with an intense breeze. He forcefully grabbed Leon's chin and brought his face within inches, locking eyes with him. Leon did not dare to blink.

"Together, we will light the way," Lucius spoke in a hushed and intense whisper, his voice shaking with passion. "To pay your price, you will need to spill some of your own blood to conjure me up. I will be waiting."

Leon's eyes burned. He blinked, letting tears spread over his corneas, rehydrating them. When he opened them again, he found himself in an empty room, pinning himself against the wall. Stevie was still slithering in excitement. The mulch spread across the bottom of the enclosure crunched as the scales coiled around.

Leon's brain was ablaze with ignited neurons. A surge of creativity overcame him as his heartbeat fluttered in his chest. His fingers quivered with anticipation. Lucius had bestowed a gift upon him. A gift from a fallen angel.

He tore his grimoire off the shelf with a newfound urgency and began feverishly scribbling the words, the lyrics pouring out of him with a passion that could not be contained.

Leon's hands flowed with rhythmic, fluid compositions as words poured out. The chronicles of Damien Moxie's poppet and untimely death charged the lyrics being written on the page in the grimoire, the power bleeding into each verse. Leon sang them out loud, the inspiration pouring out of him as if he were speaking in tongues. The idea possessed him, giving him the innate ability to transcribe the lines in a foreign poetic language, translating them to bewitch the masses.

Lucius's plan included all of this. *How wise he was.* Leon realized that he had kept this soul that night to learn a lesson, to spill it out into this song before he traded it in. What a divine power Lucius was.

Hail Satan for this gift.

* * *

Leon was nowhere to be found as the band prepared to rehearse at Lonnie's. Dallas was noodling around on his bass, his pointer and middle fingers wildly plucking at the strings as he worked out a bass line.

"What timing even was that?" Lonnie teased, twirling a drumstick between his fingers. Dallas looked at him, squinting as he slowly played through his progression. He stopped, his narrowed eyes bulging as he played it again faster, not breaking eye contact with Lonnie. The drummer sucked in his cheeks and gave Dallas a suggestive down-turned smile. "Hmm? What time was that progression in, Dallas? I thought you didn't need a drummer to keep time."

Lonnie smiled at Jimmy, acknowledging the nod to their first meeting while Dallas's fingers still moved wildly across the bass's strings. He stopped and leaned back.

"Fuck. I don't know," Dallas conceded, his bandmates erupting in laughter. He wrinkled his brow, twisting his smile into a mock grotesque frown, and looked up through his eyebrows. "Fuck off, all of you." He gallantly flipped the bird, extending his arm and rotating it around so that each guy got their own personal insult.

"Are any spirits in?" Leon stormed into the apartment, his cadence reminiscent of Jim Morrison. "The séance is about to begin!" He flickered the lights on and off. His bandmates stared back at him with bewildered faces, all except for Cam, who was enjoying the dramatic flair.

"What are you on, Leon?" Jimmy asked, his voice tinged with amusement.

"I wrote the song," Leon announced, his eyes wild as he surveyed their faces, his hand clutching the paper fiercely. "THE song. The song that will piss people off and set the tone for us as a band."

He presented the page to Jimmy, who read it with a knitted brow.

" 'Conjure Me Up?' " Jimmy questioned flatly.

"Just fucking read it, Jimmy." Leon was running out of patience, pacing with his hands on his hips. "It's our rhapsody."

Jimmy's furrowed brow softened as he read, his concentration deepening with each verse. As he finished reading the words, a smile crept across his lips. He raised his eyes to Leon as he handed the sheet of paper to Dallas.

"We sure do," Jimmy agreed. Dallas scanned over the lyrics as fast as his eyes would let him.

"This," Dallas made a proud gesture by holding up the lyrics, "is fucking metal."

"Let me see." Lonnie snatched the paper out of Dallas's upraised hand and read it. He looked up at Leon after reading the first verse, settling back in at his kit as he read the chorus. He lifted his brows in approval as he handed it to Cam, who eagerly accepted it, placing his elbows on his knees and reading it with a smile.

"Yes!" Cam stabbed a finger into the paper's center and shouted enthusiastically. "That's it. 100% yes."

"How did you come up with this?" Jimmy narrowed his eyes, searching his friend's flushed face.

"Just a spurt of creativity, I guess." Leon brushed at the tip of his nose, shrugging his shoulders. Stretching upward, he rubbed at the nape of his neck before resting his hands back on his hips. "I was reading a book, and it just spoke to me," he said with an open palm gesture.

Leon slung the guitar case off of his back, dropped to his knees, and threw the case open. He pulled out his guitar, plugged it into the amp, and switched it on. The buzzing hum of the electricity mirrored the vibrations coursing through Leon's hands as he tuned up his instrument.

"Here's what I was thinking for the main riff..."

As Leon began to play the lead guitar riff he had composed, Cam listened intently, nodding in rhythm with the notes. Leon's guitar cried out an ominous tale. The strings painted a dark picture with its dissonant sound.

In response, Cam began to craft a rhythmic chord progression, blending it with Leon's wailing guitar.

Leon let a shuddering breath escape as a laugh caught in his chest. He repeated the riff as Cam seamlessly followed his lead.

Cam experimented with some supplementary riffs between chords. When he discovered the perfect combination, a chill lifted the hairs on Leon's sweaty neck.

"That's it!" Leon screamed, pointing his guitar pick at Cam, who threw his head back in a howl as he struck one final chord.

"Holy shit," Dallas tittered. "That was fucking magic."

Lonnie sat at the drum kit, twirling the drumstick between his fingers. "Hey, loop that again," he demanded, getting into position to make his entrance.

Lonnie counted them in with four hits, and then they were off. He began keeping time with the kick drum while emphasizing the downbeat on the second measure using the kick and snare drums. He experimented with different hi-hat options for each phrase, and once he found a rhythm he liked, he added accent notes to give the song more power. As Lonnie settled into the groove, Cam and Leon adjusted their riffs to match the rhythm he was playing. Lonnie then signaled the guitarists to end the phrase, which he concluded with a final fill.

"That fill would lead into the chorus perfectly," Leon said as he played his vision of the chorus. Cam followed his lead with the rhythm.

"Hey, bassist," Lonnie pointed toward Dallas with his chin. "If I play the verse, can you modify that bass line you were fucking around with earlier?"

"I think so," Dallas considered. "Let's give it a shot."

They ran through it, so close to everything coming together. "Take out the repeated note in the second bar. See if that tightens it up," Lonnie suggested. Dallas ran through it again, letting the rhythm flow through his fingers.

Minor adjustments were made, finessing the song with a fine-toothed comb. Leon's guitar summoned a dark tone as he added the Devil's Triad as the opening. The Devil's Triad—such a powerful sound. *Diabolus in musica*, this chord marries together a sinister collection of notes, giving the listener an unshakable sense of foreboding.

The tritone rang out, opening the song with unmistakable dissonance. They finished writing the song that would serve as track one on their debut album, a song that would define their reputation for the rest of their lives.

"Let's play it through again," Leon said, rolling his neck and repositioning his guitar strap. Lonnie counted them in, ready to play it through in completion for the first time.

Leon strummed the Devil's Triad, letting it ring out as the song began. They all sang together in deep harmony. As the bass built up to the first drum beat, they began chanting together in deep harmony, "Conjure me up." They repeated the chant, getting louder with each repetition in a crescendo. The guitars swelled, and Leon played the main riff that led into the first verse.

The light of a candle
The darkness in your soul
You've come to the séance
To spill blood, to spill blood
The coven is calling to you
We are the fire. We are the flames
The sky is black and falling down
The Veil is thin

The band echoed baritone notes as Jimmy let out a howl that introduced the chorus.

Conjure me up, conjure me up, conjure me up
I'm the one you need
You've been searching for a long time
For a way to release your pain
But it's not here tonight
It's not here tonight
Burning at the stake tonight

Leon slid his pick down the strings and settled back into the main riff for the second verse.

I've been waiting for you
I've been aching for you
Lost in a lake of fire
Now, you must pay the price
No going back. Let it begin
We'll dance in the shadows of night
Dance in the fire, dance in the flames
Feasting on fear

Leon's bluesy, gritty guitar solo followed the chorus. Like a scream from his instrument, the notes added a raw, emotional layer to the song. The solo closed with a drum break as Jimmy moaned.

Wake up, wake up
You know you're bound to die
Don't make a sound, don't breathe a word
There is no one to hear you scream

After strumming the Devil's Triad following the last chorus, Leon let the notes ring out until they dissipated. The band ceased with the exception of Dallas, who slowed the bass line to pluck a deep staccato melody that laid the foundation for the song's finale collective chant.

Conjuring me up
We will light the way
With our eyes closed

A heavy silence hung in the air as they exchanged glances. None of them were willing to make a move, not daring to disrupt the magic moment they had conjured.

Leon held his breath, his lungs burning from the lack of oxygen. "So what do you think?" A smile budded on his lips, already knowing the answer.

A laugh gurgled in Dallas's chest, a warm and triumphant sound that bathed Leon in ecstasy. He had single-handedly presented their future as a band on a silver platter for them.

"This is it," Cam proclaimed, slinging his arm around Leon's neck and drawing him in. "Nice job, brother."

"Where did you get the idea again?" Jimmy asked, suspicion rising in his heart. He wondered how Leon could pull this masterpiece out of thin air just when they needed it. Beyond that, it was so dark. Leon had always allowed himself to be enveloped by darkness, embracing the good with the evil. Jimmy had never opened that subject with Leon, hoping he wasn't dabbling in something he couldn't fully understand. Damien Moxie's death deepened his suspicion; the glint in Leon's eyes that night made his gut sink. A silent prayer rattled off in Jimmy's mind, asking for protection as he waited for Leon to answer.

"It just…" Leon's eyes darted off to the left as he pursed his lips, "came to me. I was reading a book, and it just," he snapped his fingers. "Clicked."

Jimmy took in a slow breath. "Is this the image that we want to lean into?"

"Jimmy," Leon moaned, drawing out the last syllable of his best friend's name. "If anything, it'll set us apart. Sabbath isn't Satanic, but their songs are dark. They have a Gothic vibe. Who's to say we can't modernize that and use it to get ahead."

"I agree," Lonnie said, setting his sticks on his drums.

"I will say," Leon taunted, "that you can't sing about a séance without ever having done one."

"What…" Jimmy said flatly.

"You guys are going to look like a bunch of posers," Leon teased, "happy to cash in on the image but never tip-toeing into anything supernatural."

Cam's spine straightened. "What are you saying? Do you want us to do a séance ?" His eyes widened, and he beamed at Leon. "Are we going to do one?"

Leon flattened his lips into a tight line and shifted his eyes down, shrugging in confirmation. "It would only be ethical. To not to be a band of posers."

"I'm in!" Cam pointed at Leon, bouncing on the balls of his feet. "I'm so fucking in."

"Me too," Dallas said. "It sounds like it could be fun."

"Whatever." Lonnie shrugged. "When can we get this over with."

"Tomorrow. Tomorrow is Devil's Night."

"Devil's Night?" Jimmy's palms prickled with sweat.

"The day before Halloween." Leon laid his guitar into the case, buckling it with one quick flip. "The veil is thin, and the spirits are out." Leon wiggled his fingers at Jimmy, moaning like a ghost. Jimmy slapped his hand away as he prayed for the white light to surround them all, especially Leon.

17

Devil's Night

On the night before Halloween, the veil separating our world from the realm of the supernatural is especially thin. On this night, known as Devil's Night, it is believed the Devil himself wanders the Earth, unleashing chaos and destruction. Many take part in their own destruction, using it as an excuse to run wild. On Devil's Night in 1983, Leon was thrilled to lead his fellow bandmates in a séance that involved performing acts considered blasphemous, as October 30, 1983, fell on a Sunday—the Lord's Day.

Leon drew an inverted pentagram on his tabletop before adorning it with a velvet curtain. He carefully positioned the Ouija board on the table, turned off all the lights, and lit enough red and black candles to fill the apartment with a warm glow. Pouring a generous amount of red wine into his ritual chalice, he placed it neatly next to a black bandana intended to be used as a blindfold. A pen and paper lay beside the blindfold as Leon fully planned on acting as a vessel, allowing the spirits to communicate through him.

"I don't think we should be doing this," Jimmy muttered as he examined the planchette. "I mean, do you really know what you're doing?"

"Don't be such a pussy, Jimmy," Lonnie said, taking a seat at the table. "It's not like it's real anyway. Leon's just seen one too many horror flicks."

"That's just Jimmy. He's been a wet blanket on fun since we were kids." Leon smirked at Jimmy, lowering his register into a mocking voice. "Wanna play "Stairway to Heaven" backward?"

"Fuck you guys," Jimmy said, sitting beside Cam.

"Hey, hey, now," Dallas scolded, sitting between Cam and Lonnie. "This is supposed to be fun and bring us together as a band." He smiled widely and grabbed Lonnie by the chin. "Isn't that right?"

"Get your fucking hands off of me," Lonnie snapped, jerking his head away from Dallas.

"Enough," Leon roared, taking his seat. "It's time to begin. Is everyone ready?"

Everyone exchanged brief glances of trepidation. Cam gave Lonnie a dubious expression. Lonnie then looked to Jimmy; they locked eyes and offered each other subtle nods. Dallas didn't take his attention off of Leon, who ceremoniously lifted the chalice full of red wine with both hands.

"We drink to this band, our brotherhood. We drink to our success, our fame, and our legacy." Leon sipped the wine and offered it to Jimmy. Leon nodded as Jimmy studied him warily. After taking a taste, Jimmy passed the chalice to Cam, who then passed it to Dallas, who in turn passed it to Lonnie.

"Seriously, do I have to?" Lonnie grimaced.

"Just fucking drink it."

Lonnie huffed as he sipped, taking only a taste so as not to drink any backwash. Leon instructed them all to join hands. Closing his eyes, Leon let his shoulders drop and began his opening monologue.

"We have gathered here tonight to communicate with the spirits still roaming the Earth after their physical bodies have died. Let us create a sacred space to lift the barrier between this world and the afterlife. We invite anyone who wants to connect with us to come forward and make their presence known. Let us start this séance with an open heart and a clear mind."

Leon opened his eyes, squaring his jaw as he looked down at the planchette. "I need everyone to put two fingers here."

"Sounds like another normal night for me," Dallas smirked, putting his pointer fingers on the planchette.

"Do you always have to be so graphic?" Jimmy said as he followed suit.

Cam placed his hands on the spirit board, marching his fingers over to the planchette. He bit his lip as his fingers landed on the planchette with a dramatic flourish. Cam glanced at Jimmy, who snickered at his playfulness.

"Is this, honestly, necessary?" Lonnie folded his arms over his chest. "Can I just watch?"

"No," Leon said firmly. Lonnie rolled his eyes and slapped his two fingers on the wood plank with a huff. Satisfied with everyone's participation, Leon paused for a beat to signal the start of the session before posing his first question.

"Are there any spirits here tonight?"

The planchette remained still for a moment before jerking forward an inch. Cam's eyes widened in disbelief as he exhaled through parted lips. Dallas snatched his hand off of the planchette. "What the fuck?" He rose from his seat and stumbled backward, knocking the chair out from under him and bumping Lonnie's shoulder with his hip.

"Dallas—" Leon rumbled.

"Sit down, Dallas," Lonnie gestured to the board with his head. "Leon's moving the damn thing."

"I'm not moving anything. Spirit is."

"Yeah, okay. Whatever," Lonnie snapped, shrugging him off. "Sit down so we can get this over with."

"You do not break contact, Dallas. Sit down and put your fingers back on the planchette."

"No." Dallas scoffed defiantly.

"Dallas!" Leon's chin snapped to the empty chair, the rest of his body statuesque. His eyes never left the board, but they blazed with a fury that only Jimmy had seen before. "Sit. Down." Leon's voice deepened, and a sense of unsettling evenness coated the command.

Dallas swayed and grumbled as he sat back down at his place at the table. He reached his two fingers toward the planchette and hesitated, looking to Jimmy for confirmation. The singer nodded but was starkly pale in the dimness. Dallas slowly put his fingers on the empty space on the planchette, barely touching it before Leon barked out his next question.

"Are you alone?"

Dallas's ears burned in the deafening silence. He waited, stiffening, for the pull on his fingers, but nothing came. He let out a breath to steady his nerves, feeling more stable with each passing stagnant second.

"Can you give us a sign that you're here?"

The B string on Leon's guitar rang out from across the room, crisp and confident as it cut through the anticipatory silence. They all jumped from the unexpected noise, none of them expecting a response. An unsettling, cocky smile spread across Leon's face as Jimmy grimaced.

"How long have you been dead?" Leon's excitement grew, not letting the rest of his bandmates process what had just happened.

"N—"

'For Christ's sake," Lonnie rolled his eyes, breaking contact with the board to run his free hand through a stray hair that had fallen onto his forehead. As soon as he put his finger back down, it moved to:

"E—"

Jimmy muttered the Lord's Prayer under his breath as the planchette moved to "V." His spine stiffened as the wheels scratched over the board.

Cam's whole body bounced in his seat. He took shallow breaths as his eyes followed their hands across the board, keeping a mental tally of everywhere they'd been. His fingers shook as the wheels stopped briefly over the "E" before looping toward the "R."

"You never died?" Cam blurted out. He gave Leon an apologetic shrug. Leon paid him no attention as the planchette gradually moved to "NO," concealing the hand-painted crescent moon's face with a hooked nose and sly grin.

"Were you human?" Leon asked, eliciting an anxious glare from Jimmy. Jimmy searched the faces of his bandmates, but no one would reach his gaze. It felt like he was watching them from above, an untethered spirit, powerless to be heard. As if he were the only one to feel the weight of the air in the room or see the blackness forming in the dark behind Leon.

The planchette wandered toward the center of the board and paused before returning to "NO."

"Of course not," Lonnie rubbed his temple, keeping one hand on the planchette to appease the guitarist.

"Did you ever kill anybody?" Leon said in a voice just above a whisper.

"I'm sorry," Dallas said sarcastically, lifting his fingers off of the board. His Adam's apple bobbed as he swallowed. "Are we just going to ignore the fact that it said it's not human?"

"Do not break contact! Put your fingers back on the planchette, Dallas. We didn't say Goodbye." Leon commanded. Dallas hesitantly put his fingers back on the wooden plank as it started to move.

The planchette scratched slowly across the board by a weighted, mysterious pressure. It carried their sluggish fingers, like a puppeteer directing the limbs of a marionette. The weight of ten twitching fingers pressed light grooves into the wood as the planchette squeaked across the board, filling the room with the scent of aged wood and lemon polishing oil.

"M—"

"Here we go again," Lonnie stomped a boot into the floor, shaking the table.

Cam's stomach fluttered. "A—"

"N—" Jimmy clenched his jaw, holding his breath. "Y."

MANY.

Jimmy's head filled with a muffled pressure; the thump of his body pumping blood made it heavy. He squeezed his eyes shut. Even the candlelight was too bright. The darkness dulled the nausea roiling in his throat.

"Who did you kill?"

"Stop—" Jimmy's voice got lost in the clatter. The planchette flew off the board violently despite moving slowly throughout the session. It left a scuff on the wall.

"Jimmy, pick that up," Leon spat, his eyeballs vibrating in panic as he stared at his fingers, still poised over where the planchette had been.

Small white circles floated across Jimmy's vision. "Maybe we should—"

"Pick it up, Jim," Leon singsonged the words like a warning. "Pick it up. Pick it up. Pick it up." The pace picked up with each repetition. Jimmy slowly leaned away from Leon as the spit started to fly as he raised his volume with each repetition. "PICK IT UP!"

Jimmy stumbled out of his chair and bumped into the wall. He lowered himself to the floor and felt around for the planchette. He refused to take his eyes off Leon, who was swaying from side to side in his chair like a demented Jack-in-the-box. Jimmy's fingers found one of the wheels of the upturned planchette. He grabbed it and quickly rose to his full height. Leon reached out a hand, his palm glistening with sweat in the candlelight.

"Thank you," Leon said. He sounded completely normal. "Okay." Leon set the planchette back on the table and let out a sigh, smiling at all of his friends. "Everybody," he mimed, putting his fingers on the planchette in an exaggerated gesture. "Let's get back to it," he said, nodding encouragingly around at the rest of the band. One by one, they replaced their fingers, sharing wary looks. Leon looked satisfied: the circle was complete.

"When will I die?" Leon asked, clenching his teeth and squaring his shoulders, not daring to look at Jimmy. He avoided looking at the others and continued to focus on the planchette. The letters came fast, with barely enough time between them to process where they had been before.

Y-O-U-N-G

"This is getting out of hand," Jimmy interjected.

"Shut up," Leon snapped, turning his attention back to the board. "Why are you here?"

Their fingers remained utterly still on the wooden plank. Cam burst out in a fit of laughter in the growing silence. "I'm sorry," he blurted and covered his mouth with his hand, his shoulders shaking violently. Leon glared at him, forcing him to quickly put his fingers back on the planchette. "It's just... I'm sorry. I'm so uncomfortable."

Dallas snickered. "That makes two of us."

"You ruined it," Leon curled his thin top lip at Jimmy.

"I didn't do anything wrong."

"Will we get signed?" Dallas raised his eyebrows as he addressed the board. Lonnie glared at him. "What?" Dallas shrugged. "I wanna change the subject. We could get some useful information outta this."

They all fell silent, Cam's laughter trailing off as his fingers began to move. The planchette glided steadily to "YES."

"See!" Dallas knocked his body into Lonnie. He bounced off of the drummer, who barely recoiled from Dallas's weight. "Will we be successful?"

It moved back slowly before returning to "YES."

"Fucking A right we are." Dallas bobbed his head, smiling proudly at their fingertips. His leg began to shake with excitement, bouncing off the ball of his foot.

"Can you tell us a joke?" Lonnie interjected with a sneer.

"Guys," Jimmy's voice was thick with annoyance. "Seriously?"

"Jimmy's right," Lonnie said. "This is probably just Leon screwing with us."

"It's not." Leon snapped, rolling his eyes slowly from the board to Lonnie.

"Mhph," Lonnie grunted, matching Leon's stare. "Prove it then. Let's say Goodbye, and you can play medium. I love a good game as much as the next guy, but this blows."

"It's a joke because you guys aren't asking serious questions." Leon hissed, his tone dripping in venom. "You need to be respectful to Spirit."

Lonnie cocked his head to the side and narrowed his eyes at Leon. "Just fucking close it out."

"Whatever," Leon grumbled, rolling his shoulders back and straightening his posture. "Thank you, Spirit, for speaking with us tonight. We are now going to cease communication. It is time for us to say Goodbye."

With that, the five of them guided the planchette to 'GOODBYE' and removed their fingers.

"What now?" Dallas asked.

"Leon is going to play psychic medium." Lonnie shot Leon a smug look. "Isn't that right, Leon?"

"That's right." Leon folded the bandana and laid it over his eyes, knotting it under the crown of his head. "I need you all to be respectful; this is sacred."

"Oh, absolutely," Lonnie mocked, jutting out his jaw and rolling his eyes. "We will."

"I need us all to gather hands again," Leon directed, laying his hands palm-up on the table.

"Oh, for fucks sake." Lonnie sighed.

"Is everyone's hands joined?" Leon was growing impatient. Dallas held out his hand, gesturing for Lonnie to place his hand in his palm. Reluctantly, Lonnie complied.

"Let us create a sacred space to lift the barrier between this world and the afterlife." Leon recited.

"Didn't we already do this?" Cam whispered to Jimmy, who shrugged as he widened his eyes and pushed out his lower lip. "I invite any spirit who wants to connect with us to come forward and make their presence known by using my body as a vessel. You may speak through me or use my hands to write. Let us start this séance with an open heart and a clear mind."

"How are you going to write if our hands are joined?" Lonnie mumbled to Leon, who sat still as stone.

"Is there anyone that wishes to come through?" Leon asked, ignoring him. "Please give us a sign that you're here."

A knock echoed from the middle of the table and pierced the silence. Jimmy, Dallas, Lonnie, and Cam exchanged uncertain glances, looking from the center of the table where they heard the knock to each other. Cam chortled quietly, and Lonnie's spine straightened. A lock of Dallas's hair lifted up.

"What the fuck," Dallas whispered.

The room was silent until a low moan reverberated through it, quiet at first before growing louder. Leon's jaw dropped as he let out a primal and guttural groan, simultaneously accompanied by an unnatural, high-pitched screech. The dual-voiced wail made everyone freeze in their seats. Jimmy stared in horror, his stomach dropping. They all suspected Leon of faking the Ouija board session, of putting on a show for their sakes, but that sound was unexplainable. It was inhuman.

The mysterious sound trailed off and faded into a raspy and ragged breathing pattern. Air rattled wetly in Leon's lungs. A death rattle.

"Lonnie?" Leon beckoned in a voice that didn't sound like his own. The corners of his mouth turned down, twitching as it gaped open. He looked like a fish, his mouth bobbing lazily. In the dim light, it almost looked like Leon had developed jowls. The skin on his face appeared to hang limply over his bone structure—nearly skeletal. Wrinkles formed over his young face, etching a lifetime's worth of story into his skin. Lonnie turned his attention and snatched his hand away from Leon at the familiar voice.

"What the fuck?" Lonnie croaked. Leon, still blindfolded, reached out his arm and grabbed Lonnie's hand back, holding it tenderly.

"Watch your mouth, Lon," the hoarse voice demanded.

"Pop?" A crack formed in the drummer's facade.

"I never did—" The words stumbled out of Leon's mouth as if he were in and out of consciousness. He licked his lips, the corners of his mouth twitching as he found the words. "I never did get to thank you for what you did for me."

"Stop it," Lonnie snapped.

"I mean it. I couldn't even count on my own son to do it. He just kept crying every time I brought it up. But you..." Leon smiled. "You were a man."

Lonnie's face hardened as he stared at Leon. A single tear fell from his eye, soaking into his shirt and staining the fabric with a perfect, dark circle. He clenched his jaw and averted his eyes, fixing them on the table to dispel the emotion from his face.

"Don't get soft on me now," Pop said through the guitarist's lips.

"You're not real," he murmured, keeping his voice as even as he could. "Cut it out, Leon."

"I am just as real as you are. I'm just...somewhere else." Leon's fingers crawled out of Lonnie's grip and slid up his hand and around his wrist, tightening as his croaky voice deepened. "You listen to me, Lon. You need to surround yourself in the light. Darkness is around you all the time. The Devil feeds on low vibrations and is closer than you think. I will always be around you to surround you with light."

Lonnie's breath caught in his chest as Leon's hand crept back down. Leon pried open Lonnie's tight fist with his fingers. Although he would never admit it, Lonnie squeezed Leon's hand. Despite knowing that he was physically squeezing Leon's hand, he knew in his heart that his grandfather was squeezing back.

Lonnie felt Leon's hand grow slack in his own. Leon pulled his hands away from Lonnie and Jimmy, folding them neatly in his lap. He straightened his spine, sitting starkly straight in the chair.

"Oh, Cam." Leon's voice was his own now. Cam smiled and shifted in his seat, excited that it was his turn despite the mocking tone. "There's no one here for you. There is no one looking out for you in the spirit world like there's no one looking out for you in this one."

Cam's smile slowly faded, and his broad shoulders deflated as Leon continued.

"Not even a twice-removed uncle is coming to say hello. What a shame. Is that why you love childish stories? You can escape into your fantasy land so you can forget that daddy has one foot out the door with his mistress, and mommy is too self-absorbed to realize that you're all but raising your brothers and sister. That's why you're so invested in this band. That's why you jumped at Jimmy's invitation to jam. You think you found *a family* here." Leon scoffed, his voice laced with condescension as if it were so ridiculous that Cam would consider them family.

Cam swallowed and looked down into his lap. He sat silently, nodding to himself. He puckered his lips as he lifted his head to look at his bandmates. Their eyes all filled with a look of pity, except for Jimmy—his eyes filled with understanding. Cam continued to nod as he cocked his head to his shoulder in agreement. Jimmy turned to look at Leon, his face contorted with disgust.

"It's okay," Cam whispered to Jimmy, and Jimmy snapped his head over to Cam. He softened his features, looking at Cam's smile. "Really, it's okay."

The temperature in the room dropped. Goosebumps crawled up Jimmy's arms as Leon slowly swiveled his head to face him. Despite the blindfold, Jimmy could feel the intensity of their connection.

"Jimmy," Leon crooned, singing the name. "Sweet, pathetic Jimmy. There's no one on this side for you, either. Not that you'd recognize from a hole in the wall, anyway. She won't even come near me. She's too scared. Just like you, Jimmy—a coward." Jimmy bristled while Leon laughed maniacally. "I'm sorry, Jimmy. I didn't tell you who she is," Leon continued. "You're mother's here, Jimmy. Your real mother, the one that died giving birth to you."

"She died?" Jimmy asked in a hushed tone.

"You didn't know?" Cam whispered. Jimmy shook his head. His parents never told him; he never really wanted to know.

Now, he knew.

"Such a shame, really," Leon continued. "Her parents moved here from Portugal when she was ten years old. They worked their asses off to give her a good life. And how does she repay them? She gets herself pregnant five years later. Despite it all, Jimmy, she loved you. She loved feeling you grow inside her womb, moving and kicking. She is standing behind you now, illuminating you with light. Doesn't it get old, Jimmy? Always being so goddamned nice? Being so fucking good all the time? Doesn't it get boring? And you've found yourself a girl. Who's just. Like. You."

Leon's voice slipped into a mocking falsetto. "Heather," he scoffed. "Gag me with a spoon. You two are made for each other. So good, so sweet." He spat the word 'sweet' out like a slur.

"You'll marry her, Jimmy. You will be happy with her for a little bit. Your marriage will be cut short. Very short." Leon raised the chalice, toasting with the remaining wine. Jimmy thanked God that Leon had a blindfold on because he didn't think he could handle seeing Leon's eyes at that moment. He could picture them in his mind's eye. Yellowish, like a cat. Psychotic. Hungry, like an animal, preparing to rip him apart in a raw feast.

"Till death do you part!" Leon burst into laughter, downing the wine in one gulp. A dribble of redness stained his chin like blood. He threw his head back as he swallowed the wine, slamming the chalice onto the table. It shook with the impact. Leon hunched over the empty cup, his shoulder blades protruding. His head snapped up as his mouth broke into a cocky smile.

"Dally!" Leon drawled affectionately in a husky, honey-soaked voice. Dallas's eyes had begun to bug out of their sockets.

"Holy fuck," Dallas sputtered.

"Did you miss me? It's been a while."

"Bruce—" Dallas uttered in disbelief as he looked across the table at Jimmy. "That's my brother. Bruce. He...he..."

"Died, Dally!" Bruce said through Leon's mouth. "I died! It's okay; you can say it. And you're one needle in the arm away from being me, little brother. You wouldn't want to disappoint Mom and Dad more than you already have. I mean," Leon paused as his head lulled toward his shoulder, a cockier grin spreading across his face. Dallas shifted uncomfortably in his seat as the honeyed voice continued. "They already have one dead son and another that's a strung-out queer. Male, female, bi or straight, ole' Dally doesn't discriminate."

The energy in the room shifted. Dallas shook his head frantically as he looked around at each of his bandmates before looking back at Leon. Lonnie ripped his hand away from Dallas, wiping his palm on his jeans. He shot Dallas a look filled with daggers.

"I'm not gay."

"I know you're not, little brother. But just because you drive a Chevelle most of the time doesn't mean you don't test-drive a Camaro every now and then. You're telling me that these guys don't know? Seriously?"

All of the color drained out of Dallas's face. He felt like he wanted to heave, either from nausea or rage; he couldn't tell which. His mouth was too dry to speak.

"Look, Dallas," pseudo-Bruce said in a soft voice. "It doesn't matter what or who you like to ride. You can put whatever you want wherever you want except for a needle in your arm. You understand me? You're just like me, Dally, and I don't want you to be. But you're weak."

The flickering candles scattered around the room danced wildly, their flames casting eerie shadows. The candles placed on the table in the center of the sacred circle extinguished themselves, leaving Leon visible only from the candlelight behind him.

Leon threw his head back as he began muttering, quiet at first. They all leaned forward, trying to make out what he was saying. Lonnie was the first to realize that he wasn't speaking English. He shot out of his seat and stumbled backward, knocking his chair over as Leon spewed words in an ancient, foreign dialect.

Leon spoke in tongues, whipping his head violently back and forth. All of the shades around the apartment flew up, rolling around the bar at the top of the window as the ends coiled around and around. City lights flooded in, breaking up the darkness, as a strong wind swirled around the room, extinguishing the rest of the candles one by one.

The wind stopped as Leon fell silent, his chin falling onto his chest. He sat there limply as all of his bandmates, their faces twisted in horror, watched him. His hand slowly reached behind his head to untie the blindfold. All of the candles spit flames back onto their wicks, illuminating the apartment once again.

"Holy shit," Leon groaned as he pulled his blindfold off, rubbing his eyes. He ran his fingers through his bangs, unsticking them from his sweaty forehead. "I feel like dog shit."

No one said a thing. Leon surveyed all of their horrified faces. Dallas looked ghostly with his dyed-black hair and colorless complexion. Jimmy's face was also pasty in the dim lighting despite the warm glow from the candles. He sat in his seat, dazed, with sadness swimming in his eyes. Leon turned to Lonnie, who was looking through furrowed brows not at him but at Dallas. His lips curled, and his chest heaved with angry breaths.

"What happened?" Leon asked. "Why do you look like that?"

"Are you fucking kidding me?" Lonnie rasped.

Leon looked at the paper and pen on the table before him. The paper was blank. The pen was untouched. He rolled his shoulders forward. "It didn't work then."

"No, no. It worked," Lonnie berated. "You're a fucking freak, do you know that? What the fuck was that."

"I—I don't..." Leon trailed off. A relieved breath hitched in his chest. "It worked then. "What did I say?" Leon pried. "Tell me everything."

18

Sleep Paralysis

The events that occurred at that table left an indelible mark on the minds of all five of those men, and the memory of that fateful night continued to haunt them, echoing throughout the years.

Leon sat with wild eyes as chaos ensued around him. His head pulsated, feeling ten pounds too heavy. He wanted nothing more than to kick them all out and go to bed. They were all being too loud, saying things that he couldn't care less about. He wanted someone to fill him in on what had happened. Hours had been lost, but no one would oblige him. Dallas accidentally brushed his hand against Lonnie's when getting up from his chair, unleashing a barrage of rage from the drummer. The bassist locked himself in the bathroom, pushing past Lonnie to escape his abuse. Jimmy held Lonnie still by his shoulders and spoke to him in hushed, urgent whispers. Lonnie dismissed Jimmy's words, his face contorting as he pulled away from his grasp. He settled into a dominant stance, yelling into Jimmy's face. He gestured toward the bathroom with bulging eyes.

Leon couldn't make out what Lonnie was saying. His eardrums thumped in his head, scrambling all the words. He squeezed his eyes shut and lowered his head onto his steepled fingers. His body weight was tethered to the chair, and all of his energy had gone with the spirits.

Cam coaxed Dallas out of the bathroom, who pushed past him to get to the door. His eyeliner had been rubbed away, revealing small, bloodshot eyes.

He pushed past his bandmates, keeping his eyes on the cigarette burns and beer stains on the carpet. Jimmy pushed Lonnie's shoulder blade toward Dallas. Stumbling, Dallas slung his jacket on in a hurry and bounded for the door. Lonnie clenched his jaw, shooting Jimmy a sharp look before going after the bassist. As Dallas opened the door, Lonnie reached over him and slammed it shut.

"What the fuck?" Dallas whipped around, shoving Lonnie away from him. He fell into the side of the couch, catching himself on the tattered arm. The heel of his boot tore a small hole in the worn leather, a blemish that would blend right in with the rest of the scuffs and tears. The drummer felt a familiar boiling in his stomach, the impulse to punch someone spreading through his fingertips. His knuckles popped from the tension but released upon seeing Dallas huddled against the wall. A man who was larger than life had been reduced to wringing hands and slumped shoulders.

Dallas twisted his rings around his fingers, keeping his eyes down. Jimmy took a step toward him but was pulled back by Cam, who gestured with his eyebrows to let them be. Jimmy shifted his weight, watching Lonnie with unease as he lifted himself off the couch's arm. Leon rolled his head back, huffing a deep sigh while racking his chewed-off nails along the side of the chipped wooden chair.

The bassist flinched as Lonnie extended his arm to grasp his shoulder firmly. Dallas leaned back, putting as much space between himself and his bandmate as he could without backing down by taking a step away. The combination of drugs and emotion had turned the skin around his nose red and raw. His eyes darted from Lonnie's stern face to the rest of the band behind his back, observing every move. He tightened his lips as Lonnie squeezed his shoulder.

"I'm sorry," Lonnie muttered in a low voice. Though his spine remained rigid, his piercing blue eyes softened. "I didn't mean to freak out like that."

He loosened his grip and looked at his bandmate in earnest. Unsure of what to do with his hands, Dallas lightly scratched behind his ear before crossing his arms. The room was silent, save for the rubbing of leather stretching over Dallas's movements. He sucked in his cheeks, clicking his tongue in consideration. Nodding his bent head, he straightened his posture to stand at full height. Despite this, he didn't stand as tall as he usually did.

"It's…" Dallas shifted his weight, twisting the toe of his snakeskin boot over a hole in the carpet. He kicked at it gently, toying with a piece of spongy carpet padding. He straightened himself again, puffing his chest out. "You're fine."

Dallas shrugged it off, but Lonnie could hear a waver in his voice. Lonnie looked through the window of Dallas's facade, his chest tightening with guilt.

"I've just, I've never been…around…anyone…" Lonnie rocked his head from side to side, stumbling over his words.

"Mph." Dallas jutted his chin up. "Right. Like what, Lon?" He bit the tip of his tongue, twisting his mouth to the side. "Someone like me?"

"Jesus," Lonnie pinched the bridge of his nose. "No, no, no. I don't mean it like that. I mean—"

He looked at his bandmate through pleading eyes, but Dallas hardened. Lonnie took a deep breath, rubbing his hand through the back of his shaggy brown hair.

"I just mean," he reiterated slowly, "that I don't know what I mean."

Dallas clicked his tongue.

"Look, just don't go running off with a guy, okay?" Hurt washed over Dallas's face. "Or girl," Lonnie quickly added, "I don't give a shit. Just don't screw the band over, okay? "

"Get over yourself," Dallas leered.

"I—uh. Fuck," Lonnie hissed, shifting his weight uncomfortably. He cast his eyes down, blowing air from between his teeth as he raked his brain for words. "Uh..okay. I'm going to regret asking this, but um… I'm…" he hesitated, balling his hands into fists. "I'm the best-looking guy in the band, right?"

Dallas raised an apprehensive eyebrow, dipping his chin to look at Lonnie head-on. His bandmate was edgy, holding tension in his limbs, in his face. He almost winced as if immediately regretting the words. Lonnie's eyes averted to the ground for a split second before returning with a pain that could either be physical pain or forced tolerance. If there was one person in the world who wasn't tolerant, it was Lonnie. Lonnie hated hearing other people chew. Lonnie never wanted to share a bottle of vodka. Lonnie would swirl your brains with his drumstick for looking at him the wrong way. And Lonnie was trying to accept his bandmate to the best of his ability. This stupid joke was an olive branch, his way of making things right.

"Shit," Dallas snorted. "You wish."

Lonnie's face relaxed, erasing the wince, though his ice-blue eyes remained sharp on Dallas. He flipped him off with an upside-down smile.

"Hey." Dallas put a hand on Lonnie's shoulder, mirroring the gesture that his bandmate had just done to him. "Your grandfather, I'm really sorry—"

"It's done," Lonnie said, stiffening under Dallas's touch. "I did what I had to do, what he'd asked of me. It's done. I've filed that away. People die, it's okay."

Dallas knew by the look on Lonnie's face that not another word would or should be uttered about this. Ever. He gave the drummer a firm squeeze before releasing his grip on his arm. Lonnie nodded once, putting the subject to rest.

Glass clanged together as Cam reached into an almost empty fridge. Rogue pieces of rice littered the cracked glass shelves, and spilled soy sauce clung to a beer bottle. Cam gathered the beer bottles, unsticking one from the shelf, figuring this mess was probably from the night that they named the band. He extended one to Leon, who looked at him through squinted eyes.

"What the fuck are we doing?" Leon ignored Cam while massaging his temples. Cam considered the bottles in his hand and placed the sticky one next to Leon before giving Jimmy the other. Cam smirked, realizing that Jimmy had seen what he had done.

"Do you all want to sit in a circle and sing "Kumbaya" now? Wanna braid each other's hair?" Leon ripped his hands through his ginger frizz.

"Pipe down," Jimmy barked as he cranked the bottle cap off with his teeth and spat it at Leon.

"Fuck off." The cold beer bottle tingled on his clammy forehead.

179

Come the witching hour, the night had become too eerie to part ways. No one wanted to go home to their empty apartments or lone beds, so they all decided to camp out at Leon's after the chaos died down. They rationalized it to Leon as having strength in numbers, having just gone through a brutal bonding experience. He agreed to let them stay in a huff, perturbed that there were other people breathing his air, sitting on his furniture, and drinking his beer. He just had the energy sucked out of him, and no one cared. He threw some blankets into the middle of the floor before curling up on his mattress, covering his eyes with his flattened pillow.

The rest of them exchanged glances, not wanting to make the move that would poke the sleeping bear. Lonnie said fuck it, stomping over to the pile and grabbing a threadbare blanket off the top. He snatched it up, pulling it over his lap as he flopped down on the couch. All of the air puffed out of the leather like a deflated air mattress.

"Fucking perfect," Lonnie mumbled, situating himself to try and get comfortable enough to sleep. "Just fucking fantastic."

Dallas curled up in front of the door like a cat, ready to slink out the door at the first sign of trouble.

"I'll take the floor," Jimmy said, lowering himself onto the stiff carpet. He balled up a blanket to use as a pillow and handed the last one to Cam. "You can take the other end of the couch," he said.

"Thanks, man." Cam attempted to fit his large frame into a comfortable position, resembling a Great Dane who believed he was a lap dog. He rutched around clumsily, eliciting a sharp warning stare from Lonnie.

They had forgotten to turn out the lights, a small coincidental detail that no one decided to point out, but darkness enveloped Jimmy as he drifted into slumber. The pungent scent of the sweat, mildew, and wasted liquor ingrained into the splotchy carpet filled his senses, lulling him into sleep. An hour later, he awoke in Leon's apartment, the city's neon lights casting an eerie glow. *Had someone turned off the lights?* His eyes struggled to adjust to the dimness.

A soft touch brushed against his big toe. Wiggling his foot, Jimmy tried to shake off whatever had touched him, but he couldn't move, no matter how hard he tried.

Another touch, more forceful this time, jolted Jimmy out of his drowsiness. It was not a gentle prod but a sharp pinch that sent a shiver down his spine.

He struggled to lift his head, but he couldn't move it. He attempted to move his foot again, but it remained immobile. Fear set in at the realization. Jimmy's body was unresponsive, as if an invisible force had seized it. His mind, however, scrambled in a state of panic, sending frantic SOS signals throughout his body. *Move. Do something.* But his limbs remained still, defying his will.

He began to panic, his head unmoving on his makeshift pillow. His arms remained pinned at his sides, and his fingers had curled into talons, scratching at the carpet. Sharp pains tingled in his hands as they contorted. His whole body prickled in a nervous sweat. Jimmy wanted to heave, to expel this horrible sinking feeling out of his body, but couldn't turn his head—he would choke if he vomited. Swallowing down the bile rising from his gut, he rolled his eyes around in their sockets, desperately relieved that he had autonomy over one part of his body. *There*—he saw something, moving his eyes toward the shadow he felt lurking to his right.

The sound of tiny sniffs filled his right ear. Something cold and damp touched his hand as little claws dug into his wrist, pulling itself up onto his arm. His eyes rolled to the side, straining to see what was in the shadows as little feet clawed at his skin, climbing onto his body. Tiny nails pierced his skin, burning as they drew pinpricks of blood. It crawled up, briefly trying to burrow in his armpit. Jimmy came nose to nose with a rat. Its beady eyes stared back at him, its nostrils flaring as it inclined its neck to touch his face. He wanted to jerk his head, to sit up and throw this rat across the room. But he could only lay there as the rat sat down on his chest, its bulbous body sitting up straight. Agonizing time passed like hours had elapsed, with the rat getting heavier each hour. The stupid rodent weighed on him as if hundreds of pounds were pressing down on his sternum.

Giles Corey, the man pressed to death during the Salem Witch Trials, came to mind as whiskers brushed against his cheeks. He imagined this was the kind of pressure he endured with every boulder placed on his failing body.

Jimmy's breath rattled in his chest, the weight making breathing harder and harder. Air rasped out of his barely-parted lips, sipping in as much air as his body would allow under such duress.

A breath hitched in his throat as a new shadow cast upon him. Relief washed over Jimmy as Leon stood over his stiff body.

Thank God.

Leon's name danced on the tip of Jimmy's tongue, but instead of screaming for his friend, his vocal cords let out a raw moan. Leon reached down, his face brimming with serene patience, and picked up the rat with tender care. Jimmy gasped as air permeated his lungs—relief. He sucked in greedy breaths even though it burned, squeezing his eyes shut at the sweet piercing pain.

When he opened his eyes, Leon no longer cradled a rat in his hands. Instead, a creature of wonder, so pure, met his gaze with dead eyes. Leon caressed a lifeless bird as its limp body bled.

Blood poured out, spilling over Leon's hands as he clutched it tightly. A red, sticky stream dripped onto Jimmy's leg, making his limbs itchy. He wanted so badly to move—to scramble away from Leon, to wipe away the blood—yet he was cursed to lay there, doomed to watch as Leon tilted the dove to showcase a wound on the bird's breast. It looked to be a stab wound, a puncture to the heart. He pushed his fingers into the corpse; a thick squelch squeezed his fingers as they made contact with the gore. Feathers rustled as he jostled them around, digging his fingers deep inside of the dove.

Leon put one foot on either side of Jimmy's frozen body, lowering himself until he straddled his chest. His knees dug into helpless collarbones as he pulled his fingers out of the bird. They glistened with blood in the dim city lights. The corners of Leon's mouth pulled back into a grotesque grin as he slowly reached out his bloody fingers to touch Jimmy's lips.

Jimmy could taste the sticky metallic liquid as it was spread across his lips. Leon mumbled, mucus rattling in his throat.

"Take the blood on your tongue. If you don't, you'll die young."

He repeated this phrase over and over as he rubbed the blood onto Jimmy's mouth. With each repetition, he put more pressure on the gesture, attempting to pry Jimmy's mouth open to force blood in. Jimmy pursed his lips as hard as he could, clenching his jaw to the point of cramping.

Leon's fingers slowed, smearing the blood in a final wipe. In his other hand, the corpse of the dove lay wrenched in tense fingers. Leon wrapped it in both hands, squeezing, wringing out any gore left in the poor animal. Blood poured on Jimmy's chest, soaking his shirt in a thick, sticky pile.

"It flicks its tongue to taste, and it listens to its Master. Faster, Jimmy, thou must make haste before I slash your throat to sip and splatter," Leon chanted in a hushed voice.

The chant became more frantic, being repeated in a hurried whisper. Leon rolled his neck, the vertebrae crunching as though a demon were inhabiting his body, stretching and popping bones and muscles to make room. Throwing the dove aside, Leon hunched down, his shoulder blades protruding like broken wings. Jimmy could see each individual knob of Leon's spine through the fabric of his shirt. He crouched, putting all of his weight on Jimmy's chest as he looked at him through pale eyelashes. Hot, stale breath burned Jimmy's nostrils as bloody hands wrapped around his throat, the dove's blood making Leon's hands too slick to get a good grip. They slipped and slid over Jimmy's windpipe, squeezing harder and harder until Jimmy's mouth popped open, his eyes wide as he gasped for air. He gulped for oxygen, his mouth bobbing like a fish.

Leon dipped forward until his breath tickled Jimmy's ear.

"I can smell your fear, James. It makes me hungry," he whispered. Frizzy red hair haloed his pale skin as he released his grip. As Jimmy's eyes refocused, thanks to getting oxygen to his brain, he realized that Leon's eyes were black.

Utterly, bottomlessly black.

A chill tickled Jimmy's sweaty body, instantly making him shiver and shake. His bladder was about to betray him as he lay vulnerable on the floor, watching motionless as Leon stood up, sliding viscous fingers off of Jimmy's neck. He planted a foot on either side of Jimmy, smiling down at his friend with a demonic expression of elation painted across his face. The smile continued to grow, tearing at Leon's cheeks as it stretched all the way up to his temples, like a Cheshire cat from hell.

Falling asleep on the couch made Lonnie think of falling asleep at his grandfather's bedside, matching his breathing to the rise and fall of the ventilator. He had always been a light sleeper, which was why he always volunteered to take the night shift in his grandfather's final days. Groaning would lull him out of his dreams, knowing it was time to administer the next round of pain medication. If he gasped, he knew to take the pillows out from under his head to extend his airway. Lonnie jolted awake, hearing his Pop gasping for air.

Except he was in Leon's apartment.

Lonnie shot up, seeing Jimmy seizing on the floor, laying flat on his back.

"Jimmy!" Lonnie shouted, throwing the threadbare blanket off of his lap onto Dallas.

"What's the matter?" Dallas panicked and threw Lonnie's blanket off of him, scrambling to get up. He stumbled, having not even been awake a full second by the time he was on his feet. Cam swung his legs off of the couch, ready to lunge at the disturbance. He pushed his golden brown hair out of his paling face upon seeing what was causing the commotion.

Lonnie fell to his knees, clutching Jimmy's face in his hand. The drummer watched as Jimmy's eyes bulged, darting frantically around the room. Jimmy's jaw hung wide open as tension pulled it to one side. He lay in Lonnie's hands, gasping for air, his entire body rigid as his hands stiffened into offensive claws. Lonnie's heart rose into his throat, and panic overcame him as he slapped Jimmy across the face to snap him out of the episode.

The sound of the connection between Lonnie's hand and Jimmy's cheek startled Leon awake, his head throbbing under the weight of the pillow. The lights blinded him when he threw the pillow off his face. He swore under his breath and whipped around to see why Lonnie was yelling. His stomach dropped at the sight of the band gathered around his friend's seizing body. Jimmy's eyes followed him as he crossed the room, and they bore into him with such raw terror that it made his blood run cold.

Jimmy threw Lonnie onto the couch and scrambled backward like a crab away from Leon, his body bursting into motion. "What the fuck, Leon?" Jimmy screamed, gagging on the influx of air he gasped in as he regained control over his body.

Cam steadied Lonnie, who watched with horror as Jimmy cowered away from the guitarist. Dallas jumped back at the sudden movement, his eyes so wide with shock and surprise that white completely surrounded his brown irises. Leon gawked back at Jimmy with a perplexed expression.

"I didn't do anything," Leon said with hurt in his eyes.

"You were standing over me with black eyes. You had this creepy fucking smile on your face that stretched to your ears. And—"

"No," Dallas muttered under his breath, shaking his head as he stepped away from Leon.

"Hold on," Lonnie said, placing a hand on Leon's shoulder. He pushed him down gently on the couch between himself and Cam. Dallas perched himself on the arm, not wanting to get too close to any of them. "Let's take a seat so we're not crowding Jimmy. Jimmy, tell us what happened."

"No," Jimmy said. "You tell me what you saw first."

"We didn't see anything," Leon snapped, defensive.

"We just saw you," Cam's voice was calm as he locked eyes with Jimmy. "You were laying on your back, and your eyes were bugging. All the veins in your neck were popping out. It looked like you were having a seizure or being tortured or something." The band stared at their singer as he processed what he had just been told. Silence hung in the air as he mulled it over, breathing heavier with each passing second.

"I don't know what just happened." Jimmy looked at the floor, his mouth twisted in disgust. He looked like he was about to be sick as he recounted the nightmare from the beginning, wiggling his toes as he told the story to make sure he was still able to move them.

"Oh my God," Dallas whispered as Jimmy got to the part about the rat. He winced, squeezing his eyes shut.

"There was no rat, Jimmy," Leon said.

"Let me finish," Jimmy snapped. His eyes grazed the floor up to Leon.

They were pained as he told them about the dove. Wincing, he held out his hands, cupping them as if there was a delicate white bird in his palms. His fingers tensed, digging into the air.

"Jesus Christ," Lonnie interjected, shaking his head, trying to erase the mental image like it was an Etch A Sketch.

"There's no blood," Jimmy rationalized, rubbing his hand over his mouth. "I know that. But I felt it. I swear to God, I felt it. It was warm and wet, and it got itchy as it dried."

Leon looked at his friend with horror. He hadn't told anyone about his ritual or Lucius. *He couldn't know about that. No one knows what I did. No one can know.*

Jimmy reached up and ran his fingertips along his lips, ensuring once more that there was no blood.

"Then you took your hands off my throat, stood up, and smiled down at me. I blinked, and you were normal, looking at me like I was the one being fucking creepy. And I could move my head again, and you were all looking at me like I was the one that was fuckin—"

"We were just worried," Lonnie said.

"Fuck that," Dallas scoffed. "Yeah, we were scared. I'm not pussyfooting around this."

"Leon, I don't know if I can do this with you."

"Jimmy," Leon began.

"No, Leon, I'm serious."

"Jimmy, he didn't do anything," Cam said, running his palms on his pants.

"Seriously, Jim," Lonnie said. "We were standing here watching you go through it. Leon looked just as wigged out as the rest of us."

"I don't believe it," Jimmy shook his head and pointed at Leon. "You have always been a little off. It never bothered me. I've always just accepted it as who you are, but this is taking it too far."

"Jimmy, honest, I didn't do anything."

"You made us all come for a séance. You are dabbling in something that you don't understand."

"Jimmy—" Dallas interjected.

"Dallas, stay out of this," Jimmy said as he stood up. He jabbed his finger at Leon, his lips curling away from his teeth in a sneer. "You need to get right. I don't know what you have going on personally or if you need to get right with God, but you need to change something, or you will be the destruction of this band."

Leon scoffed.

"No," Dallas shook his head. "Jimmy's right. Something real fucked up happened here tonight, and I don't want to be a part of it."

"Guys—"

"Listen," Lonnie cut Leon off. "I hate to say it, but this whole night was fucked. I thought you were fucking around with us, playing a little game, but I was wrong. And I don't believe in this stuff. Not really, but there's some bad shit here. I feel like there are eyes on me. Something is watching us have this conversation, and I don't like it. We shouldn't have stayed here tonight."

"Are you fucking serious?" Leon said. "Nothing happened. There's nothing here besides us. You, me, Jimmy, Dallas, and Cam. And Stevie. Flesh and fucking blood. You are all blowing this out of proportion. You're scared. Whatever. The séance is just an anecdote we can use in interviews when we make it big."

Lonnie scoffed, throwing his head back. "Leon—"

"No, seriously," Leon said. "When they ask about our number one song, our *rhapsody*, we'll have something interesting for them to print. They'll say, "How did you come up with the idea for "Conjure Me Up"?" and we can say that we conducted a séance and the lyrics were written on the paper from beyond or 'conjure me up' was spelled out on the Ouija board. Something like that, we can figure out the story later. But people will eat that shit up. It's cool. It'll scare people, it'll be controversial, it'll get media coverage. It will be different."

"That's all fine and good," Dallas agreed. "But *this*," he pointed around the room, gesturing wildly with both hands, "is not okay with me. We can push the envelope all we want on stage, but what happened tonight won't happen again. I need to get fucking blessed."

"I'm not rehearsing here anymore," Jimmy said firmly. "And I'm not staying here anymore either. We can rent a storage unit like Dallas's old band for all I care. I'm not coming back here."

"We can rehearse at my place as long as we rehearse after the ice cream shop closes," Lonnie offered.

"For fucks sake, Jimmy—" Leon sighed.

"That would be great, Lonnie," Jimmy cut Leon off, not taking his eyes off of him. "Can you help me put my shit in my car? I'm going to stay with Heather."

Lonnie, Dallas, and Cam wordlessly got up to help Jimmy.

"Cam?" Leon questioned. "Really?"

"Sorry, man," Cam shrugged. "I don't feel comfortable either. The energy is bad. Like, something is way off. It's heavy."

After they left, Leon found himself alone in the shadows. He heard a growl from behind him, and a heavy presence loomed, pressing down on him. He knew that someone was watching him, displeased that four innocent souls had just walked out the door, slipping from his grasp. Leon would find a way to fix it.

* * *

When Jimmy got to Heather's, it was seven o'clock in the morning. She was curled up with a cup of coffee and a notebook, drafting a new chapter for her book. He walked in, plastered on a smile, and kissed her.

"This is a surprise," she said brightly, but the worried look on her face betrayed her. "Are you okay?"

"Yeah," he breathed, attempting to deflate his rigid posture. "Why?"

"Well, it's early, and you look like you've seen a ghost."

She reached up to grab his face, but he flinched away from her touch. Rolling her shoulders back, she straightened herself up into a defiant stance. Jimmy's eyes darted from her to the floor as he rubbed sweaty palms on his pants.

"Tell me what's wrong."

"It's stupid," he said, shaking his head dismissively. "We did this séance at Leon's, and I guess it just freaked me out a little."

"You did?" Heather's eyes widened, and the corners of her lips perked up. What happened? Tell me everything." She paused, looking at Jimmy with expectant eyes. He remained silent, unwilling to disclose Leon's prediction that their future marriage would be short-lived.

"Why didn't you invite me," she slapped him good-naturedly on the arm. "I want to do a séance!"

"No, you don't," Jimmy reassured her. The smile faded from her face as her expression grew serious.

"Why? What happened?"

She poured him a cup of black coffee, and he took it, holding it with both hands. He traced his thumbs over the hand-painted blue border around the lip of the mug. The dark liquid reminded him of the darkness that overtook Leon's eyes. He took a sip to break up the stillness.

Jimmy recounted everything to her, from the candles to the spirit board to Leon and his blindfold. Her mouth gaped open as he told her about his friend speaking in tongues and how they lost hours.

He took a deep breath and sipped his coffee. It tasted strong and slightly bitter, just as he liked it. The heat warmed up his belly, the acidity burning his throat as he told her about his nightmare, which he still wasn't entirely sure was a dream.

"When I woke up, they were all standing around me like I was the crazy one."

As he finished speaking, he avoided making eye contact with her, keeping his eyes on his coffee cup. An oily film jiggled on top as he swirled the cup gently.

"Jimmy—"

"I won't go back to that apartment," Jimmy shook his head definitively. "Leon has always been a little fucked up. That's just who he is. But last night..."

He grappled with himself, unsure how to feel. The darkness was growing. That gloom could envelop them if he let it grow too big.

189

Should I be scared of Leon? Is he just odd, or has he become dangerous sometime over the years? When did that switch flip inside his head?

Heather flattened her lips into a straight line, the corners dragging down in a sympathetic expression. She took the cup from his hands, set it on the table, and drew him into her arms, running her fingers through his black hair. He wrapped his arms around her waist, hoisting her into his lap. He held onto her like a child seeking comfort from his mother.

His mother. Leon said she was always watching over him. He hoped that was true. He looked up at Heather's beautiful face, hoping that his mother had a hand in bringing her to him. Jimmy prayed that Leon was wrong, that their marriage wouldn't be cut short. He couldn't bear the thought of hurting this beautiful, kind soul. She deserved nothing but love.

Leon had always been synonymous with darkness. That darkness had always been there, small at first inside of his little boy body. Just a little seed buried deep inside the child's subconscious. What came into the world as a bad seed grew as Leon did, growing big enough to swallow the light.

Swallow them up. Swallow *him* up to be devoured in the belly of the beast.

What should I do? Is there anything that can be done?

"I'm scared," he admitted, burying his face into her chest. "I think something is wrong with him."

19

The Conjuring

After the séance, Jimmy vowed never to step foot in Leon's apartment again, and he kept his word.

The singer reasoned with the rest of the band to get a designated rehearsal space despite incessant protests from Leon. All but the guitarist agreed, and they began renting a storage unit at the same place where Dallas brought them to party on Jimmy's birthday. This decision turned out to be a game-changer for them. Since no single person owned the unit, it served as a neutral and collaborative space where they could freely write and play. They could set up their equipment and leave it there, saving them time and energy. The time they spent lugging their instruments and amps back and forth between Lonnie's and Leon's apartments could be spent actually rehearsing. Plus, being out of the apartments meant that Lonnie could finally take the towels off of his drum kit during rehearsals, and they could blast their amps at full volume without worrying about noise complaints.

Jimmy felt free in that storage unit, no longer having to endure the eerie presence of Baphomet on the wall, looming over him while he sang. For that, he was endlessly grateful.

The dust from Devil's Night settled, and the band fell back into a groove; however, a lasting impression had been made on the group. A mark had been painted. A piece had been chipped away, forever tainting Psychosomatic Slaughter with a blemish that could not be fixed. They still rehearsed their songs, running through their setlist like usual, but something shifted. Their equilibrium had been disrupted.

Jimmy constantly kept his guard up, never allowing himself to be too comfortable around Leon, having made that mistake too many times in his life. He tried with all his might to keep the chemistry alive on stage, still slinging his arm around Leon's neck while belting out a note. But it no longer felt natural, like he was crossing a boundary that screamed DANGER. The connection didn't feel right anymore. The action felt stiff so as not to feed off of Leon's energy. The relationship soured, spoiling behind the scenes as he kept Leon at arm's length off stage. Jimmy wrestled with guilt over this feeling, this fracture. Leon was his blood brother; they had made a pact sealed in blood. Blood was thicker than water but could not be thicker than Jimmy's moral compass.

Once the facade of normalcy fell back over the band, they polished their rhapsody until it was ready to be played for their manager. Deanna was floored the first time she heard "Conjure Me Up." She jumped up and down, cheered them on, and screamed, "That's it! That's it!"

Their rhapsody, mixed into their arsenal of music, generated more buzz than ever. The Roxy Theater booked Psychosomatic Slaughter for a couple of shows, and they played extended runs at the Whiskey A Go-Go and the Troubadour. A&R reps barraged Deanna, all wanting a piece of the up-and-coming band. Deanna had become their trusted confidant, manager, surrogate big sister, and mother. She was fiercely protective of her boys and their music, rejecting record executives and A&R reps who wanted to change their sound, refine their image, or rewrite their songs. She handled those rejections so they could concentrate on their music.

The pumpkins on porches rotted, being replaced by paper snowflakes in windows despite the warm California weather. Deanna burst into the storage unit the first week of December, breaking the cardinal rule of never interrupting rehearsal. She brought with her a rush of cool air, refreshing the dank and musty fog that lingered around the guys. She mumbled an apology and stuttered over the big news: Psychosomatic Slaughter was scheduled to headline at the Whiskey A Go-Go on New Year's Eve, a moment that would mark a new chapter in their career.

"This is the big time, guys," she warned them. "A&R reps are flocking to me. I've been shooting down the bad ones, and I've been playing hard to get for most of them. I'm flooded with calls to meet with record companies. These guys will be at this show, so this needs to be the best God damned show you've ever played."

Headlining New Year's Eve represented a major win. The band was ecstatic to ring in 1984 as headliners. Their performance would set the tone for the rest of the year. Influential people in the industry would be watching them closely, vying over who would get a piece of the action. Leon itched with expectancy, hoping for a bloodbath. He wanted to sit back and watch, playing the soundtrack while they ripped each other's throats out with their teeth, jamming their thumbs into eyeballs, all for a chance to make their record. It was a good omen, a whisper from beyond that their time was approaching.

Leon ran through the band's setlist alone to drown out the Christmas carols that floated in like a draft from the street. There was only one piece missing that he needed: the keys to the Kingdom. Psychosomatic Slaughter was on the precipice, standing before the gates, waiting for an invite inside. All he had to do to get those keys was ask for them.

Leon prioritized the guitar and his band over absolutely everything else in his life. He would rather starve than not have his music, welcoming an empty gut that ripped and tore itself apart out of hunger if that meant he could have his music. He would sacrifice anything, everything, to get those keys. There would be conditions attached to any help he received, and there would forever be strings attached to him—he knew that. But the thought of achieving this dream, despite the pang of guilt that ran through his gut, a residual effect from his childhood, made it worth it.

Shaking his father's voice out of his head, Leon prepared his altar. Leon's confidence blossomed with each ritual he performed. With every hex cast or rite conducted, he meticulously recorded the experience in his grimoire, noting all of his research on each subject. As he transcribed, he could feel his power mounting as he honed his craft. He faithfully anticipated adding the ritual that would change his life in his sacred book.

Leon lit a single candlestick. It stood tall in the center of a bowl filled with an offering of red wine. He held the athame loosely against the scar on his palm, the exact spot that he cut in 1976. *Jimmy*. His blood brother. His hand quivered, a twinge of guilt running through his body. *Fuck it*, he thought, shoving down any feelings that could get in his way. Jimmy would not ruin this moment for him, not again.

Leaving all traces of morality behind, Leon thrust the blade into his flesh, sending anguish up his arm and across his hand's nerves. He seethed out a breath.

I am ready, Lucius.

I conjure you.

I conjure your power, your glory, your being.

I conjure you, Lucius. The serpent. The wolf.

My soul is yours.

The blood pooled in his hand, running down the heel of his palm and streaming down his arm. He watched the dark liquid glow against the candlelight. Bringing his hand to the candle, he chanted through concentrated breaths. He squeezed his hand into a fist, letting the flood fall in a steady trickle. Leon anointed the candle with his essence, pouring the blood down the sides. The blood ran freely onto the candle, crying sticky burgundy tears as it mixed with the black wax. Blood oozed down the candlestick, combining with melted wax as it rolled down the sides before hardening into dark, bloody beads. The candle's single flame licked his palm, and a burning sensation radiated from his hand and ran throughout his body.

The room's energy distinctly changed, growing humid and thick before the temperature dropped. Something blocked the hum of the refrigerator behind him as the vibrations in the air shifted. Someone loomed there, poised behind Leon's hunched shoulders.

He's here! Hail Satan!

Leon squeezed his eyes shut, feeling the anguish rushing out of his body in a labored sigh. He pulled his shoulders back and held his bleeding hand against his chest, caressing it as blood soaked into his shirt.

Lucius rounded the table, flattening his palms on the other side of the burning candle. Stooping to Leon's eye level, he wore a smug expression, his lips turned up in pride. The candlelight contoured his cheeks, carving out his face with severe shadows. His dark, angular sideburns swallowed all the light. The Devil's eyes glowed through the darkness, and the candle wick reflected in his serpent-like pupils.

"I've been thinking about what you said to me." Leon raised his gaze to meet the Lucius's, speaking slowly and softly. "Every day, I've thought about it. I want to let you know I'm ready for the slaughter." Leon swallowed hard. "I'm ready."

"You do realize the price," Lucius's eyes darkened, a flicker of a smile on his lips.

"Yes," Leon said. "I turn over all humanity to you. I renounce all societal conditioning, all moral conditioning, all religious conditioning. My soul is yours."

"Very well," Lucius purred, his lips peeling back from his teeth in satisfaction. "You've made a wise decision. You will be a legend."

Pushing himself off of the table, Lucius stood to his full height. He reached over the candle to grab Leon's arm. Holding it by the wrist, he rounded the table; the thud of his heavy leather boots sounded dull against the carpet. He caressed Leon's arm, pushing his sleeve up.

"This is a deal that needs to be bound in blood." Lucius stroked Leon's palm, running his finger in the open cut. His eyes blazed at the sight of blood pooled into a tempting puddle.

Leon hissed as Lucius cupped his hand, bringing it to his mouth. The Devil's teeth grew pointed, like an animal's, and his eyes glowed brighter as he sunk his teeth into the wound and drank away Leon's soul.

He sucked away what was left of Leon's morality, swallowing his remaining humanity. Leon's eyes rolled back into his head, the whites of his eyes peering up at his darkened ceiling. He swayed back and forth, feeling lighter the longer Lucius drank. Grinding his teeth, he willed himself the strength to remain upright. When he pictured this moment, he wasn't expecting it to feel so good, almost erotic. The weight of his conscience was gone, and it was liberating. Goodbye, Jiminy Cricket.

Lucius smiled at Leon, his pointed, stained teeth haloed in red.

20

Devil's Luck

December 31, 1983

The green room at the Whiskey A Go-Go was electric with exhilaration. Dallas took a quick bump from the pocket he'd sewn onto his bass strap and washed it down with a swig of Jack Daniels, the dim light casting a shadow on his face.

Lonnie tapped rhythms on his knees, channeling his nervous energy through his hands. He studied the signatures that graffitied the dark backstage walls, scanning to find the perfect place to make his own mark. Meanwhile, Heather expertly lined Jimmy's eyes with bold black eyeliner, running her finger along the lines to diffuse it. With a scowl on his face, Leon ran scales on his guitar, and Cam diligently tuned his instrument, playing a few practice chords. They hadn't experienced this mix of nerves and excitement since their first house party gig.

Deanna rounded the corner with Lisa, a drink in hand. She flashed them an eager smile, holding her drink up to cheer the band.

"Here's to rocking the fucking house down tonight!"

The band whooped with her, banging their instruments in a rowdy ruckus.

"Come in here," She extended her arms and gestured for the guys to gather around her, flicking her fingers toward her palms. "Come on, huddle in."

She proudly smiled as they gathered around.

"This is it boys. Give them hell, have fun, and put on the best fucking show you've ever played."

Huddled in their pre-show ritual, the five of them slung their arms over each other's shoulders. Leaning in, they chanted *break a leg, shatter some skulls,* and gave a loud holler as they broke apart. Cam ruffled Lonnie and Jimmy's hair as he pushed out of the huddle like an overexcited child. He jumped in place, pumping his arms into the air. Heather ran over to Jimmy, throwing her arms around his neck to give him a good luck kiss. Leon stood on the wings, looking at the amber hue of the black stage as the lights shone down on it.

As the lights went down, they strutted onto the stage and took their places. The hum from the amplifiers and microphones radiated through their bodies, which were already buzzing with adrenaline. The crowd cheered as the emcee's booming voice washed over the darkness.

"Welcome to the stage, ready to rock us into 1984, Psychosomatic Slaughter!"

That was their cue: the five of them began chanting the beginning crescendo of "Conjure Me Up," the lights fading up to illuminate Leon as he rang out the Devil's Triad. They exploded into the song, playing off of the crowd. The lights momentarily blinded Leon, and the audience appeared as a large mass, swaying and moving together. Heather danced in the wings with a broad grin, moving fluidly to the music.

As the crowd thronged around him, a floating figure parted the sea of people on his side of the stage. Lucius halted amidst the mass of fans, fixing his gaze on Leon with darkened eyes. He was effervescent in the middle of the crowd, like a beast among men. The Minotaur—freed from the labyrinth to participate in the decade's debauchery and decadence. His ferocity was alluring, albeit jarring, as no one in the crowd dared to stand shoulder-to-shoulder with the towering man. It was almost as if an invisible ring smoked out around him, tempting the young souls around him to take a step into his circle. He would smile at them, a snake charmer's smile, enticing them to take that step. Though many toes danced in the smoke, no one was brave enough to take the full plunge. Instead, they would rebound back into the gyrating crowd, wasting their youth with a soul unburned by the embers in

Lucius's eyes.

A sly grin crept across his face as he hoisted his Jack Daniels bottle in the air, raising a toast to Leon from the masses. A striking Psychosomatic Slaughter patch adorned his chest in the promised spot on the vest.

Leon's heartbeat quickened at the sight of him, and he could not take his eyes off the patch. It was beautiful, stitched neatly around the edges, and the embroidery was so bright and new compared to the old, faded patches surrounding it. Leon saw a piece of himself with his idols, a peer among their sacred covenant.

As they ran through their set, Leon was energized by Lucius's presence, determined to prove himself worthy of the spot on his chest. Jimmy introduced the band at the end of their set at the clock chimed 11:58.

"Thank you for spending New Year's Eve with us tonight!" Jimmy huffed and puffed into the microphone, his long black hair stuck to the contours of his cheeks with sweat. He beamed at the screaming crowd as he got the signal. "Let's make 1984 the best fucking year! Chant it with me!"

The venue echoed with a chorus of voices as the countdown began. "3... 2...1...Happy New Year!"

Heather burst onto the stage and planted a spontaneous kiss on Jimmy while the rest of the band dove into the crowd to kiss the first woman they saw, sending the crowd into a frenzy. Leon ripped through an electrifying improvised solo to keep the energy soaring. Chuckling to himself, Leon thought, *let them have their fun. The hard work has paid off. This is our year.*

Lonnie ran his drumsticks down the hallway wall, and they ran back to the green room. Dallas hollered behind him as he skipped through the doorway. Leon slung the guitar off his shoulder, placing it on the guitar stand before joining the fun. Playfully punching Dallas in the shoulder, the two of them howled together. Cam joined in as Jimmy entered, his arm resting around Heather's neck. She stood back as Jimmy joined the wolf pack, the stench of sweat stinging her nose. Cheering them on, she poured a celebratory drink. A shadow sobered their high when it fell over their light, casting a mysterious air over the room.

"Oh shit." Dallas froze, looking at the massive figure leaning in the doorway. Lucius had to stoop to enter the room. Lonnie puffed up his chest, furrowing his brow as Jimmy stepped in front of Heather, pushing her behind him.

"Gentleman," Lucius cooed. "Fantastic show you put on."

"Thank you," Leon said. "I'm glad you were able to come tonight." He spoke those words with such sincerity.

The stranger's presence sent a surge of irritation through Jimmy's mind and body. He looked to Leon, who appeared to be comfortable with the newcomer. Dread punched Jimmy in the gut, unable to stand being in the same room as this person. Leon's eyes locked with his for a split second before darting around, revealing an emotion he couldn't grasp.

Guilt?

Jimmy's brain screamed warning signals as he observed the stranger, who barely looked human. The man's face appeared too perfect, and his size was almost too immense to be mortal. He resembled a painting, as if an artist had re-imagined a modern portrait of Lucifer on Earth. He emanated a black aura that absorbed virtue and integrity and twisted it, spitting it out in a deformed mass.

Lucius shifted his gaze to Jimmy, the smile on his face fading. He narrowed his eyes and subtly adjusted his stance, hooking his thumbs through his belt loops.

"Glad I could make it," he said, not taking his eyes off Jimmy, his eyes remaining dead as he pointed to the patch on his chest. "I'm a big fan."

Lucius's piercing green eyes hooked into Jimmy, causing the singer the most intense discomfort he had ever felt, tormenting him with the most dreadful emotions known to humanity. Despair, anguish, and murderous rage manifested as shaking hands. No one else seemed to notice the exchange in energy as if Jimmy and the Devil were the only two people in the room. Lucius relished in every tremble, sizing Jimmy up.

Something snapped inside Lucius, causing him to tear his gaze away and smile wide at the rest of the band. Immediate relief washed over Jimmy as the intense stare broke.

"I know for a fact this is going to be a big year for you boys." The Devil winked at Leon.

Jimmy wrapped Heather in his arms, running his fingers over her curled auburn bangs. They talked in hushed whispers, scanning their eyes up and down Lucius's body.

Dallas turned, discreetly pulling a pill out of the pocket on his bass strap. He stuck it under his tongue and wiped the base of his nose in an attempt to cover up the action. His eyes flashed to Lucius, who had caught him in the act. Guilt filled Dallas's eyes as he washed the pill down with some vodka. The colossal figure gave him a wink and a nod, the guilt vanishing.

One of Lonnie's spare cymbals crashed to the ground, averting everyone's attention away from Lucius.

"Thank you again," Leon said, taking the opportunity of the distraction.

"Watch that one," Lucius growled, gesturing toward Jimmy with his eyes. "He could make things difficult for you."

Leon nodded. *I know.*

"Listen," Lucius hushed his tone. Everyone else in the room fell away as if Lucius had hit a pause button on the entire party. "If I were you, I'd sign with Behemoth Records. I have a good feeling about them."

Deanna entered the room with a man as if on cue, her body physically recoiling upon seeing Lucius. She stumbled through an introduction and shared a confused glance with Lonnie, who was shocked to see Deanna's usually powerful bravado falter. Picking at the chipped red fingernail polish on her thumb, she shifted her weight as Lucius excused himself, never once breaking eye contact.

Deanna stood to her full height, rolling her shoulders back as she blossomed back into the dominating presence they were all used to. She cleansed her lungs with a fresh breath, clearing her throat.

"Guys," she beamed. "I want you to meet Rodger Andrews from Behemoth Records."

III

PART THREE: Sacrificial Lamb

Beginning in 1984

21

Sign Your Name In Blood

Rodger Andrews: a man of undeniable confidence. He could walk into a room and instantly command the attention of everyone there without uttering a single word. He exuded effortless coolness and a commanding aura. It came off as condescending—he knew that, and he didn't care. His confidence was well-earned, and with some major clients under his belt, he geared up to add Psychosomatic Slaughter to his impressive roster.

He wore a gold hoop in his nose, which shone off his smooth mahogany skin. Even under the meeting room lights, it looked airbrushed. Red strands wove through the inky dreadlocks thrown over his shoulder.

Gold and platinum albums lined the walls, and the band surveyed the lineup of clients with whom they were now peers. Stars filled their eyes as they scanned the framed records. They settled into oversized leather chairs around an equally oversized wooden table, shining as brightly as the awards adorning every square inch of the room. Rodger rattled off his pitch to the band from his place at the head of the table.

For the first time in meeting with an A&R rep, Rodger Andrews was the only one who truly understood the band. Instead of trying to change them, he appreciated and embraced the darkness of their lyrics and heavy instrumentals—those elements fueled their image. He took them for what they were: a breath of fresh air on the scene.

"I love the aesthetic that you guys have. It's edgy. It's grungy. It's dangerous with leather and decadence. It's Gothic, which means we could do a lot in terms of imagery. The music videos, the album cover, the marketing—we could lean into that Gothic metal energy and shock people with something they haven't seen before, going beyond bands like Sabbath." He turned his attention to the individual members of the band, giving them each a stroke to their ego. This tactic always worked well for him; it got him the gold records on the wall, special thanks in the liner notes, and an impressive contact list filled with connections to the dark underbelly of the industry that he liked to indulge in. Rodger was an expert at buttering up the talent. He could make them melt into putty in his hands.

"The Cliff Burton look on Lonnie perfectly offsets Dallas's theatrics on stage. We've got the yin and yang of understated and dramatic," Rodger said. Lonnie scoffed in response. "I'm serious. This whole band is a match made in heaven."

"You're saying all the right things," Dallas teased.

"You were able to deliver a captivating performance that left the audience spellbound on New Year's Eve," Rodger said. "And that was in a small venue. I've never seen anything like it. Imagine that same energy in a stadium."

Rodger turned his attention to Leon, his eyes darkening as a wicked smile contorted his features.

"You're a hellhound," he said, narrowing his eyes at the guitarist. "You have this animalistic energy and unbridled passion that lets you shred the guitar like prey, like a raging rock demon ready to take on the world. It's genius." He paused, waiting for a response from Leon. One never came. The guitarist sat stone-faced, unfazed by the flattery. He kept his yellow-green eyes fixed on the man at the head of the table, his pupils expanding like a cat ready to pounce. Leon would not be a mouse in this game.

"Look," Rodger leaned forward, resting his elbows on the table. His fingers interlaced, forming a triangle under his chin. "I don't want to change you or make you more marketable. I don't want to make you more glam or metal or this or that. What you have is something special that can't be formulated by a marketing team. It's rare, and I have no interest in messing with perfection. That's not my job. My job is to give you the tools to create a badass record.

We will need to find a producer, a studio for recording, a manager—"

"I will continue to be the band's manager," Deanna interjected. Rodger raised his right eyebrow, scanning the band for objections. He was sure they would come, but they didn't. He scoffed, studying all of their faces.

"Is that what you all want? You'll need someone who can handle the big time, and I don't know that this," he hesitated. "This *woman* can handle the...pressure."

"She's kept us out of trouble so far. On paper, our noses are clean," Dallas's mouth curled in a sly expression.

"She can handle us," Lonnie sneered. "Better than any man could."

Deanna shifted her eyes down and pursed her thin lips into a closed-mouth smile.

"Thanks, hon," she said in a soft, sweet voice. She turned to Roger, wiping the smile off her face as her voice turned cold.

"I am the manager for Psychosomatic Slaughter," she reiterated slowly and evenly. "I've gotten them where they are, and I will *continue* to get them to where they need to be. Understood?"

Rodger looked to Jimmy, his last hope of sense and sanity in this motley lineup.

"You heard the lady," he shrugged, looking Rodger in the eye with indignation. "She's our manager. End of story."

Deanna sucked in her cheeks, smiling at her victory. She cocked her head to Rodger, raising her brows in defiance.

"I'm looking forward to working with you, Rodger."

"Well, alright then," Rodger conceded, the corners of his lips turning down in an impressed expression. "Let's make them the bad boys of rock and roll."

* * *

Leon buzzed with excitement on the drive home from Behemoth Records. This opportunity became possible thanks to him—thanks to Lucius. Between the lyrics he belted on the radio, his voice croaking over Bon Scott's, he praised his savior. He didn't even care that he sounded like dying roadkill when he sang; he was too busy basking in his win and hailing Satan to care.

As he shifted into park in front of his apartment, Leon turned his key and killed the engine. He took a moment to drink in the dilapidated building, marveling at the unexpected beauty hidden within its worn walls. Once the money began flowing and Lucius held up his end of the deal, he would bid farewell to this place. It was within those walls that Psychosomatic Slaughter was born, and it would always hold a special place in his heart. That apartment, with all its flaws and imperfections, would forever be sacred ground to him.

Leon sensed a familiar energy emanating from inside his apartment as he climbed the stairs to his door. He stilled on the stairs, pausing as he swayed on the rotting wood, listening for something or someone. Leon was met with silence but could feel a tingling throughout his body. Blood surged through the vein that Lucius drank from. The emptiness inside where his soul used to be burned with euphoria. A warm, boozy smell filled his nose; the notes of vanilla, tobacco, and pure sex intoxicated him. His heart pounded as he hastened his steps.

Swinging open the door, he found Lucius comfortably seated on his couch. The worn leather enveloped his large body, and the wooden frame creaked under the pressure of his immense weight as he stood. With a proud smile, Lucius opened his arms and greeted Leon as he stepped inside.

"It's done!" Lucius boomed, proudly holding Leon by the shoulders.

"It's not done yet," Leon said humbly. "We still have all the paperwork to sign and hoops to jump through, but it's as good as done." He took a deep breath, the sigh making him feel free. "Thank you, Lucius."

Lucius held his hand up, cutting Leon off. "No need to thank me. You paid for a service. You are just reaping the benefits of your payment."

Something lurking behind Lucius drew Leon's attention away from his savior. A decently large object shrouded in a sheet stood propped up against Stevie's enclosure. The serpent slithered itself into a writhing coil at the corner, looking over the gift as if on guard. It flicked its tongue, winding its head to watch its owner as Leon noticed the present.

Leon furrowed his brow and craned his neck to catch a better glimpse at the mysterious gift. Lucius casually glanced over his shoulder, pretending to be unaware of the intrigue.

"Ah!" Lucius strode across the room in two fluid movements. "How could I forget? I have a little something for you."

Lucius lifted the gift, which was objectively small in his massive hands, and unveiled the most exquisite instrument Leon had ever laid eyes on. The guitarist's breath escaped him as his eyes fell over a vintage 1958 Gibson Gold Top. A rare gem in the world of guitars, and it was now his, a treasure beyond compare.

Leon always played a Les Paul copy because all of his idols—Frank Zappa, Jimmy Page, and Randy Rhodes—played that guitar. Now, he finally has a real one of his own. He took in the finely etched lettering on the stock, spelling out "Gibson" in curling, metallic letters. The guitar was a masterpiece, with a flawless golden finish that shimmered in the light. Lucius handed him the instrument, letting the heavy weight of the mahogany body drop into his hands. Leon ran his fingers over the finish, with faint tiger strips on the body, making it look like an open flame.

"I—I don't know what to say," Leon said, barely above a whisper. "Thank you, Lucius."

"You can't make a record without the proper equipment. You need to sound as good as you can. This music will be played throughout generations. I wouldn't let you be immortalized with a shitty guitar. Go ahead, try it out."

Leon secured his tried-and-true strap on the guitar, tenderly slinging it over his shoulder. He felt the guitar's weight—the body was a much more solid instrument than he was used to. He imagined this is how Robert Johnson felt at the crossroads with his prized acoustic. Plugging the guitar into the amp, it buzzed to life with a hum. A chill ran down his spine as he strummed the Devil's Triad. The tone of the guitar was so rich, so warm. A full-bodied sound reverberated out of the amp as Leon ran a couple of scales, the guitar perfectly in tune. For as long as he played the instrument, Leon never once had to tune it. He ran through his "Conjure Me Up" solo and was dumbfounded by how incredible his song sounded on a real Gibson. The guitar didn't only enhance his music. It transformed it, infusing every note and chord with its rich, warm tone. When played, it became an extension of his own body, a replacement for his soul to make him whole.

"Lucius, this is just too much."

"Your soul," Lucius said, touching Leon's shoulders, "was golden. You earned this."

* * *

Behemoth Records signed Psychosomatic Slaughter to a worldwide record deal. Deanna hired an attorney to draft the contracts, and after completing all the necessary legal procedures, they each received a significant advance— more money than they ever had.

Upgrading their instruments and equipment became their initial priority, although naturally, they wasted a chunk of the money on alcohol, drugs, and tattoos.

Jimmy gave his parents a portion of his advance as a token of gratitude for their support. They fought him over it at first, but they could see that this gift meant a lot to him. Leon couldn't fathom why Jimmy would feel the need to give his money away. It was Leon's hard work that put the money in his hands. Rage filled his heart as he watched it get squandered and given away.

After a relentless quest, Jimmy finally found the perfect vintage Art Deco ring for Heather. The emerald-cut center diamond, flanked by baguette-cut diamonds tapering into the band, reminded him of her. Classic and timeless, it retained its charm even after decades. He envisioned a future with her, where every line on her face and every strand of gray hair would only enhance her beauty. It symbolized their love, and he eagerly anticipated the moment she would wear it.

Struggling with his demons, Dallas cashed his portion of the check and stashed it inside his snakeskin boot. He always kept it strapped to his ankle, not trusting it to be off his person. A chunk of the money went to clothing, threads he could wear on stage. Velvet, satin, elaborate embroidery—all got paired with leather. Dallas loved the texture of his clothes; the sensation of touch was so important to him. He loved the feeling of fabric, like how he loved the feeling of getting high. He would slink away, his bandmates none the wiser, to buy drugs, popping any pill that he could get his hands on and washing it down with a cocktail of cocaine and Jack Daniels. It became customary for Dallas to stumble into rehearsal with sallow skin and bloodshot eyes.

Bruce's warning rang through his head on a loop. Every time he would begin to hear the words repeating again, he would take another pill to dull the memory until his mind was silent. That memory had become more of a demon than the drugs.

22

Hell's God

It took two months after signing to find a producer everyone could agree on. They recorded demos with producer after producer before finally adding Steve Wilak to the team. Steve, a creative at heart, took Psychosomatic Slaughter's sound and elevated it without stripping the essence of what made them authentic and raw.

Steve spent months with the band, each member pouring their heart and soul into recording every single demo, trying to work out the perfect track list for the first album, which they titled *Hell's God*. The title came from Leon, yet another sneaky tribute to the driving force behind their eminent success, much to Jimmy's dismay.

Leon became extremely hard to be around, but it wasn't necessarily anything he did or said. It was his energy. Being around him made people shift in their seats, even in the happiest moments. Feelings of discomfort clouded the band's celebration of getting their big break. He lowered the vibration into a low, rumbling feeling of dread. He drained the joy from the room, creating an unsettling feeling deep within. It was as if he were a dark shadow, a black hole sucking in and devouring any form of light, cheerfulness, or laughter.

Leon became an energy vampire, operating at the lowest of frequencies.

Deanna walked around on eggshells to avoid disturbing the band's fragile equilibrium. Cam, Dallas, and Lonnie were able to record a clean backing track for each of the songs that they were considering for the album. On those days, the band was on fire. The energy pulsed through the air as the instruments filled the live room with reverberating sounds that resonated through the soles of their feet. They recorded pure, chest-vibrating rock and roll.

Leon's dedication to perfection took its toll on the band. During his days in the studio, he would record solo, making the techs record the songs verse by verse, breaking up the recording of each song. Every note that he played oozed charisma, never letting himself fall into the routine of playing the same song he'd been playing night after night on the Strip. He would improvise a little with each take, controlling the takes that were used in the final cut of the song. These days in the studio were tedious, but the days blocked for vocal recordings were Hell on Earth.

The energy in the recording studio was palpable, and Leon's darkness wormed its way into their sessions like a PK manifestation. If things didn't go his way, playbacks would sound warped. Takes wouldn't be recorded despite the rolling tape. Jimmy doubled over while recording a ballad he wanted to include on the album, a song that Leon couldn't bare to listen to. The guitarist would only allow for one cheesy love song on the album, not two. The phantom pain shot through the singer's chest, ending the session abruptly. The idea to add the song was scrapped, and Jimmy never had chest pains again.

Jimmy loved the band to its core—he loved their songs, the deeper structure of each one, and their melodies. He would die for his band; the lineup had become his family. Their appearance was distinctive, their energy unmatched, but their branding told a different story than he wanted to tell. The Satanic imagery made him feel sick to his stomach.

As they devised their tracklist, Jimmy became increasingly vocal about his dissatisfaction with the album's direction. Foreboding took up residence in his gut, growing at the thought of the band walking into the mouth of corruption. Of evil. He worried that this album would be their mark of the beast.

"Don't you think this will turn people off?" Jimmy yanked off his headphones and addressed the control room through the microphone. He stared at Leon through the glass wall that separated the live room from the control room. The guitarist sat with his elbows firmly planted on the table, his fingers steepled in front of his deadpan face. Neither of them broke eye contact, but Leon moved slowly to push the intercom button. His voice filled the room with a *click*.

"No," Leon said plainly.

"Well, it turns me off," Jimmy snapped back, throwing the headphones onto the ground. The spiraled cord wrapped around the mic stand, making it wobble. Jimmy didn't bother to steady the equipment.

"Here we fucking go," Lonnie mumbled under his breath, getting up to sit in the lobby to get away from the confrontation that was bound to ensue. Dallas and Cam followed suit, trading their chance to weigh in on the direction of the album for peace and quiet.

"It goes against what I believe in to sing songs like this. "Conjure Me Up" is a staple. It's our rhapsody, we need it. *Hell's God* is an edgy title. I understand that we need an image and we need to brand ourselves. I get that. What I don't get is why we need songs like "Beelzebub" and "Disciples of Hell" on here. For Christ's sake, Leon, why does every song on the album have to be about drugs or the occult?"

"Give it up, Jimmy," Leon growled. "You have your stupid fucking ballad on the track list. What more do you want."

"That's not the point," Jimmy roared, exacerbated. "Don't you think it's a little too much? Let's write about something else. Life. Parties. Sex. *Anything* else."

"No." Leon's monotone voice disconnected him from the conversation as he stared at Jimmy with a disassociated expression. "No," he repeated, taking his finger off the intercom, punctuating the verdict with a click.

Jimmy held his gaze, fury blazing in his eyes as he stormed out of the studio. He whipped the door open and bounded through the control room without looking in Leon's direction. Leon stared straight ahead at the now empty live room, the eyes in his reflection looking back at him from the mirrored glass. He leaned forward, returning his fingers to the steepled position in front of his lips. "He'll come around," he said to an empty room.

Cam jumped when he heard the door slam. Jimmy grabbed him by the shoulder and dragged him out the front door. He stopped, letting go of Cam's muscular body to put a cigarette between his lips.

"Am I the one being difficult, Cam?" Jimmy repeatedly flicked the lighter, frustrated at Leon and at the lighter that wouldn't give him a flame. He gave up, pulling the unlit cigarette out of his mouth. The sun was so bright in his eyes, so jarring from the dim hole that was the recording studio. "You're a rational guy. Hell, you're the most grounded person in this band. Tell me the truth. Am I overreacting?"

Cam's mouth tightened into a thin line. He pulled out his lighter and flicked it once, holding the flame out to Jimmy. The guitarist considered his words while Jimmy exhaled a plume of smoke.

"Think of it like a movie," he said slowly, the metaphor coming together as he spoke. "We all have a role to play."

The corners of his mouth turned up, waiting for it to click for Jimmy.

"Think of Gene Simmons," Cam reasoned. "On stage with KISS, he is the Demon," Cam put up a set of Devil horns and waggled his tongue around. "Offstage, he's just plain ole' Gene Simmons. On stage with Psychosomatic Slaughter, we are all playing a role. But you're still Jimmy Ballard at the end of the day."

Jimmy lowered his eyes, took a long drag, and threw the cigarette to the ground, snuffing it out with his boot. Shifting his weight, he gazed up at Cam. His one eye was squinted to shield from the sun, causing his lip to curl. Jimmy nodded, bumping his fist against Cam's muscular peck. "Alright," he murmured. "I can do that."

Cam clapped him on the arm, the corners of his lips turning up as he puckered his lips out. "Thatta boy."

Dallas and Lonnie sat on the couch in the lobby. Jimmy and Cam were still outside, and Leon remained holed up in the studio, either too proud or too ignorant to come out. Lonnie leaned back on the couch, spreading his knees apart as he stretched.

"We're never gonna finish this fucking record," he sighed, looking to Dallas

215

to commiserate. Dallas lounged on the other side of the couch, his boot heel digging into the cushion as he propped his chin up with his knee. His eyes were fixed on the dirty baseboard across the room, starting off in a disassociated trance. Picking his head up off the back of the couch, Lonnie took a hard look at Dallas.

"You okay?" he asked, laying his head back down facing Dallas. The bassist didn't move. Instead, he took a deep breath.

"Yeah." His chin didn't move from his knee.

"Are you sure?" Lonnie bounced his leg with the ball of his foot. "You've seemed off lately."

Dallas pivoted his head to look at the drummer, leaning away from him to rest his back on the arm of the couch. "I don't know," he crossed his arms. "I've just been thinking about the séance and..."

Lonnie let the silence hang in the air, waiting to see if Dallas would finish his sentence. When he didn't, he clucked his tongue. "Are you still upset with what Leon said? Shit, man, that was months ago. No one cares about that."

"I care about that," Dallas snapped. His eyes softened, looking at the drummer's reddened face. "But no, I'm not upset about that. It's not what was said. It's who said it."

The plastic faux leather of the couch squeaked as Dallas readjusted. He looked up, finding understanding in Lonnie's eyes.

"That was Bruce. There is no doubt in my mind that that was my brother. And since then, I've thought about him a lot. I was always the kid brother who would get in his way. I had to do everything he did. Hell, that's why I play bass. He hated it, mostly because everything he taught me I did better. I just wanted to be like him so bad. Fuck, even this jacket is his." Dallas scoffed at himself as he rubbed a knuckle between his eyebrows. "I mean, was his."

Lonnie sat frozen on the couch, not sure what to say. He had never been good with emotions or conflict. In his mind, emotions belonged in a box. You put them away and store them in the back of your mind. If you do that, you never have to open that box again and feel pain, anger, or sadness. You put the feeling away so you don't have to deal with it.

"I miss him and I hate that because now, I realize he wasn't a good person," Dallas said, rubbing at one of the patches sewn onto the worn denim of Bruce's jacket. "He was mean, and he was a bully. Heroin controlled his life. Drugs made him into someone that I didn't know anymore. At the end, I could barely recognize him. And now that I'm older, and we are making a record, and we're on top of the world, I still find myself wanting to be like my brother. And that scares me."

Dallas's eyes looked dull, like the light had taken a vacation. His spark smothered under the weight of his brother's ghostly thumb. The black rimming his eyelashes made them look even duller. They were bloodshot, the veins feathering into the whites in his eyes.

"Dallas—"

"It's everywhere," Dallas said in a voice merely above a whisper. The muscles in the lower part of his eyes pinched, making his eyes look small and deranged. "I can get it everywhere. I just want to see what it's like. What is so good that you feel the need to die for it—"

Jimmy and Cam came back in, re-energized from their time in the sun. The sound of the opening door cut off Dallas's sentence. The bassist jumped, scrambling to look over his shoulder at his bandmates.

"Let's make a record," Jimmy beamed, passing the guys on the couch, oblivious to the conversation that had been in progress. Dallas got up to follow them back in, but Lonnie hesitated. The drummer swallowed his anger, the only emotion he knew how to handle, and reached out for Dallas's shoulder. His hand rested gently on the bassist, even though what he really wanted to do was shake him out of this funk, to shake the idea of heroin out of his head. Lonnie opened his mouth to speak but was interrupted by Dallas shrugging off his hand and walking right by him back into the studio.

Day after day, they inched toward the finish line. After months of built-up tensions and creative differences, they finally settled on a track listing.

1. Conjure Me Up

2. The Hanged Man
3. Sweet Nothings
4. Queen of Destruction
5. White Horse
6. Beelzebub
7. Jack in the Box
8. Crying Wolf
9. Shire on Fire
10. Walking on Water (acoustic)
11. Disciples of Hell

Behemoth Records was at its wit's end with Psychosomatic Slaughter, but their persistence paid off on March 10, 1985, with the release of *Hell's God*.

The "Conjure Me Up" music video hit number one on the charts upon its release on MTV in May of 1985. Unlike the production for the album, the making of the music video went off without a hitch. Dallas and Jimmy suggested incorporating Heather into the music video as a dancer. She danced in the wings at every show, her movements so feminine and graceful. The way she moved was Gothic, so fluid and whimsical. Lisa dressed her up in layers of black lace and satin, painting her lips a deep mulberry color a few shades darker than her auburn hair. The mix of fabrics moved with her as she danced through a graveyard while hooded occultists chanted the backup vocals. Jimmy stood backlit with light surrounding him, carving out the sharp contours of his face as they sang. In a hauntingly beautiful scene, Leon took center stage in the mausoleum to play his solo while the rest of the band played their song amidst the eerie woods that encircled the graveyard. The video skyrocketed the band overnight, getting requested for play daily. "Conjure Me Up" climbed to number two on the Hot 100 chart the week of the music video release.

* * *

In 1986, Psychosomatic Slaughter geared up for an epic tour of the United

States, kicking off at the iconic The Ritz in New York City before rocking the stage at CBGB. Lonnie was ecstatic to perform at these legendary venues, especially CBGB. The band had lined up some major gigs at famous venues, including The Fillmore in Philadelphia, Grande Ballroom in Detroit, and First Avenue in Minnesota.

Before setting out on tour, Jimmy proposed to Heather, and she happily accepted. She packed up and traveled with them from city to city.

Dallas indulged in life on the road, taking advantage of his big hotel rooms and close vicinity to strip clubs to whore around, get high, and party the entire tour away. Night after night, he indulged in a cocktail of drugs, orgies, and rubbing boots with the dangerous vagrants that lived in the shadows, lurking in each city they played. The distractions made him feel good, dulling the pain that the séance left behind.

With major success comes money, the root of all evil. They could all see Dallas slipping down the slope of addiction, powerless to stop him. They watched as his teeth began to grey from smoking crystal, forced to turn a blind eye as he popped a pill to stop his hands from shaking. White powder rimmed the base of his nose before shows, needing an upper to turn on the performer that lay abused inside his body. He turned a deaf ear to everyone. They all indulged, why did the issue only involve him?

Only Leon knew that Dallas had developed a taste for heroin. Curiosity got the best of the bassist, scoring an ounce during the recording of the album after his conversation with Lonnie. He kept it strapped to his boot, trying to prove to himself that he could break the family curse, but Bruce's voice wore him down. *You're just like me, Dally. You're weak.* Leon's only priority was to ensure he had enough smack to function like a human being and play bass.

Dallas's favorite mistress cost him a pretty penny, but the way she made him feel was well worth the hefty price tag. She knew her worth, and he knew that she was bad news, for she had destroyed the hearts of many men like him. He wasn't the first victim, and he certainly wasn't the last. She was a heartbreaker. A homewrecker. A destructive little minx, seducing man after man.

Dallas knew that she would lead him to destruction, but he didn't care—he had an appetite for it. A longing for numbness. He needed her now, his addiction to her raged beyond rationality. Being without her made the sun too bright and his stomach sick. He didn't just love her; he was in love with her—in the trenches. The withdrawal from her would leave him feverish and sweaty, but he loved everything about her so thoroughly that he came to love the pain. At least she was making him feel.

Every day, he would look forward to the preparation—the foreplay to his pleasure. He would twist the needle onto the barrel of his syringe, making sure it was secure and tight. He relished the sound of the metallic flick of the lighter igniting beneath his spoon. His spine tingled as the drug sizzled as it warmed, melting into a bubbly pool, ready to be sucked up. Dallas's vein bulged, pulsing under the strain of the band secured onto his bicep. Pulling the band taught with his teeth, he kept the tension, watching as the needle impressed against his skin. The skin dimpled around the tip, tinted blue from the veins running below. Exhaling through his teeth as he pierced the skin, he watched the length of the needle disappear into his arm. He was entranced by the feeling of her swimming through his bloodstream, pluming out of the needle as he pushed the plunger down.

* * *

The tour was a mega success, selling out shows across the country. In each city before the shows, Jimmy visited homeless shelters with bags of supplies and food he bought from local stores, hauling in armfuls with Heather. He'd listen to their stories and even invite them to the shows if they were up for it. Leon hated him for it. It's just like Jimmy to be such a goddamned martyr, acting like such a good guy. He wished that Jimmy could indulge and have fun with the band. Instead, he holed himself up with his perfect little wife-to-be, giving out charity as if he were better than Leon. It got old, especially when those little acts of kindness began making headlines and being a topic of discussion in interviews. Everyone wanted to know about the hard rock hottie with a heart of gold. Leon raked his fingers across his jeans during these interviews, channeling all of his rage into gnarling his fingertips every time precious seconds of an interview were wasted on Jimmy's kindness. They were supposed to be talking about their music, not Jimmy's Jesus act.

During their stints on the road, it became harder and harder for Dallas to find privacy for his torrid love affair. The tour bus offered no place of solace; he had no place to slink away to get high in the shadows of shame. Lonnie closely observed Dallas as insomnia consumed his nights, noting the bloodshot eyes that accompanied the sleeplessness. He noticed Dallas's constant need to wipe his sweaty palms on his clothing and the frequency with which he wiped away blood from his nose.

* * *

After returning to Los Angeles, they dove into crafting an EP while eagerly awaiting their upcoming European tour, which kicked off in England in March 1987. Their faces graced the covers of Rolling Stone, Kerrang!, and CREEM Magazine. Their album soared to platinum status, solidifying its place as the most successful debut rock album of all time.

In the midst of all of the success, Leon bought a home in Los Angeles. Saying goodbye to his apartment was bittersweet, but the house was too perfect to pass up. Despite its unsettling history, including previous owners with eclectic renovation tastes and a 1930s murder on the books, he felt at home the second he walked through the front door. The house had an eerie charm that intrigued him. No one except for him was allowed in this sacred space, his Devil's den, especially after the séance incident. This rule didn't need enforcement; it was an unspoken rule that Leon extended no invitations, which was okay because no one wanted to be there.

Surrounded by his taxidermy and oddities collection, Leon felt most at ease spending time alone despite the occasional presence of lingering ghosts. The day that he signed the lease, he hunted down a pair of stuffed ducks dressed in Victorian clothing. Teenage Leon would be ecstatic to know that he finally possessed his very own set of ducks, among the other spoils that came with being a rock star. Yet, for him, Lucius's company was all he needed to stave off the loneliness.

Leon poured his heart and soul into creating the next musical masterpiece as he sat with his guitar. Despite the thrill of life on the road and the adoration of his fans, he couldn't shake the feeling of fleeting success. The thought of whether they had hit the big time too quickly gnawed at him. Would he spend the rest of his days trying to surpass his first album? Had he sacrificed everything for this? Surely, there had to be more to it all.

23

The May Queen

"You gave me your soul. I gave you success. What more could you possibly want?" Lucius lounged on Leon's dark purple Victorian couch, his large arms draped over the ornately carved wood that framed the back. The furniture groaned under the weight of the massive man, loudly protesting as he shifted his weight to rest his ankle on his knee.

"I want more," Leon growled, pacing before him. His motorcycle boots thwacked dully against the shag carpet. Lucius smiled, running his hands over the velvet upholstery as he watched Leon unravel. "I don't want to fizzle out. For our second album, we need to exceed our current level of success. Anything less will be a failure. I won't be a failure. I will *not* fizzle out."

"Then you're going to have to give me more." Lucius leaned forward, wrapping his fingers around the wine bottle sitting on the coffee table. Bringing it to his lips, he took a long sip. Wine hung on his lips like blood. Lucius licked it away, looking like a wolf about to lunge on its prey.

"Anything," Leon sighed, his shoulders relaxing. He took a step back, his eyes fixed on Lucius, and knelt before the purple couch. Lucius cast his eyes down to meet Leon's, sitting as still as a statue. The Devil rested the wine bottle on his knee and rapped the side of the glass bottle with his wolf's head ring. Leon held firm in his posture, reminiscent of a downtrodden churchgoer, kneeling before the cross, pleading on their knees before a statue of The Virgin Mary. Lucius appeared quite statuesque, with his marble skin and long black hair, as Leon, in a desperate bid, pleaded for salvation from the only entity who could save him. "What do you want?"

"Well..." Lucius hesitated, rolling his neck to the side. The leather jacket squeaked as Lucius crossed his arms over his broad chest, exuding a confidence that was more than only arrogance; it was a display of power. He looked at Leon out of the corner of his eye, a smirk playing on his lips. *Cocky son of a bitch.* "Your soul is already mine. You have nothing left to give."

Leon snapped his eyes shut. His jaw clenched in a visible display of frustration at the mind games ensnaring him. The emotion pouring out of Leon was so intense that it seemed to materialize as his own PK manifestation, like the one that plagued the recording process for *Hell's God*. Only this time, his personal poltergeist was no match for the entity sitting before him. The energy crackled in the air. A twinge of excitement flickered in Lucius's eyes as he watched Leon's face contort—he reveled in this game.

"Unless..." The weight of the looming request pressed down on Leon's shoulders.

"Unless?" Leon repeated, his voice betraying his uncertainty. "Unless what?"

"I can give you more, but then I need more. But you have nothing else to give. So you need to take."

Leon pondered this. "Take?"

"Take." Lucius's eyes darkened, his green irises almost glowing. "You gave me your soul, and I gave you success. If you want more, you know what you need to do."

His words hung in the air, heavy with implication, as he got up, towering over the guitarist. He strode around the room, the tension so thick it was almost tangible. Reaching his hand out, he petted a mounted jackalope head, its glassy eyes seemingly following his every move.

"You mean I need to give you a sacrifice?" *Of course*, Leon thought—*the fee. I need to pay a fee. Nothing is free in this world.* His father's face flashed in his mind's eye. He winced at the thought, a cold shiver running down his spine.

Lucius grunted, tapping the jackalope's glass eye. The sound of his nail hitting the hard surface clinked as the Devil contemplated the word. "Sacrifice?" He turned down the corners of his mouth in heavy consideration, jerking his head and cocking it to one side. "No. An offering," he said, the inflection of his voice rising. He snapped, pointing to Leon with the tip of a finger gun. His unblinking eyes lit up. "You offered me the gift of your soul, and I offered you the gift of fame. Give me another soul, and I will give you more fame, wealth, and legacy." He paused, making sure Leon understood what was at stake. He stooped to look Leon directly in the eye. "Give me another soul, and I make you a legend."

"A virgin sacrifice?" Lucius's scoff took Leon aback.

"How very Puritan of you to assume I care about that. It's 1986, Leon, not 1686," Lucius laughed. His smile faded into a harsh line as he looked at Leon through deep-set eyes. "I don't care about the vessel. No—it does not matter if the vessel is tainted so long as the soul is pure and intact. As long as a soul drives that vessel, I will take that life force."

Leon soaked this in, nodding.

"That's all," Lucius said in falsetto, throwing the words out as he threw his hands up in a carefree gesture. The corners of his mouth turned up in a smile. "Don't you think that's fair?"

It's more than fair.

* * *

David Lee Roth served as one of Dallas Jacobson's idols. He looked up to Roth as a trailblazer—he admired his stage presence, the way the man made love to every camera he saw, and how he handled women on the road. It was said that David Lee Roth had a foolproof system for his exploits on tour: he would signal to his road crew that he found a woman that suited his fancy in the crowd. They would then hand-deliver an all-access pass to the chosen girl for use after the show.

Dallas adopted this little trick for himself. The roadies condoned this

225

unique arrangement because of the fact that they, too, held power in this situation. They were the keepers of the passes and the gold star stickers. If there was a golden star on the lucky lady's pass, it was a signal to Dallas that the roadie had the first go with her, and she was definitely up for anything.

For Dallas, this was his favorite kind of foreplay. Once his girl had her pass in hand, he would lock eyes and play to her all night until he could take her home after the show.

Psychosomatic Slaughter returned home for the holidays and revisited their favorite haunts. Leon mastered the secret signal and discreetly passed it to the roadie during a fateful performance at The Roxy. As a result, the roadie granted a special girl an exclusive all-access pass, courtesy of Leon Holman.

Dallas winked at Leon, indicating his appreciation of the guitarist's use of the gesture. Besides his music and getting high, there was nothing that Dallas loved more than watching his bandmates use the roadie trick. The bassist strutted his way across the stage to play beside Leon. He watched the roadie make his way through the crowd, a deliciously indecent smile spreading across his lips as the roadie passed by beautiful woman after beautiful woman. His face contorted when he saw the girl accept the pass, shooting Leon a perplexed expression. Dallas returned to the other side of the stage, not wanting to play to Leon's girl.

She stood alone in the third row, with long, mousy-brown hair. There was nothing special about her round, makeup-less face, albeit the thick eyebrows that framed her brown eyes. She was a plain girl, not necessarily ugly, merely unremarkable. To Dallas, she would have been only a blur, a face that he scanned over only to forget a second later.

Leon, however, thought she was absolutely perfect. Something intrigued him about her, a unique quality that set her apart. She stood alone, with no friends standing by her side, bobbing their heads together to the music. No man held her on his shoulders so she could get a better view of the band. There was no one to wait on her after the show. She was independent, free to make her own choices. She could come back with him, and no one in her life would ever know.

With the heat of the lights still radiating off his skin, Leon wiped his face with a towel, drying the gleaming sweat from his brows. His ginger hair frizzed at the root from sweat. He ran his hands through the length of his hair, waiting for her in the green room after the show. The roadie escorted the girl back, and her confidence caught him off guard. The moment she walked into the room, she broke into a smile with yellowed teeth. It was the most beautiful smile that Leon had ever seen with her pure, beautiful soul shining through that expression.

"There you are," he greeted her with a charming smile.

"Here I am," she chirped, touching her chin to her shoulder in a cutesy gesture as she kicked her foot behind her. Her black miniskirt showed off her long legs, and the fringe of her leather jacket swung as she moved.

"I'm Leon, it's nice to meet you." He held out his hand, feeling like the occasion called for a level of formality. Though she didn't know it, this was business. A pending transaction.

"I'm Pamela, it's nice to be here." Her hand was soft in his, her energy transferring to him, soaking into his skin. It tingled—playful and carefree. There was so much life in her eyes, an appreciation for it. He knew at that moment that she was the one.

"Are you up for a party?"

"I'm up for anything," she batted her eyes in a show of flirtation. *What a shame.* He could have liked her, but fate was not something he could change. Her story had been written. She had been put on this Earth for a reason, meant to be in that venue for that show, and was destined to receive Leon's invitation. She was destined to belong to Lucius.

Leaving the venue was a daze. Leon put forth his best mask, the most charming self that he could muster. He performed the song and dance well, putting her under his spell, whisking her to the car. Gently, he closed the passenger side door as she settled inside. There was precious cargo in there to be transported. She trusted him so easily, a shameful truth that the guitarist was grateful for. He was in control—in control of the car behind the wheel, of how her night would go and how her life would ultimately end. He was in control of her destiny, of her soul.

Leon rolled the windows down, letting the wind whip through his hair. Pamela stuck her head out the window like a dog, giggling into the breeze.

She settled back in her seat, took a pack of cigarettes from her jacket pocket, and lit one up. Resting her hand outside the window, she blew the smoke into the wind. Smoke trailed their drive as she puffed away while she hid a smile forming on her lips by taking a drag on the cigarette. Leon took a peek over at his prize.

"What are you smiling about?" he teased, mirroring her expression. She threw the cigarette out the open window and glanced over at him.

"I'm just havin' a lot of fun," she said, scrunching her nose at the end of her sentence. The sun had kissed her there, a hint of a sunburn spattered across her creamy complexion. She ran a hand over her bangs, self-conscious because she knew they were cut a little crooked, in a rare moment of vulnerability.

"I can't believe you picked me out of all those beautiful girls," she admitted.

"Why wouldn't I?" Leon asked, his tone casual and confident, not taking his eyes off the road. He placed his hand on her knee and slid it up her thigh.

"I don't know, it just feels like I got really lucky on my trip here," she said, her voice tinged with gratitude. If there was one thing that Pamela knew, it was that she was undesirable. Not in a self-loathing way, but a self-aware way. She was painfully normal. Not too thin, but not fat. Not beautiful, but not ugly. Outgoing, but never the sexy, daring, mysterious or magnetic girl that got her drinks paid for at the bar. Pamela just existed, never noticed in the crowd. Until now.

As she pondered this thought, Leon pondered on one word that she said: *trip.*

"First, I score tickets to see my favorite band. Now this? God's looking out for little 'ole Pammy."

"Someone sure is," he agreed, his tone reassuring.

As the perpetual outcast, Cam seized the opportunity to become the resident party host, a role that gave him a sense of importance and belonging. It had become a band tradition to head to Cam's after the local shows. He insisted on throwing the after party—it was as if Jay Gatsby joined a band

and offered guests sugar bowls full of cocaine. He didn't do any of it for himself; he did it for everybody else. Fans, other musicians, and groupies flooded the house with drunken sex, shared drugs, and a sense of never-ending youth. Cam was unfazed by the state of his house come morning or the fact that he got stuck with the booze tab. None of that mattered; he just wanted to be around people.

Pamela's eyes filled with wonder as Leon escorted her inside Cam's house. No one looked her way as if she were invisible. She stuck out as the obvious outsider, and yet…

The only person who seemed to notice Pamela was Jimmy. Heather laughed with Dallas's entourage when Leon and Pamela walked in, the singer's hands resting on her hips. Jimmy couldn't believe his eyes—Pamela wasn't Leon's usual type. He usually went for busty, leather-clad blondes with thigh-high boots. This girl was the complete opposite: her jacket swallowed her up, and her long legs were cut off at the ankles thanks to a choice of sensible shoes. Leon looked absolutely enamored by her, and Jimmy couldn't have been happier. This girl seemed like a breath of fresh air. He raised his drink in a silent salute to his friend as Leon led Pamela to the makeshift bar at the far end of the room. Leon shot his friend a wink before turning back to his lucky lady.

"Care for a drink?" He let go of her, and she settled into herself, accepting that she was one of the beautiful people for the night.

"I'll have what you're having."

"I like that," he nodded appreciatively, pouring her some bourbon. "Where are you from?" Leon handed her the glass, running his fingers along hers as she took it from his hand.

"The Midwest," she answered, not flinching as she swallowed the liquor. Leon narrowed his eyes, a smirk spreading across his lips.

"Can you be…a little more specific?"

"Indiana." She giggled, indulging him. "I used to live on a farm, actually. So I'm no stranger to getting a little down and dirty."

Her jaw went slack as Leon sucked on his teeth, a whisper of a laugh dancing on his lips. She scoffed at herself, tapping her finger against the rim of the cup in an attempt to let go of some of the embarrassment swimming in her body.

"I'm so sorry. I can't believe I just said that. Anyway, I took a couple of Greyhounds, slept in a couple of bus shacks, and backpacked the rest of the way here."

"By yourself?"

"I'm a big girl. I can take care of myself," she teased, her smile fading. The sting of loneliness burned deep in her heart. "Yeah, it's just me." She attempted to smile once more, but her lips only curled slightly as she released a deep sigh through her nose. "My dad's a drunk and is in and out of jail for this or that. My mom won't leave him even though he hits her, and I just said fuck it and left." She flushed and looked up at the ceiling as she took a shot of Jack Daniels. This girl could handle her liquor.

She is alone. She's perfect.

"I'm sorry," Leon said as he took a shot in solidarity, gently tapping it on the table before throwing it back. "I've lived that story too."

"Yeah," she said, distant. "It's okay. I've met some really cool people along the way." She winked at him. "But I'm all I've got."

"You can have me," Leon said, his eyes darkening.

"I am a lucky girl," she quipped. "I get to play groupie for the night."

"Play groupie," Leon snorted.

"Believe it or not, I usually don't do this," she nudged him playfully. "But I wasn't going to pass up the chance to see Psychosomatic Slaughter."

"And..." he gave her a wolfish expression. "You're not going to pass up the chance to fuck the guitarist, right?"

"Nope," she smiled, popping the 'p' in the word playfully. She bit her bottom lip, trying to hide a smile. "I mean, I'd prefer the singer, but you'll do."

Red rage flashed in Leon's eyes. Everyone always wanted Jimmy. *Jimmy fucking Ballard.* But he had to give it to her; she was quick. She had wit. And she also had a pure soul.

"I'm humbled," he said, grabbing her by the chin and pulling her into him. "What do you say we head back to my house?"

"I get to see your lair?" she flicked her eyes playfully across his face.

"Absolutely."

Leon bent the one rule he had for his house for her. Once in his lair, she barely looked around at all the glass eyes that perceived her from their mounts on the wall or at the collection of jarred specimens. Her undivided attention remained on Leon as she pushed him onto the velvet couch. Propping a foot on his knee, she raised her eyebrows and ran her tongue between her teeth. Leon pursed his lips to conceal a smirk, obliging her as he slowly unzipped her leather boots, one after the other. She guided Leon's knee to the side with her toe, spreading his legs apart to make room for herself. Lowering herself between his knees, Pamela ran her hands over his thighs, slithering up his body to run her tongue along his strong jawline. Delicately small hands fumbled with his belt buckle as she slid her tongue back down his body, snagging his nipple ring between her teeth.

Leon panted, he'd never been more aroused. It wasn't the way that her tongue rolled around his tip; it was the way that she looked up at him while doing it. Her eyes—the windows to the soul—burned with passion. Leon allowed himself to be seduced by her spirit, succumbing to the intensity of her soul, getting off on the fantasy of taking that fire for himself. For Lucius.

Pamela pulled back as she got him to the edge, running a finger over her lips with a teasing wink. Slipping off her skirt, she revealed a red thong hanging off of her wide hips. She looked so juicy—Leon wanted to take a bite and devour her right there. Pamela turned her back to him as she unclasped her lacy black bra. She playfully tossed it to the side and peeked over her shoulder, gathering her hair in an impromptu updo. Leon reeled from the torrid affair that he had just had with her soul, uninterested in the show she was putting on with her body until he saw *it*.

When she gathered her mousy hair in her hands, Leon laid eyes on the most fascinating piece of art that he had ever seen in his life. An anatomically correct heart adorned her back, spattering her pale skin with muted colors. He found himself under scrutiny by the eyes in the ventricles and valves of the organ. The amount of eyes was uncanny, transforming the heart into some kind of creature. One eye, directly in the center of the organ, bore into the hole where his soul should have been. It was larger than the rest, its unblinking stare keeping a protective watch over its host's body. The other eyes kept watch elsewhere. One swirled into the oblivion of hypnosis. The vertical slit that was a cat's eye stared fixated out of the right atrium. Another cried blood for the heartache that Pamela had endured throughout her lifetime. Some were rolling, and some were wary, but they all came together to make up one being. One organism.

"Don't move," Leon commanded in a low voice.

"Yes, sir," she simpered as she heard him shuffling around behind her.

He pulled out his Polaroid camera and asked her to pose for him. She obliged, her stomach twisting with butterflies. The thought of being remembered by Leon, the guitarist for her favorite band, made her want to cry with joy. The camera spit out photo after photo. Leon's favorite was of Pamela on her knees with her back to the camera, holding up her hair to show off a tattoo unlike anything he'd seen before. He caressed the inked skin, tracing its curves.

"This is exquisite," he crooned, biting the tip of her ear.

"I'm glad you think so. I didn't get it for me to enjoy."

Fuck.

Leon throbbed, spinning her around and hoisting her up. She wrapped her legs around him as he brought her to the bed. He threw her down, running his tongue up her thigh and tasting her. He hoped that her blood would taste this good.

As he caressed her naked body, he thought of the soul living within, the life force swimming through her veins. He wrapped his hand around her throat, pushing her into the mattress. Her pulse quickened under his thumb, the vein in her neck bulging the tighter he squeezed, the life force thumping hard under the pressure.

She moaned in ecstasy, her back arching as he pumped into her. The harder he went, the tighter she squeezed, her legs hooked around his waist. He groaned with pleasure at each of her whimpers, seconds away from his climax, thinking about how the blood would flow down her breasts and into his mouth when he slit her throat.

The two of them lay in a pile of sheets and sweat when the deed was done and done again. Leon ran his hand over the curve of her waist, kissing her up her sternum to suck on her neck, right above the pulse. Her breasts glistened in the moonlight as she ran her fingertips over his shoulder blade. Drunk off of her, off of her life force, he tore himself away from her. *You will have her completely soon enough,* he reminded himself.

Leon opened the drawer to his bedside table and pulled out a joint, lighting it with a match. He relaxed at the sound of the sweet sizzle from the paper as he inhaled, letting the smoke fill his lungs.

"Can I tell you a secret?" Leon blew out the smoke, inspecting the joint between his fingers as he handed it to Pamela.

"Who am I going to tell?" she asked, taking a long, greedy puff. She rested an arm above her head, her breast lazily swaying with the movement.

"I want to see you again." Leon's eyes darkened, grabbing her gently by the chin and turning her head to look at him. Her wide-set eyes looked so innocent, freckles littering across the bridge of her sun-reddened nose. She narrowed her eyes, jutting her chin out of his hand.

"Am I your dirty little secret?" she smirked around the blunt, drawing in a drag.

"I just don't want to have to share you with Dallas," Leon lied, putting on his most convincing jealous act. Like Dallas would want her anyway. "If he got a look at you, it would be a done deal, and I don't share well."

She pretended to consider this, playfully pursing her lips and rolling her eyes to the ceiling. "Mmm, okay." Pamela rolled toward him and kissed him lazily on the lips, as if it were as natural as walking, putting one step in front of the other. It made her feel good, the idea of being wanted, even if she was just a groupie to him. Even if it was just sex. He wanted her, and she would take that attention, that faux display of love wherever she could get it.

Hunger roiled in Leon's groin. He began the clock in his head, a ticking countdown to the next night.

"Perfect." He kissed her neck, the exact spot that he planned to slit.

24

Unholy Communion

Days of rest became so few and far between as Psychosomatic Slaughter flourished in front of the eyes of the world. Booked and busy, the members of the band had little time to go off by themselves and play. In the little time he had, Leon gathered his supplies, burrowing them away for future use. He didn't know what he might need or what the mood might call for, so he bought it all: duct tape, wire, tarps, bags, rope, and even a handsaw that may come in handy.

As their schedules died down to celebrate the birth of Jesus Christ with their families, Leon prepared for a different kind of celebration—a rebirth. A communion with the first blood he was about to shed, a moment of great transformation for him.

Leon retreated into his lair, drawing all the curtains to shroud his preparations in secrecy. He hid away from the sun, shunning its rays as if he would turn to dust in the light of day. Nightfall would prove to be busy, and the night would be his ally. He rested, gathering all of his strength for the slaughter. Like a creature of the night, he prepared for his evening hunt, his late-night feed.

Leon, rising with the moon as the sun went to sleep, meticulously readied himself for the night ahead. He made his bed atop a plastic mattress protector. Various tools sat carefully arranged in his bathroom, and his athame lay poised on his bedside table. The golden chalice, spit-shined and cleaned, gleamed as Leon poured himself a glass of red wine. Leon toasted Lucius, his heart pounding with anticipation for the woman who would soon be at his door. He tossed back the wine with a hard swallow, his tongue lingering on the rim of the cup as the doorbell rang.

The chiming bell sent a tingle of excitement through his groin. He stood poised at the door, taking a moment to steady his shaking hands before swinging it open. He hadn't been this excited since Psychosomatic Slaughter's first show. Leon felt like a virgin again, filled with erotic anxiety.

The door opened, and there she stood, radiant in red. Her satin slip dress clung to her ample figure, hugging her in all of the right places. A vision in this color—how fitting it was for her to wear the color of blood. Of passion. She dressed the part so sweetly, convincing Leon that she knew what this night meant for them—for him.

He rested his arm on the door frame, holding a scarf in his free hand. The silk felt smooth in his hands; the black and red geometric pattern matched her dress perfectly.

"Wanna play?" Leon coaxed her as he pulled her into him.

"Yes, sir," she cooed, smiling salaciously. Her wide eyes drank him in as she held out her wrists for binding. He grabbed one, spinning her around to pin her arm behind her back. She squealed as he pressed her body against his.

"It's gonna be like that then?" she purred, rubbing her ass against his crotch. The silk allowed for fluid movements as she slid down his body. She felt him harden as she stood back up to her full height. He ran a finger beneath a spaghetti strap.

"That will come later. I'm just getting started." He breathed in her ear, pulling the blindfold out of his back pocket. Leon lowered it over her eyes, tying it carefully so as not to pull her hair. Running his fingers through it, he neatly arranged the strands around the scarf, draping a lock over her bare shoulder. Leon caressed her, giving her a false sense of kindness for her last moments alive.

He spun her around to face him, crashing his mouth into hers. Hoisting her up, she wrapped her legs around his waist, squeezing like a serpent. He carried her to the bedroom and lowered her onto the bed. Flicking off the thin straps holding her dress up, he ran his hands down the length of her body, bringing the dress with it. She wore nothing underneath, primed and ready for him. Picking up one of the hundreds of candles illuminating the room, he poured the hot wax onto her open thighs. She gasped, letting her hands explore her own body.

She sat up, running her hands on the sheets in front of him, searching for his body. Finding Leon stiff and pressing up against his pants, she ran her tongue along her lips as he felt for his zipper. As much as he wanted her to strip him down and submit to him, that's not why she was there.

Stay focused.

He grabbed her wrists, pinning her to the bed, and ran his tongue up the length of her torso, tasting the salty sweetness of her skin. Flipping her over, he pulled her arms behind her back. He began to tie her wrists to her ankles before stopping himself.

"May I?" he growled. After all, even monsters like vampires and demons need permission—he was not going to be an exception.

"Please do," she consented.

"Thank you," he smiled as he hog-tied her. With a final pull of the rope, he ran his fingers through her hair, toying with the blindfold's knot. He pulled on it gently, and the silk fell from her eyes. As her eyes adjusted to the dim candlelight, her smile faded when she realized they were not alone.

"Who is that?" she asked in a shaky voice. Looking at the enormous man standing in the corner, his menacing expression sending shivers down her spine. She wanted nothing more than to cover herself as every hair on her body stood on end, but she couldn't move. She tugged at her restraints, but Leon tied them well. The rope bore into her skin, burning as she fought.

The stranger in the corner appeared unquestionably feral. Rabid, chartreuse eyes stared at her through rouge strands of wild black hair. Leon stepped in front of her, her eyes falling to the athame in his hand. Struggling, she kicked and flailed, trying to loosen the ties around her limbs to set herself free, to no avail. Leon held his chalice in the other hand, circling the athame around the lip of the cup. The metallic sound grated in her ears.

"What the fuck are you doing?" she screeched like a banshee. Tears blurred her vision, turning the two men into rippling blobs. Crouching down, Leon reached out to stroke her face. She pulled away the best she could, twisting her neck in an unnatural position. Drool dribbled down her chin as she cried, her mouth frozen in an open, silent scream. "Why are you doing this?"

"I want to see the life fade from your eyes when I sacrifice you to Satan." Leon's mouth spread into a grin as he twirled the tip of the athame on his front tooth, his voice unsettlingly even.

Her eyes flickered with realization, tears spilling over as they darted back and forth between the two men. A guttural shriek rose in her body. The sound of her scream made her own blood run cold. He watched as she struggled to free herself, screaming and crying. He pooched his lower lip out in faux sympathy for her torture.

"Please, I'm not a virgin," she pleaded with the man. Her eyes widened, the whites completely encircling her irises, hoping that she had just discovered the loophole that could help her survive. She swiveled her head to look at Leon. "You know I'm not a virgin."

"Sweetheart," he singsonged with an air of condescension. "I don't care, and neither does he."

Her stomach sunk as the last glimmer of hope faded away. Snot ran into her mouth, and the salty taste mixed with the bile rising in her throat. She gagged on the eminent death staring her in the eyes.

Leon snickered as he climbed onto the bed and encircled her, putting a foot on each side of her body. Lowering his weight onto her, he constrained her, keeping her still. Her muscles grew tired with the added weight. She fought less and less before succumbing to fatigue. Gnarled sobs shook her body as she accepted her fate.

Leon leaned down, his face only an inch away from her tear-stained face. Crouching around her, he placed his hands on the footboard; his fists balled around his two ritual items. "He doesn't care about your body. It's just a vessel carrying the true prize. The purity of your soul is the only thing he cares about."

Leon caressed her face, his guitar-callused fingertips stroking her red cheeks. The stench of a hundred burning wicks and her own mess overpowered her—she had soiled herself. He jumped off the bed and squatted, resting his chin on the footboard. His normally green eyes looked almost yellow. He smiled at her with dead eyes.

"I'm sorry, I just wanted to look at you one more time. Are you ready?" he asked, widening his eyes as he got up and climbed back on the bed. Leon placed a foot on either side of her body, bouncing her helpless body as he found his footing. His thumb gently caressed her face, moving a strand of hair off her tear-stained cheek. He lowered himself so that his lips grazed the tip of her ear.

"See you in hell."

Leon yanked her head back, causing her to reflexively let out a gasping groan. He pulled her hair hard enough that he was able to look into her pleading eyes as he slashed her throat. Tears spilled out the outer corners of her eyes, her last expression one of betrayal, pain, and sadness. They quickly glazed over as Leon severed her windpipe, and the blood began to flow. He brought the chalice under the wound to catch the stream of her blood. The blood poured over it, spilling over the side of the cup and over his fingers. It coated his hands in hot, sticky liquid.

Lucius lunged at her, seizing her by the shoulders and holding her wound to his mouth as Leon held out the chalice to Lucius, who was sucking the blood directly from her throat. Leon let go of her hair, letting her head roll lazily onto her shoulder blade. Her corpse lay on the bed, crumpled and bloodless from Lucius's feast.

"To us," Leon toasted to Lucius over the body. He drank, feeding on her life essence, the energy of her soul. *Pure.*

The blood ran over his tongue, sweet like nectar. It was thick, coating his throat with her life force. He drank it greedily, needing more. More. Tilting the chalice, he sucked down as much blood as he could, gulping air loudly as the cup ran dry.

"Thank you for your contribution, my child," Lucius got up, taking the chalice from Leon. He ran his finger along the inside of the empty cup, collecting the rest of her blood, and stuck it in his mouth, slowly pulling it out, relishing the last taste of her essence. "Your transaction is complete."

Leon bowed his head to Lucius, the sweet taste of her blood still on his tongue. "Thank you, sir."

"Now," Lucius bellowed in a casual tone. "What to do with her." He enunciated each word, turning up the ends of the words in a questioning twist as if he were helping a child play a game.

Leon looked upon Pamela's shell. He crouched beside her face, stroking the hair off her cheekbones and throwing it onto the flat plane of her back. Her skin looked so beautiful in the candlelight, and her eyes remained frozen in her final look of fear.

"I want more of her." Leon's eyes moved over her body, scanning her flesh. The corners of his lips turned up, admiring his work.

"Then take it," Lucius commanded in a whisper, a sinister grin on his lips.

"I want to show you something, Lucius." Leon moved her nearly-decapitated head off of her back and untied her limbs. The plastic tarp under the sheet rustled as her arms fell to her sides and her feet fell into the pillow at the head of the bed. Leon ran the tip of his knife lightly along her spine, revealing her naked back and the tattoo painted there.

"It's beautiful," Lucius ran his fingers over the lines of ink that feathered into the creases and cells of her skin. "Such a shame that this art will go to waste."

He gave Leon a sly, suggestive look, indicating that he knew what Leon was planning. Leon narrowed his eyes and smirked in agreement. "You have a beautiful mind, Leon."

He ran his eyes over her body, choosing which tattoo he wanted to start with. Wanting to get a feel for the process, he picked up her lifeless arm and made an incision with his athame up the palm, gliding over the inside of the wrist. He carefully carved out a section of skin that was tattooed to look like an ornate gemstone bracelet. The knife knocked too far into one of the black lines, creating a sloppy and jagged edge. Leon didn't fret over this, he was glad he decided to practice first before doing the real piece. Handling it with care, he ran his fingers over the wet backside, feeling the residual blood on the underside of the layers of tissue. He pulled at it, pleasantly surprised with how durable the skin was. Stroking it one last time, he tossed it to the side. It was an ugly tattoo, nothing he wanted to immortalize.

The process was easy enough now that he had a feel for it. Leon wiped the athame on the comforter, cleaning it off to start on her back. He ran the tip of the blade from shoulder to shoulder, wedging the blade gently between her skin and fat. Tracing a rectangle across her back, he sliced into her, running the knife down the length of her body. The skin easily peeled off the fat as he ran his blade between her hide and the corn-like jelly.

A low vibration purred on his lips as Leon began to hum the tune of ABBA's "Slipping Through My Fingers." The song always made him so angry—the wallowing, the sadness that overpowered the delicate piano and string accompaniment. He had always ground his teeth together hearing the lyrics about a mother's love—it gave him a headache. He could never relate to the maternal lament, but it resonated with him now as he ran his fingertips against the smoothness of her skin, feeling the wet, bloody underside. *Did she have a mother missing her, reminiscing over her daughter's fleeting childhood?* He wondered as her skin slipped through his fingertips.

His insides warmed with a cozy sensation he had never experienced before. Leon let the patch of skin slip through his grip as he hummed, singing the words in his head. He would never lose her. Pamela's memory would be preserved, ensuring she would live on through all eternity because of him. She would continue through his legacy, through his greatness. Her sacrifice was for the music, the imprint that he would make. Her life force would live inside of him forever, fueling him. She could never be lost to time.

The sensation of running his fingers along the pores and the peach fuzz felt therapeutic. He understood why children clung to blankies—why they would rub the silky trim against their eyes to soothe themselves to sleep. It was calming, this little patch of skin. The inscribed eyes glared up at him, watching him trace their lash lines. He put a palm over the feathered ink, obstructing the eyes' view of him. Flipping the patch over, he patted the underside of the skin dry.

"What are you going to do with it?" Lucius's voice was heavy with interest.

"I have a book," Leon answered, still holding the piece of skin. "It's a personal grimoire. I've recorded rituals that I've done in there, the things we have done together. I've penned every single lyric in that book. It deserves a special cover."

"Beautiful," Lucius whispered, pride in his eyes.

He set down the skin and considered the body lying limp in front of him. Without the skin, he could see all of her muscles—every delicate knob of her vertebrae. He could see the white peaks of her shoulder blades. They glistened in the candlelight. When you peel back the skin, humans are just simply animals. Complex compositions of biological matter. Just...meat.

Tilting his head to the side, Leon extended the incision down her hip, running along her thigh. He peeled the skin away, her sustenance glistening. Cutting off a bit of her meat, he consumed his unholy communion. Lucius watched through darkened eyes, the tip of his tongue curling to touch his top lip as the corners of his mouth drew up in a feral smirk. He relished the taste of this moment for Leon.

The raw meat on Leon's tongue melted in his mouth as her juices mixed with his saliva. He consumed her, feeling more powerful with every bite. Her raw humanity, her power, seeped into his body. He would forever hold a piece of her inside himself, the memory of tasting her. Her body provided him with nourishment, her residual life force charging him like a battery. Leon became invincible, her strength becoming his. His being had been elevated, his feast opening up a new plane of reality. He could see more clearly, his sight turning almost bionic with every swallow. Like a ravenous animal, he clawed at her carcass, tearing away fistfuls of meat. He tore at them like a starving man, gluttonous.

Leon wished each of his bandmates would set their pride aside and join him. They needed this as much as he did. He knew they wouldn't, especially Jimmy. Oh, how he wished he could share this moment with them.

Dallas.

Poor Dallas—the weak link in the band. A slave to his addictions, slowly losing himself in the track marks that bruised his forearm. Leon had the opportunity to give his friend a gift, the chance to bask in this moment with him. He would share his power, turning Dallas's weakness into strength.

Leon flipped her over to find her mouth hanging limply open; the silent scream etched into a permanent expression of horror.

Perfect.

He wrenched her lower jaw to open her mouth more. The pressure on the skin drug the rest of her face down, her lower lash line pulling grotesquely away from her eyes. Leon ran his blade along her creamy cheeks, giving her a Glasgow grin. Tugging on her chin, her skin separated in clean lines on both sides of her face. He gave her chin a firm twist that completely separated her jaws. A crack reverberated in his ears; the communion had also enhanced his hearing. The combination of her power and his pure adrenaline created a lethal substance, an inhuman strength that coursed through his veins. He was on a high, one that drugs never were able to give him. She gave him a high that could never be topped—sweet, sweet Pamela.

He reached into her mouth with pliers and pulled out one of her molars. The roots ripped as he yanked it out, and he clutched the dingy yellow-stained tooth in his hand. Leon wrapped his fingers around it, anointing it with intentions for Dallas and enchanting it to do its duty. Setting it on the bedside table, he observed the teeth still intact in her gums, glancing between the extracted tooth and the hole it left in her mouth. Dallas really needed him—he needed her. He needed the rest.

Wrenching the pliers back into her mouth, Leon began to harvest the pearly jewels. The roots ripping as he tore each one out sounded like a pumpkin getting its seeds pulled out on Halloween. The roots hung out, shredded and useless, as he placed them in a pile. This treasure would be worth the price, worth the time. Satisfied with his endeavors, he left the teeth to dry.

Leon thumbed through the Polaroid photos, taking in the image of her naked body. The white bottom border of the square photo had a thumbprint of blood imprinted on it from Leon picking it up. "My Muse," he wrote beside the bloodstain. His muse would remain forever young. Time could never erase her, for her DNA now coursed through him. This legacy was hers, still alive beyond the veil into the abyss into the unknown with Lucius. Together, they would guide him to greatness.

Leon rolled her back over, observing the delicate structure of her body. It was pure poetry—the veins, muscles, and bones coming together to create perfect harmony. She looked more beautiful to him in death, her skin shed, than in life.

The beauty of the spine infatuated him. These delicate bones created the body's most important support system. So much trust, so much responsibility rested on these bones. If they could be trusted to support human existence, they could be trusted to support his surrogate soul.

Leon ran a wire through the vertebrae next to the spinal cord, beading each bone onto the wire. He pulled the wire through the last of the cervical bone in the vertebral column. A bit of nervous tissue from the spinal cord got pulled out with it. Leon pulled at, stretched, and balled it between his fingers to feel its wet, spongey texture. He wrapped the wire around the base of the spine, gingerly securing it around the pubic bone to keep the connection intact.

Severing the connection between her humerus and her scapula on both sides, he wrapped the wire coming out of the top of her vertebral column around her clavicles, reinforcing the section together. With a hefty grunt, he wrapped his fingers around the rib cage and hoisted the bones out. The remains were wet and heavy in his hands as goopy threads ripped and tore. He pulled the pelvis loose and hoisted out the entire section from her pelvis to her clavicles, connected by her reinforced spine. He held it above the crumpled shell of what was left of her gore and skin. Placing the bones on the bed beside her desecrated remains, he caressed the rows of ribs, sticky with tissue. Running his fingers between each one, he pulled out the muscle and tissue, relishing the slick texture of them on his skin. The organs were removed and tossed onto the heap of discarded skin and bones.

Once only the desired section of the skeleton remained, Leon prepared to sculpt his masterpiece from her bones. With a handsaw, he ground away at the rib cage, halving it vertically under the armpit. He pulled away the

243

top of the rib cage by the sternum, tossing it aside on the pile that used to be Pamela.

Leon marveled at the frame of shoulder caps, the clavicle still attached, leading down the vertebrae to the pelvis base. He always meant to buy a stand for his prized instrument, the apple of his eye. This would do. This would do, indeed.

Hail Satan for this sacred gift.

25

Rats

Blood stained the porcelain claw foot bathtub. Leon looked down upon the remains, mulling over what to do with her now that he'd moved her. Lucius leaned against the door frame, his thumbs resting in his belt loops as the smell of gore wafted through the room. He bounced the toe of his boot against the checkered tile floor, the chains on the boots jingling.

"Did you know, Leon, that rats are a lucky omen? They represent wealth. Prosperity," Lucius's eyes widened. "Excess."

"N—" Leon shook his head, interrupted by a small squeak. A brown rat sat perched on the pedestal sink. Its little nose crinkled as its nostrils flared, smelling the raw flesh and muscle laying in the bathtub for the taking.

Leon's eyes fixed on the rat, its every move captivating him. He turned to Lucius, who raised a knowing eyebrow. The rodent descended from the sink, its landing on the tile marked by a distinct *thwack.* It scurried across the floor to the bathtub, where it stood on its hind legs, stretching and sniffing. Lucius reached down and picked up the rat, gently placing it on the heap of Pamela's flesh, hair, and organs. He stroked the top of its head as it flicked its tail, taking in the feast it had been placed upon.

It decided to start with her eyeball, holding the optic nerve between its tiny pink paws as it took a bite out of her iris. Its sharp claws pierced through the cornea, creating little pinpricks through the filmy layer. The fleshy part of the eye squelched between its little teeth as it chewed.

Without warning, a small splash broke the tranquility of hearing the rodent's large teeth tearing away at creamy eye jelly. The water in the toilet rippled, and to Leon's astonishment, a second rat clawed its way up through the pipe. Another rat followed, emerging from the toilet bowl. They hit the floor with a wet splat, their paws slapping against the floor. Water dripped from their whiskers as they left wet trails leading to the bathtub.

The pitter-patter of twenty more rats resonated through the hallway, their fleshy toes smacking against the bathroom's black and white tiled floor. The house filled with the sound of a hundred rats, causing the walls to reverberate and the floors to vibrate. They scratched inside the walls, waiting their turn for the feast. Leon watched in wonder as they poured in. Lucius opened the window, and a chorus of squeaks filled the room. They greedily tore into Pamela's remains.

They piled in front of the tub, fighting each other for the chance to gorge themselves, climbing over each other's bodies. Their claws dug into faces, and they trampled tails that whipped wildly as they fought their way into the tub to eat away what was left of her jaw and chin. Red drips spilled out of their mouths as they ripped and tore at her flesh.

Gnawing on the chewiest pieces of her, rodents ate away at her fat. They nibbled at the rest of her skin, their teeth tearing at feathered ink that had aged since she got the little star tattoos at 16. The rats tore away at her lips as strings of skin hung from their mouths, the holes in her gums where her teeth once were looked like bottomless voids. Leon watched in awe as these rats ate the rest of the evidence, basking in choruses of squeaks and crunching teeth. It was so easy.

"I need you to do something tomorrow with me, Lucius."

"More than I've already done?" Lucius leaned against the pedestal sink that was stained with soap scum. "Greedy, greedy."

"It's just an errand," Leon quickly added, holding his hand out in a steady gesture. He noticed that his palms were stained pink from the blood, and he realized he had never washed his hands of her. He merely wiped off the excess blood and continued with his project. "I just can't do it alone."

* * *

Rosenburg Funeral Home greeted guests with an open foyer that consistently smelled of sickeningly sweet flowers due to the ever-present floral arrangements adorning the two chapels on either side. Beige velvet curtains hung on the windows, tied back by ornate tassels. The floral burgundy carpet was squishy beneath Leon's boots as he stepped in behind Lucius. A grandfather clock at the end of the hall chimed as a short, stocky man greeted them.

"Welcome in, gentleman. What can I do for you?"

Lucius underwent a sudden and startling transformation. His once-imposing figure now appeared hunched as if carrying the weight of an invisible burden. Deep furrows formed on his forehead as he knitted his brows in distress. This unexpected change in Lucius, from a powerful figure to one of vulnerability, was disquieting. Leon studied the Devil in amazement, almost wholly convinced by the act himself.

"Mr. Gilmore, I presume," Lucius said tentatively. The man held out his hand, his fat fingers enveloped by Lucius's oversized palm.

"Yes, sir," Mr. Gilmore said, his tone and expression full of genuine caring, a welcome relief within the somber walls of the funeral home.

"Great," Lucius nodded, the corners of his mouth pulling down. "My name is Griffin Alanzo, and this is my brother, Damon. We called earlier about getting a consultation. Our dad is rapidly declining in health, and we are preparing for the worst."

"I'm so sorry to hear that." Mr. Gilmore's eyes crinkled at the corners, exuding empathy for them. The light gleamed off his shiny head, where a sparse comb-over barely had any strands to cover. He was a small, mouse-like man, barely reaching Leon's chin, with spectacles precariously perched on the tip of his nose.

"You called earlier?" His nose scrunched, making his glasses even more crooked. "I don't have a consultation in my books, but I would be happy to talk—"

In an instant, Lucius transformed once more before their eyes, his hunched figure expanding into his usual intimidating form. His formidable presence returned, and his unwavering gaze bore into Mr. Gilmore as he spoke. His once-knitted brows smoothed out, his shoulders squared, and a confident smirk played on his lips. The subtle movement around Lucius's eyes intensified, driving his piercing stare deep into the core of the man's being. Mr. Gilmore's head snapped up to meet Lucius's direct gaze.

"Follow me this way, sir." The entranced funeral director turned with mechanical precision, hypnotized into a subservient trance. Lucius took a step after him, shooting Leon a sly wink, a silent communication that the plan was in motion. He nodded subtly down the hallway. The perfect opportunity had arrived.

As Leon strolled alongside them down the seemingly endless hallway, he couldn't shake the feeling that he was intruding on someone's home as they passed by comfortable sitting rooms and lounges. Mr. Gilmore and Lucius entered a cozy office, with Lucius shutting the door firmly behind them.

Leon strayed and continued onward, passing by paintings of serene landscapes and rosy-cheeked, cherubic faces adorning the walls.

Opening every wooden door he came upon, he finally found the one he was looking for. As he stepped into a sterile white room, the building's facade gave way.

A stainless steel slab sat in the center of the room, surrounded by a long counter with numerous drawers and cabinets. The air was heavy with the scent of chemicals, evoking memories of high school biology class. He began to explore the contents of the cabinets, uncovering vacuum-sealed bags of embalming tools, makeup, and coiled wire. Leon picked up a large, hooked needle from among the array of tools. Tapping the tip of his finger on the point, he wrapped the needle in a couple of rubber gloves to dull the sharpness before stuffing the needle in his pocket. He stole a couple more pairs of gloves—he would need them.

His eyes sparkled as he spotted the amber bottle. Greedily grabbing the formaldehyde from the cabinet, he stuffed it into his jacket, careful not to make a sound. He then opened the door on the far side of the room, which led him out to the hearse garage. As he strolled around the building, he waved to Lucius from outside through the office window. It was time to go.

* * *

Leon felt like a kid again as the familiar stench of formaldehyde burned his sinuses, making his nose run. It stung his eyes, and he blinked away the tears coming to his defense. Dipping the tip of his turkey baster into the bottle, he squeezed the rubber top and watched as it sucked up the chemical. He rubbed it thoroughly into her tissue with a gloved hand. Flipping her hide over, he repeated the same process, tenderly massaging the liquid into the outlines of her tattoo. He ran his finger over the lines that had feathered out into the tiny cracks and crevices of her skin, satisfied that they would never diffuse any further because of him. He never wanted those beautiful, brilliant colors to fade, so he applied a little extra fluid to those spots.

The skin lay in Leon's palm, the center of the eye gazing up at him as the preservation fluid set in. Its stare thanked him for the appreciation, for treating it with love and care, and for recognizing her power. He placed the skin on a towel to dry, giving it a long look before pulling his beloved grimoire off the bookshelf.

Opening the grimoire was like talking to an old friend. It welcomed him and his conversation. The book fell open to the next blank page, creased from years of love. Leon scrawled the details of the sacrifice onto the page, writing about how the satin scarf tied around her eyes matched her dress. He recounted the look in her eye at the sight of Lucius looming in the corner. The way her blood tasted sweet, like honey. Leon told the book about his muse—and the art inscribed on her back.

He could trust his grimoire with the safekeeping of the Polaroid photos. Running his thumb over the tattoo on her back, flesh and blood immortalized in the throws of lust, he tucked them into the pages.

Once the book held the knowledge of his sacred ritual, he closed the book and laid his palm over the black leather cover. A smile whispered across his lips as he reached for the tattoo and placed it delicately in the center.

It was perfect. *Exquisite.*

Leon threaded the large hooked needle with thick black thread that he had run through some black candle wax, anointing it to protect this piece of art and his sacred writings. He made his first connection through the skin, tugging on the thread gently so as not to pull it right through the skin. Gingerly binding the leather cover with Pamela's adorned leather, he crisscrossed his stitches to ensure they were completely secure. The more stitches he sewed, the more he became comfortable in the movements, pulling the thread through her skin with ease.

Clipping the last of the thread, Leon held the book in front of him. He admired his handiwork, the clean stitching around the tattoo. Now, Pamela would be there with every song that he wrote, fueling his lyrics with the power of her sacrifice.

* * *

As Jimmy spent Christmas Day with Heather and their parents, Leon spent the holiday with Pamela. He washed her bones with tender love and care, gently scrubbing each one with dish soap and water. Cleaning them carefully with a toothbrush, he inspected each section as he gently scrubbed the remnants of life off of them. He brushed away any remaining tissue, running his fingers over each of her smooth bones, admiring the intricacy of his creation.

Once they were clean, he bathed them in water mixed with bleach to degrease and preserve them further before letting them dry. He let them soak, whitening them into pearly brilliance over the following days.

26

Til Death

Jimmy and Heather tied the knot before the band set off for London. Leon should have been supportive in this profound moment in his best friend's life. It should have been a happy and joyous occasion, but Leon viewed his position as best man as a chore through jaded eyes.

Heather, a vision of beauty, graced the aisle in her wedding dress adorned with delicate lace sleeves that tapered into a point at the back of her hands. Her eyes, a reflection of the joy in her soon-to-be husband's, emanated an ethereal beauty. Leon's stomach twisted at the sight of her. His expression soured, the bile and alcohol burning in his throat. Jimmy let a tear fall from his eye as he took her hands. Leon's lip twitched up in a smirk.

Pathetic.

As Jimmy lifted her veil, a wave of emotions washed over him, his heart swelling at the sight of her radiant smile. She looked absolutely angelic, as if she had descended from the heavens. But the soft scent of Heather's perfume made Leon's stomach churn.

He hated the vows—the choked-up ramblings of two stupid, foolish people making promises to each other. Leon made it his mission to get Jimmy so fucked up on the European leg of the tour that he would violate every single one of those vows. What a waste of time this was, this facade of wholesome love. They were rock stars, not the fucking Waltons.

Mrs. Ballard sat down at Leon's table during the reception, beaming with motherly pride after the rice was thrown and the drinks were poured. He sat up a little straighter, trying to hide his boredom of watching Jimmy's aunts and uncles swaying on the dance floor.

"I want to show you something." She opened her clutch and pulled out an old photo. She gazed at it with a warm fondness, offering a closed-lip smile. She tilted her head in a sentimental reminiscence before passing it to Leon. "I found this the other day."

When Leon looked at the photo, he saw himself and Jimmy as teenagers, sitting in Jimmy's childhood bedroom with guitars in their laps. In the photo, Leon was teaching Jimmy how to improvise a guitar solo. They looked into the camera with brooding teenage annoyance that Mrs. Ballard dared to interrupt their sacred rehearsal to capture this memory. As Leon picked up the photo to take a closer look, he huffed a laugh at the innocence on Jimmy's face and the dissociated anger in his own. He remembered that time so vividly; they were so focused and driven. That was his brother, his blood brother. Looking at this memory, he realized that they had kept their promise to each other. He had fulfilled all of his promises and was debt-free to everyone.

Dad should be proud of me for that.

"This," Leon huffed another laugh and flicked the photo. "This is something."

He placed the photo back onto the table and slid it back to her. She gave it another long look.

"You boys," she shook her head in wonderment as she looked at the photo. "You used to play for hours—hours upon hours, day in and day out." She closed her eyes, letting herself get lost in the memory. "You boys were always so talented." Her voice filled with pride.

She shifted in her seat, bouncing with happiness. Leaning forward, she grabbed Leon's hands, holding them in her own. "I remember when you boys decided one day, out of the blue, that you wanted to be in a band. I thought it was a passing phase. But you...you stuck with it. You stuck together. Look at you now."

A gentle and maternal warmth radiated from her fingertips as she held his face by the chin.

"You really did it," she giggled, scrunching up her shoulders into her neck as she leaned back in her chair. A deep sigh escaped her lips as she settled back, watching her son dance with his new bride on the dance floor.

"I'm so proud of him," she said to no one in particular, never taking her eyes off Jimmy.

Leon clenched his jaw, looking at the photo that was lingering on the table. *He* is the one who worked hard. *He* is the one who sacrificed everything. *He* was the glue, not fucking Jimmy.

Mrs. Ballard's gaze drew his eyes away from the photo. He looked at Jimmy, who beamed with love and happiness. Leon wanted to wipe that smile right off his stupid face.

"Can I keep this?" Leon tapped on the photo.

"Hm?" Mrs. Ballard's reverie broke. "Oh, yes—yes, sweetie, you keep this." She laid her hand on top of his, sliding the photo in front of him. "I'm so happy that everything worked out for you boys. I'm so happy you've stayed friends for all these years."

* * *

Jimmy enjoyed time with his new bride, and Leon spent his time with the only woman in his life. Pamela's bones had soaked long enough. Leon dried them off, patting the smooth surface with an old towel and running his fingers over the bumps and ridges. How amazing the human body was, these pearly little treasures hidden deep within each and every person. The bleach whitened the bones to a nearly artificial brilliance. He slid his fingertips across the knobby bones as he secured the vertebral column, working his way up to lovingly recreate the curve through the thoracic vertebrae. The stunning beauty of the spine captivated Leon, a remarkable masterpiece that could stand on its own. He brushed a coat of polyurethane on it, preserving her beauty from the ravages of time.

Even in death, Leon could appreciate her beauty every day, her body a constant reminder of her sacrament to him. She gave him this gift, and he was able to give Dallas an even more valuable one.

Leon jingled her teeth in his hand, bouncing them around. He poured them into a mortar, the porcelain-like remnants *tinged* off of the side of the stone bowl. Pestle in hand, he ground the tool into the teeth. They crunched under the pressure, breaking into teeny-tiny fragments. He pressed the pestle into the fragments, swirling it around until it milled into a fine powder. Pouring cocaine over the teeth, he cut the drug, stirring the mixture.

Leon scooped a bit out with his pinky nail, snorting it with a sharp inhale. His heart squeezed with the sheer power he had unleashed upon himself. The cold head rush was instant, burning his nose with a familiar pleasure. His hands trembled as he held the essence of her life, creating the most intense high he had ever experienced. It was perfect—*she* was perfect.

He poured the mixture into a small baggie and flicked the corner, envying the high the bassist would get. Leon was thankful that he could give Dallas the gift of her strength—of her power. After all, her sacrifice was for all of them. *How lucky Dallas was to have him.*

The polyurethane dried and cured, denoting that Leon could finally give his guitar a proper home. He placed the body in the pelvic bone, sensually caressing the instrument. The curve of her hips hugged the base of the guitar, and the spine ran up the neck of the instrument. It was absolutely flawless, an exquisite homage to Lucius and the guitar that had been bestowed upon him. The clavicles secured the fretboard, while the shoulder blades and rib cage framed the entire guitar.

She was breathtaking.

Leon wouldn't trust anyone else to safeguard his cherished guitar as much as he trusted Pamela.

27

Stranger Danger

The two founding members of Psychosomatic Slaughter practically lived at *For the Record* in the early days. It was a surreal experience for them to sign their own posters and records at a place that had become like a second home—a full-circle moment that warmed Rufus's heart from the second the date was booked. His boys were coming home, and he couldn't wait to have them.

The band came in through the office's loading door to avoid the hoards of fans lined up outside. It was the exact loading dock where Leon had taken hundreds of smoke breaks and made hundreds of dollars dealing. Jimmy was home the second he walked in the door, greeted by the smell of dusty instruments and the artificial scent of plastic records and tapes. Posters still hung on the walls, but instead of Lynyrd Skynyrd and Led Zeppelin, their own faces were staring back at them, shining on the glossy paper.

"Rufus," Jimmy greeted, opening his arms to the old man and embracing him tightly. Rufus drew back, holding Jimmy by the shoulders and taking in his face with kind eyes. He tapped the singer on the cheek.

"Good to see you, Jim," he said warmly as he turned to look at Leon. Rufus was eager to have all the boys back in his little store, but Leon was his buddy. Never having kids himself, the red-headed little shitface was the closest thing the old man had to a son. He poured hours into teaching him how to play guitar, sharing his love for music with a kindred spirit. There was always a spiritual connection with the kid, filling his heart with happiness to be a part of his life and to watch him grow into success.

The man before him had grown out of the fiery passion from childhood. Leon stood stone-faced, surveying the record store that used to be his home away from home—his real home—as if it were his first time stepping foot in the store. His posture looked rigid, uncomfortable in the place that used to be his solace. Rufus laid a hand on Leon's shoulder, barely touching him as if he were a bomb about to detonate.

"Hey, kiddo," he said, drawing his hand back when Leon stiffened. "You made good on your promise. I knew you would."

"We sure did." Leon's smile didn't quite reach his eyes. Although the corners of his eyes crinkled, they couldn't hide the emptiness within. Leon shuffled, shifting his weight onto his other leg. The squeaky rustle of the guitarist's leather pants filled the space between them. Rufus narrowed his eyes, worried that fame was going to his head. He cleared the awkwardness out of his throat.

"You boys ready to rock and roll?" Rufus asked over his shoulder as he walked toward the door.

"Let her rip," Dallas yelled. He bounced on his toes as he shrugged off his denim jacket, revealing a tight black t-shirt. He buttoned the wrists on his fingerless leather gloves, rubbing his palms together in excitement.

They autographed poster after poster, record after record. Cam handed out guitar picks like candy on Halloween while Dallas signed every pair of boobs thrust his way. Rufus watched as Jimmy connected with the fans, engaging in genuine conversations with each one. No fan left Jimmy's presence without a hug or a handshake. His warmth emanated from him, but it couldn't thaw the coldness of the band's lead guitarist at the other end of the table. Leon didn't attempt to hide his uninterest, taking sips from his flask and hastily moving fans along, leaving sloppy autographs in his wake as he directed them out the door.

The young woman next in line had the same green eyes as Leon, accentuated by burgundy eye shadow. The same russet hair, with a faint scent of jasmine, fell over her thin, pale shoulders. Gone were the days of pigtails and dolls. Heavy-handed blush added color to her face, and her thin lips were painted to match her eyes.

Jimmy's eyes widened in realization as he recognized the young woman, a smile spreading across his face. He couldn't believe his eyes; he would recognize her anywhere.

"Emmy Holman?" Jimmy's voice filled with pride as he rounded the table, his hands outstretched towards Leon's kid sister. She embraced him in a familiar hug, burying her face in his shoulder.

Cam's head snapped up, his eyes wide with surprise as he leaned over to Lonnie to ask if he knew that Leon had a sister. Lonnie shrugged with a frown—he had no idea. The only family they knew Leon had was Jimmy. They looked to Leon, whose eyes remained fixated on the album he was signing for a fan, pretending not to notice the girl who shared his genes.

"Jimmy!" she pulled back, taking in his face. "You guys did it!"

"You're so grown up!"

"Little Emmy comes in here all the time," Rufus put a hand on each of their shoulders. "She's become a fixture in this place just like you little rugrats were."

"What can I say? I have my brother's taste in music." She gave Jimmy a good-natured shrug, shoving her hands into the pockets of her oversized bomber jacket, a Psychosomatic Slaughter patch sewn onto the shoulder.

"And she never fails to tell everyone coming in that her brother is one of the biggest rock stars in the world," Rufus chimed in before turning to her. "I remember you tagging along with the boys. You must have only been about yay high," he barred his hand at his knee. "You were so happy that they let you come that you didn't even care that they were using you as their pack mule. They loaded up your little arms so full of albums that you could barely see over it."

"And then they made me put it back," she added with a playful eye roll.

"I'm sorry," Jimmy laughed sheepishly.

"That is one of the only memories I have of my brother. I want to make more. That's why I'm here. You know my parents," she said to Jimmy with a wan expression as she trailed off. "He's my only chance at family."

"It's been so good to see you, Emmy." Jimmy pulled her in for one more hug, planting a kiss on her ginger hair. "I hope to see a lot more of you."

"Thank you, Jimmy." Emmy squeezed his hands and released them. "I hope so, too."

She made her way down the line, meeting each band member. Dallas started to say something inappropriate to her, earning him a slap on the back of the head from Lonnie.

"That's Leon's sister," Lonnie whisper-snapped, leaning forward to look at Leon, who was still none the wiser that he had a visitor. "Knock it off."

Dallas zipped his lips, giving her his famous, sleazy smile and a wink. "Knock 'em dead, kid."

At last, she slid up to Leon, placing her poster before her brother. Leon barely looked up as he signed it.

"Thanks for coming out," he said, completely monotone.

"Leon." Her voice was light, prompting him to look up at her. He flicked his eyes up, annoyance filling his expression.

"Yeah?" He drawled, and they stared into each other's matching eyes.

"Don't you recognize me?" she asked, hoping. Her smile faltered as he looked at her with an unchanging expression. He shrugged one shoulder.

"Should I?"

Jimmy's heart sank as he watched Emmy's entire face fall.

"Yeah," she tried to laugh off the rejection, but her voice trembled. She fidgeted with her fingers, twisting a mood ring to offset her discomfort. "I'm...your sister." Her voice was laced with hurt, willing her brother with her eyes to accept her. After he'd left, she bore the brunt of their dad's anger and their mom's neglect. She resented him for a long time, but the older she got, the more she understood him and why he left. How he'd left. Family had become a word synonymous with obligation, and she wanted that to change. After all these years, she needed him.

Leon flicked his eyes down and put the cap back on his marker. He pushed the poster toward her, tapping it twice in finality.

"I don't have a sister."

Jimmy's heart broke for her as her celery-green eyes brimmed with tears.

She looked up at the fluorescent lights, doing everything she could to keep them from falling onto her youthful cheeks. The rest of the band looked on with sorrow filling their faces, watching the pain Leon's rejection was causing weigh down the girl. Dallas looked away, sniffing at the table. He knew the pain that brothers caused all too well.

Jimmy sucked in his cheeks, looking to Rufus, the only other one in the store that knew the extent of the truth. The old man's lips pursed in a taut line as he shook his head in disappointment.

"Next," Leon called out, looking at her once more before leading his eyes over to the exit, silently guiding her with his gaze. She gave her brother one final pleading look before shuffling away.

As the hoards died down and the last of the fans wandered out, Leon took the opportunity to sneak out back and have a cigarette in peace.

"Jim—" Rufus whisper-shouted, pulling Jimmy aside. "What the fuck is wrong with Leon?"

Jimmy glanced toward the door that Leon had slipped out of, a knowing look crossing his face. He took a deep breath and turned to Rufus, his eyes filled with sympathy.

"He's—he's Leon," Jimmy shrugged. "He's difficult, but he's talented as hell."

Rufus crossed his arms, eyes darkening. "Jim," he said, lowering his voice. "You know him better than anyone."

"He's my brother," Jimmy nodded, shifting his eyes comfortably.

"So you know better than anyone that there's something wrong with him," Rufus said sharply. "I practically raised that boy. I spent every day with him." Rufus shook his head sternly. A sick feeling crept into the old man's stomach. "That man," he pointed at the door as Leon pushed through, running his fingers through his frizzy red hair as the breeze from the door blew it in his eyes, "I don't know that man. That's not the same kid. He's different."

Jimmy couldn't tear his eyes away from Rufus. He already knew, he sensed the shift a long time ago. Frankly, he'd been too scared to look too hard at Leon for fear that he wouldn't recognize the stranger that Leon had become.

Jimmy wasn't ready to accept that Leon wasn't Leon anymore and that the darkness inside of him might have finally grown too big and had swallowed him up.

"Keep an eye on him, Jim," Rufus said as he cast his eyes down. "Best of luck to you boys."

28

Hail Satan

In 1987, Psychosomatic Slaughter ventured out of the country and saw firsthand the mark they made on the world. People loved them even outside of their home base. For the first time, their leather boots set foot on European soil, and they had to ensure that this concert was perfect. After starting off their tour in America with a bang, they aimed to make rock and roll history with the biggest debut tour of all time, making their mark on Europe during their first overseas show in the heart of London. It needed to be flawless.

They spent hours rehearsing, fine-tuning every aspect of their performance. As the sun set and the stage lights went on, Psychosomatic Slaughter completed their soundchecks, tuned their instruments, and lined their eyes with black liner.

Leon wanted so badly to share Pamela's power with his band. Despite all of their ups and downs, they became a family. Those guys were his brothers. He wished for the gift of Pamela's life force to flow through their bodies, giving them the strength to face the future with hope and determination. But some needed her more than others.

Dallas's vibration was so low that he depended on substances to get him through the day, using sex as a crutch to make his life exciting. He squandered away the gift Leon had given all of them: the gift of fame and immortality through their music. Dallas needed her life force the most. One taste would do the trick.

"Dallas," Leon called as they headed to the stage. Excitement raged through each of the members; they all buzzed with the energy from their foreign crowd. Their giddiness was infectious as they made their way to the stage, a stark contrast to Dallas, who had made it a habit of isolating himself to shoot up before shows. There was no helping him, for addicts have the deafest ears. The bassist would rather shoot up and die than listen to his bandmates—the harder they tried to help him, the more he pushed them away. When he was good, he was great. The high gave him the pseudo sense of a spark, but when that high faded, it was a dark and barren winter in Dallas' eyes. It was a vicious cycle.

"What's up?" Dallas slowed his pace, tucking his bass off to the side to keep from hitting Leon. He raked at his forearm like a misunderstood woman scratching at the seams of her yellow wallpaper. Angry red lines scored his pallid skin. His eyes were shadowed by deep purplish bags.

"Don't tell the guys I got you this, I know they've been on your ass hard, but…" Leon murmured, holding the baggie under his thumb, partially concealed by his guitar pick. Dallas's eyes glistened looking at the drugs. He broke into a wide smile, snatching the baggie out of Leon's hand as he ran his tongue over his teeth. He dipped his pinky in and snorted a bump, unable to wait another second, and rubbed the remnants over his teeth. A chill ran through Leon as he watched Dallas massage the side of his nose.

Did his eyes look clearer?

Dallas straightened up, exuding an air of self-assured arrogance as he rolled his shoulders back. The zombie that had been playing bass in their band, the stranger that Dallas had become, melted away before Leon's eyes. There he stood, the familiar bass player Leon had always known. His skin began to glow, lighting from within as blood colored his pale cheeks. The blemishes on his arm faded, the red punctures disappearing. A spark ignited behind Dallas's eyes, lighting life back into the man. The grey hue faded from his teeth as Dallas broke into a wide, mischievous smile. Leon hadn't seen that expression in years.

"You're my favorite person in the whole entire world," Dallas tucked the baggie into his bass strap. "Did you know that? I love you." Leon knew and hoped she would serve him well with every bump he took.

When they took the stage, it was clear that the English audience adored them as much, if not more, than their American fans. The energy from the crowd fueled their performance, and Leon drew his inspiration from Dallas. He uttered a hail Satan as he watched Dallas deliver an immaculate performance. The bassist was once again filled with infectious vitality, spreading his energy into the crowd. He was on fire the entire show, radiating cockiness through his larger-than-life expressions. Even his bass sounded clearer, supercharged by his Master's aura. Leon caught a glimpse of the 19-year-old version of Dallas, the one he truly missed, devouring the stage with the stars in his eyes and a hunger in his heart that he wore on his sleeve. Leon thanked Pamela, wherever she was, for her contribution to the band and for bringing Dallas back to full strength.

"I think it's about time we meet the band," Jimmy screamed into the microphone, swinging his arm in a grand gesture across the stage, landing on Lonnie.

"On the drums, we have Lonnie Herring."

Lonnie's drum solo was a moment of pure connection with the crowd. They cheered him on, screaming as he smashed the cymbals to close his performance. He stood up while keeping the beat on the kick drum, twirling a drumstick in his right hand while pointing at the crowd with the other. He gave the audience a crooked smile before sitting back at his kit.

"On the bass guitar, give it up for the King of Sleaze, if you please." Women in the crowd went wild. "Dallas Jacobson!"

Dallas stepped into the spotlight, situating the bass on his crotch, and stroked it slowly, bending his knees and thrusting into the instrument. He twisted the bass to lay correctly, improvising a nearly inaudible lick over the lustful whoops and hollers. Dallas stepped out of the spotlight and grinned at Jimmy, sticking out his tongue and shaking his head. His eyes looked bright, and his complexion appeared clearer than it had in years—he was the glowing picture of health. Jimmy could not have been happier, seeing that spark fire back up in the bassist. Dallas had come around as if he had turned back the hands of time to undo all the damage he had done to himself for this performance.

As Cam was introduced, Dallas scooped out another bump, charging himself up.

"And last, but certainly not least," Jimmy put the microphone back into its stand, picked the entire thing up, and walked across the stage toward Leon. He slung his arm over Leon's shoulder. "My brother. The one who started his dream with me eleven years ago. On the golden guitar, Leon Holman."

As Leon played a bluesy solo, he improvised over a minor pentatonic scale. Jimmy positioned the microphone stand at the front of the stage and disappeared into the wings to watch from the sidelines. Watching Leon play to a crowd of Brits, it sunk in for the first time for Jimmy that they made it. Psychosomatic Slaughter hit the big time. Taking a shot of Jack, he reveled in the realization. His heart vibrated in his chest, both from the reverberation of Leon's instrument and the rush of his accomplishment. Their accomplishment.

Leon walked towards the front of the stage to the microphone stand. As he let the last note of his solo ring out, the crowd erupted in a frenzy of excitement. Leon tipped his head back, basking in fans' thunderous applause and cheers as the stage lights blinded him, flushing his face with the heat of the lights. He flicked his pickup selector repeatedly, creating a vibration through the stadium. The distortion from his guitar faded as he smiled into the microphone. The audience's cheers grew even louder, their energy matching his.

"When we first started our band," Leon said, his voice echoing over the shouts of the audience. "We were told that to succeed, we needed to find our rhapsody. Are you ready to hear it?"

The crowd eagerly awaited the song that defined Psychosomatic Slaughter, cheering and whistling in approval. Leon ran a hand over his sweaty forehead, combing back the clumpy strands of red hair that stuck to his skin. His fingers shook with anticipation.

"There is one person we need to thank for inspiring this song. For being the driving force. Let's conjure up some noise for him!"

He strummed the Devil's Triad, building up suspense for the song. Cam beamed at Jimmy as he played a chord, letting it ring out over the stadium. The improvisation Leon was styling at the front of the stage layered perfectly over it. This was their best intro for the song to date. Dallas plucked a slow, melodic rendition of the song's bassline, gearing up to let the song rip.

"Hail, Satan!" Leon chanted. Jimmy's smile quickly disappeared as he locked eyes with Lonnie, who looked both concerned and startled. Even Dallas, who had been carefree just moments before, sobered as he glanced back and forth between the two. Cam, who had always admired Leon's fascination with the occult, couldn't help but let out a gasp. Despite the warmth of the stage lights, Jimmy couldn't shake the feeling of cold dread creeping through his veins. "Give me a motherfucking Hail!"

"Hail!" The crowd repeated. Jimmy's ears filled with the sound of blood beating through his heart, drowning out the crowd in a muffled haze.

"Satan!" Leon cried.

"Satan!" The crowd chanted back.

"Hail Satan!" Leon chanted. The crowd repeated it back again. Leon struck the triad once more, signaling the band to begin their chant. Jimmy's fingertips tingled as he wrapped them around the microphone, adding his voice to the crescendo. Despite the sinking in the singer's gut, the band played the song flawlessly, not missing a single beat, leaving the audience in awe.

Psychosomatic Slaughter's European debut concert was a resounding success; however, the band itself began to unravel when Jimmy caught up with Leon backstage.

"What the fuck was that?" Jimmy spat, grabbing Leon by the shoulder and whipping him around. The stock of the guitar almost hit him in the jaw, but he didn't flinch.

"What do you mean?" Leon lifted the guitar strap and passed his guitar to his guitar technician, who whisked it away to safety. Leon took a step away from Jimmy, looking at him with a deadpan expression.

"Hail Satan?" Jimmy questioned with bulging eyes. Heat radiated off his skin despite the chill still living in his bones.

"Oh, Jesus Christ." Leon rolled his head back, staring up at the rafters as he twisted the top off of a bottle of vodka. He flicked the top off, sending the cap flying. "Here we go."

"What that fuck was that?" Jimmy asked again. "Hail Satan? What the fuck is wrong with you."

"It was good showmanship," Leon retorted, taking a swig of the liquor. "That's what the fuck it was."

"I think we're beyond that."

Jimmy stood in front while the rest of the band watched in silence. Cam still had his guitar slung over his body, but it didn't seem like they would be returning to the stage for an encore.

"Oh," Leon spat, scrunching up his face in disgust. "Come off it, Jimmy."

"No. This is going to be all over the news. I can hear it now: Psychosomatic Slaughter conjures up Satanic Panic. Christ, Leon!"

Heather ran up to the band, asking why they weren't on stage yet for their encore. She stopped in her tracks the second she felt the tension radiating off of Leon and her husband. Her smile fell as she looked from Jimmy to Leon, who leered at her with an unsettling smirk on his face.

"That's perfect," Leon sneered, jutting an open palm in Heather's direction. "Just fucking perfect. You know what, let's go back out there, get this fucking show over with so you can go back to the hotel room with your perfect little wife."

"This isn't about me or Heather. This is about you trying to make this band something it's not."

"Whatever, Jimmy." Leon threw the bottle, shattering it against the wall. Droplets of vodka flew across the room. "Fuck the band, okay? Go back to your hotel room with this little cun—"

Jimmy lunged at Leon, but Lonnie pushed him back. Lonnie's fist landed square on Leon's jaw, knocking him into the wall. Lonnie picked him up, holding the guitarist up by the shoulders of his leather jacket.

"You two have known each other since you were kids." Barely above a whisper, Lonnie struggled to keep his emotions in check as his voice fought the frustration to stay as even as possible. The anger simmered just beneath the surface. "You have been friends for years, and I'll be damned if I let Jimmy throw that all away to lay your sorry sack of shit ass out. Don't think I care about saving your face or your friendship. No—I just know that Jimmy'd never forgive himself for that. But if you ever, ever call her that again, I won't stop him."

"Lonnie," Dallas took a step toward the drummer, who was hunched over Leon.

"Shut up, Dallas," Leon spat. "You're just a worthless—"

His sentence was punctuated with a kick to the stomach. Lonnie landed another blow in the guitarist's eye. The wild boar head ring on his hand left a gash on Leon's eyebrow. Blood dribbled onto his pale eyelashes.

"Don't you call him a damned thing."

"Or what, Lonnie?" Leon rattled out a laugh that transitioned into a breathy cough. "What? Did you think I was going to call him something? What was I going to call him, hmm? Nothing you haven't called him in your head, I'm sure." He paused, watching Lonnie's face turn red with rage as the drummer pulled his fist back to deliver one more punch. "Junkie. A worthless junkie. Is that what you thought I was going to say?" Leon's eye had already begun to swell shut. Despite this, he looked at Lonnie with a nasty smirk on his lips.

"You don't get to call him a damned thing," Lonnie repeated as he pushed Leon down and spit at him, his saliva landing on the floor next to Leon's face. He stalked out, clapping Jimmy on the shoulder. "Show's over, friends," he shouted as he walked.

Cam and Dallas followed suit, leaving Leon on the floor and looking up at Jimmy. Heather leaned in close to Jimmy, whispering in a hushed panic. She pulled on his chest, trying to turn him away from Leon and tell him that it was okay and not to worry about it. Jimmy stood firm, staring at Leon with a burning hatred that Leon had never seen before.

"Go back to the room, Heather," he said gently, his tone betraying the malice in his eyes. She held onto his arm, her desperation evident in her grasp, trying one more time to get him to come with her with a leading hand on his chest. She gave him a tight smile, realizing he wasn't going to come with her. She ran her fingers over his chest, still damp with sweat from the hot stage lights. She turned and walked out slowly, looking over her shoulder at Leon as she left.

"You've pushed me around long enough." Jimmy's voice quivered with a sense of betrayal once Heather's footsteps faded from earshot. He swallowed hard, causing his Adam's apple to bob up and down. "You've done it for most of my life. I could handle it—you trying to make yourself feel better by talking down to me. But I will not let you disrespect my wife. That is where I draw the line. I'm going home—with Heather. Try and finish this tour without me."

* * *

The members of the band retreated for the night, and in the harsh light of day, the situation became even more complicated. The tour had a series of sold-out shows on the horizon, and the contracts had already been signed. They couldn't afford to back out now. There was too much riding on the tour to call it quits.

Leon sent Heather a bouquet of flowers the next day. He didn't give a shit how Jimmy felt or what Heather thought of him—as long as they could see the superficial olive branch he was extending. Making amends meant nothing to him—Leon's sole motivation was to save the band from the tension that Jimmy and his distraction were causing. Heather was to Psychosomatic Slaughter as Yoko was to the Beatles: a distraction—a snake in the garden tempting Jimmy to taste her fruit.

Jimmy's eye was off the prize, and Leon would make sure everyone saw his apology display because visibility made it real.

Fucking stupid, Leon thought. It took all of his strength to swallow his pride. As Lucius told him, "Sorry gets you nothing."

The constant pushing became unbearable, and Leon had crossed the line for the last time, challenging Jimmy's reputation for being able to let go of grudges. Jimmy struggled to remember what had initially made them friends.

The tension between Jimmy and Leon spilled over onto the stage, putting the rest of the band on edge. They struggled to maintain their professionalism, but each show was filled with sharp glances and passive-aggressive movements across the stage. Audiences became mere spectators to the ever-mounting drama fracturing the band. An act of sabotage was committed when a new song was added to the setlist of their Hamburg show, a song they all had a hand in writing but Leon. Rage fueled the guitarist, walking off the stage and refusing to finish the concert. The night ended in chaos as the fans rioted at their show being cut short. A fan died after being trampled to death at the foot of the stage. Jimmy took time to visit with the mourning family, while Leon refused to give a statement. He didn't care about the backlash the headlines caused. Those headlines fueled the band's infamy. It was Pamela at work, ingraining Psychosomatic Slaughter into the history books.

Cam, who was usually just happy to be alive and in a band playing guitar, retreated into himself, opting to stay in his hotel room rather than enjoy the sights and scenes of Europe. His love for the music was the only thing that kept him going.

Dallas snorted the rest of Pamela to cope with the stress. The teeth made him feel euphoric, more so than any other drug. Outwardly, he had been healed. His smile was bright, his body was strong, and his creativity was flowing. He played better than ever. With each show, they performed with an electric stage presence that distracted crowds from the tension playing out on the rest of the stage. The teeth made him human again and separated him from the conflict of the band. As long as he had his mistress—his drugs, he was happy. Until he had none of Pamela's life force left to snort.

Having crashed hard from that high, his skin became sallow again, and the tract marks that the magic of the sacrifice concealed came back with a vengeance. Sunglasses constantly sat propped up on his prominent nose as the light made his head feel as if it were splitting in two. Dallas chased the high that Pamela had given him by overindulging in everything. Sex. Heroin. Horse tranquilizers. The bottle.

It was after their show in Stockholm that the drugs caught up with him.

Lonnie was coming back from the ice machine to find Dallas running down the hallway naked and screaming about a hallucination that was looming in the corner of the room. He kept screaming, *"There are worms in his eyes!"* Lonnie assured him that he would check the room and led Dallas back there after much protest. The room had been trashed: the footboard was cracked, and Dallas had put his bass through the television screen. There was a buffet of pills spread across his bed, and the bruises on his arm indicated that the cocktail of drugs wasn't mixing well. Wrapping his arms around Dallas, Lonnie constrained his friend, talking him through the visions that he was seeing.

Bruce isn't going to hurt you. He loved you. There are no worms in his eyes.

As Dallas's hyperventilation eased into slow, deep breaths, he rested his head on Lonnie's shoulder. His neck rolled as he placed his hand on Lonnie's thigh. He began to ramble nonsensically, babbling as his head lulled onto his chest. Throwing his hand off of his leg, Lonnie hauled the bassist into the bathroom. He pulled him into the shower and stuck his fingers down Dallas's throat, the water from the shower washing away the vomit. Lonnie stayed with him that night, keeping watch as Dallas shivered himself to sleep despite sweating profusely under the blankets. He tipped sips of water into Dallas's mouth until some semblance of color came back into his face. They never talked about that night again, but Dallas was endlessly thankful to Lonnie for being there. He wished he could have been that person for Bruce.

Through the detoxes and the eventual relapses, Lonnie was there. He dedicated the rest of the tour to helping Dallas sober up, offering himself as a crutch to be leaned on. He became an unwavering beacon for Dallas, a backbone to keep him standing. An unspoken agreement sprouted between the drummer and the bassist, but more importantly, an unbreakable bond formed between the two most unlikely members. Outside of their music, they had absolutely nothing in common. Lonnie was always guarded—his heart was an impenetrable fortress surrounded by a brick wall and barbed wire. He boxed up his emotions and filed them away into neat little boxes onto the shelves of his mind, tucked away so as to not cause him to feel.

Dallas was impulsive and wild, always wearing his heart on his sleeve. He felt everything too deeply and took that pain out on his body, whether it be through sex, drugs, or just general recklessness. Lonnie would never have the capacity to understand the depths of Dallas, but that didn't matter. He didn't have to understand what made him tick. A brotherhood that had been forged in the trenches had blossomed; there was mutual respect, a pure platonic love that never had to be expressed. It just *was*.

* * *

After a long and tumultuous tour, the band was tired and worn out, sitting in tense silence on the private plane ride back to Los Angeles. As the minutes ticked by, Leon's mind raced with a calculated plan to mend the fences that Jimmy destroyed. His callused fingers tapped on the corner of a photo. He couldn't sit still any longer. Leon walked over to Jimmy and cleared his throat.

"Heather," Leon laced his voice with as much understated guilt as he could muster. "Could you give me and Jimmy a minute?"

Heather glanced at Jimmy, who gave her a small nod and tilted his head toward Cam and Dallas. She squeezed his bicep as she gave him and Leon privacy.

Leon sat in front of Jimmy, who stared at him expressionless.

"I...I just wanted—here."

Leon extended his arm, clasping the photo in his hand, letting the gesture speak for him. Jimmy snatched the photo from him, his eyes softening as he took in their round, teenage faces, a wave of nostalgia washing over him. The corner of Jimmy's mouth quirked up, flipping the photo over and reading the date written on the back. He looked up at Leon with wonderment and confusion as he recognized the handwriting.

"Where did you get this?"

"Your mom gave it to me." Leon shrugged, keeping his eyes downcast on the photo. "At your wedding." He waited another second before flicking his eyes up and meeting Jimmy's gaze. The longer he could play the role of

271

weak prey, the better—just one more second, one more feigned moment of meekness. Leon finally looked up at Jimmy and saw the kind eyes he had always known his friend to have as the hardened mask melted from his friend's face.

What a sucker.

"I don't want things to be weird with us." Leon twisted his face in an expression of pain. "We're here because these kids," he took the photo out of Jimmy's hands and held it before him, "had a dream. We made it happen. We can't bail now."

Cam's head perked up, trying to look like he wasn't eavesdropping and hiding it poorly. Dallas and Lonnie exchanged glances.

Examining Leon's face, Jimmy processed this as Leon kept his eyes open wide and the corners of his mouth turned down.

God damn it. Leon couldn't keep this expression much longer. The muscles in his cheeks twitched in protest at the unnatural expression.

"We've come too far," Leon tried again, feeling his mask slipping too much for comfort. "I'm sorry."

Someone coughed in astonishment. Leon found it difficult to accept changes to his song lyrics, let alone admit defeat in an argument and apologize. Jimmy nodded and drifted his gaze over to Heather before glancing back at Leon expectantly.

Fucking asshole.

"Heather," Leon said without missing a beat. "I apologize for everything that's happened this tour. Can you forgive me?"

"I forgive you, Leon," she said with a slight nod, "but I won't forget."

What a fucking bitch.

Leon sucked in his cheeks, biting his teeth into the tip of his tongue until he tasted blood. It took everything Leon had not to say anything to ruin all of the work he had just put in. Instead, he nodded in acceptance and turned his attention back to Jimmy as he swallowed his bloody saliva.

"When we get back, I want you to come over. You can see the house, and we can write like we used to. Just you and me, like when we were kids."

Jimmy tried to find the words, opening and closing his mouth while his eyes appeared to flinch.

"No weird stuff, I swear," Leon quickly added. "I won't make you play with an Ouija board."

Jimmy twisted his lips, looking down in his lap to hide his smile.

Almost there. Just a little more.

"We're the glue of this band," Leon lowered his voice and leaned in toward Jimmy. "We are at the heart of this thing. We need your soul to be in it if we're going to make another album. A better album." The Devil knew Leon's soul was already too far in it.

Jimmy's warm brown eyes met Leon's hard green ones. Leon fought to keep the emotion in his eye—this could not be the moment to falter. He held his breath, willing all of the kindness into his eyes that he could muster. It took all of his energy to care so much for that long. Jimmy grinned and nodded, holding his palm out to Leon, who looked at the faint scar running across his lifeline. Leon pressed his scar to Jimmy's in a clap, sliding their fingers down each other's palms into a handshake.

Bingo.

* * *

The plane landed in Los Angeles under the stars. The cool night air filled their lungs as they stepped out onto the tarmac, stretching their legs as they made their way down the stairs to set foot on American soil.

Good ole' America. The fresh, crisp smell wafted through the trees of the valley, mixing with the stink of aviation fuel and the budding of corporate greed, creating an air that smelled like home.

The band began to part ways, walking like zombies off of the runway as they made their way to their own corners of the universe for the first time in months. As they retreated into their own little bubbles, Leon's was burst by the sound of Jimmy's voice yelling out to him. He turned to find Jimmy holding Heather by the shoulders and kissing her forehead before they parted ways. She looked to Leon before she left, leaving the heart of the band alone on the tarmac.

"Are you dead set on going home right away?" Jimmy asked, shoving his hands in his back pockets, his oversized belt buckle glinting red from the plane's beacon lights. Leon shifted his weight, balancing his guitar case on his leg.

"What do you have in mind?" Tilting his chin up, he sized up his lifelong friend.

"Gimme your keys."

"No," Leon took a step back. *What game is he playing?*

"C'mon Leon. Give me your fucking keys." Jimmy held out his hand, smirking. A muscle under Leon's eye twitched—he had the upper hand right now; he had Jimmy eating out of his scarred palm. Narrowing his eyes at Jimmy's open palm splayed out before him, the guitarist weighed his options.

Jimmy was never the vindictive type, Leon thought. *He didn't have the capacity to play the game of life strategically.* Jimmy never had to be the manipulator, molding the thoughts and actions of those around him, stringing them up to dance as he pleased. No, that was Leon's role in their friendship. He was the one who held the strings. Dance, Jimmy, dance.

Leon unclipped his keys from his belt loop and tossed them to Jimmy. He would indulge the singer, making Jimmy feel important and spontaneous could play to his benefit.

Jimmy drove them down familiar roads, passing through Burbank before pulling into their favorite spot a half hour later.

The moon was full—so bright and beautiful it lit the way to Dante's View. Silver lay in streaks on the dirt and dust, illuminating their hike up the trail. Jimmy's eyes were heavy, and his legs were tight after a continuous flight out of Europe, but he powered on, fueled by the soul of the little boy who still lived inside of him. Leon dragged his feet, determined to maneuver his pawn across the board and regain Jimmy's favor.

Having returned home, the cityscape looked even more beautiful now than it ever had. They had been detached for so long, not just from nature, but as people. Jimmy pondered the purpose of success without anyone to share it with, feeling a pang of sadness for the guitarist. Hoisting himself on the wooden rail, Jimmy smiled back at Leon, his face glowing in the moonlight.

"It's like we never left," he said, swinging his legs over the fence. Leon leaned his hands on the rail Jimmy was sitting on and squinted out at Los Angeles and the city lights that faded into treeline. The Hollywood sign cast harsh shadows in the trees, a silent witness to their shared memories.

"It looks different now," Leon muttered with a tinge of nostalgia in his voice. "It used to look so big and magical."

"You don't think it does anymore?"

"No," Leon twisted his toe in the gravel, taking a pack of cigarettes out of his pocket. He knocked the bottom of the box before sliding one out. The calm of nature's sounds was interrupted by the flick of Leon's lighter. Smoke polluted the sanctuary, blowing into the trees.

"You know, the last time we came here was on my 18th birthday." There was a pause hanging in the air, and the silence made Jimmy fidget with his fingers. Leon sucked on his cigarette, the orange tip glowing as he inhaled. Ashes littered the breeze. "I'm excited to write with you tomorrow. I've missed it."

With another drag, Leon dropped his arm, letting the hand holding the cigarette dangle over the rail. He reached out, giving the rest of it to Jimmy.

"Me too."

IV

Part Four: Face The Music

1987

29

The Devil You Know

For the first time since the séance, Leon welcomed Jimmy into his home. Walking through the door, Jimmy couldn't help admiring the intricate woodwork adorning the house's supports. The old floors creaked under their feet, showing the age of the home. As he followed Leon inside, Jimmy fell under the intense gaze of a taxidermy bear standing proudly on its hind legs; its death mask paused in mid-growl. Dead, glassy eyes looked through Jimmy at every turn. The walls were lined with framed moths, bird skulls, and mummified fish.

A familiar presence followed them, looming through the house. An eerie feeling crept through Jimmy's body, sending alarm bells to his brain. He wrote it off as the past haunting him, the ghost of Halloween night from many moons ago. Nevertheless, there was something else in the house, someone else besides Leon. The air seemed heavy like stagnant energy was making the house stale. The singer shook off the hesitation budding in his gut, writing off the feeling as nerves from old wounds.

Leon led him into the music room, and Jimmy halted at the sight of Leon's gold top guitar resting upon a throne of bones. The skeletal guitar stand appeared to be meticulously hand-crafted, the most intricate piece of art that he'd ever seen. The bones gleamed around the instrument, majestically displaying it as the room's focal point.

"Wow—" Jimmy stammered, crouching to look at the stand more closely.

He reached his hand out to touch it, wanting to see if it felt as silky-smooth as it looked. His fingers grazed the clavicle, and he ran his finger down the length of the spine. The polyurethane rubbed smoothly against his fingertips. Jimmy tapped on one of the shoulder blades as he stood back up. "It looks so real. Like it could be human."

"It's cool, right? Fucking expensive but cool."

An unexplainable wave of nausea plunged through Jimmy's core. "Yeah," he agreed tentatively. "Where did you get it?"

"Dude," Leon chuckled, waving him off as he cracked open a beer from the fridge in the corner of the room and handed it to Jimmy. "What, do you want one?"

"No," Jimmy said, more to himself than to Leon. "Where did you get all of this stuff?"

"Around the country. While you were holed up in your hotel room with Heather, and the guys were getting shitfaced on tour or wasting time at the Tropicana, I was curating my collection."

"Where did you get this one, though?" Jimmy asked, pointing to the guitar stand.

"That one was a local piece," Leon paused. "But, now that I think of it, I think it originally came from Indiana."

Jimmy pursed his lips, considering. "What animal is it?" he asked, but he already knew the answer.

"It's human," Leon confirmed, his tone light as air as he opened a beer for himself.

"How is that legal?" Jimmy stumbled back, sitting down on the velvet purple couch. There was so much to look at in Leon's house, but he couldn't concentrate on any of it except for that damn guitar stand. There was something about it that drew him in like a plea. Leon grabbed his gold top guitar from the grip of the pelvis, giving Jimmy an unadulterated view of the curvature of the spine. Each knob glinted in the light, the sparkling midsection a sight that made Jimmy feel weak. That was a person—someone with their own desires, thoughts, and dreams, reduced to an object to collect dust in Leon's house.

"The person this once was donated their body to art. How hot is that?"

When Jimmy didn't respond, Leon raised his beer bottle to him in a toast. "Just like old times," he said with an unnerving grin as he took a sip. The taste of the hops, weak and purely American, brought back memories of Leon's old apartment. It was the same cheap beer that they would drink in the ragged apartment off the Strip.

The awkwardness dissipated as they drank and wrote; however, the nagging voice in Jimmy's head remained, monitoring the bones. He distracted himself long enough from the skeleton stand to write a song with Leon, though the pull of the piece kept stealing his glances.

He thought the song might actually be the best they'd ever written. The lyrics were thoughtful and retrospective, like a heavy metal "Landslide." Verses recounted the years while the chorus kept the heart of the dream beating. Jimmy read back over the words, touched by their work and surprised that Leon let the session take such a sappy turn. A few years ago, Leon would not have entertained the idea of this song, let alone help pen it. *Maybe he had changed for the better.* It felt natural, like they were kids again chasing after a dream. Leaning back on the couch, he watched as Leon noodled around on the guitar, closing his eyes and feeling the rhythm of what he was playing. Leon tilted his head back, bending a note and making the guitar scream. Jimmy scrawled the title of the song across the top of the page: "Blood Brothers." A full circle moment, the singer felt at peace with the homage that this song paid to their lifelong friendship, letting go of the unease that he felt within those walls.

Jimmy's eyes wandered back over to the guitar stand, his thumb absent-mindedly stroking the scar on his palm. He thought about what that person must have been like in life. Were they a man or a woman? Jimmy knew by looking at the curve of the hips that this skeleton belonged to a woman. The longer he looked at it, the sicker he became. A phantom wail pleaded in his head as a rush of heat washed over him. His instincts screamed at him to get out of that room.

"Where's your bathroom?" Jimmy asked, tilting the empty beer bottle toward the door. "I've had one too many of these."

"It's down the hall and to the left," Leon said, not bothering to open his eyes. His fingers continued caressing the strings, making the guitar sing. "You'll have to go through my bedroom. The door should be open."

Jimmy put the bottle down and followed the shrine of dead organisms down to Leon's bedroom. As he stepped into the bedroom, a sense of trespassing washed over him, as if he had entered a realm he wasn't meant to. The ornate bookshelf, adorned with leather-bound editions, and the intricately carved wooden walls were like a Gothic twist on Versailles. His curiosity pulled him towards the bookshelf, where he eagerly scanned the titles on the spines. Amidst the vintage collection, one book stood out - its modern-looking black leather cover defying the surrounding antiquity.

No writing embellished the spine of this book, and Jimmy's fingers tingled with wonderment at what was inside the titleless book.

Jimmy carefully slid the book out, his eyes immediately drawn to a smaller tan patch of leather that had been hand-stitched on the center of the cover. A collection of eyes, both unsettling and strangely beautiful, peered up at him from the most unique piece of art he had ever seen. He couldn't resist running his fingers over the array of eyes embedded into an anatomically correct rendition of a heart.

He opened the book and found the original lyrics to "Conjure Me Up" scrawled in messy handwriting, letting out a chuckle before eagerly flipping through the remaining pages. His eyes darted over handwritten rituals, mysterious lyrics, and cryptic writings, accompanied by detailed accounts of each ritual.

Jimmy tilted his head in confusion, returning to the page with the lyrics before flipping back through the rest of the book. His eyes flitted across Damien Moxie's name as he scanned the details of the poppet Leon sacrificed and burned. Droplets of black wax dribbled across the page, hardened into tiny seals. Jimmy's stomach churned—he remembered smelling Damien cooking from the inside out from that electric shock and the gut feeling that Leon had welcomed that death as a happy accident. Now, he learned, it was no accident.

Jimmy thumbed through more lyrics interlaced between dove slayings and dreams of demons when he read one line that stood out to him:

I can give you success, I can make you a legend, but I am going to need pieces of you. Pieces of human morality. The slaughter of all of the societal conditioning, the religious conditioning, the moral conditioning.

Leon had circled the word and made a note in the margins: *A Psychosomatic Slaughter.*

Adrenaline coursed through his body, his palms sweating, the moisture seeping into the handmade paper pages. His heartbeat rose into his throat as the beer he had just drank threatened to make a reappearance all over this God-forsaken book.

As he turned the pages faster, a couple of Polaroid photos slipped out, piquing his interest and startling him back to reality. The photos showed a naked woman, holding her breasts and flashing bedroom eyes at the camera. He felt a sense of déjà vu as he gazed at her; there was something familiar about her. In his haste, he fumbled and dropped one of the photos. As he stooped to pick it up, he found himself gazing at a frozen moment in time, capturing Pamela sitting naked on the bed with her back to the camera. Blood stained the white border at the bottom, next to Leon's handwritten words.

My Muse.

A shudder ran through Jimmy as his chest constricted. A breath hitched in Jimmy's throat. Gravity weighed down on him, pushing the light from his eyes. The book before him looked hazy. His heart pounded so fiercely, the blood so thick in his ears that it muffled his hearing, drowning out the sound of Leon's guitar playing from the other room.

30

Crucify The Flesh

"You shouldn't have done that."

Jimmy whipped around to find Leon leaning against the door frame with a coy smile on his face.

"What did you do?" Jimmy's heart skipped a beat as he tried to keep his voice even. His stomach lurched at the sight of his friend.

"Do you like my little art project?" Leon gestured to Jimmy's hands. The corner of his mouth ticked upward. "I think for an amateur, I did a damn good job."

"Leon," Jimmy pleaded, holding up the Polaroids of Pamela. "What the hell is this?"

"Come on, Jimmy," Leon drawled, rolling his eyes in exasperation. "Use your eyes."

Looking into the frozen frame of the lustful young woman, it clicked. "I remember her," he whispered to himself. Jimmy studied the book in his hands, the knowledge refusing to penetrate his understanding. His eyes darted between the photos and the cover. The design wasn't drawn on there with a pen, copied from the muse—it *was* the muse. Ink feathered out into little cracks and wrinkles, showing the age as the tattoo settled into the skin. The book fell from his hands, splaying open on a scribbling of Satanic devotions.

"You cut off her skin." Jimmy shook his head in disbelief, the words coming out like a question as he struggled to fathom the man who had suddenly become a stranger to him. He heard the flick of a lighter, followed by the smell of cigarette smoke.

"Mhmm," Leon hummed, his eyes closing. He rested his head against the door frame and took a long drag. Jimmy's face twisted in an expression caught between disgust and confusion.

"W-Why?"

The sound of Leon's lips popping off of the cigarette filter was the only answer Jimmy was offered. Leon rolled the back of his head on the door frame, back and forth. The sound of his skull grinding against the wood sent chills up Jimmy's back.

Leon stopped to meet Jimmy's eye, glaring through his eyebrows as he exhaled smoke through his nose. He stared at Jimmy through his ginger eyelashes with a knowing look.

"Jim-my," Leon singsonged.

"What else did you do to her?" He swallowed hard and let the photos fall from his fingers, unable to keep the muscles in his fingers tensed any longer.

"I drank her blood. And consumed her flesh." Leon dropped the bombshell on Jimmy with the same casualness one would use to predict a chance of rain in the afternoon. His detachment from the situation, his actions, and his reality shook Jimmy to his core. Leon was completely void of any emotion. "I also made that guitar stand in the music room." Leon gestured over his shoulder, taking a step into the room. "The one you liked so much."

A noise caught between a gag and a laugh escaped Jimmy's throat as Leon's mouth stretched into a wide, toothy grin.

"Why? W-why?" It was the only question he could think of asking.

"Do you believe in God, Jimmy?" Leon asked in answer, snuffing his cigarette on the top of the dresser. Ashes poured over the wood, burning a ring into the stain.

"What?" Jimmy exhaled a mix of disbelief and revulsion. His face contorted as he instinctively took a step back. He stumbled over the book covered in Pamela's flesh.

"I never believed in God," Leon's eyes blazed, shaking his head firmly.

"But, for there to be a Devil, there needs to be a God. And there is a Devil. I know him very well."

Jimmy's blood ran cold as he as he met Leon's intense gaze. The adrenaline surged through his veins, leaving him stunned and motionless. Under the weight of Leon's stare, his skin crawled with goosebumps.

"Fuck, Leon, you're fucking crazy," Jimmy breathed, resting his hands on the edge of the bed, the feel of the rich velvet comforter grounding his spinning head. Leon encircled him like a wolf circling its prey.

"Oh, get off your high fucking horse, Jimmy," Leon scoffed, never breaking eye contact as he circled the room in slow, steady steps. Jimmy's exasperated yell reverberated through the room, expressing his disbelief at Leon's audacity.

"Do you believe," Leon yelled over him, enunciating each word before whispering dramatically, "in *God*?" Leon splayed his hands over the front of his body on the word 'God,' as if bowing at the end of a performance.

"What does it matter?"

"Answer the God damned question," Leon rasped, a small string of drool dribbled down his lips. The veins in his neck protruded. "Do you believe in God?"

Leon appeared feral. *Deranged.* He stared up at Jimmy through his hair, his pale eyelashes pushed up against his brow bone. The whites of his eyes looped underneath the pupils, creating an unsettling illumination of madness.

"Yes," Jimmy whispered in a conceding breath. Leon closed his eyes, turned his head to the side, and passionately nodded, the corners of his mouth drooping.

"Good. Now. What is Jesus then, Jimmy?"

"The son of God."

"A *sacrifice*," Leon hissed. He raised his voice, booming in the cadence of a preacher. "Jesus, the son of God, was a sacrifice for humankind to absolve us from our sins so that they may be accepted into the pearly gates of Heaven's eternity."

Leon lunged over the bed at Jimmy, grabbing him by the shoulders. His breath was hot on Jimmy's face, reeking of Jim Beam and stale cigarettes. It reminded him of the way the old Holman trailer used to smell.

"When you go to church, you are given wine to drink, for that is his blood. You are given bread to eat, for that is his body. How is what I did any different from what is done in churches every Sunday morning?"

"You're fucking sick," Jimmy muttered. Leon's grip intensified, violently shaking Jimmy.

"How is it different?" Leon sprayed Jimmy's face with spit. His voice calmed as he reiterated, "We're both just drinking the blood of the sacrifice, right?"

"Why are you telling me this?" Yelling back into his face, Jimmy shoved himself away from Leon. Grief swirled in his stomach, weighing him down. A pained moan escaped his body as he crouched to the floor, so guttural he could feel it in the root of his being. The Leon he had known and loved was dead—dead and gone and replaced by a heartless, soulless monster. Burden lay on his shoulders, keeping him on his knees. The burden of knowledge broke his heart, shattering a lifetime of trust and memories. "What is wrong with you?" Jimmy's voice shook as he struggled to inhale a breath.

Leon returned his stare, an insidious fury in his eyes. Jimmy used every ounce of strength to stand up, his legs buckling under his own weight. Straightening his spine, he tested a step. He didn't fall over, so he took another one, gaining speed.

"Stay the fuck away from me." Jimmy passed Leon and crossed in front of the bed, his eyes fixed on the door. The frigid air in Leon's laughter stopped him in his tracks, and he turned to face the redhead.

"That'll be pretty hard to do, considering we share a stage and a tour bus." Leon threw his head back and rolled his neck to look at his friend. "You'd better just come to terms with it."

"You're out of the band," Jimmy said, his voice trembling. The sentiment felt so trivial in light of the reason. The band—it felt so small, so stupid to even bring up. "You're done. I'm calling the police."

"No, you aren't," Leon chuckled playfully, sitting on the corner of the bed. He leaned down, propping himself up with his elbow. Jimmy's eyes widened at his cavalier attitude.

"You're not going to just get to get up every day free from this. You're fucking insane."

"You will **not**," Leon dictated slowly, "call the police. And you will **not** kick me out of this band. It's my band."

"Your band?"

"My band!" Leon roared, jumping to his feet. He hit the ground with a loud thud. "You have been given everything your whole God damned life, Jimmy. You've never worked for a single fucking thing."

"I haven't worked? Are you fucking kidding me? I'm as much a part of this band as you are. We're the heart of it," Jimmy screamed, picking up Leon's palm with the scar. "Or at least we were."

"You didn't do anything to get us where we are," Leon snatched his hand away. "You didn't do this. It was me, Jimmy. It was all me. It's mine. You can thank **me** for our fucking success. Do you think the power of friendship got us here? Be for fucking real. It was me. *My* talent. *My* deal. "

Frozen in fear, a million thoughts floated through Jimmy's mind. He thought of the little boy he met all those years ago, with the choppy red hair and peanut butter sandwich—that little boy who grew into the friend who taught him how to play guitar, driven by a shared passion. They had been each other's shadows, the brothers that they had never had but were able to choose. Yin and yang, they balanced one another—the light and the dark. At one time, passion lit Leon's eyes. There was a spark, determination, loyalty. That spark had fizzled out like a black hole sun, letting the darkness overtake it.

Jimmy searched Leon's eyes for something but found nothing—they appeared to be completely empty. It was like looking into an abyss—like taxidermy. Leon's physical body, the shell, was right before him, but he looked into glass eyes. There was no humanity, no remorse, no *soul*. The pieces fell into place.

"You sold your soul," Jimmy whispered in disbelief.

"Yes, I did," Leon snapped, indignant. In a rage, Jimmy seized Leon and threw him against the wall, tipping the nightstand.

"Was it fucking worth it?"As Jimmy stood there, pinning Leon against the wall, his face was distorted in anguish for the friend he no longer knew. Leon was quiet, with a silent sneer on his face.

"Yup," Leon remarked, pursing his lips in a smug look of defiance. "And you are not going to fuck this up for me. You're not going to make the sacrifice I made to be for nothing."

"What the *fuck*, Leon?" Jimmy shook his head, the hurt thick in his voice. An expression of clarity spread across Leon's face. All of the muscles around his mouth and eyes softened as he looked through Jimmy. Lunging, Leon grabbed Jimmy by the shoulders, shaking him roughly. His eyeballs bulged as an epiphany lighted his eyes.

"Do you see what my soul got us? It gave us everything. Can you imagine what could happen with two?" Reaching down, Leon picked up Jimmy's hand, the one with the matching scar. Jimmy snatched his hand away, his shoulders rigid. He pushed away from Leon, creating space between them as he sized up the stranger, the threat that his friend had become.

"No," Jimmy snapped. "God, no. Who are you?"

Leon's face remained unchanged as Jimmy's breath hitched in his chest. There was nothing more for him to do. There was nothing he *could* do. "Oh my God," Jimmy moaned. "God, oh God!" A fate worse than death—at least if Leon had died, he would still be Leon. He wouldn't be a void of a human, a monster among men. Jimmy lurched toward the door, backing up weakly. Grief seized him, and he sank into a crouch, burying a mournful cry into the crook of his elbow. "God!"

"Jimmy?"

Jimmy turned to see Leon standing before him, his expression filled with sorrow. He rose to his full height, standing face to face with Leon. Before Jimmy could open his mouth to reply, Leon's yellow eyes grew cruel, quickly wiping away the sympathy. In a single rapid motion, Leon slashed Jimmy's throat with the dagger hidden under his leather jacket sleeve.

"It's a shame that your God couldn't save you."

Jimmy gurgled. Blood splattered across Leon's expressionless face. His best friend—occasionally his only friend—slunk to the ground with a wound so severe that his body was nearly severed from his head in a spray of blood.

As Leon beheld the heap that once contained Jimmy, the dagger slid out of his fingers and clattered on the ground. Staring blankly, he stood above his friend's body.

A minute passed.

Then five.

The spray of blood ran like tears down Leon's cheeks. It coated his skin, tingling as it dried. The itch spread across his face, and flakes of blood rained down over his hands as he scratched it off.

As he backed away from the rapidly spreading blood, realization slammed him like a ton of bricks in his chest. Neurons fired throughout his body, electrified by adrenaline. His organs heaved with a sickening sinking ache. Leon extended his hands in front of him with fingers locked like talons. He raked his nails across his blood-soaked face and let out a heartbreaking howl.

He longed to feel something—anything at all. Tears should have been flowing for Jimmy, but he couldn't cry. Numbness engulfed him as he grappled with the stark realization that his very humanity had been sucked and drained from his veins. An intense feeling of emptiness overwhelmed him. For the first time since he sold his soul, fear gripped him. *Was this the true experience of being soulless, of losing all sense of humanity?* The thought of the band flashed in his mind. *How could Psychosomatic Slaughter go on without Jimmy?* He spun around, searching the vacant room.

"Where are you?" Leon shrieked. "Where the fuck are you?"

He turned back to Jimmy, his knees giving out on him when he looked at the lifeless body encompassed in a pool of blood. There was so much of it—he didn't remember Pamela having this much blood. *Of course, she didn't; Lucius sucked her dry.* It spread under the soles of Leon's boots, leaving bloody patterns on the floor as he paced around the room.

"Lucius!" Leon thundered. "I conjure you! I conjure you, Lucius! Where the fuck are you?"

Leon let himself fall against the wall, crumbling to the floor.

He crawled over and picked up Jimmy, carefully supporting his head.

Jimmy's eyes stared past him, a cloudy film coating them. He cradled Jimmy's head like an infant, trying to preserve what little tissue and bone still connected his head to his body. He was a monster—he had done this.

He took a needle and thread out of his nightstand and carefully stitched Jimmy's wound closed, a neat X pattern repeating across his throat, back below his ears.

"I'm so sorry, Jimmy," Leon set Jimmy down, looking at his bloodless face. He was so pale. As Leon gazed at Jimmy, he delved deep within himself, seeking any flicker of emotion. Instead, he encountered a void where empathy, love, and brotherhood should have been. All he encountered was a raw, animalistic instinct for self-preservation. It was a primal response, one that reduced him to the level of a wild beast, no different from a wolf.

He sat there. Waiting. Hour after hour, and Lucius never came. The pool on the floor had dried and congealed into a deep brownish sludge. Jimmy's jaw had dropped, his mouth hanging grotesquely open. Leon stared at Jimmy's body, stitched together like Frankenstein—a feeble attempt to fix his mutilation. He breathed in deeply, calming his shaking limbs. His body went rigid, and his eyes darkened as he stood up and calmly opened the door and walked down the stairs to gather his supplies.

Leon tied Jimmy at the ankles, neatly crossing one over the other. He put his hands on the dried blood, skimming the top. It had completely dried. Only a few flakes of blood were on his fingertips. Beyond any sort of feeling, he cut his palm open in the place most familiar to him. He traced the blade across the scar for the third time in this life to draw a cross on the wall.

He picked up Jimmy's body once again, the stiffness of death setting in. Leon leaned against Jimmy's body, pinning his wrist to the wall as he hammered a nail into his right palm. Jimmy slumped, and the weight of his limp body crashed into Leon. Leon grunted out of pain, out of frustration at the neck stitches that were almost pulling free as Jimmy's head lulled to the side. The skin around the threads pulled, stretching with the pressure.

He nailed the left palm to the wall. This side came easier for him. Flesh kept the nail in place, but it took a couple of hits from the hammer to get through the bone. Each hit brought with it a nauseating crack as it rigidly slid further through Jimmy's hand, binding it to the wall.

He kneeled on the floor in front of Jimmy, nailing his bound feet to the baseboard. The nails crunched through layers of skin, bone, and cartilage. When he was done, he looked up at Jimmy's drooping head, his face covered with his long, black hair. Leon stood up, brushing his friend's hair away from his face. He leaned Jimmy's head against the wall.

Leon couldn't stand looking at the limp jaw hanging open, so he took his needle and thread once again and stitched Jimmy's mouth shut. Standing there with a ringing in his ears, his shuddering breath was his only companion.

"Come on, you sick fuck," Leon taunted. "Come to me! I conjure you!"

Nothing.

"What else do you want from me?" Leon ripped a chunk of his own hair out, throwing it to the side as rage filled his body. "I HAVE NOTHING LEFT!"

He threw a lamp into the wall and hurled his bedside table across the room, crashing it into his bookcase. Rogue books rained down, blood soaking into their pages. Leon smashed his prized guitar into the blood pool, leaving a sticky, clumpy indent in the middle. He did it again, letting the guitar body sit in the impression in the middle of the pool. The guitar left a trail of clots behind as it was drug out. A picture flashed in his mind of his mother smashing his guitar from Rufus—that pathetic, ramshackle instrument.

Is this how she felt?

His fingers tightened around the neck as he swung the guitar into the wall. The plaster crumbled as the wall hung onto the instrument.

Leon threw a bottle of whiskey in the middle of the blood. The bottle smashed, and amber liquor spilled over the blood, settling on top. Leon pushed his palms into the middle of the pool, pushing the whiskey around, mixing it into the blood, liquefying it. He rolled his hands over the floor, smearing the mixture. The broken glass tore at his palms, adding his own blood to Jimmy's. The liquor burned his open skin.

Leon dragged the blood around the floor, crafting a huge pentagram with Jimmy's crucified body at the top point. Leon threw his head back, tossing his hair out of his face as he surveyed his work. He took a deep breath, rolling his head to the side to crack his neck.

Jimmy's filmy eyes glared at him. Leon blinked hard, shaking his head, trying to erase the image out of his mind. He couldn't take it anymore. He scooped out Jimmy's eyes, pushing his thumbs into the sockets. Slimy wetness glazed his fingers as he dug into the socket and pulled out Jimmy's eyeballs by the optic nerve. Holding the eyeballs in his palm, he considered them for a moment. His blood stained them as he rolled the eyeballs around, placing them at one of the bottom points of the pentagram.

Leon tore Jimmy's shirt open, cutting it with his bloodstained knife. He pushed the fabric aside, exposing Jimmy's chest. Leon drove the blade into Jimmy's belly button, twisting the blade and ripping the knife up and out over the sternum. Gravity pulled the intestines out, the organs spilling into a sloppy pile at Leon's feet. He picked them up and put them at the westernmost point. He picked up the pancreas, setting it at one of the bottom points.

Muscle memory took over as he cut into the corpse. Leon stuck his hand into the body cavity, reaching up through the slice he made up the abdomen and into the rib cage. He fumbled around blindly, his fingers feeling around in the lumpy, lukewarm insides. He found what he was looking for, wrapping his fingers around the organ before yanking it out, grunting with force. Leon stared at the heart in his hands. Instinctively, he squeezed it, causing stagnant blood to dribble out of the vessels and down his forearm. He couldn't put it down. Instead, he just leered at Jimmy's body.

"Well done, Leon," Lucius clasped Leon's shoulder in a fatherly gesture, standing behind him. The Devil locked his gaze on the guitarist, a little smile curling on his lips. He squeezed Leon's shoulder as he drank in the sight of his handiwork. A single tear fell down Leon's cheek. The arms that had once comforted him as a child when he had no one else to turn to were now nailed to the wall, crucified. The heart that had accepted him his entire life now rested in the palm of his hand, useless.

"I'm proud of you, Leon."

With heat radiating from the fingertips wrapped around Jimmy's heart, Leon's stomach rose into his throat. *I'm proud of you.* That was the first time he'd ever heard that—he never made anyone proud. Leon's lips trembled, and his body shook as laughter ignited. After tearing his eyes away from Jimmy, he gazed at the floor with trembling hands. There was blood everywhere. All over the floor. All over himself.

The muscles in his stomach contracted as he burst out laughing. In pure joy, he tossed his head back and let his laughter consume him. Lucius beamed and turned Leon around. He took the heart out of Leon's hands, giving it a firm squeeze in appreciation before he dropped it on the floor. He placed this other hand on Leon's shoulder and fixed his eyes on him.

Leon's smile melted as he became engrossed in Lucius's eyes. They glowed, red and unblinking. Lucius's smile widened, stretching over his face until his cheeks looked like they were going to tear. His teeth grew long and pointed. Leon realized Lucius's tongue was split like a serpent as his jaw sagged to make room for the expanding expression. A decaying odor struck Leon as the Wicked One's mouth opened.

His hands brushed up Leon's neck and cradled his face. Jimmy's blood smeared one side of Leon's face as Lucius firmed his grip on his cheeks. A cold sweat spread throughout Leon's body as Lucius drew him closer. He could hardly hear Lucius above the deafening boom of his heart in his ears.

"You fulfilled the commitment you made to me. Your mortal body shall die, and I shall take what belongs to me."

31

Non Est Anima Mea

Leon opened his eyes to find wet, gloomy stone walls glistening like coals in a fire. Heat radiated on his face as if standing too near a flame despite the frigid goose flesh prickling up his bare body. He clenched his fists, finding his arms to be shackled above his head, clasped at the wrist, and propped up against the wall. The stones behind his back secreted a cold slime that sent chills up his spine as his vertebrae clicked, clicked, clicked up the stone as he sat up straighter. He could see that shackles had also been used to bind his ankles, keeping them anchored to the ground. His toes had gone entirely numb.

He could move a little, but not much, enough to move away from the stones grinding his spine like a washboard.

Leon choked on the horrible stench of rot.

Of *death*.

The air hung around him, thick and musty. A sickly sweet, suffocatingly pungent aroma mixed in. It smelled overwhelmingly like cherries. *Cherries?* An aroma of a rotting bloom; *that was it*. A dying sweetness, a cherry ripening past its prime, rotting to return to the earth in a sticky slime. This assault on his nose blended with the smell of sulfur, the acidic decaying odor scorching Leon's throat and burning his eyes. He was confined to hear desperate pleadings and shrieks for mercy, screams of anguish, and sobs of despair. Choruses of men setting their pride aside and begging for Jesus bounced off of the stone, mixed with the cries of mothers begging for their children.

"You piece of shit, little son of a bitch."

The words crept over the nape of Leon's neck. Hot breath that smelled like rot and ethanol overpowered him, tickling the little hairs inside his ears. He knew that voice. That voice had called him that and worse many, many moons ago.

A lifetime ago.

Dad.

His father looked the same as the last time he had seen him: worn down despite still grasping onto his youth. Rotten teeth gave way to more rot as he sneered at his son, helplessly cowering into the wall. Black goo ran out of his dad's mouth. Leon's shackles rattled as he shook.

His father leaned down, the rosary he always wore swinging off of his neck. Except, this wasn't Nana Holman's rosary as he knew it.

The cross hung inverted.

Heaving breaths escaped his body, and he shuddered and gnawed to get some air. Leon was met with only decay and the strong grasp of his father, whipping his head back. Ginger hair snapped at the root with force, wrenching Leon's face upwards. He was nose-to-nose with the man who taught him how to ride a bike, the man who introduced him to rock and roll. The man who beat him bloody for forgetting to put the toilet seat down despite every surface of the bathroom being encrusted in grime and mold. The man who force-fed him a helping too big. The man who starved him for two days after he threw up that helping. The man who threw him against the wall for stealing a guitar that he didn't steal.

"I told you, boy." The thick black liquid dripped onto Leon's face. He recoiled with each droplet. Leon's lips curled away from his teeth, and tears streamed out of the corners of his eyes, running down his neck in streams. "I told you that you never take anyone's charity. You don't accept help from nobody."

The hand gripping his hair released, throwing the side of Leon's head into the stone wall. A white light burst in Leon's vision. He couldn't tell if his eyes were open or closed. All he knew was that the crack that just echoed through the cell was his skull splitting. He raised a shackled hand to his temple, shocked to feel no sticky blood.

"Your debt may be paid," his father's singsong voice echoed in the cell. "But look at where it got you."

Leon raised his head, trying to figure out where his father had gone. He wouldn't be able to handle another blow like that. He wouldn't survive. He couldn't.

Heaving, the weight of the world pushing down on his shoulders as fear roiled in his gut. He vomited up bile all over himself, unable to move without the room spinning.

I'm not alive.

Leon let out a guttural cry, a primal sound that came up from the root of his very being. His head fell into his lap, his limbs curling around himself to protect what was left. His body? He was fragile.

His soul? He thought that to be gone, for he had sold it. But the pain—the pain of his actions knocked out what little wind he had left in him. Deflated, the full burden of his decision climbed on his back to weigh him down. The soul that he sold waited for him in this pit of hell, waiting to become whole with his body again. The sinking realization of all of the hurt he had caused throughout his life crashed into him threefold. He felt all of the pain he inflicted on Jimmy, both the physical and the mental torture he put his friend through. It was at that moment that he truly understood what the Hell was. What it meant to be in Hell. The turmoil was a part of the punishment, a repercussion of dealing with the Devil.

"Leon?" The damp stone walls echoed with a female voice turned hoarse by cigarettes. "Oh, how I've missed you, honey."

"Ma?" Leon's voice broke. He reverted to feeling like a young child—a small boy who loved his mother. A little boy whose mom cherished him before waking up one day and deciding she didn't anymore. She always adored babies but not the people that they grew up to be. Her affection was conditional once he was old enough to walk and talk. She loved him less with each milestone.

"It's me, baby," she whispered, crouching to hold his face between her cold hands. She didn't look to be much older than he was. The smoker's lines around her mouth weren't there. Her skin looked smooth, like porcelain. He could see the woman that his father fell in love with when he was capable of such an emotion. He could see the person she was before life, and a series of poor choices had run her haggard.

"It's going to be okay. I'm going to visit you every day."

Leon looked into his mother's eyes as she patted his head, smoothing out his sweat-matted hair. It was like looking into his own celery-green eyes. She gaped at him, unblinking, and turned her head to the side.

"Ma," he crumbled into her, trying to collapse in her arms, but the chains kept him back just enough that he couldn't completely let himself break. He strained for her, stretching his neck out to her so she could keep petting his hair.

"I'm going to come here every day and slice open your chest," She said in a sickly-sweet voice. He swallowed hard, the muscles in his neck tightening as he froze. Her fingers became longer, revealing her bony knuckles as she took the hand caressing his cheek and stroked it down his exposed sternum. "Just like you did to young little Jimmy Ballard."

"Oh," Leon whimpered. He pulled his neck back, slumping to try to cover his eyes with his shoulders. The pain cut him deep inside at the memory, only this time, he felt the full extent of Jimmy's injuries with it, along with all of the guilt he wasn't capable of before. "Jimmy."

"He's not here, Leon. You know that. It's just going to be us from now on." Her hands caressed his face, her cold fingers tilting his chin up to look at her. "I'm going to crack your ribs, one by one, and I'm going to slice open your *chesssst.*" She began to hiss, her green eyes yellowing around angular pupils.

She snarled, lowering her voice to speak slowly, her face only inches away from his own. "Then, I'm going to reach into your body, and I'm going to pull out your heart. And you're going to watch me take a bite. Bite after bite after bite. Watching me take bites out of your heart, sucking the blood out of your arteries in excruciating agony."

She carefully slipped her skeletal fingers away from his chest and onto her cherubic face, patting the round, protruding apples of her cheeks. She smiled tightly, her mouth widening into a hideous grin that extended from ear to ear. Her mouth tipped upward at the corners. The flesh on her cheeks spread to the corners of her mouth as if someone had used thumbtacks to secure them to her temples. Her eyes did not flinch as they fixed an unwavering gaze on him.

She sat there in a hideous squat, her body contorting along with her face. Her spine's knobs began to protrude from underneath her thin, pale skin as her posture grew more rounded. Only the yellowish whites of her eyes were visible when her eyes fully rolled back.

"Aren't you excited, honey? My little Prometheus, this is what you wanted."

"No!" Leon cried as he lunged himself forward, forgetting the chains. They quickly reminded him of their presence, yanking him back against the stone wall.

"No?" A figure said from the shadows. It towered behind Leon's mother in the cell's entryway. Leon shut his eyes and let out a heart-wrenching wail. He heard the damp clomp of hooves slowly walking across the stone floor. The sound got louder and louder until it stopped in front of him. Leon recognized the beast immediately.

"Leon," Lucius's voice was honeyed.

From the waist up, Lucius looked like himself. His Herculean figure was naked, with dark, coarse hair trailing from his stomach down to an animalistic bottom half. His legs were that of a goat, but they were long and muscular. His feet bore large black hooves. Large, leathery wings protruded from his back, and the membranes between each digit created sharp points. Peridot-green eyes made his pale skin look translucent. His black coily hair cascaded down to his chest, with massive goat horns curling out from the top.

"You fucking bastard," Leon's arms shook in the shackles.

"Did you not get what you wanted?" Lucius's smile was deranged. It was too perfect. The teeth were too long, too sharp, and too white. Leon

299

cowered away from this beast that he once worshiped and called a friend.

"This is not what I wanted. This is not what you promised."

"The Devil is a liar, honey," Leon's mother sneered.

"What did I promise you?" Lucius crooned.

"You said you would give me success. Fame—you would make me a legend!"

Lucius took a step toward Leon's mother, his hooves echoing against the damp rock. He reached up and fondled her body while running his serpent tongue up her cheek. She leaned into him, throwing her arm around his neck and caressing his horn as he squeezed her breast. Lucius laughed, a nasty sound.

"There is no greater fame than infamy."

32

Face The Music

"Today is a sad day for Psychosomatic Slaughter fans. The band's singer, Jimmy Ballard, and lead guitarist, Leon Holman, were both found dead this morning in Holman's home. Bassist Dallas Jacobson found a gruesome scene before calling 911. Ballard was found crucified and dismembered. He was pronounced dead at the scene.

Jacobson found Holman unconscious, covered in blood that appeared to be Ballard's. He was rushed to Saint Muriel's Hospital, where he was pronounced dead at 8:43 this morning. It is suspected to be a murder-suicide.

We have contacted representatives for the surviving members of the band and have received no comment. The band had just wrapped up a successful tour following their breakout debut album, Hell's God. While having one of the most successful debut albums of all time, controversy has followed this group since the beginning. The band came under fire only months ago after Holman rallied the crowd at a stadium to chant "Hail, Satan" during their first show at the Manchester Apollo Theatre in London, England. Following the incident, a fan died in a riot that ensued at their concert at Markthalle Hamburg after Holman stormed off the stage.

Parents have shown their concern for the dark imagery used in rock and metal music, claiming that there are Satanic messages interlaced in the lyrics. People across the nation believe that society has reached a dangerous point of deviance. Parents worry that their teens are conducting devil worship by listening to bands such as Psychosomatic Slaughter. It is believed by many that Holman, the band's main lyricist, penned lyrics weaving in Satanic rituals, causing listeners to be a part of said rituals unknowingly. It could be speculated that these tragic deaths could be tied to a ritual sacrifice for the Devil.

This is a developing story that we are actively investigating. We will update you as more information becomes available."

* * *

News of the betrayal riddled the headlines. Parents lashed their scornful tongues, blaming the Devil for corrupting their teenage daughter, who wept for another pure soul gone too soon.

Dallas took the news the hardest, having been the one to find the gory scene. He cursed Leon's name as his boots made footprints in the dried blood, condemning him to Hell for what he'd done. There may have been some solace if Dallas knew that Leon was, in fact, in that wretched place for all eternity.

Through the wreckage, two bodies still needed to be laid to rest. However, many couldn't fathom that fact. Reminiscent of life, Jimmy was the star, even in death. He was the one with the memorials on the Sunset Strip and the candlelight vigils held in his honor. While Leon's life was also lost, his memory would always be shrouded in the shadows with whisperings of how Judas betrayed the light once more. And so it goes, history is damned to repeat itself.

Jimmy was returned to the Earth in a beautiful ceremony, surrounded by everyone he loved. Roses littered the top of his casket, and the ground drank the spirits that had been poured out for the slain angel. The band, now a mere trio, hung behind after the mourners had gone, and Heather had no more tears to cry. They paid tribute to their singer, allowing themselves to crumble and cry into the dirt that now separated them. The weight of his loss was so great that Mother Earth even cried for sweet Jimmy, raining down her tears onto Lonnie, Cam, and Dallas.

Mother Earth did not cry for Leon. No roses were laid upon his casket, and the ground in his plot was dry. The only shadow cast around his grave was the stranger shoveling dirt onto it, a solemn and tragic sight.

After a few weeks of hard thinking, Rufus stood over the lonely grave whose headstone was flat against the Earth. It almost blended in with the grass, which had grown long around the marker as if trying to conceal the atrocities committed by the person below the surface. He muttered curses into the wind at the lost potential and cried for the little boy he once loved. Before turning away, he noticed something glinting in the light despite the overcast clouds. Rufus's eyes narrowed at the lone wolf ring propped upon Leon Holman's name.

* * *

Death is a constant and inevitable part of life. We often push it to the back of our minds, thinking it is far away from us. We believe that we are untouchable and have time on our side. However, death hits us like a ton of bricks when we are faced with it, leaving us disoriented and lost. Memories make it hard to navigate through the fog of grief. Death is so definitive, so final. You cease to exist. Ashes to ashes. Dust to dust. What is born will return to the Earth, but the soul… the soul lives on. Where that soul ends up is up to you. The fabric of your life determines that. The small moments. The encounters with others. The decisions we make.

Music, like souls, lives on as a legacy. Generations will hear a frozen moment in time. The music of Psychosomatic Slaughter lived on, as did the lore of the Devil and the Angel at the center of the band.

Character Anthems

These songs were a significant source of emotional inspiration for the central characters of Psychosomatic Slaughter. Consider these to be the personal anthems of these characters.

Jimmy Ballard: "After Forever" by Black Sabbath
   This song, penned by Geezer Butler, a Catholic-raised bassist for Black Sabbath, showed the world the band's softer side. Many people at the time claimed Black Sabbath practiced devil worship, but with its pro-God lyrics, this song aimed to change that perception. It is the perfect anthem for Jimmy Ballard, our primary hero and martyr. While Psychosomatic Slaughter was portrayed as a band of darkness, much like Black Sabbath, I want people to remember that Jimmy was a source of light and goodness in the dark.

Leon Holman: "Me and the Devil Blues" by Robert Johnson
   You can't help but feel uneasy listening to this song. It features a haunting acoustic guitar and has an eerie antique sound. The lyrics are from the point of view of a man being invited to walk with Satan so that the Devil may retrieve his soul. Like the song, Leon has a way of evoking unease and exuding an unsettling aura. It also parallels Leon's experience. It is particularly appropriate considering this song is from the record that made him fall in love with music in a whole new way, establishing his passion for the occult, the blues, and the guitar. Robert Johnson helped pave the way as inspiration for his eminent demise. If you haven't already, give this entire album a listen.

Dallas Jacobson: "Young Lust" by Pink Floyd

This song is cocky, smooth, and dirty, just like our favorite bassist. In Pink Floyd's 1982 masterpiece *The Wall*, we watch Pink settle into a life of debauchery as a rock star. This song is about falling victim to the sex, drugs, and rock and roll lifestyle. In this story, Dallas is the band member who falls into the so-called "life" the hardest, allowing himself to indulge in all of the perks that come with fame and indulge too much. His raging drug addiction comes to the forefront as the band rises to fame and allows him to trust in Leon (and his gift of ground-up sacrificial teeth). This song exudes the grit, sexual magnetism, and sleaze I wanted Dallas to radiate. This character was my favorite to write, and honestly, he may be my favorite band member overall. I spent so much time honing his character, giving him the arc he deserves. When I want to feel all of the good feelings I experienced when writing this book, this is the song I put on.

Cameron "Cam" Tulley: "Rivendell" by Rush

The whimsical sound of Geddy Lee's soft vocals, the medieval-inspired flutes, and the fingerstyle guitar is exactly what Cam would love to play at night to unwind and draw his fantasy maps. He would use this song as the soundtrack to create new D&D campaigns or create the perfect atmosphere for reading (or rereading) a fantasy novel. This song is enchanting, magical, and cozy—exactly Cam's style.

Lonnie Herring: "Bastard" by Mötley Crüe

This song is a massive 'fuck you' and perfectly captures Lonnie's attitude. He is arrogant, takes no bullshit, and will be ready for a fight at the drop of a hat. He won't hesitate to throw a punch to defend himself or his friends. When I imagined Lonnie, I saw an air of haughtiness with ample eye rolls, an unrelenting middle finger, and a cigarette dangling from his lips. This song oozes that vibe.

Lucius Wolfe: "Devil's Dance" by Metallica

When James Hetfield sings this song, he plays the serpent's role, tempting the listener to succumb to him. The song perfectly encapsulates the Devil's seduction to the dark side thanks to the sleazy bassline, gritty guitars, and dominating vocals. This song inspired me to write about Lucius's enticing personality and the appealing aura that he would use against Leon to seal the deal for his soul.

A Thank You Letter From the Author

I have always dreamed of writing a book. Ever since I was a child, I have enjoyed crafting stories. As a little girl, I wrote about fairies. As I grew older, I wrote about kidnappings, possessions, and creature features (I have always taken a creepy approach to writing thanks to the Stephen King obsession I fell into around nine and never grew out of).

This book's inspiration grew from my obsession with classic rock bands and the lore behind myths like backmasking, the 27 Club, and selling souls for talent. I've always been fascinated with how horror and rock and roll go hand in hand, but I could never find a book that scratched my itch.

I wanted a story about a band like Mötley Crüe, Guns N' Roses, or Metallica with an unhinged member making a deal with the Devil, inciting horrors and sacrifice. Since I couldn't find a book exactly like that, I decided to write it myself. As it goes, I wrote the book I wanted to read.

Writing this book took me a lot of time (two years, but who's counting?) for various reasons. One of the main reasons was my lack of motivation to put my thoughts on paper, followed by fear, falling down research rabbit holes, and self-doubt. Imposter syndrome was a real pain in my ass throughout the process.

To be honest, writing pieces of this book and certain characters were also pretty scary for me. While writing certain scenes, I had to take a break (and pray a little) and step back, as they were pretty intense and overwhelming. Despite this, I loved writing the character of Leon, my little psychopath, although it was daunting. However, writing Lucius was even more challenging. While most people find themselves rehearsing arguments or performing concerts in the shower, I rehearsed conversations between a rocker and Satan. Frankly, I did some of my best work in this novel while rinsing and repeating.

Throughout the process, there were so many people in my life who supported me. Even people from high school that I had never talked to before reached out to me on social media when I shared writing-related milestones (if you made it this far, I hope that you enjoyed the book and aren't judging me too harshly as a person—this story is one hell of a first impression).

I am extremely lucky to have a support system of amazing people in all facets of my life, encouraging me to fulfill a lifelong dream.

My husband, Michael, was especially instrumental. He listened patiently as I talked on and on about 1980s hair metal bands, and he indulged my playlists during car rides. He talked me through self-doubt and cured many spells of my imposter syndrome. He pushed me to write even when I didn't feel like it and provided me with unwavering support throughout the writing process. I am grateful for his patience with my hyper-fixation with Guns N' Roses and the genre as a whole, as well as my book-buying addiction. You are my life partner, cheerleader, and best friend. I love you so much for this and more.

My mom was my biggest supporter while writing my damn book (which I started calling "this damn book" around month 7). She was always the first to read new pages and the first person I would message with ideas. I would often ask her, "Is this too dark?" to which she would reply, "No, sweetie," with words of encouragement, telling me that it was a great idea. I am grateful to her for supporting me in my writing, even though it is dark, twisted, and macabre. As I wrote each draft, she read and reread each and every version. She proudly tells all her friends about her daughter's book about murder, rock and roll, satanic sacrifice, and cannibalism. Thank you, Mom, for this and for letting me watch scary shows and movies with you when I was a kid. You shaped me into the person I am, and I'm so grateful for that.

Allie, my writing buddy. While our genres are at different ends of the spectrum, thank you for being there to commiserate with me about being a writer. Thank you also for being one of my first readers and providing excellent, detailed, and brutally honest feedback. Having such a creative, whimsical friend in my corner means so much.

Rob—"The Undertaker." I love talking with you weekly about all things horror. Thank you for patiently waiting for this book and reading it with such a critical eye. Thank you for sharing your knowledge on working in a funeral home, embalming, and the stages of death with me. You entertained my questions on skinning, organ removal, and rigor mortis and provided me with gruesome details to make this book that much more realistic and horrifying.

The managing partners at my day job were also so supportive of my writing, not at all turned off by the subject matter. Andrea and Julie, you are the coolest bosses around. You were the first to demand a copy of the book. Thank you for reading it and letting me keep my job after reading my disturbing little brainchild. In all seriousness, I appreciate you taking a genuine interest in the book and taking the time to read it and give me feedback on my draft.

Sarah Derr brought my vision for Pamela's tattoo to life by doing the cover art, design, and layout for my book cover. As soon as I saw your work as a tattoo artist and a graphic designer, I knew you were perfect for this project. You polished my crude idea for a cover design, making it shine brighter than I could have imagined. I am so grateful for you and for the vision you brought to life. Thank you for your partnership, attention to detail, and talent. Your love for the genre and the art of tattooing shines here.

Lexi, you were my #1 hype woman behind the camera. You made me feel beautiful, like the lovechild between Elvira and Morticia Addams. Thank you for taking the most gorgeous author photo.

A special shout-out from me to me for stepping up as editor, marketer, and publicist. I couldn't have done it without you.

And last but not least, thank you to the readers who took a chance on my debut novel. If you made it this far as to read the acknowledgments, you rock.

As I've said, this book culminates two years of work. This is the first book

I have written to completion, and I wanted everything to be perfect. While I am incredibly proud of this story, it is not perfect. I was told in college that writers (and artists in general) never finish a work; they merely abandon it. I have found this to be wholeheartedly true as I wrote this book. But through each draft (there were many) and each change (Dallas used to be named Kelly, and there is a scrapped Black Mass scene sitting in the garbage can), I genuinely feel as if I wrote the perfect version of this story.

I hope people enjoy reading it as much as I enjoyed dreaming it up and writing it. Whether you love or hate this book, I hope you will go on this journey with me as a reader. I have many other stories to tell and want to take you along for the ride.